The Loyal Friend

A. A. Chaudhuri is a former City lawyer. After gaining a degree in History at University College London, she later trained as a solicitor and worked for several major London law firms before leaving law to pursue her passion for writing. She lives in Surrey with her family, and loves films, all things Italian and a good margarita!

Also by A. A. Chaudhuri

She's Mine

A. A. CHAUDHURI

The Loyal Friend

CANELO
US

San Diego, California

Canelo US
An imprint of Printers Row Publishing Group
9717 Pacific Heights Blvd, San Diego, CA 92121
www.canelobooksus.com

Printers Row Publishing Group is a division of Readerlink Distribution Services, LLC. Canelo US is a registered trademark of Readerlink Distribution Services, LLC.

This edition originally published in the United Kingdom in 2022 by Canelo.

Published in partnership with Canelo.

Correspondence regarding the content of this book should be sent to Canelo US, Editorial Department, at the above address. Author inquiries should be sent to Canelo, Unit 9, 5th Floor, Cargo Works, 1–2 Hatfields, London SE1 9PG, United Kingdom, www.canelo.co.

Publisher: Peter Norton • Associate Publisher: Ana Parker
Art Director: Charles McStravick
Senior Developmental Editor: April Graham
Editor: Julie Chapa
Production Team: Beno Chan, Julie Greene

Design: Brianna Lewis

Library of Congress Control Number: 2022947662

ISBN: 978-1-6672-0529-8

Printed in India

27 26 25 24 23   1 2 3 4 5

'*Revenge proves its own executioner.*'

John Ford, *The Broken Heart*

Prologue

There's a violence about the weather tonight, a kind of insanity that seems to accord with her own state of mind. The rain is brutal, lashing down with such ferocity even turning up her wipers at full throttle had felt almost pointless. She's amazed to have made it back to her flat unscathed.

She opens the door and steps into the pitch-black darkness, fumbling for the switch on the wall to the right, sighing with relief when the light comes on. She heads straight for the bathroom, ignoring her growling belly as she does so, taking her mobile phone with her, laying it on the bathroom stand.

She turns on the shower and strips off her clothes, taking a second to admire her naked body in the mirror as it starts to steam up before untying her long blonde tresses and stepping inside the cubicle.

She closes her eyes and tilts her head up to the ceiling, enjoying the sensation of the water running over her, trying to blank out the last few days. The feeling that she is being hunted.

She hears nothing but the sound of the powerful jets rebounding off the cubicle's tiled floor.

Not the bathroom door opening. Nor the footsteps approaching. Nor a voice saying *filthy bitch* under its breath.

But she does hear the cubicle door crashing open.

Her attacker repeating the same vile words.

And with that, her fear is so great she cannot find her voice to try and save herself.

No one will hear her.

And very soon, she hears nothing at all.

Chapter One

The present
Tuesday, 31 July 2018

The woman pulls back the thick powder-blue curtain a fraction and peers out of her bedroom window, sees the familiar black Vauxhall Astra pull up and come to a standstill. She waits with bated breath. No sign of its passengers just yet, causing her tension to rise, her mind to wonder what they might be talking about, why they are here.

What they might have discovered since she last spoke to them only three days ago.

Finally, the driver and passenger doors open, and she sees the detectives exit the car, serious expressions etched across their faces, not unusual in their line of work, but there's something about their demeanour that worries her; a kind of singularly determined look that tells her they mean business, that they've made some kind of break-through.

She watches them cross the road, eyes darting left and right as they do so, then approach the front door. Watches the more senior officer raise his right hand and press the bell.

It's so quiet in her bedroom, the sound seems to reverberate around her in one thunderous echo. It's grey

3

outside today, chilly too; more like mid-autumn than late summer – she's even had to turn on the central heating. But it's the sound of her bell being pressed by her visitors that sends a shiver up her spine, rather than the cool temperature.

She cannot dither a moment longer. Even though the last thing she wants is to go downstairs and open the door to her visitors. She leaves the bedroom, being sure to close the door behind her, then slowly makes her way down to the hallway, the sound of her breathing and the natural creaks of the building all that can be heard. Then she inhales deeply before opening the door to her callers.

They're standing there with grave expressions, and when she asks them what's happened, how she can be of assistance, they say there's been a development in the case and enquire if they might come inside.

She cannot refuse them. She must stay calm, act surprised, exude an air of innocence. Be the best actress she possibly can. It shouldn't be hard; she's been doing that for so long now it's become second nature, donning another face for the world. Hiding the truth, her past. The things she has done and kept secret from others. In any case, she's not the only guilty one here. Far from it.

She latches onto that thought, flashes her most congenial smile, says, 'Yes, of course, officers, anything to help,' then leads them inside and says a silent prayer that her secret is still safe.

Chapter Two

Natalie

Eleven days before
Friday, 20 July 2018

I shiver as I trudge along the Thames Path heading for my yoga session at The River Club, where I belong, last night's storm still making its presence known. Gone is the oppressive oven-like heat that's tortured us for the past fortnight, and in its place an almost wintry breeze seems to cut through me like I'm some sort of ethereal being. Yesterday's storm has cooled things down markedly, and I'm thankful for it, having never been one for the heat. It's never sat kindly with my pale skin. Nor my naturally anxious state of mind. Although at least now that I'm fitter, I can take it better. A stone lighter than this time last year, it doesn't sap all my energy, take the breath out of me, like it used to. I have Jade to thank for that. It's not been an easy path, granted. In fact, it was bloody tough to start with, and I'd almost quit at the first hurdle. But she'd encouraged me, got me through the worst, helped me climb a mountain that at first had seemed insurmountable. Looking back, it's hard to believe I'm the same person I was before Jade walked into my life.

As I stride along, making sure I keep to the right and don't cross over onto the cycle lane like I notice some thoughtless people do, I fish out my phone and check to see if Jade's messaged me back. I sent her several texts this afternoon, anxious to know why she's not replied to any of my calls or messages since Wednesday night's Body Attack class, checking she was OK. She'd looked so out of sorts that night, as if something was weighing heavily on her mind, and it had me worried. She didn't even stop to chat afterwards like we normally do. And that upset me. It made me think she's not over our row on Monday, even though we made things up on the phone the following afternoon and agreed to put it all behind us. To be honest, things have been a bit strained between us for a few weeks now, and it's set me on edge. Could well be the reason why my sleep's been so disturbed lately.

Thursday morning, I woke up feeling like utter crap, and when I finally crawled out of bed, having only managed a couple of hours' kip, I ended up pulling a sickie, my usual morning routine thrown completely out of kilter. I'd felt so guilty, particularly as Jane's such a nice boss, but as I'm not in the habit of being sick, she was very understanding and said the library would manage without me for a day. Consequently, I spent most of Thursday afternoon slumped in front of the TV but must have dropped off early evening, as I woke up on the sofa around three a.m. on Friday still in my sweater and joggers. Hungry and disorientated. The dregs of a cup of camomile I seem to remember drinking before nodding off still on the table in front of me. I'd also neglected to tick off all the items on my day planner. For the third day in a row. That distressed me somewhat. It's vital I have confirmation that I've followed my routine, done everything I should have done. But at least I managed to put myself to bed afterwards and get some sleep.

As I walk, I yawn widely. Hopefully, tonight's yoga will help settle my mind, and I'll sleep like a baby later. I don't function well without a good eight hours. Sleep's always been a problem for me, and for a while I fixed it with pills like lorazepam. Until my therapist pointed out that these were causing me to experience vivid dreams and other unpleasant side effects, and were therefore not a long-term solution. She said following a routine, a good diet, avoiding caffeine and stress was the healthier, more sustainable option.

I was tempted to leave the class just this once, but if I don't stick to my routine it'll be so easy to fall back into old habits, and I can't chance that. Finally, I arrive at the club at dead on 6:15 p.m. like I always do, but as I race across the car park and approach the double doors leading to the main entrance, hoping to catch Jade before the class starts, I hear a voice call out my name from behind.

'Natalie, is that you? It is, isn't it? Why the rush?'

I stop dead in my tracks, feel my skin crawl. *Susan.* Her voice is unmistakeable. A sort of low, raspy drawl that unsettles rather than comforts you. A voice that can't be trusted. Just because it always seems to have an angle to it. She knows damn well it's me. I mean, we see each other three times a week almost without fail; have done for the best part of a year. We know each other by the mere sight of our Lycra-clad bottoms, for God's sake. Mine a sort of rounded peach, hers more of a sagging pear. We've been at coffee mornings and gym socials together, including Jade's thirtieth last month. A night when everyone got hammered. Except for me, who as usual remained stone-cold sober. We don't socialise because we enjoy each other's company, but by sheer circumstance, the club being our common denominator. We practically live at

7

this place. For me, it's become a sort of home from home. I think it has for Susan, too, even though she'd never stoop so low as to admit it. She thinks she's too good for the likes of us. And that's why she enjoys playing her mind games. Exuding a toffee-nosed air of superiority over me and others. That's the kind of person she is. No wonder her husband always looks so bloody miserable.

I take a lungful of air and will myself not to be goaded by her condescension, even though there's a part of me simmering inside that wants to punch her lights out and wipe that infuriating smirk off her face. But I can't go there. That would never do.

I turn around, give a false smile. 'Oh, hi, Susan. Yes, it's me. I just don't want to be late for the class. Need the loo first. Assume you're doing it?' Just as I say this a wave of tiredness overcomes me. My head hurts too. That kind of muzzy, vice-like fatigue that grates at your temples, makes your eyelids heavy but at the same time flicker involuntarily.

She rolls her eyes, glances at her watch. An Omega. I'm sure the other day it was a Rolex. The week before that a Gucci. She drips designer like the King's Road. I instinctively fiddle with my Timex from Argos, feeling incredibly awkward.

'There's fifteen minutes to go, so you're well in time,' she says. 'Jade won't start without her number one fan, anyway.' Her eyes linger on me before she proceeds to examine her immaculate French-manicured nails, making me feel conscious of my own bitten down ones, another smirk creeping across her face as she raises her head to meet my gaze once more. What did she have to say that for? I'm not some stalker, I'm Jade's friend. Maybe she's jealous because unlike me she has no real friends. And who would wonder, the way she goes on. It's pathetic, really. She's pathetic, even if she doesn't see it. Dressed in Nike purple and white leggings with a matching zip-up top, I notice she's also wearing pristine ASICS trainers, not that there was anything wrong with the pair of Reeboks she was wearing on Wednesday. Her dyed auburn hair is tied back in a low ponytail, but she's wearing less make-up than usual. I can't help wondering what's triggered this uncharacteristic lack of vanity. Usually, she arrives at Jade's classes made-up to the max, her hair blow-dried like she's just stepped out of a L'Oréal ad, as if she's trying to make a point and feels the need to compete with the younger blood in the class, including Jade. Even though she doesn't stand a chance in that department because Jade's young and fresh and way out of her league, and no matter how much make-up or how many expensive treatments she has, that's never going to change. Having said her piece, Susan gives me the once-over, like I often catch her doing – a kind of disparaging look as if she can't bear the sight of my cut-price leggings and t-shirt – then allows herself a self-satisfied chuckle. I notice the crow's feet around her eyes crease up as she does so, while her mouth seems crinklier around the corners too. Less foundation and concealer failing to cover the telltale signs of her smoking addiction. Despite her regular exercise classes, and her protestations that she's a health freak, regularly starting her days with green smoothies and hot lemon tea, we all know she smokes like a chimney. You can't hide it – the acrid smell on her breath, a smell that infests a smoker's body like a malignant disease, no matter how many tabs of spearmint gum they chew on. My father was the same. Then again, he was a walking disease in himself. Rotten to the core.

9

'Well, run along then, we don't want to keep the boss waiting.' Susan stirs me from my thoughts, giving a gentle flick of her wrist like I'm an insignificant fly she's swatting away, her knuckleduster four-carat diamond and platinum engagement ring glimmering in the early-evening light as she does so. Once again, I swallow her superciliousness, force down the anger her tone stokes in me.

The club is situated a little way back from the river path, bordering the quaint leafy village of Thames Ditton. As a premium member, I don't have to check in at reception. When I swipe my card at the turnstile, it automatically registers my attendance at tonight's class, and so I waste no time dawdling in the foyer waiting to be attended to by Karen on reception. I simply walk in, swipe my card and immediately make my way towards the Ladies at the end of the corridor. I always have a pee before my class. It's an unspoken ritual, I guess, even though I could probably hang on until the end. Having done my business, I'm out like a flash, sprinting up the stairs until I reach the second floor where studio two is situated. A year ago I'd never have opted for the stairs. I'd have taken the lift at any given chance because even a few stairs would have had me gasping for breath. It brings a smile to my face. Makes me realise how far I've come. Makes me think of my vile foster parents, Cath and Brian, and what they would have said, seeing me like this. No longer the fat waste-of-space loser child they regularly made a point of telling me I was. They tried to starve me, like they did all the children; couldn't understand why I didn't lose weight. Said I must have been genetically disposed to obesity, to being a freak of nature. They didn't know that my best friend in the whole wide world secretly gave me crisps and chocolate which I stuffed my face with whenever I could – a crutch to make myself feel better.

I reach the second floor, exit the fire doors and turn left towards the studio, but just as I do, I see several familiar faces striding towards me. Including Susan and Grace. Grace is a regular too. She joined the club at the same time as me. I notice she has a somewhat vexed look on her face, although that's not exactly unusual – she has a lot on her plate, and invariably arrives looking rather harassed. But just now she appears more troubled than usual. Vivien and Shelley are there too, plus Jill and Callie, with Bruce the token guy in the class lagging behind, as well as a few others who come to Jade's classes on and off but aren't regulars like us. A few of them motor right past me, not making eye contact, a kind of 'pissed off' vibe emanating from them.

Why are they coming this way? Why aren't they standing outside the studio waiting to be let in? Looking at their expressions, I suddenly get a bad feeling. Something's wrong with Jade, I can feel it in my bones. And I'm sensing it's the reason she's not responded to any of my calls or texts. Just as I'm thinking this, I happen to look up and catch Susan's eye.

'Class is off,' she announces. She almost sounds glad, triumphant about the fact. Disappointment floods my insides. Maybe Jade had a row with the guy she's been seeing? He's nothing but trouble, but she thinks he's God's gift. Doesn't see the reality of the situation like I do. Or perhaps it's not man trouble. Perhaps she's sick? She has looked a bit peaky of late.

'Why?' I ask. My gaze automatically falls on Grace, just because I see her as being the more approachable of the bunch. Even though she can be a bit vague at times.

She gives me a sympathetic glance, hesitates a second then opens her mouth as if on the verge of responding, but before she can utter a word, Susan answers for her.

'Jade didn't show.' She says this particularly loudly. And somewhat derisively. As if she wants to make the point that Jade's bailed on us all.

In light of current circumstances, i.e., the fact that Jade's nowhere to be seen, I shouldn't be surprised by this revelation. Even so, I find myself saying, 'What? Why? Are you sure?'

Susan scowls. 'Course I'm sure.' She looks around her. 'You can't see her, can you?' She shrugs her shoulders. 'And no, I haven't a clue why. How the hell would I know? It's not a big deal. So, our instructor didn't turn up. Why are you getting so worked up about it?'

Talk about defensive. It's not an unreasonable question to ask.

I hear Dr Jenkins' voice inside my head telling me everything's fine, that I need to stay calm. That I cannot afford any trigger points. 'I thought Martin might have explained why,' I say. 'Passed on a message from Jade, or something. I mean, he is the gym and class coordinator. We've been going to her classes for a year now, and she's never just not showed up. It's not like her.'

I wonder to myself if any of them noticed Jade looking out of sorts on Wednesday night, like I did. Maybe not. They don't know I've tried calling her, like, a million times since, that she hasn't responded to me once, not even by text.

My gaze flits from one face to the other, but all I get back in return are the same blank expressions. Susan shrugs her shoulders again. 'From the look on Martin's face, and the little he's said, I think he's as much in the dark as we are. He seemed quite pissed off, actually. Can't say I blame him. Even if she's got herself in some sort of trouble, the least she could have done was call to say she can't make it. It's bloody inconsiderate of her to let us down like this without any kind of explanation.'

'Trouble?' I frown. 'Why would you think she's in trouble?'

'What is this,' Susan snaps back, 'the Spanish bloody Inquisition? Look, I know you worship the ground Jade walks on,' I feel myself redden at this comment, 'but let me enlighten you – she's no angel. Like all of us, she has a life outside of this place, and I bet she has secrets even you don't know about. Everyone has.' She pauses, her eyes narrowing. 'I'm sure even you do.' I instinctively flinch, feel a sudden tightness in my chest. 'Point is,' Susan carries on more lightly, her gaze switching to the others as if seeking their endorsement, 'it's pretty clear Martin couldn't give any insight on the matter. But it's bloody slack, as I said. They could have got a temp in if she'd given them more warning. Martin, bless him, was very apologetic, said we could have a drink on the house. But that's all well and good. What a waste of my precious time. I could have been watching *Real Housewives* with a glass of Shiraz at this very moment. I deserve it after three days on the Type O diet.'

Christ, not another bloody fad diet. I bet secretly she stuffs her face with Walkers crisps and Dairy Milk at night. She must do, else she'd be stick-thin, which she most certainly isn't. I think about her comment about Martin being pissed off. All the women fancy him. Except me. And Jade. She told me so. Which surprised me. I mean, he's handsome, fit. Knows he's both of these, the way good-looking people do, but still has a certain unassuming

13

charm about him. In essence, he's the male counterpart of Jade. Which is why I always saw them as the perfect match. Plus, I've seen the way he looks at her. It's obvious he likes her. And it makes me wonder if he resents the fact that his feelings aren't reciprocated.

'I'm a bit cross too, I have to admit,' Grace says with a sigh, running her fingers through her unruly fringe, the lines on her brow which, unlike Susan's, actually moves, creasing. She looks dog-tired, like she has all the cares of the world on her shoulders. 'I was so looking forward to tonight's class. I had such a shitty day. Mum's dementia seems to be getting worse. I spent most of the day at the home trying to convince her it was daytime and that she needed to change out of her nightclothes. She was about to go to bed when I arrived at ten a.m. The nurses have given up, say it's normal, that they can't do anything about it and we need to let nature take its course. But I can't stand seeing her like that. I'm just glad Dad's not around to see it. It would have broken his heart. I never take the kids. It's too upsetting for them, even though Jim says they need to spend time with their grandma. I know I need to be tougher, more practical about things, but I can't bear for them to remember her like that.'

Grace receives sympathetic glances all round. She has it tough. Unlike Susan, who as far as I can tell worries about nothing and nobody but herself. At this moment she's pretending to look concerned about Grace, her head cocked to one side, every now and again nodding as if she knows exactly what Grace is going through. But really I bet her mind is still focused on missing *Real Housewives*, or perhaps whether she should get her toes painted rose pink or fuchsia pink at her fortnightly pedicure tomorrow.

'I could really have done with a session to de-stress,' Grace goes on. 'Jim's locked upstairs in his study all day so he's not much company. I feel like I'm going crazy sometimes, not talking to anyone. Before I know it, the kids will be grown and gone, and it'll just be me roaming the house talking to four walls.'

'Oh, but you and Jim will have more time for one another then,' Jill says. 'I was so worried when the kids went off to university, and I think Bill was too, although he'd never admit it. For years, our conversations, everything we did, really, had revolved around the kids, and with both our parents being up North we never did date nights or weekends away. But we surprised ourselves. Got to know each other again. The last twenty years have been like a second honeymoon. Next week we're off on our third cruise of the year.'

Jill gives Grace an encouraging smile, who responds with a weak smile of her own. Her eyes still with that faraway look in them. And is that a tear I spot? 'Thanks, I hope you're right.'

'I know I'm right,' Jill says. 'Look at me, I'm sixty-five and I have more energy now than I did when I was your age. My forties were the most stressful years of my life. That's what kids and elderly parents, along with trying to maintain a career, do to you. I thought I was on the verge of a nervous breakdown at one point.'

'Anyway,' Susan says, her tone ringing of boredom, 'who fancies a drink in the bar? Especially as the first round's free, thanks to Jade's no-show. I suggest the £8-a-glass Chablis. I think I need one just to quash my irritation at having driven all this way here for nothing!'

Any excuse. Besides, she's only a twenty-minute drive away.

I glance at the others, who look equally put out. And as I do, a familiar rage hurtles through me. I mean, I can understand Grace being upset, she's got a lot to cope with, but I had expected the rest of them to show a bit more concern for Jade's well-being. But all they can worry about is their own inconvenience. Yes, it's disappointing not being able to have our session after we've all made the effort to get here. But it's not life-shattering; it's not world famine or anything. I know for a fact that Jade loves working here, so whatever caused her not to show up can't be good. As I think on this, my heart plummets to my stomach, an almighty lump developing in my throat thinking about all the grim possibilities. The worry must show on my face because I catch Susan eyeing me suspiciously.

'Are you all right? You've got a weird expression on your face.'

I feel a familiar trembling coming on and so I clench my fist again, will myself to keep control of my emotions. Just as Dr Jenkins encourages me to. The way my child psychologist would instruct me to after what happened and the trembling started. There might be a harmless explanation; I can't think the worst before I know for sure what's happened. I need to take things one step at a time, and not get ahead of myself.

But Susan's next remark doesn't help matters. 'I'm surprised she didn't let you know she wasn't coming. I got the impression you two were close. Best friends, even. Do you know anything we don't? Jade must have said something to you, surely?' She pauses. Then adds, 'Unless you've had some kind of falling-out?'

Fuck. I wonder, did Susan hear me and Jade argue on Monday? Or was that a lucky guess? All eyes are on me, and

16

I suddenly can't breathe. It's always a bit stuffy up here, it's why the air con in the studio is such a heavenly contrast. But I'm sweating now. Why the hell would I have been rushing to get to the class if I knew she wasn't going to show up? What a stupid question to ask.

Don't get angry.

'It's come as much of a surprise to me as it clearly did to you.' I pause, then say boldly, turning the tables, looking at each woman in turn. 'That is, I'm assuming it *did* come as a surprise to all of you?'

Silence, and I wonder what that tells me. Nothing, perhaps. Maybe they just feel sheepish for bad-mouthing Jade without knowing the facts behind her no-show. But then Vivien, who's American, pipes up. She married a high-flying investment banker donkey's years ago and settled here in the UK.

'Sure surprised me,' Vivien says in her trademark Texan twang. 'Jade seemed fine and dandy on Wednesday.' She chews on a piece of gum, a ploy designed to curb her appetite, and which perhaps accounts for her rake-thin physique, while twiddling one of her large gold hooped earrings just about visible under the mountain of bleached-blonde hair. 'As it happens, I was in touch with a friend earlier who does Thursday classes, and she mentioned Jade covered Shona's Zumba class last night. Said Jade was as perky as a peach, made it really fun.'

Which makes it even more of a worry, I think to myself. *What on earth could have happened in the last twenty hours?* Whatever it is must explain why she hasn't responded to my latest texts.

'It's so annoying,' Callie says. 'My first night off the maternity ward in three days, and no class.' She rolls her eyes. 'I've done nothing but snack on crap from the

17

vending machine these past few nights, and I can feel it round here big time.' She pinches her sides for emphasis.

'Smoking will cure that,' Susan says drily. 'Works a treat for me when I need to shed a few pounds. Obviously, I don't make it a regular habit.'

Liar.

Just then, Grace seems to mutter something, but I can't quite catch what she says. 'What was that, Grace?' I ask. Everyone looks her way, her eyes wearing the same fretful expression, her mouth twitchy as she bites her bottom lip, then replies, 'Oh, nothing. Just that I feel bad for moaning, as disappointed as I am not to have had the class. I mean, I'm sure Jade wouldn't have failed to show up without a word to anyone without having a good reason.'

Finally, someone who shows a little compassion.

Susan lets out an exaggerated sigh. 'Yes, perhaps. But she's always struck me as the flighty, self-centred type. Maybe she got a better offer. Like a hot shag. She's an incorrigible flirt. You must have noticed. Despite her butter-wouldn't-melt demeanour. We can't get bogged down with it, though. She's only an instructor, after all. They'll get someone new in for next week if she's a goner.'

A goner? I so want to ignore Susan's insensitive comment, tell myself I have better things to do with my time than get into some petty slanging match with her, but I can't stop myself on this occasion. 'How can you say that? We all went to her thirtieth. You were practically attached to Jade at one point that night. Pouring your heart and soul out to her, from what I saw.'

Susan widens her eyes. 'I didn't know I was being watched.'

I catch Grace's eye – she knows, she was there at the time – and stand my ground, even though once again

Susan's managed to portray me as some kind of stalker. 'I was plastered,' she says. 'I would have attached myself to a postbox if it had happened to be standing next to me. And besides, I attend most of the social events here. I'm a sociable person and I like to put money into this place.' She casts her gaze around. 'God knows, it could do with a major refurbishment.'

If it's so bad, why the hell do you come here? I want to scream. Maybe it's because here she doesn't have to compete with clones of herself.

This time I do ignore her. Turn my attention to Grace. 'Did Martin mention if he's tried calling her?'

'No, he didn't say much, like Susan said. I should imagine he has, though. I mean, it'd be the first thing you'd do, right?' She looks around and receives several nods. 'Poor guy, he seemed a bit snowed under. Apparently, there's a private function on later this evening from eight thirty, and he's stuck here till late manning it.'

'People have better things to do with their time than go chasing after unreliable gym instructors,' Susan says.

Again, I ignore her. I'm better off finding Martin, just in case he's had any joy reaching Jade in the last ten minutes. If not, I'll try her mobile again, and if that proves unfruitful, I'll go over to her place. We're friends, and she wouldn't just ignore my messages, even though on Monday we both said some things we shouldn't have in the heat of the moment. She knows I was only looking out for her. All I wanted was for her to realise she's worth more than she gives herself credit for. That she doesn't have to let her past dictate her future.

Chapter Three

Jade

Before

I've finally met the man of my dreams. The man I've been picturing since I was a little girl. The one who will make me whole. Make up for my shitty past. He's everything I'd hoped he would be. Kind, caring, attentive. We had the most magical day yesterday. He said I'm what's been missing from his life all these years. Then pulled me tight to his chest and hugged me so hard it almost made me cry. It was as if he couldn't bear to let go. As if I had become his everything, who he'd cherish for all eternity.

I see how sad he is, though. Behind the armour he wears. I know he wishes he could turn back time and do it all again; thinks about how his life could have been so different had he not tied himself to *her*. I assured him we can all say that. Look back and wish we'd made different choices. Else we'd be living perfect lives. OK, so he's made some pretty crap decisions, been too trusting, gullible even, not to mention lived much of his life treading on eggshells where she's concerned, just because he's too afraid of what she might do. But then again, I've also been naive. Let myself be walked all over. But as the saying goes, what doesn't kill us makes us stronger. It's never too late for second chances, and now he and I are being offered a second stab at happiness with each other. I told him he needed to grab life by the horns before it passed him by. No matter how guilty she makes him feel. She's been in the driver's seat for so long now, it's as if he's resigned to it. Bullied into submission. But I told him he needed to wake up, that this is his time, *our* time, and that he shouldn't feel guilty about seizing his chance to escape. That I'm a big girl, who knows what she's doing and that he can trust me. He'd smiled at me when I said all this; removed his snug red woollen scarf and wrapped it around me, as we'd sat on a bench in the frosty morning air.

I just hope my words were enough, and that he stays true to his own. I'm not sure I'm strong enough to be let down again, despite the danger we might be placing ourselves in.

He has become my world, the light in my darkness, and there is no way forward without him.

Chapter Four

Natalie

Friday, 20 July 2018

I leave the others, turn on my heel and make for the stair-well, hearing Susan mutter something under her breath. I'm sure it's something derogatory, but I don't care; I have better things to think about.

I scurry down the stairs to the first floor, making sure I take the left-hand side, intending to stop off at the gym where I know Martin can often be found, either super-vising or giving a PT session. I exit at the doors, turn left and walk along the corridor until I reach the entrance to the gym. I peer through the glass and try my best to spot Martin, but, craning my neck this way and that, I see no sign of him. I go inside just in case I missed him, ask around, but to no avail. I'm disappointed but decide to try downstairs. If he's staying late for a function, he must be around somewhere. Heading back towards the stairwell, I fish out my phone just in case Jade's texted. But she hasn't. I try her number again, but she doesn't pick up. I feel almost sick at the thought of what might have happened to her. I just have this sixth sense that she's in trouble.

I reach the ground floor and head for the bar. It's still quite early at just on ten to seven, soft music playing in the background, but I spot a few regulars having a drink, some of them perched on stools at the counter, others, including Grace, Vivien and Susan, sitting at tables. They're tucked away in a corner, three large glasses of white wine in front of them. They certainly didn't waste much time getting their freebies in. It makes me doubt the sincerity of their supposed 'disappointment' at the class being off. I'm also more than a little surprised that Grace took Susan up on her offer. I'd have expected her to rush off home. Having said that, she did seem particularly worked up this evening. Clearly, she needed the drink to unwind with no yoga on offer. Still, seeing them cosied up together, like some sort of conspiratorial clique, stirs something inside me. *Frustration? Anger? Jealousy?* I'm not exactly sure what it is, but I do know I resent them for being so blasé about Jade's non-appearance. Grace happens to glance up and catch my eye. Something of a sheepish look in hers. I have no choice but to go over, courting a disdainful glare from Susan as I do.

'Any luck?' Grace asks, following this up with a hopeful smile.

I shake my head. 'No sign of Martin in the gym. And I can see he's not here, so I'll go and ask at reception on my way out.'

Grace picks up her glass, takes a sip, her eyes locked on mine over the rim. 'Maybe he's in the function room?'

'Yes, maybe,' I nod.

'Can't tempt you with a drink?' Susan's tone smacks of insincerity. I'm not a fool; I know I'm the last person she'd want to have a drink with if she could help it, so why does she bother asking? It's like she enjoys making me feel uncomfortable. She also knows I'm teetotal. The least fun drinking partner she could wish for.

I shake my head. Say with a sharpness to my voice, 'Funnily enough, I'm not in the mood.'

She doesn't bat an eyelid. 'You would be if you actually drank alcohol. Exercise is all well and good, but there's nothing better than a shot of vodka hitting your bloodstream.' She holds up her glass. 'Or a silky-smooth Chablis.' I watch her take a protracted sip. Watch her swallow it down her stringy, sun-damaged turkey neck, and at the same time can't help wishing she'd choke on it. 'Mm. Tastes like nectar. That's where you go wrong, Natalie. Right now, you're more wound up than the Duracell Bunny. If Jade's in trouble or she's done something wrong, they're not going to tell any of us. So, if you want my advice, I'd just leave it be.'

Her advice is the last thing I'd take. 'That's the second time you've mentioned Jade having done something wrong. Why would you suppose that's the case? Why aren't you more bothered about the fact that she could be hurt, or ill?' I let my gaze drill through her, delight in watching her eyes flicker with apprehension.

Even so, she's quick to regain her composure with a firm shake of her head, before throwing back more wine. 'I'm not supposing anything. Look, just forget what I said. I meant nothing by it. What I'm trying to say is, if it's personal, they're not likely to tell you. It would be a breach of confidentiality.'

'It's true, honey,' Vivien chimes in. 'Come and have a drink with us. Even if it's only a Coke. My treat.' She grins, revealing a perfect set of gleaming white teeth. It's hard to know which bit of her is real and which is fake. She clearly doesn't know me very well either: Coke is a complete no-no for me.

I politely decline, say my goodbyes and practically sprint out of the bar, almost colliding with Martin, or rather his torso, in the process. 'Oh, sorry, Martin!' I gasp. 'Wasn't looking where I was going.'

He's not in his sports gear today. Instead, he's wearing the club's branded navy-blue polo top and grey trousers, his dark blond hair parted at the side. Perhaps he's been in a meeting, or busy getting the function room ready. There's no question how handsome he is. I've even caught Grace glancing his way, blushing like a teenager with the biggest crush when he happens to walk by and say hi. Tall, broad-shouldered, I know from what Jade's said that he's a hit with most of the female staff as well as the clientele. Martin would have been a much better choice for Jade than *him*. But she told me he's too young. That she needs someone older, more mature.

'That's OK. I can't apologise enough for there being no class tonight. So disappointing, I know.' He looks genuinely sorry. 'Can't think what came over Jade. Have to say, I'm not best pleased. And neither is my manager.'

'I take it you haven't been able to speak to her, then? To be honest, I'm more worried about her than there being no class. She's not picking up any of my calls or messages. I just hope she's not hurt or in trouble.'

I fix my gaze on Martin but it's hard to read his expression. I can't tell whether he knows something more than he's letting on.

'I'm sorry, Natalie, I know you two are close, but I've not spoken to Jade. No one can get through to her.'

'Oh.'

'I've tried calling, left voicemails, as has Karen.' His tone becomes sharper. 'Frankly, I'm pretty ticked off. The very least she could have done was pick up the phone. It doesn't look good for the club's reputation, our instructors not bothering to show up without a word of explanation.'

'Yes, but it's unlike her,' I say in Jade's defence. 'She's never done anything like this before, has she? Let you down, I mean.'

'No,' Martin shakes his head, 'she hasn't, that's true. Usually she's very reliable.'

'What if she's had a car accident?'

'I don't think so. I checked the local travel updates and there've been no reported incidents in the area.' *Is it me, or is he really not that bothered? Or am I just taking out my frustration on Martin?* 'I would go over to hers myself, see what's what, but there's a function on here tonight and I have to be around.'

I give him a nod. 'That's OK, don't worry. I'll go over and check on her. I was going to anyway.'

Martin thanks me and I agree to let him know if I manage to get to the bottom of Jade's absence.

It's gone 7:30 p.m. by the time I leave the club, heading back along the Portsmouth Road towards Surbiton, where Jade rents a flat on the second floor of a converted period building on one of the many tree-lined avenues branching off the main high street that's dotted with charity shops, pubs, cafes and convenience stores. She gave me a set of keys around eight months ago, when she'd asked me to look in on her place while she was away on a two-night training course. I'm only a five-minute walk away, she said, so it made sense. I'd offered to give them back, but she'd insisted I keep them, just because I'd become such a close friend and she trusted me to keep them safe. It touched my heart that she felt she could count on me like that. So much so I had a duplicate set of keys to my place made up for her. I didn't tell Dr Jenkins, though. I didn't think she'd approve. She knows what I'm like. That letting someone into my personal space is a big deal, a big risk for me. For so long I've been precious about my stuff, always needing everything just so. So, I can't exactly blame her. But it felt right somehow. I felt that Jade and I had struck up enough of a bond for me to let her into my home. And it was a good feeling, being able to trust again after being let down by so many people in my life. After losing the person I counted on the most.

Jade's keys are attached to my own house keys, so there's no chance of me losing them. It's summer, and still light, although not as bright as we've been used to in recent weeks, now that the temperature's cooled and the days have been cloudier. At least the wind from earlier has died down, losing that piercing chill.

I'm nearly at the bottom of her road, having turned off the river path some five minutes ago and taken a street leading up towards the centre of town, passing my own house along the way. I check my phone again just in case she's messaged, but it's wishful thinking. I try calling once more, then, when I get no joy, send a text: 'Hi, you OK?' But there's still not a peep from her. Finally, I reach her building. Standing there, I glance to my right and notice her car is parked a little way up on the other side of the road. That's a good sign, surely? She must be in. But if that's the case, why hasn't she responded to any of my calls? Or Martin's? I stand there for a few seconds, looking up towards her window on the second floor, hoping to God she's in, hoping to God she's safe.

Hoping to God I won't live to regret the day Jade walked into my life and I allowed her to throw it off track.

Chapter Five

Natalie

One year before
July 2017

My alarm clock's shrill ringtone wakes me with a start at seven a.m. The same hour it goes off every morning without fail. Weekends too. I'd probably set it to the same time if I ever were to go away on holiday. But that's never going to happen because I've got no one to go on holiday with. I try not to dwell on this. At any rate, it's my choice to be alone, my life is better for it, while a change of scene would rattle me, and that wouldn't do. Wouldn't be relaxing at all. I am a creature of habit. I like things 'just so'. Have done ever since I left foster care, went through college, got a job and a place of my own. Everything in my home has its set place. It pacifies me, suits my character. Makes me feel safe, in control. The exact opposite to how I felt growing up as a child and which caused all the bad stuff to happen.

I live in a two-bedroom cottage house in Surbiton, just off the Portsmouth Road which runs parallel to the Thames Path. It's small, but it has the advantage of a decent basement where I have enough tinned food and water stocked to feed an army in the event of some major national crisis. Unlikely, I know, and I hope and pray it never happens because I loathe basements, but you can never be too sure, and being prepared is everything.

I love being by the water. It keeps me calm, centres my mind, and it's so freeing being able to walk to and from work along the river road every day. Also, as has been the case with everything in my life since leaving foster care, it gives me routine. My therapists have always said that's so important for me. Having routine. Feeling settled. Not putting myself in any kind of threatening or stressful situation.

After rising, I immediately shower for fifteen minutes. I set an alarm for this too, just because I don't want to go over the allotted time. That would really derail my morning, and I can't have that. I have fine shoulder-length brown hair, so it doesn't take me long to wash and towel-dry it. I can never be bothered with hairdryers, let alone fancy preening items like tongs or straighteners. I'm not fussed by that sort of thing; it would be self-indulgent of me, and besides, I've never been a looker, so it probably wouldn't do much good. I cut the ends myself, because I can't face setting foot inside a hairdresser. I can only imagine the looks I'd get were I ever to do so. I'd die of humiliation, and I wouldn't begin to know what to ask for. And the stress of not knowing would probably send my blood pressure through the roof. It's not like I'm searching for love or have anyone to impress. I have Ernie, my goldfish, for company. Ernie is the perfect companion; he knows his place and never does anything to wind me up or hurt me. I love watching him glide through the water. Whenever I do, I feel my underlying stress ebb away, a sense of peace descending over me. Other than Ernie, I am content to be alone. Being with someone scares me; it would cause too much disruption to my ordered lifestyle, and I can't take that chance. While the very idea of being intimate with a man terrifies me.

After showering I brush my teeth for exactly two and a half minutes using an electric toothbrush, then get dressed in my high-neck blouse and ankle-length skirt, put on my glasses and pad to the kitchen, fill the kettle and boil some water for my first cup of decaffeinated tea of the day. I'll have three more at Kingston Library, where I work as a full-time library assistant. No more, no less. I don't bother with much make-up, just a neutral lipstick and lick of mascara; foundation is too much of a faff. My decaf tea is taken with a splash of milk, no sugar. Sugar would only raise my anxiety levels. As would caffeine. I also pop two slices of square wholemeal bread in the toaster and fish out the low-salt margarine from the fridge in preparation. While I wait for the water to boil and my toast to pop, I go to my day planner and tick off 'shower, teeth, dress' for the appropriate day, then slide the marker pen back into its slot above the whiteboard. Every night, when every item on my checklist is complete, I will wipe this clean, write a new date and plan in preparation for the next morning. That way I'll know exactly what I've done and where I've been.

A few minutes later, I'm sitting in front of the TV in my tiny living room, watching *BBC Breakfast*. I don't have a lot of furniture, just a beige fabric two-seater sofa, a small coffee table and a twenty-eight-inch TV – along with Ernie in the corner and a potted plant. Too much stuff would overpower me. Things must be clean, visible and tidy.

It's hot and stuffy in my flat, not surprising as we're in the throes of a heatwave, but I'm too scared to leave the windows open overnight in case of intruders. There've been a spate of burglaries in the area in recent weeks, and the idea of someone breaking in and going through my stuff terrifies me, even though I don't have much of value. Just my laptop, the odd item of jewellery and some petty cash I keep in a jar in the kitchen. I can literally feel every inch of my fair-skinned body expanding, sweat accumulating between the rolls of fat around my waist and sliding up my back as I sit blowing then sipping my tea. You'd think with my relatively healthy lifestyle I'd be stick-thin, but the fact is I eat too many carbs – bread and pasta are my biggest weaknesses – and that, coupled with not much exercise, isn't a good combination.

The tea only makes things worse and so I only drink half, toss the rest in the sink, load the dishwasher, cross breakfast off my list, gather my things and leave the flat, making sure to double-lock it before I do. You'd think it would be a relief to get outside, but it's almost as suffocating in the open air as in my flat. I cross the road to take the river path to the centre of Kingston. The air is still, no breeze at all. I pass several early-morning runners, feeling seriously inadequate next to their toned physiques, jogging mothers pushing their babies in buggies, office workers like me heading towards their destinations but striding more purposefully, many of them having removed their suit jackets which are slung over their backs or draped across the crease of their elbows because of the heat. None of them appear as harassed or out of breath as I feel, though. I mean, I know I'm out of shape, but the heat only serves to accentuate this fact, and I find myself wheezing as I quicken my pace, conscious that I'm a little behind schedule. The idea of being late, even by a few minutes, disconcerts me, and so I'm aware that I need to make up for lost time. I shuffle along faster, growing hotter by the minute, feeling my ankles swell in my sensible court shoes, the sweat now dripping down my back and drenching my armpits, making me wish I'd brought a change of top. No doubt Sam, one of my colleagues at the library, a stuck-up sort who looks like she belongs behind the beauty counter at John Lewis with the amount of make-up she plasters on, will have something demeaning to say the moment she spies me. She normally does, even if it's just with her eyes. But I never say anything in response, despite wanting to. I'd love to answer her back, yell at her to piss off, but I know it would only lead to no good and I tell myself she's not worth my time and energy.

Finally, having made it to Kingston town centre and crossed two sets of traffic lights at the busy one-way system, soaked with perspiration and feeling like I'm about to pass out, I reach work and enter via a side door reserved for employees. The familiar smells of books and coffee greet me as I walk in and all at once a sense of calm filters through me, knowing I'm in the one place that brings me peace. Books have been such a comfort to me since I was a child. Offering an infinite number of worlds I could get lost in. But most importantly, a welcome escape from reality.

Jane, my manager, is a coffee addict. It's only 8:45 a.m. but she'll be on her third mug already. All day she flies around like a bee on speed; small wonder, with the amount of caffeine she puts into her system, and I fear that one day she'll keel over from a heart attack, or something. I never touch coffee, and I wonder how Jane possibly gets any sleep at night. She's a wiry woman in her late forties, with short brown hair and spectacles permanently perched on the end of her nose. I know she has a husband, but no kids – I always wonder what happened there as she seems the maternal type, but I daren't ask and besides, I don't need other people's complications in my life. She hears me approach, looks up immediately with her thyrotoxic eyes and I catch the look of horror on her face. Evidently, I look a fright. I certainly feel like one.

'Dear God, Natalie, are you OK? Your face is as red as a beetroot! Come and sit down. I'll fetch you some water.'

I let her steer me to a chair, say thank you, then wait for her to bring me a glass of water. She's back in a flash and instructs me to drink it all. I do as she says and before long, my body temperature has cooled considerably, but I still feel exhausted. I'm so unfit. It's pretty sad, but the idea of exercising in itself is exhausting.

'How's that? Feeling better?'

Jane's eyes lock on me, full of concern. She's a kind person, calm too despite her caffeine habit; the ideal boss for someone like me, and I tell her I'm grateful. But just then, Sam, who's never on time, flounces through the door and my mood instantly drops. She's wearing a strappy red summer dress with white wedges, her glossy chestnut tresses bouncing off her bare shoulders. Her gaze latches onto me, and I see scorn in her eyes in contrast to Jane's pity.

'What on earth…?' she begins. Jane explains how I'm feeling rather overheated.

Sam dumps her Louis Vuitton bag (I'm sure it's fake) on the floor, pulls out a nail file and begins to work on her right thumbnail, which looks perfectly fine to me.

'Oh, you poor thing,' she coos, pulling a sad face. 'Look, don't get me wrong, but I do worry you might have gone and brought this on yourself, Nats.' (I HATE it when she calls me Nats; only Jack was allowed to call me

33

that.) 'I don't mean to sound harsh or anything,' *no, course not*, 'but there really is no excuse for slovenliness in this day and age. There's a leisure club a short distance from your house, isn't there?' *Yes.* 'If I were you, I'd join it. I work out six times a week. You don't get to look like this without putting the work in.' She flashes a pearly-white smile and does a twirl, and I literally want to kill her. Plus, I'm sure she's had a few nips and tucks here and there.

'I don't like gyms,' I reply meekly. I hear my voice. So docile. Pathetic, even. But I daren't be more belligerent. Don't let on that the merest thought of stepping inside a gym and exposing my unsightly bingo wings and love handles to a bunch of self-serving judgemental narcissists has me breaking out in a cold sweat.

She rolls her eyes and shakes her head. 'Now how would you know that, Nats? Have you ever been to one? Anyway, The River Club is more than a gym,' she waffles on. 'It's a social club, there's tennis and a bar, and again, please don't take this the wrong way, but I'm guessing you could do with pepping up that area of your life? I so hate to think of you being lonely. I mean, it's like you're middle-aged or something.'

Another sad face. I count to five inside my head, take a deep breath. The answer to her question is no, I haven't ever been inside a gym, so I guess she has a point. But there's a reason for that. One of her is bad enough – the thought of mixing with a roomful of Sams is my ultimate nightmare. I'd rather slit my wrists. As for being social, I can't think of anything worse than trying to make small talk with a load of strangers I have nothing whatsoever in common with. It would drive me mental. I'd rather talk to Ernie. He's no trouble. I can trust him. He doesn't talk back.

I simply shake my head.

'Now, now, Sam, don't get on to Natalie,' Jane interjects. 'She's not into gyms. Not everyone is.'

'Oh my goodness, is that the impression I gave? I really wasn't getting on to her, Jane!' Sam looks positively affronted that the thought should ever have crossed Jane's mind. 'I'm just trying to give Nats some gentle advice.' Yet another patronising look. 'Now's the time to start, when you're still *relatively* young. It'll catch up with you before you know it, and the damage will be irreversible. Anyway, I've tried my best out of the goodness of my heart to make you see sense. But now I have some cataloguing to do. See you later.' I watch Sam pirouette off and disappear through the double doors leading out on to the library floor, and feel an immediate sense of relief.

A quick glance at my watch confirms it's fifteen minutes to opening. I tell myself that I'm OK, that I need to get a grip, get on with my work.

'You OK now?' Jane asks. 'You're on the desk this morning, so you won't be on your feet too much.'

She smiles kindly and I smile back, while at the same time feeling so lame. She's treating me like some ninety-year-old OAP, rather than a twenty-nine-year-old woman who shouldn't need to be sitting down to catch her breath after a relatively short walk to work. Anyone would think I'd run a marathon.

A few minutes later, I'm sitting at the circulation desk, the doors having just been opened to the public. There's a slow trickle of customers through to eleven o'clock, and then things become steadily busier with the under-fives' rhyme-time group arriving with their bleary-eyed mothers. A cavalcade of buggies pours in and parks up at the front in the allocated spaces, various irritable and overheated toddlers strapped in and arching their backs in protest the moment they enter the familiar-looking premises and sense their impending freedom. The place has gone from pristine pin-drop silence to something of a war zone. The air filled with crying, shrieking, shuffling, and a cacophony of stressed-out mothers' voices. I think how lucky these kids are to have mothers who take them to the library; mothers who want them to be happy and grow into normal adults with healthy minds and no hang-ups or issues. I'm certain these kids are loved and adored and given the best start in life. I only hope they appreciate the fact when they get older. I for one can't imagine being a mother. Putting someone else first. I have a hard enough time concentrating on me.

I watch the mum and toddler group disappear into the children's section of the library, happily closed off from the main part, so only the faint sound of 'Old MacDonald' can be heard through the doors. I've just finished stamping five books on the Second World War for a polite elderly gentleman who trundles off breathlessly once I'm done, when a gorgeous, slim, long-limbed woman, maybe in her late twenties, appears holding what looks like a bunch of flyers. I immediately recoil, conscious of my appearance in the face of such perfection. I'm not sure what she wants; I have a feeling she's not the 'library' sort, and this sets me on edge. What *does* she want, my naturally suspicious mind can't help wondering?

'Hi,' she says, her face breaking into the broadest of smiles. It's a warm, genuine smile. Not one of the fake, condescending smiles Sam's in the habit of giving me.

'Hello,' I find myself stuttering, still on edge. My glasses slip to the crook of my nose on account of the sheen on my face that's developed in the space of a few seconds, and I push them back up. 'Can I help you?'

She holds up the flyers. 'I'm new to the area, just started as a fitness instructor at The River Club. Do you know it?'

Might have guessed. She looks like she spends hours in the gym. Still, her pleasant demeanour isn't in line with my usual impression of gyms and the egomaniacs who inhabit them.

'Yes,' I nod, 'it's actually not too far from where I live.' Inside, I think what a coincidence it is that only a few minutes ago Sam was lecturing me to join.

'But you're not a member?'

From out of nowhere Sam appears. She must have been listening in on our conversation like the sneak she is – so much for her cataloguing – because she then gives a little chuckle and says, her gaze directed at the blonde: 'Natalie? Gosh, we all love Nats to bits, but I think it's pretty clear the answer to that is no, even though I so wish it wasn't.' Her eyes give me the once-over, and I feel so ashamed I want the ground to swallow me up. She carries on. 'Poor thing nearly passed out walking here this morning. I keep telling her she needs to get fit, else one day it'll catch up with her, and then, well, I hate to think what the consequences will be. It doesn't bear thinking about.' She gives a prolonged shake of her head.

The blonde eyes me compassionately, then shoots daggers at Sam. 'You know, that's pretty unkind. I wouldn't be surprised if it's unhelpful comments from the likes of you that have put her off joining a gym.' Sam looks gobsmacked, opens her mouth to speak, but nothing comes out. I grin inside. I'm enjoying the show immensely, and although I don't know her, I love the blonde for standing up for me. Just because no one, aside from Jack, has ever done that. 'Gyms can be pretty intimidating places, I know,' she continues kindly, directing her gaze at me and purposely ignoring Sam. 'I've worked out at a few, so I can totally see where you're coming from. But The River Club really isn't like that. You should give it a go, or at least, give my class a go.' She hands me a flyer. 'Beginner's Body Attack.'

The word 'attack' puts me off instantly. It sounds threatening. Sets my pulse racing. Accords with my general impression of gyms.

'I've only just started the class, which is why I'm handing out flyers. The first one's on Wednesday, six thirty p.m. I'm also planning a Monday and Friday yoga class. I think you might like that. It really centres the mind, gets rid of any stress, which, forgive me if I'm barking up the wrong tree, I'm sensing you have.' Another smile as I feel my cheeks burn. 'But let's face it,' she continues, 'none of us are immune to stress these days, life's too bloody crazy. Plus we all have our own demons that haunt us and need to be expelled, and to my mind, exercise is the best way to achieve that. As it happens, I have a few free passes for friends.' She delves into her handbag and pulls out a pass for one class and one gym session, then offers it to me.

'For me?' I'm startled at her kindness but remain unconvinced. I start to shake my head, say, 'I don't know, it's really not my thing,' but just as I do I catch the smug look on Sam's face, a look as if to say, *I knew it, I win*, and it's as if a fire is lit inside me. The blonde holds my gaze, giving me an imploring look as if to say, 'Come on, go for it, prove this bitch wrong,' and then I chew my lip, find myself taking the flyer and saying, 'OK, sure, why not? I'll give it a go.'

I glance at Sam, who looks stunned, a sense of satisfaction swelling inside me.

'Great,' smiles the blonde. 'I'm Jade, by the way.' She hands me the flyers. 'As I said, I've not long moved to the area, so I'll leave these here if that's OK with you. If you could put them on the counter for anyone who might be interested to pick up, I'd be grateful.'

I nod. 'Of course, no problem.'

A wink, followed by another smile. At the same time I notice a couple of teenage boys loitering to the right, pretending to look at the historical fiction section but clearly more interested in researching Jade. Jade seems to sense this. I'm guessing she's used to such attention. I watch her glance their way, flash another smile, and it's like they have no idea where to look. She gives me another wink. 'Thanks, Natalie. See you Wednesday, six thirty sharp.' Jade gives Sam a last jubilant look before swivelling round and making for the door, her high ponytail swishing from side to side as she does so.

Just to see Sam cut down to size was worth it. But I'm also having kittens thinking about how I'm going to work up the courage to walk into that class on Wednesday.

Chapter Six

Susan

Friday, 20 July 2018

I'd much rather have gone straight home and collapsed on the sofa in front of Netflix with a bottle of red than hang around talking to Grace and Vivien. As much as I quite like Grace, and have some modicum of sympathy for all she has on with her kids and her mum and her dull hermit husband, she can be a bit of a wet blanket droning on about how hard she has it all the time. I mean, she doesn't *have* to do so much. She could just say no, fuck it, you pick up some of the slack. It's what I'd do. And even though Vivien's harmless and quite fun, and we do have rich husbands and Botox in common, her Texan drawl does rather grate on my nerves after a while. Plus, she's not exactly the brightest tool in the box. But having said all that, spending time with them was more appealing than the prospect of facing Lance when I got home, his comment this morning before he left for work still ringing in my ears. 'You might want to think about cutting down on the booze, Susie, it's not kind to the waistline.' And then he had the nerve to follow that up with a spiteful pinch on the hips!

Bastard.

I mean, I know I've put him in a worse mood than usual. I'm not so naive not to realise that after our fight on Wednesday night he has more reason than ever to hate me. But I had expected him to be a bit more conciliatory. Now that I have him by the balls. Bloody men. So frigging arrogant, the lot of them.

'Right, well, duty calls, so I'd better get going,' Grace says. She knocks back the rest of her Chablis and makes to get up.

'No time for another?' I don't know why I ask this. It's not like I'm having a particularly good time. Not like these two women are my ideal drinking companions. But then again, I'm not sure who is any more. The best days of my life were my university ones. Hanging out with Tamara and her socialite friends. The River Club is the last place I want to be this evening. For more reasons than the lack of scintillating company. But I guess it just goes to show how I'll do anything to avoid going home. Plus, I don't want my desire to get away to look too obvious. That's why I turned up to the class in the first place. Even though I had a good idea it wouldn't be on.

Grace shakes her head, looks at both me and Vivien with those big blue soulful eyes of hers. 'I'd love another one. Love a bloody bottle, to be honest, but I really must be getting home, Jim will wonder where I am. And there's the boys' karate club in the morning. Not to mention an article I need to finish for Monday. Honestly, going solo isn't all it's cracked up to be. I sometimes wonder if I should go back to a paper or magazine. I kind of miss the buzz of an office, along with the regular pay.'

Just listening to her rabbit on nearly sends me to sleep. The way she cowers to her husband not only bores me to tears, it makes my blood boil. I also find her a bit secretive at times. I mean, she's been to my house for coffee mornings, but she's never once returned the invitation. It's a bit rude; makes me wonder what else she's hiding other than a tedious husband. Then again, maybe I ought to be concerned. Maybe he's violent or verbally abusive. She seems the type who'd fall for a controlling man. Maybe he forbids her from having friends over. I say I *ought* to be concerned, but right now I've got enough of my own problems to worry about anyone else's. I need to keep my wits about me. I stifle the urge to yawn, then roll my eyes. 'Who fucking cares? You can't let a man control your life. I certainly live by that motto. Let him do bloody karate club for once. It's not like he goes into the City or anywhere far, like Lance. No frigging excuse, as far as I'm concerned. Don't let him walk all over you. Stand up for yourself, woman.'

Grace gives me a faint smile, and I can tell that although she's grateful for the pep talk she won't take a word of what I've just said on board. *Why the hell do I bother?* I'm too fucking generous for my own good. 'Thanks, I appreciate the thought,' she says, 'but it's my turn tomorrow. He's still working on his book.'

Argh, not that again. He's been working on that bloody book for as long as I've known her! 'Besides, to be fair to him,' she prattles on, 'he's been pretty good lately helping out with the kids, doing his fair share of the school runs, club drop-offs and pick-ups. Not like when we were living in Southampton when I was doing it all.' She sighs heavily. 'It's a bit sad that it's taken Dad's death to make him see the light and realise how much I do for him and the kids and that I need some help now and again.'

Dull, dull, dull.

'Right! So why do you still sound like he's doing you a favour? He's not the only one who has a career to manage. You have too. And forgive me if I'm missing something, but I'm guessing he had a hand in creating those kids of yours? Unless it was the immaculate conception, part two? Let him shoulder some of the burden for once. It's the twenty-first frigging century, equal rights, work–life balance and all that jazz. And you have your mother to look after. I mean, I know she's in a home, but you're the one who visits her. I bet he doesn't. I bet he doesn't even visit his own parents.'

Just as I say this, I realise that's rather rich coming from me.

'Well, she is *my* mother,' Grace says, 'and his parents are up North. You know what men are like. They're crap at keeping in contact, even when it comes to their own parents. It is stressful, though, you're right. Now that I'm in my late forties, I really do miss having a sibling. I could so have done with a blood relative to shoulder some of the burden. It all falls on me.'

'Exactly! Which is why he should step up and take the load off you. Men, it's so typical, always wanting their cake and eating it.'

Having said my piece, I down the rest of my wine.

Vivien frowns. 'Is everything OK with you and Lance? Haven't seen him in the gym much lately.'

I study Vivien for a few seconds. She looks concerned, but I wonder how genuine she is. Whether it's more a case of her fishing for gossip. Just because it's the kind of thing I'd do. We're quite alike in that way. It's why I tolerate her company, I guess.

'Oh, you know, same old, same old. We're like passing ships. He's a workaholic. Four nights a week he's either working late at the office or out with clients. It comes with the territory when you're a partner at a major City law firm. But I knew exactly what I was getting into when I married him.'

'Doesn't that upset you?' Grace asks. She's standing over the table now, ready to go. I wish she bloody would, it's getting on my nerves. Over her shoulder I notice three dishy young men walk into the bar. They've clearly been in the gym, all hot and sweaty. What I wouldn't give for one night of hot no-strings-attached sex with one of them. Better for the skin than any fancy cream or treatment, that's for sure. 'It would me.' Grace stirs me from my delicious fantasy. 'I'd wonder what he might be getting up to. I mean, you know what men are like, how they can be led astray. Especially when their wives aren't around to keep an eye on them. Or have busy lives themselves. They're so much more likely to buckle under peer pressure, or have some kind of midlife crisis.'

'No,' I lie. 'Like I said, I knew what I was getting into. And we wouldn't have the lifestyle we have if he wasn't in the profession he's in. It pays for my winter skiing trips to Courchevel, and my spring sojourns in Cannes. Not to mention my summer breaks in Portofino. I'd rather not know what he's up to.'

Grace flops back down on her chair. 'There's more to life than money and five-star holidays, though, isn't there?' she says. 'All I've ever wanted was a man who loves me for me. Who's loyal. A family with kids who feel they can tell me anything, give me grandchildren. Health and happiness. Loyalty and respect. Total honesty. Isn't that what's most important in this life?'

Vivien and I exchange a glance. Then burst into fits of laughter. 'Jeez, sugar, you really do live in a fairy-tale world,' Vivien says. 'Yes, maybe, but let me tell you something, honey – money helps. I love Frank, but I'm not *in* love with him, like when we were in our twenties. I don't hang on his every word, looking up at him with puppy-dog eyes, and I for certain don't want to spend every minute of my waking day with him. Heck, I'd frigging kill him if I was stuck with him 24/7. Passion fades. The kids leave you. And when it does, and when they do, money helps. Helps take the load off, helps take your mind off the fact that you're one step closer to the grave, but also how the men in our lives can be such utter shits.' She grins broadly, then raises her glass to mine and we toast our men and the money they earn to keep us in the style to which we've become accustomed.

I don't let on that, unlike Vivien, I don't love Lance. Not one bit. I don't even like him, to be fair. In fact, sometimes I just wish he'd fuck off and die. Even though I know how unlikely that is to happen, he's so sickeningly fit; as fit as the day I married him. Unlike me. But then again, he hasn't pushed three babies out of his vagina, has he? I think I'm owed a little leeway on that basis. Maybe the answer is to hire someone to bump him off, and then I'll get the lot – I know he's left everything to me in the event of his death, and then the kids in the event of mine – because I was there when he made the will. Unless he's changed it without me knowing. He'd better not have done. Hopefully, after our little chat on Wednesday he'll have put a halt on any change of heart he might have had in recent weeks. Thirty years ago I could never have imagined wishing him dead. Whereas now, everything he does sets my teeth on edge: the way he chews, the way he always leaves the stalks of his broccoli on the side of his plate and can never be bothered to put them in the food recycling bin, meaning I end up having to do it; the way he chuckles when he thinks he's made a hilarious joke even though all his jokes are toe-curling; the way he shouts at the TV when Arsenal are playing – referring to them as 'lads' or by their first names, as if they're his best mates from school; the way he still leaves the toilet seat up after three decades of marriage; the way he leaves stray black hairs in the sink after he's wet-shaved (refusing to use an electric razor because it doesn't leave as neat a finish, like anyone will notice or give a fuck), despite having the gall to complain about my hair plugging the shower! Once upon a time, way back when, I literally worshipped the ground he walked on. The sun shone out of his tight, perfectly formed arse, and I'd have done anything to make him mine. I would have sunk to the lowest levels imaginable.

I did, in fact. Although he can never know that.

Grace stands up again, clutching her gym bag. 'Well, thanks for the company, ladies, it was nice to catch up. Hopefully tonight was just a blip and Jade will be back on Monday. Can't think why she wouldn't show without a word. Maybe Natalie will get to the bottom of it.'

That freak, I think to myself. She's so odd. With her OCD mannerisms. Specified gym clothes for specified days. Always standing in the far left-hand corner at the back. Doting on Jade like she's got some lovesick lesbian crush. There's something very wrong about her. And she had a particularly weird look about her tonight. Almost like something was working overtime in her brain and she was on the brink of erupting. It's like she's in a trance half the time. I see the way she clenches a fist at her side even though she thinks she's being discreet. It's not normal. I noticed it on Wednesday. As we waited for Jade to start the class. Her eyes were glazed and locked on Jade. Not because she was concentrating. It was more like she was sizing her up. Mad at her, even. Just recalling that look in her eyes gives me the creeps. I need to be on my guard with her. It was slack of me earlier, but I couldn't help myself when she commented on my *heart-to-heart* with Jade. I was so rat-arsed at the time I had no idea she was watching. But now that I know she was, and how close she and Jade are, it makes me wonder what else she knows. The last thing I need is her sticking her nose in and spilling secrets she has no business spilling.

'Yes, maybe,' I say. 'Perhaps something came up at the last minute, or she had a flat tyre or something. Very likely she'll be back on Monday. Have a great weekend.'

Did I sound convincing? I'm not sure, but they seemed to buy it.

Vivien and I watch Grace walk off, and then against my better judgement I order another glass of wine.

It's force of habit.

Something to mask the void in my life.

But also, and more importantly, my guilt.

Chapter Seven

Natalie

Friday, 20 July 2018

I press the buzzer for Jade's flat and wait. I'm hopeful that she's home, having seen her car parked across the road, but still unnerved by her failure to answer my calls. There's no response. I try again. Still nothing. With a growing sense of alarm brewing inside me I fish out my own key and turn it in the lock before stepping into the communal hallway. The light has almost faded as I take a last look around me at the desolate street, the shadows of the trees and distant street lamps towering over me, making me feel small and vulnerable, especially as I see no other human presence. It's odd for this area, and the still relatively early hour; usually there are some signs of activity, being so close to the main high street: drinkers pouring out of the pub, or into the local McDonald's, craving grease to mop up their inebriation; commuters heading home from the station, either walking or looking to catch a bus. But tonight it's deathly quiet, the shadows of the inanimate my only apparent company. It's not the best of evenings weather-wise, so perhaps I shouldn't be surprised. Even so, the lack of human activity makes me nervous, and I realise how defenceless I'd be in the face of some random attacker hovering close by, waiting to pounce. Or perhaps wondering what I am up to as I linger at the doorway looking around anxiously. Guiltily, even, from where they are standing.

But it's not like I haven't been here before; the neighbours must have seen me come and go umpteen times. Must know that Jade and I are close. That we hang out a fair bit. Even so, I can't help feeling conspicuous. Also, a sense of déjà vu. Maybe it's just that I'm worked up. Not knowing what's happened to Jade. Not sleeping these past few nights, my routine all over the shop.

I gently shut the door and instinctively look towards old Mrs Denby's flat, half expecting her to burst out of it, the usual cross look masking her face, before proceeding to give me the third degree as to what I am up to. But the door remains shut. Not a word out of her. Thank God.

Gingerly, I creep up the stairs, my stomach growling because I've not eaten anything since the low-sugar, high-protein bar I had at 5:30, like I always have one hour before my class. By now I would have been home and already eaten my veggie lasagne and salad. Prescribing a set meal for each day stops me stressing about what to cook. Keeps my meals regular, my blood sugar levels even. But tonight hasn't been normal by any standards. And neither was last night, waking up in the early hours to find myself still reclined on the sofa, fully clothed and starving. It's unnerving; against everything Dr Jenkins has tried to instil in me. But I must try and overcome my own anxiety for Jade's sake.

I reach the second floor and hover in front of Jade's door. I put my ear to it, listen out for any hint of movement, the sound of her voice, someone else's voice, including her lover's or possibly even another man's.

Although I'd never give Susan the benefit of being right, I know what Jade can be like – she can be rather flirtatious when it comes to men, and so I wouldn't have put it past her to have some random guy in there with her. But I hear nothing. My heart is beating double time, my mind racing with a whole host of morbid thoughts as I insert the key into the lock, my hand quivering as I turn it and push the door open. Taking a cursory look around her tiny hallway, nothing seems out of place, but then I spy her car keys on the hall table. No house keys, though. It doesn't mean she's not here; they could be in a jacket pocket, or lying around elsewhere. But if that's so, why hasn't she appeared? Why haven't I heard a peep out of her? I'm suddenly having palpitations at the thought – the thought of why Jade's not made a sound since I entered her flat, and I almost don't want to go a step further. But I force myself to. First trying the kitchen, then the living room. 'Jade,' I call out, 'Jade, are you here? Are you OK?' A part of me wonders if she's asleep on the sofa or has her headphones on like she often does when moving around the flat, meaning she hasn't detected my presence. But I suspect it's wishful thinking.

There's no sign of anything amiss in the living room, or kitchen either. The wildly imaginative side of me had pictured overturned furniture. Or some other evidence of violent intrusion. I'm relieved there's nothing so awful. But it doesn't stem my sense of unease, the fluttering in my belly. I do spy an unwashed cereal bowl and coffee mug in the sink. Dried grains of muesli still stuck to the rim of the bowl, the last dregs of coffee swimming at the base of the mug. It looks like they've been there for some time, possibly yesterday's rather than this morning's breakfast, and this strikes fear in me. Just because I know

50

that, like me, Jade doesn't leave mess. She either washes up immediately or loads the dishwasher, which I find is empty.

Her entire flat, although small, is generally kept immaculate. She told me she rented it unfurnished, and it's clear from the way it's been decorated that she has a naturally artistic eye. I've always liked coming here. Although it's compact and modern, the cosy mix of furniture, colours and textures lend it character. The colour scheme is harmonious, with everything from the side lamp in the living room to the toaster in the kitchen working with the rest of the rooms' earthy tones and natural colours. I know she doesn't have a lot of money, and so it's been a case of quality over quantity. A modernist chair taking centre stage in the living room; an art deco vase in pride of place on a table in the hallway as you walk in. I'm certain it's her keen sense of style that attracts men as much as her looks.

I feel my guts churn again as I pluck up the courage to venture towards Jade's bedroom, terrified of what I might find. The door is shut. I place my hand on the knob and turn it, push it, preparing myself for the worst. But when I step inside the room and look around, I'm not sure what to make of things. I find that her bed is empty, the covers intact, as if no one slept in it last night. I know Jade likes to keep things neat and tidy, but the way the bed is made, it almost looks too perfect. Not a crease in sight, while the pillow is smoothed out. Conversely, three drawers are pulled out from the chest to the right of her bed. I walk over, see that they contain pants, sweaters and jogging bottoms. It's unlike Jade not to have closed them. It's like she was in a rush, didn't have time. Perhaps an unexpected emergency or a last-minute errand? I think about how it was sheeting down with rain last night. What if she'd popped down the road for milk or some other essential she'd realised she was lacking, not bothering to take the car, but then got set upon by some lunatic on the way home? All sorts of nasty images flash through my mind – of her hurt, or worse, lying dead in a ditch somewhere. What if she was taken against her will? I squeeze my eyes shut, clench a fist at my side, desperately trying to blank out the thought, stop myself from thinking the worst. I've always had a vivid imagination. As a child I'd experience night terrors so real, I'd wake up in a cold sweat, scared and breathless. Jack would be the one to calm me down, tell me it was just a dream. But my brother's not here now. There's no one here to comfort me, reassure me everything's going to be OK, and I must try and get some answers alone.

There's only one room I haven't tried yet: the bathroom. I'm not sure why I've saved that for last, it's not like I know what awaits me in there. Perhaps because it's the most private space in Jade's home. Or maybe it's just chance that I've made it my last port of call. Another deep breath, and as I make my way to the bathroom door I notice it's slightly ajar, while I can hear a soft, steady *drip, drip, drip* of a tap that hasn't been quite turned off. It sends a shiver up my spine. I use my fingertips to push the door open and immediately notice Jade's mobile phone lying on the bathroom stand to the right of the washbasin. Fear accelerates in me once again, and I almost don't want to venture further and look round the corner where I know Jade's shower lies. But I do. And it's at this point that I see gym clothes strewn across the floor. Unmistakably Jade's. And I see traces of what looks like blood on the bath mat.

But I don't see Jade.

Chapter Eight

Grace

'Jim, I'm home,' I call out softly as I enter the hallway of our home in Cobham, one of the more affluent areas of Surrey. We moved here, to a house situated at the end of a quiet cul-de-sac just over a year ago, having uprooted ourselves from Southampton where Jim had taught physics at an all-boys' private school and I worked as a features writer for the *Daily Echo* newspaper. It's very different to Southampton. Quiet, peaceful, more upmarket, like I said. The neighbours, who are all retirement age, keep themselves to themselves, and that suits me and Jim to a tee. Quiet and peaceful is exactly what we wanted. No prying eyes, no gossipmongers, no intrusive questions. So different to how it was before, when the life we led made it impossible to avoid this, even more so after the inquiry. Jim, of course, has his own separate reasons for wanting to hide himself away. And I cannot begrudge him that.

There's no response. Maybe he didn't hear me. It's also possible he's fallen asleep on the sofa. He often does that, even more so lately, just because he gets tired so easily. He turned our loft conversion into his study when we first moved in. Said he needed somewhere quiet to work, somewhere he'd be able to think. It's certainly peaceful, overlooking our garden rather than the road. Although, to be fair, even the road is pretty dead much of the time. Sometimes, when I'm downstairs and it's so quiet I might hear a pin drop, I think to myself that I might as well be alone. I try not to take it to heart, even though it often feels like he wants to bury himself up there to get away from me. But on my better days, I realise he's just being practical, that he needs the peace and quiet to work on his book, having taken an indefinite sabbatical from teaching. We wouldn't be able to stay afloat were it not for the fact that Dad had made several canny investments back in the day. Not only did he leave me half the house he and Mum bought mortgage-free in the 1970s, knowing Mum's mind was going the way it was and wanting to avoid his share getting swallowed up on nursing home fees, he also made sure I inherited two semi-detached houses in Southampton he'd managed to acquire in the 1980s' property boom. I sold both to buy this place and help with Mum's care, having moved her to a lovely residential home less than a mile from here. There were other savings accounts, too. He was smart like that, was Dad. His body may have been falling apart, but unlike Mum, his mind was all there. And I'm grateful for that. At least he was still the Dad I'd always known and loved when he passed, whereas when I try and have a conversation with Mum these days, I don't even recognise the person I'm talking to.

Now Jim's in the habit of cocooning himself away for lengthy periods, we seem to spend even less time together than we did in Southampton. I understand his reasons, but it's still hard, especially when I think back to when we were young and in love and had all the time in the world. When we couldn't get enough of each other. That saccharine-sweet couple at college, uni and beyond. Always together. Joined at the hip. But now? Now I can't recall the last time we were seen out in public together. The girls at the gym must wonder why they've never met him. They're not that foolish or blasé not to wonder. I bet Susan does. I bet she wonders why I've never had her over for coffee. All their other halves, Lance and Frank for example, have been to at least one club social, including Jade's thirtieth, but Jim hasn't been to any. It's a bit awkward turning up without a plus one, always having to make up some excuse for your husband's absence, always on the lookout for someone to talk to because it's never ideal standing there like a billy no-mates, wishing you could click your fingers and become invisible because you feel like you stick out like a sore thumb, is it? Then again, I'm not sure Lance and Frank go along to socials because they necessarily want to. I know they work out in the gym, but I also get the feeling they're under Susan's and Vivien's thumbs, so don't exactly have much choice in the matter. The opposite to how I've treated Jim since we got together. I've never crowded him, I've always given him space, never made him feel it was my way or the highway. Perhaps I've been too lax, not kept him on a tight enough leash. But I never wanted to be that kind of wife. And we've never been that kind of couple. I'm also certain Lance and Frank come along to those events to avoid spending time with their wives at home. Lance especially. It's always safer in the company of strangers, isn't it? Less chance for arguments, to say the wrong thing. Having said that, I've noticed the strained look on Lance's face when Susan's had a bit too much to drink, like he's

55

embarrassed to be in her company, like he wishes she'd just shut the hell up. Being a lawyer, I imagine he has to be careful about what he says in public, so maybe he's worried about her letting out some client secret or ruining his reputation. Or worse, something intimate. I don't feel sorry for him because I find him a slippery sort, and in many ways he and Susan seem to deserve one another. But he's good at playing the game, never saying anything, just keeps it buttoned up inside the way we all do.

Everyone puts on a face in public, too afraid to make a scene, to show their true colours, what they're hiding, what they're ashamed of. I'm a classic example. The fact is, a couple's life could look like a bed of roses to the outside world, when in reality, behind closed doors, it's a gutter of thorns, lies and deceit.

And that's why I limited myself to that one glass of wine tonight, despite the fact that I was aching for another. I can't allow the truth to come out.

Jim's always been a bit antisocial anyway. Typical academic, I guess. I was the first and last girlfriend he ever had. He said he didn't need to sleep around to feel satisfied. That he knew I was the only one for him from the first moment we set eyes on each other at the sixth form gates. It's the most romantic thing anyone's ever said to me. And it's something that will be forever imprinted on my heart. Something I cling to whenever I feel low, or Jim does something to tick me off. Like pretending not to hear me just now. Or before, when we lived in Southampton, and I'd ask him if he might be able to work from home and keep an eye on Mum while I took Dad to chemo.

It gets my goat when he doesn't respond. And although I understand his reasons now for wanting to shut himself off from the world, even before the accident, when he'd regularly work late at the office or upstairs in his study while I was doing five things at once, he could never seem to spare five minutes to take a load off me. And that's something I find hard to shrug off. Even though he now claims I only had to ask, that I enjoyed being a martyr, competing with all the other 'supermums'. He says I've always been like that, a bit controlling, that I can't seem to trust anyone else to do the job for me, and yet at the same time complain I have too much on my plate. That's the way he sees things, but I don't agree. I think that's just his excuse for being crap.

The truth is, I was drowning. Drowning in other people's demands. Sometimes I felt so overwhelmed I wanted to scream 'piss off, the lot of you' at the top of my lungs and run away from my life and never come back.

Sometimes I wanted to swallow a bottle of pills and make it all go away. Including the people I loved. And that was a scary feeling. Made me feel like a failure, the worst person alive.

But it's not easy being at the behest of everyone, pulled in all directions. It's asphyxiating, bleeds the strength out of you. And it made me anxious, so much so I couldn't sleep, and I resorted to sleeping pills like diazepam to take the edge off. A habit I've not managed to kick. I was like Atlas with the weight of the world on my shoulders, or a ton of bricks that just seemed to pile up by the day, and no sooner had I got rid of one, a new brick was put in its place. Until the final slab, the size of a boulder, crushed me completely.

People used to say, 'Make sure you make time for yourself, get some rest, treat yourself, you'll be no good to anyone if you burn out.' But in reality, although I knew they meant well, it's easier said than done. Because who the hell was going to do the job for me? Especially as I'm an only child. All the little things that needed doing but which added up by the day. Jim worked a twelve-hour day. My kids were nine and eleven at the time and couldn't even look after themselves, let alone their ailing grandparents, and my girlfriends all had problems of their own. So basically, it all fell on me. I took Dad to chemo because Mum wasn't up to it. Wasn't strong enough to be there for Dad. I was his rock, and I took it all on because I loved him. But it wasn't easy. Not when I was juggling work, the school run, meals, all the admin that comes with having kids – sports, plays, music concerts, parents' evenings. And don't get me started on World Book Day. A yearly event I'd had many weeks to prepare for but allowed to get lost in the mile long to-do list I stuck to the fridge and promptly forgot about because someone had stuck some other crap over it, causing me to raid all the wardrobes at the last minute, trying to cobble something together so my child wouldn't feel humiliated being left out and quite possibly psychologically scarred for life because their crazy mummy failed abysmally to get her act together! Unlike perfect Pam, whose child would win the best costume award every year and made a point of posting about it on social media, attracting a minimum of 100 likes. I'm not complaining, I'm just saying, telling it like it is. No matter how convenient it is now for Jim to say I only had to ask.

But now, looking back, maybe he has a bit of a point. I wish I hadn't let things get to me so much, wish I hadn't tried to take on everyone's problems. I should have talked to someone, tried other forms of stress relief rather than rely on drugs to manage it all. But hindsight is a beautiful thing.

I miss Dad like crazy, but at least he's not in pain any more. And now Mum's in a home, as sad as it is, it's for the best. When all is said and done, I don't mind too much that Jim's not into socialising. I quite like keeping him away from that part of my life. It's just a bit hard when people ask to come over, or invite us round for dinner, and I have to make some old excuse like Jim's too engrossed in his work and can't be disturbed. At least the club's an outlet for me. At least I get to be with people there. Chat about inane stuff like clothes and make-up, movies and the latest book that's kept me up at night. Even though it is a bit of a trek all the way to Kingston. But then the clubs around Cobham are twice the price, and I don't have money to throw around. That's what I tell anyone who asks anyway.

I say I only had the one glass, but it was a large one, which I'm now slightly regretting. For one, because I didn't work out and it's empty calories I could have done without, and two, because I'd previously pledged to give up the booze – I'm still on the antidepressants at night so I really shouldn't mix alcohol with pills, and I'll no doubt wake up with a sore head having taken my nightly dose. I've not helped matters by not eating anything since lunchtime. My stomach feels raw and acidic. I don't know how Susan does it. Tell a lie, I do. Practice. And I guess when she suggested we take up Martin's offer of a free drink, considering the week I've had, it was just too tempting.

'Jim,' I call out again. I walk into the living room, don't see my husband at first, but then, as I look more closely, spy the top of his head lolled to one side against the back of the sofa closest to the TV. I edge nearer so that I am now facing him, see that his eyes are shut, his mouth slightly open, a hacking sound coming out of it every so often. For a fleeting moment I am tempted to pop something in it, just to see what would happen. Feel almost exhilarated at the thought. He works hard, so why do I resent seeing him like this? Perhaps because it's such a contrast to how I remember him when we first met – full of youthful energy, hungry for me. Before we had kids and our lives changed forever. Not that that came as much of a surprise; we knew it would. But it's not a nice feeling, becoming invisible to someone. He could never be invisible to me, so why do I sometimes feel invisible to him?

I cough, but it doesn't spark his attention. Feeling irritated, I slump down on the sofa with force, set on rousing him from his peaceful slumber. I don't know why I do this, it's quite cruel really, but seeing him like this, so apathetic and middle-aged compared to the likes of Martin, who I can't ever imagine being dead to the world at nine p.m. and who I admit to fantasising about every now and again, even masturbating to the idea of him screwing me against the gym equipment occasionally, makes me cross, grouchy. He needs to wake up and acknowledge me. He can't just talk to me whenever the hell it suits him. He jumps with a start, slowly comes to. 'What the…' he begins, rubbing his eyes, shifting in his seat. 'Was that necessary?'

'What?' I ask innocently. 'Am I not allowed to sit down on my own sofa?' I hear my voice, know only too well that I'm being childish. He doesn't even bother with a response. His unimpressed look says it all. We both know who's in the right here, and it's galling.

'How's your day been? Done anything nice?' There's a touch of sarcasm in my voice and he looks at me like

I've lost the plot. 'You know exactly what I've been up to. The same thing I do every day.'

'Do I?' I shoot back. I just can't seem to forget. To forgive. To let go of my anger. To stop seeing him the way I do. And that's why I'm so bloody miserable, so screwed up in the head.

He flinches.

'Sorry,' I say, 'that was uncalled for.'

'It's OK, I'm used to it by now.'

I ignore his cutting comment.

'How's the book going?'

'I'm stuck. Writer's block.'

'It's on the principles of physics. Not literary fiction. How can you have writer's block?'

'Oh, I'm sorry,' he says, 'I'm not as good at making up stories as you are.'

His words wound me. 'What's that supposed to mean?'

'Really?' He's suddenly off the sofa, pacing the room, wide awake. 'You really have to ask? Come on, Grace, how long do you think you're going to fool everyone around here? I know you chose this area because it's full of old people who don't ask questions, and all the women you hang out with are based in and around Kingston. But you're living on borrowed time. It's amazing you've kept our secret this long. Someone's going to discover our past.'

I see his eyes filling with tears and I want to scratch them out, he's hurt me so badly. But I can't begrudge him for resenting me. Even though he's as much to blame as I am.

He sits back down, asks without looking at me: 'How was the class?'

'There was no class.'

'Really? Where've you been all this time then?'

This makes me happy. Him wondering where I've been. I wonder if it's ever crossed his mind that I could be having an affair. Would he be jealous? I know I'd be jealous if I discovered he was cheating on me. I'd want him to feel the same jealousy too; I'd want it to eat him up to the extent he'd be unable to focus on anything else but his jealousy. The idea of my naked body entwined with another man's. I'd want it to tear him up inside, consume him like a poison, send him insane.

'Jade didn't show up.'

He frowns. 'Oh, that's a bit out of the blue, isn't it? You always said Jade was so reliable. Any idea why?'

I swallow hard, make a concerted effort to disguise my irritation as I pick up a copy of *Red* and aimlessly flick through the pages. 'Nope, no idea. Was a complete surprise to us all.'

'Shame,' he says. 'She was a nice girl, I thought.'

I stop flicking, give him an incredulous look. 'How would you know that? You've never met her. Unless you're hiding something from me.'

'Stop being paranoid. I'm just going on what you've told me. You're always saying she makes the classes fun rather than hard work.'

That's true.

I get up.

'So where were you?' he repeats.

I fudge my response. 'Susan persuaded me to have a drink with her and Vivien. We were all disappointed the class was cancelled, having made the effort to get there, so I thought what the heck, might as well.'

Jim rolls his eyes.

'What's that for?' I ask.

'Don't know how you can stand spending time with Susan. From what you say she's a bad egg. Shallow and not to be trusted. And a lush. You know what you're like when you drink too much. It affects you badly. You say things you shouldn't. And the likes of her will pick up on it like a shot. I bet she feeds on gossip like a vampire sucks blood. Doesn't she ever wonder why you don't invite her round?'

I laugh out loud. But it's a forced laugh. Like I want to show Jim how preposterous his accusation about my drinking is, even though in my heart I know it's not so far-fetched. I've never been able to take my booze, it's true.

'Again, how can you be the judge of that if you've never met her? You don't socialise with anyone. You don't go to the gym.'

'I wouldn't be seen dead in a gym.'

'Fine, your choice, but you let me live my life how I think is best. OK?'

He doesn't respond and I say no more, head for the kitchen to make some toast. It's too late for dinner, but I need something to settle my tummy. I call out to Jim to ask if he wants some but get no response. I'm guessing he's in a mood with me or dropped off again. I don't wake or seek him out this time. I'm not that cruel. Or that desperate for his attention. If he chooses not to hear or see me, so be it. His loss, not mine. But later, just before bed, I go back to check on him. Creep up next to him on the sofa he's moved to for some reason, and softly stroke the side of his face. Despite his scars, I will always love him. He will always be the Jim I know. The Jim who's beautiful to me.

Despite the fact he's the reason our sons are no longer with us.

63

Chapter Nine

Natalie

Friday, 20 July 2018

I feel decidedly unwell, my head swimming with so many conflicting emotions I worry I might pass out at any second. There's also a stabbing pain in my chest – part panic, but also owing to the misery I feel knowing something terrible may have happened to the only real friend I've had since Jack.

I feel fear, too, looking at the evidence before me. Fear, not just because I realise there could be someone highly dangerous on the loose who may have hurt my best friend, but also because, after taking a few seconds to assimilate the scene, I went and did something incredibly stupid: I touched Jade's clothes and phone, and then the bath mat. I don't know why I did it; I guess I wanted to take a closer look, hoping there was some innocent explanation for the blood – perhaps Jade had cut herself shaving, stubbed her toe, or something equally harmless like that. Of course, that may well be the case, but right now we have no way of knowing. And the not knowing is torture. As for the phone, I should have realised it would be locked with a pin. So fiddling with that was another futile exercise.

And now I've gone and implicated myself. In fact, I've been doing that from the moment I walked into Jade's flat, opening doors, touching things. What a fool I am. My mind is racing with all sorts of grim explanations for Jade's disappearance. At best, the possibility that someone broke in and abducted her, and is now holding her prisoner somewhere. Perhaps that explains the open drawers. Perhaps they found her in the shower, grabbed her, told her to get dressed quick, then made off. At worst, that they attacked her, killed her, then dumped her body God only knows where. In either scenario, I wonder who it could be. Was it some random intruder (that too might explain the open drawers, a burglar perhaps fishing for something of value), or someone Jade knows? I think of *him*, wonder what he was up to last night, whether something happened between them. Perhaps that's why she looked so down on Wednesday. I promised Jade I'd keep his identity a secret – she made me swear to it, just as I made her promise to keep my secrets. But surely in light of current circumstances I'm at liberty to break my oath?

I know I should think more positively. But it's not in my nature, and all I can think about is the worried look on her face during Wednesday's class.

It's all too cruel, and I find myself sinking to my knees, my entire body tingling with anxiety, my breath becoming shallower as I realise I'm in danger of losing it. I'm suddenly seeing stars as I rock forward and bend my head over in a bid to stop myself from being sick, or worse, passing out. It doesn't help that I'm so tired. I tell myself I must stay in control, that I cannot let my stress take hold of me. I conquered those demons years ago, and I cannot go back there.

I stay in the same child's pose for a while – maybe fifteen minutes – not daring to move or open my eyes, my entire body frozen with fear. Then finally, knowing I can't stay here forever, the rational side of my brain orders me to get up, to phone the police immediately. If I don't, they'll find my fingerprints and assume I attacked Jade and was trying to conceal my crime by fleeing the scene. Also, there's no telling whether someone might have seen me enter the flat. It's dark outside, and I didn't see anyone, but I can't rule out that possibility. No, it's better if I come clean, say things how they are. The sooner I do that, the sooner the police can get to the bottom of things and find out what's happened to Jade. It's the only way. Slowly I raise myself up, wait for my vision to settle. Then finally, when I'm feeling steadier, calmer, I leave the bathroom, avoiding the temptation to try and guess the passcode on Jade's phone, even though I am desperate to, just because it might reveal some clue as to her last movements. And because I know it's going to show at least fifteen missed calls from me since yesterday, along with various texts. Some might view that as a bit over the top, borderline harassment even, but I'd like to think it demonstrates concern for my friend. It also corroborates the fact that we haven't seen each other since Wednesday night, else why would I be phoning her? Anyway, I'll just have to cross that bridge when I come to it. I move to the living room and pull out my phone from my gym bag, dial 999. I can't believe I'm doing this; it's surreal and brings back memories of Jack doing the same after finding Dad's lifeless body. As always, he took control, looked out for me. He was the strong one, the one who always knew what to do in a crisis. But Jack's not here now, and I must take the reins with no one around to do it for me. And so I do, as soon as the operator answers.

'Yes, I need the police,' I say. 'I'm at my best friend's flat but she's missing. There's blood on the bath mat. I don't know if there's a harmless explanation, but the fact that she's not here or picking up her calls, and her clothes and phone are lying around with no sign of her, and her car's parked outside, is worrying. Please, come quickly.' The operator tells me to stay calm, that officers are on their way. That I should hang up but keep my phone close. I do as she says and wait. And as I do, I think about the first time I set foot in Jade's class just over a year ago. A day that changed my life. But also introduced me to the woman who may know more about Jade's no-show this evening than she's letting on.

Chapter Ten

Natalie

One year before
Wednesday, 12 July 2017

I look at myself in the mirror and feel embarrassed by what I see. Appalled, even. I can't think what Jack would make of it. Even though he always told me I was beautiful to him.

I practically live in my A-line skirts, high-collar blouses and sturdy court shoes. I never show my legs and my waist is always covered by enough clothing to disguise the excess flesh hanging either side of it. I'm not comfortable exposing the less flattering areas of my body, never have been. Plus, the thought of men leering at me turns my insides. I know what they're like, that they're all the same deep down, and so the last thing I want is to give them any excuse to feed their base instincts. All that being said, what the hell am I doing standing here in black leggings and a half-sleeve t-shirt about to lay myself bare in front of a roomful of strangers? I mean, what in God's name was I thinking? OK, so the leggings go past my calves, and my t-shirt is one size up and therefore baggy enough to cover my thighs and bottom. But this is still a huge change for me, still a massive leap out of my comfort zone, and

I'm not exactly sure how I'm ever going to step outside my front door and make it to the club without having a panic attack, let alone partake in an exercise class full of lithe, skimpily clad women who'll wonder whether I took a wrong turning and got lost on my way to Fat Camp.

Since agreeing to go along to Jade's first class this evening, I've done nothing but worry. Despite Dr Jenkins assuring me that so long as I keep to my routine, a little vigorous exercise will be good for me. Good for my blood pressure, which has always been on the high side. I appreciate her encouragement, but it's only by avoiding stressful situations like the one I'm currently facing that I've managed to keep a check on my blood pressure and stress levels in the first place.

Sam's been as patronising as ever since Jade took her down a peg or two on Monday. 'Looking forward to your class on Wednesday, Nats? Make sure you don't overdo it on the first occasion – you don't want to keel over in front of everyone. That wouldn't do. And it's always a good idea to stand at the back when you're learning the ropes. Watch the experts and learn from them.'

As usual, listening to her sarcastic comments I was forced to take a deep breath, tell myself not to let it get to me. She needn't have worried, though. If by some miracle I do make it to the class, I'll be standing as far back as possible, preferably in a corner where I can't see myself in the mirror. I assume there will be a mirror – studios always have them, according to Sam. Although she could have been trying to wind me up further. Despite dreading tonight, I forced myself to visit Primark on my way home from work yesterday, choosing the baggiest, plainest black t-shirt I could find, along with some of their £7 black leggings. I saw no point in visiting a real sports shop for proper gear because I'm 99 per cent certain tonight will turn out to be an unmitigated disaster and I'll never set foot in an exercise studio again.

I continue to stare at myself in the mirror as my timer goes off, indicating that it's six p.m., meaning I need to set off now for The River Club if I'm going to make it. Deep breaths, I tell myself. Then repeat the mantra I recite three times a day, the mantra Dr Jenkins taught me to say whenever I feel stressed. 'I am a good, kind, calm and resilient person. I won't let anything or anyone upset me. I have nothing to be ashamed of. I will get through this day calmly and peacefully.'

I say it once more just for good measure, thankful as ever to Dr Jenkins for her kindness, for ensuring I stay in a good place rather than allow the darkness to take me over. We have a session booked for tomorrow, just because I know I'll want to talk to her about this evening. Unmitigated disaster or not. I still see her every fortnight. She's like a safety net, I suppose. I don't trust myself to stay on track alone.

It's gone six, time is ticking, and I realise it's now or never. Another deep breath, and then I muster up the will to pick up my small green drawstring backpack containing my water, the free pass Jade gave me, my phone and a zip-up hoodie. Not that I'm going to need extra clothing. It's still boiling outside, and I hope to God the studio has air con or I'll never make it out of there alive.

Fifteen minutes later I arrive at the entrance to The River Club, and the same sick sensation I felt earlier returns. That voice in my head questioning, *What the hell are you doing here? You don't belong here.* Jack, telling me to be careful, that the only people we can trust are each other. In fact, as I watch a trim-looking couple kitted out in matching tennis whites almost skip through the double doors, followed by an impossibly skinny woman wearing a pink Lycra top and matching leggings with literally not an ounce of fat on her, I find myself doing an about-turn. If I'm quick enough I can make it back for *The One Show* and my tuna pasta ready meal. But just then, I'm stopped short by a voice calling out, 'Natalie?'

I glance left and see Jade bounding up towards me. She's smiling broadly, but it's obvious from her expression that she knows I was in the process of chickening out.

'Oh, hi,' I say, with something of a nervous smile. Her hair is tied up in a high ponytail like it was on Monday, she's wearing a turquoise halterneck gym top and tie-dye leggings. She looks lovely and super-fit, the opposite of me.

'I'm so bloody late, bloody car trouble!' she gasps. 'Not a great start, is it? Last thing I needed to happen before my first class. I so want to make a good impression. This is my first proper instructor position since I quit being a PE teacher and decided to retrain. I can't mess it up.'

Poor thing. I can't help feeling sorry for her. On her first day too. How can I let her down now? She reads my mind, her brow furrowing. Her almond-shaped eyes on the verge of welling up. 'You weren't thinking of leaving, were you?' I feel my face flush. Busted. 'Please don't leave,' she begs. 'I'm nervous enough as it is, and I need a friendly face in the crowd to focus on.'

I smile. Think how nice it is to be referred to as a friendly face. How unusual, just because I rarely get compliments like that. Not a surprise, seeing as I never go anywhere besides work and the supermarket. It's not anyone's fault; it's a conscious decision on my part. She narrows her eyes, replacing the sullen face with an impish look, followed by a big grin. 'You don't want to give that bitch, Sam, the satisfaction of bailing out, do you? I, for one, won't stand for it.' I can't help grinning back. 'We need to prove stuck-up snooty cows like her wrong.' She leans in closer, whispers, 'I hate women like that. My mother was the same – always made me feel inadequate, never good enough. But I didn't take it lying down. And neither should you.'

Her comment is so unexpected. As is the sudden edge to her voice that catches me unawares. In those few words she's let me into a sadness clouding her life I had never expected would overshadow one so beautiful, so seemingly perfect. I want to ask more but I can see she's keen to get moving. What I do know is that I feel increasingly drawn to Jade. Like me, she's been wronged by someone close to her, by her own blood.

And because of this I can't say no to her. Instead, I take another deep breath and somewhat hesitantly follow her inside.

Chapter Eleven

Susan

I shouldn't have driven home. Shouldn't have opted for that second glass of Chablis at the club rather than a more sensible cranberry juice. God knows I could have done with it, just because it keeps the cystitis at bay. But as usual, I couldn't resist. I needed it. Needed to blot out the emptiness. The secrets I keep.

I know Natalie's suspicious of me. She looked at me like I knew more about Jade not turning up than I was letting on, even though as far as I know she has nothing concrete to base her suspicions on. I can't let that freak show get to me, can't let her rock the nerves of steel I portray to the world. Nerves it's taken more than half my life to cultivate. That's why I needed the booze, just to take the edge off. And to give me the courage to go home and face Lance. No wonder my face has become so puffy, despite all the Botox, collagen wave treatments and fillers.

I know Lance never loved me. It was more of a lust thing between us, certainly not the romance of the century. When we met, he was twenty-two and fresh out of law school. Slim, athletic, sporting the kind of dazzling celebrity smile that sent me weak at the knees and my brain into overdrive imagining myself doing all sorts of dirty things with him. I've always had a highly charged sexual appetite, and I guess that's appealing to men in their teens and early twenties, ruled by their cocks rather than their heads. Thick black hair parted at the side, chiselled jawline, cheeks you could cut glass on, dreamy dark eyes – he was literally the movie star cliché. But he'd also seemed warm and smart and funny; perfect, really. At least, that's what I told myself back then. Problem was, all the straight girls thought the same. And so, although I wanted him all to myself from the minute I set eyes on him, I knew I had a fight on my hands. That I'd have to work hard for it, pick my moment. Especially when, after we'd been dating a few months, I found out that he was still in love with his childhood sweetheart from Barnes. A girl called Ellen who he had plans to win back.

Back then, I was pretty hot myself. Pre kids. Pre stretch marks, pre loose tummy flesh arising from childbirth that stubbornly refuses to budge no matter how many planks I do. Back when it was easy to shift the weight and everything was pert and pointed the right way up. Long limbs, big breasts, lustrous hair, ebony eyes, I always attracted my fair share of male attention, and was never afraid to go for what I wanted. We met through a friend of mine from uni. Tamara. She and I studied English lit at King's College London. Her parents were filthy rich and bought her an apartment just off Sloane Square in her final year of uni. I really fell on my feet clicking with her on our first day in halls. She was terribly glam, a bit of a snob, mixing in circles I could only ever have dreamt about, coming from the humble background I did – my dad was a postman, my mum a receptionist – and Tamara introduced me to a world I'd always hankered after. Not content with my roots, the ordinary things in life, always wanting something better for myself. Which makes me a bit of a snob too, I know. Tamara opened my eyes to a whole new world, where I swapped dinner at Pizza Express for Cecconi's, Debenhams for Harrods. My parents disliked Tamara, thought her to be shallow and self-centred, out of touch with reality. Which she was, of course. But that's what I liked about her. I liked that she didn't live in reality, liked that her life was one long list of parties and designer clothes and five-star holidays in St Tropez. And when I met Lance, a rising star trainee at the biggest law firm in London, I knew that if I played my cards right, he'd be able to offer me that lifestyle on a long-term basis. I still remember the night we met, at one of Tamara's famous house parties. Brimming with booze, drugs and too many rich kids who believed themselves to be invincible and a cut above. There must have been about forty guys at the party, but they all seemed to pale in comparison to Lance. Besides his looks, there was just something about him, a kind of star quality that radiated off him, and I could tell he was going places. Unsurprisingly, there were a lot of rich, pretty girls there too. Many of them sizing Lance up as their next conquest. The competition was palpable. A roomful of hungry tigresses, ready to pounce and grab the most beautiful lion there at the first chance. Tamara wasn't interested, though. She was already engaged to some loaded guy whose daddy made even more money than hers did. At that point, I had just started as a beauty and fashion features writer for a women's magazine. I'd always been interested in beauty and fashion, and to be honest, the training and job description sounded a hell of a lot easier than being a lawyer or a doctor. As Mum and Dad had always hoped I'd become. I've always been a bit on the lazy side. Sure, I wanted the big fat pay cheque, the extravagant lifestyle, but not the long hours of study and graft that went with law or medicine. Bagging a rich husband was my only option, and so where Lance was concerned, I didn't play coy. I flirted with him all night, laughed at his jokes, hung on his every word, and when enough booze had been consumed I asked him if he wanted to go somewhere more private and with Tam's permission, took him upstairs and shagged him in her guest bedroom. I may not have been the best at my career, but I knew I was good at fucking. I've never been shy in that department, and like I said, what red-blooded male in his twenties is ever going to say no to a good screw? Lance liked that I was risqué, experimental, and so we started seeing each other a few times a week. But then, when the cracks started to appear and things didn't seem to be going my way and I realised he was losing interest, having seen me for the shallow money-grabber I was, I did what I needed to do to keep him.

But now a part of me wishes I hadn't bothered. Because look at me now. My grown-up kids don't talk to me – the eldest, Cam, lives on the other side of the Atlantic in fact – and my husband can't stand the sight of me. Still hankers after the girl next door he lost. No matter how much I pamper myself, lie to myself that I still look like I did in my twenties, I know in my heart that no amount of work can hide what's going on inside my body. The damage I'm doing to myself with booze and occasional drugs. The fact that no number of creams can reverse the ageing process and turn back time. I also know, all these years later, that despite what I said to Grace, no amount of money can bring a person happiness. But it's too late to go back on that now. Money and a lavish lifestyle are all I have. If I lose those two things, I'll have nothing in my life, because the truth is, I'm a woman in her early fifties who's not aged particularly well, who has no special skills to show for herself and whose children want as little as possible to do with her. What man would want me now?

It's a catch-22 situation. Because I want out of my marriage to Lance, and yet I don't. Staying with him is torture. But so would be the humiliation of a divorce. I'd rather die than be cast off as yesterday's news. Being around him is a constant reminder of my conundrum. And that's why I'm at the club so much, even though right now I'd be better off staying away from it.

I pull into our driveway, my heart in my mouth as I wonder if Lance is home. I really hope he isn't. Right now, I'd prefer him to be away from the house as much as possible. He could have stayed late in the City, I guess, gone boozing with his mates. I'm not sure he's ever been one for prostitutes or one-night stands, despite his other faults. He's too bloody self-righteous. Stuck in the past, pining for his Ellen, so sweet, so fragile. Traits he's always been attracted to. Perhaps because his own little sister was the same. Women he calls soft and vulnerable. Women I call weak. In some ways I'd have preferred it if he was some philandering sex addict. Fucked another hardened bitch like me who's only after sex. That wouldn't have pissed me off so much as him still being in love with a dead woman.

Having parked up, I'm dismayed to see the lights are on in the spare bedroom he moved into around six months ago. We haven't had sex in over a year, and even before then he only screwed me because he needed a release, and I was the closest thing to hand. There was nothing gentle or loving in it. From either side, to be fair. We fucked like machines. It's the story of our marriage. It's how two of our children were conceived.

I turn off the ignition and stick a tab of gum in my mouth, although he knows my trick by now, and will no doubt make some snide comment about me trying to hide my wine and nicotine breath. I kill the lights and get out of the car, press the remote-control lock and walk towards my front door. Fearful of what might await me. Of confronting what I've done. And all the time thinking about that afternoon thirty years ago. An afternoon that will haunt me forever.

Because I did something I've come to regret.

Something I should never have told Jade about.

Chapter Twelve

Natalie

One year before
Wednesday, 12 July 2017

So far the whole 'health and fitness' experience hasn't been as bad as I'd anticipated. OK, so I've not actually done the class yet, but the fact that I've not had a panic attack or felt like this was a huge mistake is something at least. Having said that, since Jade cornered me outside, I've stuck to her like glue. A factor which has probably helped me to see the positive. As soon as we walked through the door, she was greeted warmly by several staff members to whom she apologised profusely for her tardy arrival. They told her not to worry, that flat tyres can't be helped, and in any case, she was still on time for the class with ten minutes to spare. This had seemed to ease her anxiety somewhat, and she'd proceeded to introduce me to some of her colleagues, who'd understandably wondered who this quiet, sorely out-of-shape misfit clinging to her side was. So far I've met Karen on reception, a big, beefy gym and class coordinator called Martin, whose eyes, I couldn't help noticing, lit up the moment his gaze fell on Jade; also Barry, the manager, who happened to pop his head out of the office door when we walked in, as well as several other staff members whose names I can't remember but who were all very pleasant and not nearly as scary or standoffish as I'd assumed they'd be. In fact, the whole feel of the place is way less intimidating than I had expected. Perhaps because it's not all brand spanking new and focused solely on gym fanatics.

As I follow Jade's lead, I'm relieved to see a mixed bunch of faces, shapes and sizes milling about the place. Meaning I don't feel like I stick out as much as I thought I would. This instantly relaxes me, makes me think maybe this wasn't such a bad idea after all. That perhaps I need to be more open-minded, not doubt myself so much. Even though the scars of my childhood can never be erased.

I can hardly keep up with Jade, though, as I continue to follow her up the stairs where studio three is located on the second floor. My heart sank when she walked straight past the lifts in favour of the double doors leading to the stairwell. I guess someone like her doesn't entertain using a lift unless the place is situated up a high-rise or she's loaded down with groceries. Whereas for me, taking the lift at any opportunity is a given. They're easier on the heart, don't leave me gasping for breath, and therefore keep my anxiety levels at bay. She reaches the second floor and goes to open the door, looking back down at me as she does so, her right hand on the handle. 'Hey, you OK, Natalie?'

I'm sweating now, and I already feel like I've had my workout. How the hell am I going to get through an hour's Body Attack class? Even if it is for beginners. I've looked up what the class entails, and it's frightening. With star jumps, high knees, planks and way too much running around, I'm not exactly easing my way into fitness. I wish it had been yoga or Pilates or something equally placid that requires sitting or lying down. I'm frightened of keeling over with heart failure like Sam mentioned, or worse – just because it would be so humiliating – having an anxiety attack. Looking up at Jade, I'm also slightly cross with her for never even contemplating that I might have wanted to take the lift, but I tell myself it's OK, there's no harm done, and that I can't get angry over a minor thing like that.

'Yes, I'm OK. Just a little out of breath.'

'Oh, I'm so sorry,' she says. 'I should have asked whether you wanted to take the lift. I almost always take the stairs as it's so much better for you. I didn't think twice, it's so thoughtless of me.' She looks genuinely sorry, but I can't quite decide if she's being straight with me or sarcastic. I give her the benefit of the doubt, having finally reached the top and caught my breath.

'Really, it's fine, no need to apologise. You're a fitness instructor, it's only natural. And I'm sure you're not used to mixing with the likes of me, who hasn't done a day's even vaguely intensive exercise since leaving senior school. Even then, half the time I'd pretend to have forgotten my kit or have some sort of injury.'

I don't tell her I was also too ashamed of my figure to put on the short grey gym skirt they insisted on making us wear. Ashamed and afraid of being picked on and made fun of by the skinny, pretty girls. That one day I ended up in detention because when Acid Tongue Amelia made fun of me in front of the whole class, I rugby-tackled her on the concrete netball court and she ended up in hospital with concussion.

Jade laughs. 'Don't worry, been there, done that. Especially on cold January mornings when the thought of playing lacrosse in nothing but a tiny gym skirt freezing my tits off did nothing but fill me with dread. It didn't help that I hated my PE teacher. She was a miserable old cow who took an instant dislike to me from the get-go. Made my life hell, if I'm being honest, and my bloody witch of a mother did nothing about it.'

I'm shocked. I can't fathom anyone hating Jade. Least of all her PE teacher. I'd imagined her to be a PE teacher's dream. She reads the surprise on my face. 'I think it had something to do with me making it to the national gymnastics finals, while her daughter, Ginny, who was in the same age group, didn't. Despite being pushed and pushed, poor thing, Ginny didn't make it past county standard and from then on, her mother, my teacher, took issue with me.'

'Wow, you did gymnastics at national level? That's really something. What...?'

'What happened?' Jade interjects. We've both now left the stairwell and are heading down the corridor. I'm not paying much attention to my surroundings because I'm too busy listening to Jade, even more in awe of her than I was before.

'Same story as Ginny. I was good enough to reach national level, but no higher. And by the time I reached seventeen I'd had enough. I was burnt out and I wanted a social life. Wanted to go and meet boys. Stay out late and party. Much to my mother's disgust.'

There's a sadness and a deep discontent behind Jade's sunny demeanour, and although it's not my style to pry into other people's affairs, least of all worry about them, mainly because I don't have the headspace to fret about anyone but myself, I guess the fact that she's offered me this small window into her soul, and that we have far more in common than I could ever have imagined, makes me eager to know more. Now is not the time, though. As I glance at my watch, I see that it's nearly 6:30 p.m., and judging by the sizeable crowd loitering outside in the corridor up ahead, I'm guessing they're here for Jade's class. It's crunch time, and the same discomfort I felt before leaving the house creeps up on me, my palms and underarms suddenly moist. I tell myself it's no big deal, that I'm not about to give a speech before the UN or compete in the one hundred metres at the Olympics, for Christ's sake, but even so, I know it's a huge step for me. For so long I've stuck to a set routine, avoiding large crowds, unfamiliar settings, people I don't know from Adam. Like my therapists advised me to do. Just because they knew how such situations tend to set my heart racing, and not in a good way. I don't need unnecessary stress in my life. And yet here I am, away from my house, from the library. The only two places where I feel safe and secure.

'You OK?' Jade says. She gives me a big smile, as if to say, 'Don't worry, it's going to be fine,' and my sense of trepidation is ever so slightly allayed. I repeat Dr Jenkins' mantra inside my head, count to five and inhale deeply.

There must be a crowd of fifty waiting outside the club's largest studio. Some of those gathered are standing against the wall or hovering in the middle of the corridor, locked in conversation or staring at their phones. I'm guessing that although some of them may be new like me, the majority are members, just because they look like they belong here and seem to know each other from the way they're chatting and their body language. The clamour of voices is somewhat overwhelming as we approach, and I almost feel like I want to put my hands over my ears to drown them out.

'Hi everyone, you all here for Body Attack?' Jade says, all bright and breezy.

The sea of faces before her smile and nod eagerly in return. Although I notice one woman, who must be around fifty, wearing a slightly pinched expression, like she isn't much impressed and doesn't really want to be here. I can tell her kit is top of the range, while three fingers on her left hand are covered with diamonds and her face is fully made-up. Lipstick, blusher, mascara, the lot. She catches me studying her and I quickly look away.

'Great!' Jade smiles broadly. 'Thanks so much, everyone, for coming, I've got some great tracks lined up, and I can't wait to get started and give you all a good workout. Let's go inside, shall we? I hope the air con's on, Martin assured me it should be!'

More eager nods and yeses. Jade's off before I know it, and I can't keep up with her, getting left behind in the crowd. To my dismay I find myself walking through the double doors alongside Made-up Grumpy Woman.

'She's so happy I think I might vomit,' she says.

I'm too afraid not to reply, so I say: 'I-I think she's just a bit nervous. Wants to make a good impression.'

She appears to think on this. Then says, 'You best friends or something? I saw you arrive together.'

I shake my head. 'Oh no, not at all. I happened to run into Jade at the library where I work. She was giving out flyers for the class and persuaded me to come along.'

Her eyes give me the once-over. 'Yes, I didn't think I'd seen you here before. You don't seem the gym sort, forgive me for saying so. You local?'

'Yes,' I say, wishing she'd leave me in peace so I can bag a spot in the far left-hand corner at the back and closest to the door where I can make a swift exit. So far, I can see it's not been taken, but I need to be quick. 'I'm only a fifteen-minute walk away. You?'

'I'm on Coombe Hill Road. I don't suppose you know it,' she almost sneers.

I know of it. Only because it's one of the most prestigious areas in Kingston, where houses don't go for less than two million.

I shake my head. 'Not well, no. I'm just off the river, so it's pretty convenient.'

'Oh, how charming, those tiny houses are so quaint. Not much room to swing a cat, but cute all the same.'

'Yes, I like it.' I force a smile, at the same time thinking to myself that I've met Sam's mother. This was a bad idea after all.

'I'm Susan, by the way.' She offers her hand, which I take reluctantly. 'I'm practically part of the furniture. All the staff know me. I even have my own car parking space reserved outside.'

And? Is she expecting a round of applause?

'Wow, that's service for you.' I smile again.

'Yes, well, I've been coming here since it opened. It's gone rapidly downhill, though, so much so I'm not sure why I still come, and don't join Virgin in Raynes Park. It's not much further. This place is sorely in need of an upgrade.' Her eyes travel over me once more. 'And the clientele's not what it used to be.'

I feel myself go red at her dig. Clench a fist at my side. Say the mantra.

'I'm Natalie,' I say, feeling obliged to offer my name, seeing as she offered me hers, but at the same time looking around, desperate to catch Jade's eye, hoping she'll save me from this torture. But she's on the stage, has her headset on, is fiddling with the music system, too busy setting up to notice me.

'Anyway, better find a space. Enjoy the class.'

85

Before Susan can say another word, I move away and bag the spot by the door. It feels close and humid already despite the air con being on, but I think that's largely due to me working myself up. I try not to make eye contact with anyone. The last thing I want is to get into any more awkward conversations. Meeting Susan has put me right off. The thought of having to face her every week, particularly as it's clear she spends a lot of her time here, horrifies me. I make up my mind to get through this class, then never set foot in the place again.

Chapter Thirteen

Natalie

Friday, 20 July 2018

'So you say you haven't seen or spoken to Jade since Wednesday evening?'

I'm sitting at Jade's kitchen table, two police detectives facing me. A forensic team are on their way, but for now the detectives want my help with some preliminary questions. It's 9:15 p.m. and although I'm shattered, at the same time my mind is wired. I've not felt this unsettled in a long time. Not since I was twelve and the police questioned Jack and me about our foster mum's death. I cannot go back to that dark place.

The more senior officer, DI Donovan Bailey as he'd introduced himself when he and his partner, DS Javid Singh, had first appeared on the doorstep around thirty minutes ago, offered to make me coffee, not realising this is the last thing I'd want or need. But I'd gratefully accepted a tall glass of water instead, which I now take mini sips from. My mouth is as dry as sand, and I worry that my innate nervous disposition might make me appear suspicious.

I'd initially guided them round the flat, leaving the bathroom until last, pointing out that nothing had seemed especially out of place apart from the washing-up in the sink – which was unlike Jade, who's normally a stickler for cleaning up after herself – along with the open drawers in her bedroom. And then I'd led them to the bathroom, where things had taken a more worrying turn. I'd watched DI Bailey slip on a pair of latex gloves to pick up and examine Jade's phone, then her gym clothes and underwear and the bath mat tainted with spots of blood. 'Forensics will be able to unlock the phone and see if there's anything helpful on there,' he'd explained.

'But if she was attacked, isn't it a bit strange her attacker left the phone out in the open for us to find?' I'd asked.

'Not necessarily. Especially in the case of a random attack.'

'So you think this means Jade couldn't have known him or her?'

'No, I'm saying it's possible. It could be that there's something damning on her phone they wanted us to find. Something that doesn't incriminate them, but which possibly implicates others or something they believe Jade's done wrong herself.'

'You make it sound like some kind of revenge attack,' I'd said.

'It's pure speculation. I'm not saying that's what's happened here. It's one of several possibilities. There could be a perfectly harmless explanation for her disappearance. Although, granted, leaving her phone and car keys behind is concerning. As is the way things were left in the bathroom and bedroom. Particularly as you said she's normally quite a meticulous person.'

Possibilities aside, at that point I couldn't help thinking about the numerous calls and texts I'd made to Jade's phone since I last saw her. Only out of worry. Not because

I was harassing her. But they don't know that. Don't know the strength of my friendship with Jade, how much I care for her. How much we trust each other. *What if they see me as some kind of stalker?* I'd thought. What if they assume we'd had a fight, that I'd been harassing her about something, and that she'd been deliberately avoiding my calls? They're detectives, after all, conditioned to be cynical and suspicious about everyone and everything. Even so, I had told myself not to dwell on that now. That I needed to take things one step at a time. Stop driving myself crazy with ifs and buts.

I cover myself by repeating what I already told them when they first walked through the door. 'As I mentioned, I tried calling her several times – yesterday afternoon and today, then earlier this evening after she failed to turn up to the class. I also sent her several texts. You'll see all my messages and calls on her phone once your people have got into it.'

I'd never be this upfront with them if I had something to hide. Be honest. It's always the best policy, I tell myself. Even though I know I haven't always been quite so honest about things over the years.

I explain how Martin also tried and failed to get in touch with Jade.

As DI Bailey listens, DS Singh observes and takes notes. This works me up even more. I worry I'll say something wrong, and they'll later use this as evidence against me. *Stop it, just stay calm, be truthful and all will be well. All this worrying isn't doing your stress levels any good.*

'And this is unusual for Jade? She's never done anything like this before?' DI Bailey must be in his mid-forties. He has close-cropped sandy blonde hair, but I see flecks of grey dotted around his temples and hairline. Hardly surprising, given his line of work. I'd be grey all over in his position. He's wearing a dark blue suit and tie which matches the blue of his eyes. He's quite attractive, despite having a slightly weathered look about him, and speaks calmly, not in the least bit aggressive as I often imagine police officers to be, perhaps because I watch too many police dramas on TV, where the suspects seem to get a grilling at the station. Having said that, it's early days, and I guess he has to be gentle with me at first. After all, it was me who called them here on the basis that I was worried sick for my best friend. It's too soon to judge or make assumptions. It would probably be a different story if, later down the line, something in my story didn't add up and they started to suspect me for some reason. I tell myself that even though his eyes have a kindness about them which I instinctively take comfort from, I cannot allow myself to be lulled into a false sense of security. I must be on my guard.

'No,' I say. 'I've never known Jade to miss a class, except for when she's been away or sick. And even in those situations, she gives plenty of advance notice. Ask Martin. She usually arrives at least ten minutes before the class starts to set up. It's so out of character. And now, finding her clothes strewn around the floor, what looks like her blood on the bath mat, her car keys still here, her drawers flung open, I-I just know something bad must have happened to her.'

My eyes fill with tears, and I feel familiar palpitations coming on, reminiscent of my childhood days, and which I have done so well over the years to contain. I grab my glass, put it to my lips, force myself to swallow some liquid, purely to calm myself down, steady my breathing.

'It's OK, try not to distress yourself too much,' DI Bailey says soothingly. 'Can you just go over again exactly what you touched when you got here.'

I repeat what I've told them already. 'I was stupid to touch things, I realise that now,' I say, 'but I didn't think. Didn't expect to find what I did.'

'Don't worry, it was a natural thing to do,' he assures me. 'Tell me, how long have you known Jade?'

'About a year now.'

'How did you meet? At The River Club?'

'No.' I explain our first encounter.

'And you two hit it off quite quickly? She became more to you than just your instructor?'

'Yes,' I nod. 'We just clicked, I guess. Which surprised me.'

'Why is that?'

'Well, just look at her.' I point to a framed graduation photo of Jade on the kitchen wall. Looking as beautiful as ever. 'We're like chalk and cheese. She's gorgeous and popular, while I'm the opposite. I think maybe she took pity on me at first, seeing how out of shape, how lacking in confidence I was. But she needn't have bothered. She could have just left the flyers and been done with it. But when she saw how my colleague was making fun of me, she encouraged me to give it a try. And after that first class, when I wasn't sure about coming back because it almost killed me, plus some of the clientele weren't exactly my cup of tea, she convinced me otherwise. Said I needed to embrace life rather than hide away from it, something I've always done – only because I've been too scared to do otherwise. She said I couldn't allow others to walk all over me and dictate the way I live my life. I've always been a bit of a loner, you see. Not the fittest or most confident of people, and so gyms always scared me. But her classes are different, and Jade's always made a point of saying there's a place in them for everyone, including me. After giving it a couple of goes, I realised I quite enjoyed it. That it gave me a buzz, getting fit, being with people.'

'She sounds like a good person,' DI Bailey says.

I feel myself choke up. 'She is. She's the best.' I think about our argument on Monday. I should tell DI Bailey about it, in case he finds out later and wonders why I held back. Then again, if I do that, I'll be forced to reveal what we argued about. Anyhow, we made up, it's all water under the bridge and I'm certain no one was about at the time, despite Susan's probing. The others had shot off after the class had finished and it was only me and Jade left alone in the studio. There's really no need for the police to know about it.

'How often do you see Jade out of class?'

'Sometimes one of us will have the other over for a takeaway. I don't really like restaurants as I find the whole business of having to choose a bit stressful, and it's much more comfortable and relaxing being in your own space with someone you want to spend time with rather than a load of strangers in some loud, crowded room.'

Both detectives smile, but I suspect they consider my response to be rather peculiar. I can't say I blame them; it is peculiar. I hadn't meant to let them in on my strange idiosyncrasies, but it just kind of came out. It's nerves, I think, and I worry my babbling might make it appear I have something to hide. I need to be more careful in future. I can't risk all the other stuff coming out.

'Did Jade partake in any other activities or interests outside of The River Club, that you know of?' DI Bailey asks.

'Not that I'm aware of,' I say.

Other than *him*.

'So, you mentioned calling her yesterday several times, as well as today. Any particular reason?'

'I was worried about her.'

'Why?'

'She didn't seem herself on Wednesday night. She looked disturbed, like something was preying on her mind. I wanted to ask her what was up, but she dashed off before I had the chance.'

'Does she normally teach on Thursdays?'

'No, not normally. But Vivien, another of Jade's regulars, mentioned that Jade covered a Zumba class last night from eight thirty to nine thirty. She and Shona often cover each other's classes.'

'So, she was last seen at the club last night around nine thirty, ten p.m.?'

'Presumably.'

'Did this Vivien attend the class?'

'No. She told me a friend who goes to Zumba told her. According to the friend, Jade seemed fine. But I know what I saw on Wednesday. Something was wrong. Usually, she's a hundred per cent there, in the zone, but her gaze had this faraway look to it. I think she knew I'd noticed something was up because I caught her eye a few times. But she quickly looked away. Like she didn't want to get into it.'

'And you two were still on good terms? No falling-outs?'

'No.'

Fuck. Please don't let my lies come back to bite me. We made up, we were back on good terms. I'm sure we were. I mean, I think we were.

93

'Do you know Jade's neighbours?'

'Only Mrs Denby on the ground floor. She's a bit of a busybody, if you know what I mean.'

'Meaning she might have seen something?'

'I guess it's possible,' I say.

'And the others in the building keep themselves to themselves?'

'Yes, pretty much, I think. There's a single guy above Jade on the third floor who's often away, and a couple with a newborn baby on the first.'

'I see, well, I'll be speaking to them after we're done here. For one, they'll be wondering what all the madness is about the minute forensics turn up.'

Mrs Denby's going to love that.

'And does Jade have many friends outside of the club? Locally, or further afield? Family, too?'

Friends-wise it's a good question. And now that he mentions it, I realise I can't answer him with total certainty. She's never mentioned anyone to me, except for her former flatmate in Southampton, Megan. Jade told me Megan's an exceptionally private person, likes to keep herself to herself, dislikes London immensely, which is why she's never visited Jade. For this reason, I don't mention her to DI Bailey, despite feeling guilty for holding back. He'll no doubt track her down through Jade's phone anyway.

Instead, I say, 'She often speaks fondly of her uni days in Southampton, but I think most of her friends stayed down south while she relocated back to London.'

'She's from London originally?'

'Yes, she was raised in Kilburn, north London. But she chose Southampton to get away from her mother. I think she must still have friends in that neck of the woods, but never goes back there as far as I know.'

'I take it she and her mother don't get on?'

I shake my head, explain to DI Bailey what a cow – I use more polite terms – Jade's mother was, never standing up for Jade when she got picked on, and that they've not spoken in twelve years. 'I'm sorry, I've no idea where her mother is or how to get in touch. She may be dead.'

'Maybe Jade's phone will help with that, and any other friends and family, once we can access it,' DI Bailey says.

'Yes, perhaps, but I don't think she has any other family. Her father died when she was small, and she's never talked about anyone else.'

I think back to the first time Jade invited me round to her place. When she'd told me more about her childhood. Explaining how she didn't remember much about her father, except that he was kind and that she missed him. How she felt her life would have turned out very different had he been the one to raise her. Again, I'd felt this uncanny connection with Jade. Both of us having had unhappy childhoods, both having lacked a steady father figure. Despite her being the swan to my ugly duckling.

'And you live close by?' DI Bailey asks.

'I'm at the top of Cleaveland Road, just off the Portsmouth Road. Convenient for the club and Jade's. If I walk briskly, I can be here in five minutes.'

'Natalie, can you think why anyone would want to harm Jade?'

I shake my head vigorously. 'No. Jade's never mentioned feeling threatened by anyone. Or falling out with them, aside from her mother. Everyone at the club likes her as far as I can tell.'

'As far as you can tell?'

Martin's face flashes through my mind. The fact that he's clearly had a thing for Jade since she joined. I wonder if he's still teed off she's never reciprocated his feelings. Whether that's why he didn't appear more upset about her no-show? Why he seemed more angry than worried. I also think of Susan. Her lack of concern earlier, as if she was more relieved than irritated by Jade's failure to turn up. She's always been a bit disparaging of Jade. No doubt jealous of her youth and beauty. Or could there be something else at the root of her contempt? Does she know more than she's letting on?

'Something's occurred to you?'

Fuck, he's read my thoughts. I don't want to paint Martin in a bad light, especially as he's always been nothing but pleasant to me. Then again, my best friend's life could be at stake. I can't hold back, even though I realise I'm employing double standards here in keeping quiet about my row with Jade. And *him*. I go ahead and tell him my concerns about Martin, then watch DS Singh make a note. I don't mention Susan, though. At least not yet. I'm frightened of the consequences of doing so.

'So, you attend Jade's Monday, Wednesday and Friday classes?'

'Yes.'

'And who are the other regulars? Some names would be helpful so I can speak to them tomorrow.'

Shit. Now I *have* to mention Susan. But that's fine, it's routine. Natural that he'd want names. He'll discover them from the club anyway.

'Well, there's Susan Hampson, Grace Maloney, Vivien Talbot, as I mentioned, and Jill Denver. They're always at Jade's classes. The others tend to come on and off. Sounds awful, but I don't even know their last names. We might say a quick hello before the classes start but don't really mix outside them. Apart from Jade's thirtieth last month, and the Christmas social last year. A fair number make a point of keeping their heads down, just do the classes then scoot off immediately.'

'I see.' DI Bailey glances at DS Singh's notebook to refresh his memory. 'But this Susan, Grace, Vivien and Jill…' his gaze returns to me, 'I take it you do mix with them?'

'Yes, on and off. Sometimes we'll have a coffee or a drink at the bar or see each other at club socials. I only go along to the socials if Jade's going, though. I don't feel comfortable without her there.'

'You rely on her a lot?'

His eyes drill through me.

'Yes, I do. Makes me sound a bit lame, I know.'

'Not at all.' He smiles. I can't tell if he's being genuine. When I say it out loud, it does sound lame. 'Why don't you feel comfortable without her around?'

'I guess I just feel a bit intimidated, a bit out of my comfort zone. You know how women can be, they tend to gossip and that's never been my thing. Until I joined the club, I'd pretty much lived my life between the library where I work and my house. Never been one for big crowds, idle gossip and chit-chat. To be fair, Grace isn't like that. She's a very genuine person, kind and down to earth.'

'I see. And these other women, they all get on with Jade as far as you know? They seemed as surprised as you that she didn't turn up to her class?'

How can I avoid mentioning Susan now? I must tell them everything that's niggling me if I am to help Jade. Nearly everything, at least. 'Well, it has to be said that

Susan was very blasé about it all, didn't seem much concerned. But then again, that's just Susan, she isn't the most sympathetic at the best of times, although please don't tell her I said that,' I say nervously. 'She's quite a tough character. Not one for hugs or tears, if you see what I mean.' I pause. Am quick to clarify: 'I'm not saying she disliked Jade, I'm just saying she didn't seem that bothered by her no-show. But that's just her, as I said.'

'But they got on OK? You never noticed them arguing?'

'No,' I shake my head. 'In fact, last month, when Jade had her thirtieth at the club, at one point Susan was latched onto her like they were best friends. But I think that was just the alcohol talking.'

I watch DS Singh make another note. 'When was this exactly?'

'June the twenty-third. It was quite a big do, held in the club's function room. Barry, the manager, even laid on some champagne. I think it was partly a thank you to Jade for bringing in new members with her classes. She's popular, like I said.'

'You didn't notice anything untoward that night? You mentioned Susan having a heart-to-heart with Jade. But did Jade mention anyone bothering or upsetting her? Either during the evening or afterwards? What with you being good friends, and so forth? Any men come on to her?'

'No,' I answer truthfully. 'I remember her saying what a great time she'd had. That she hadn't woken up feeling that rough in ages, but all in all it had been a blast. She had a pretty messed-up childhood, so it meant a lot to her to have friends at the club. Said it had become a kind of home from home. Honestly, she's been so happy working there. That's why her not being here tonight has come as such a shock. Why I'm worried sick she appears to have vanished without a trace.'

'You mentioned her childhood being messed up. Can you elaborate on that?'

All of a sudden, I feel bad for telling a stranger Jade's secrets. The things she told me about her past in confidence. Not for the first time, DI Bailey reads my thoughts. It's what he's trained to do. 'Natalie, I understand you don't want to betray your friend's confidence, but it's important you don't hold back if you want to discover what's happened to her. There may yet be an innocent explanation, but the longer she's missing, the more concerning it is.'

'But you still think there's every chance she's OK? That nothing bad's happened to her?'

'Until a body's been found there's always hope a missing person will turn up alive and well. But that's why I need to explore every available avenue. Even the slightest lead can make all the difference in cases like this. We don't even know for sure if it's Jade's blood on the mat, even though it seems likely.'

My heart lifts just hearing him say this. Being offered the tiniest glimmer of hope. He carries on talking: 'My crime scene officers will be here any minute now. They'll be on it like a swarm of bees, taking samples, photos, prints, and this place will be cordoned off until further notice. So, getting back to my question, what did you mean by Jade's childhood being messed up? I'm assuming it's connected to her mother not treating her kindly?'

I nod. 'Yes, it's largely that. Jade told me she wasn't a happy child. Funnily enough, I think that's why we get on so well. Even though I know that sounds a bit odd. The fact

99

is, mine was pretty unhappy too.' I don't let on quite how bad it was, how it made Jade's look like a fairy tale. 'Her father died when she was young as I previously mentioned, and her mother was a bitch, excuse my French, but that's the nub of it. Jade was a nationally ranked gymnast, and her mother pushed her to the limit. Nothing Jade did was ever good enough for her, and it was like she only cared about the glory, rather than Jade's happiness. Jade told me she hated school, that the girls were jealous of her gymnastics success and would bully her. The only thing that kept her going was this boy she met in the park who was kind to her. They were best friends, apparently, would sneak off with each other for hours at a time. He was her first kiss. Made her feel good about herself. Loved. But one day he disappeared with no explanation. He was just there one day, gone the next. Jade was lost without him for a while. She told me it's something that still haunts her. Something she can't seem to shake, he meant that much to her. Anyway, when Jade turned seventeen, she said she wanted out of gymnastics and her mother disowned her. Told her she was on her own.'

'And you said you have no idea if the mother's still alive?'

'No, like I said, Jade hasn't spoken to her in twelve years, since she left home and went off to do a PE degree at Southampton Uni. Despite hating gymnastics by the time she quit, she told me exercise was in her blood, that she needed to exercise to feel good about herself, fight her other addictions.'

'Other addictions?'

'Jade suffered from bulimia growing up. She said it's pretty common amongst gymnasts. That her mother practically encouraged it.'

'Any idea how Jade came to be a group fitness instructor rather than a PE teacher?'

'She said she enjoyed her degree, but that when she went into a school and experienced teaching hands-on, she realised she didn't have the patience teaching requires. I have to say, I can sympathise with that.'

DI Bailey smiles. 'So can I. Got two teenage kids myself, and handling them is enough of a headache. Not that I'd swap them for the world.'

I smile at his light-hearted comment, at the same time wishing my father had been like him.

'So how did Jade end up here?' he asks.

'She told me she wanted to move back closer to London, where the action is. She's a go-getter, a Londoner at heart, having grown up in Kilburn, and I think Southampton was just a bit too provincial for her.'

'I see. And you definitely aren't aware of any other living relatives?'

I shake my head. 'Sorry, no. All I know is that Jade's an only child.'

I'm so tired I think I might crash on the spot.

'Just one more question, Miss Marsden, and then I'll get someone to drive you home.'

'That's kind, thank you.' I wait with my heart in my mouth, wondering what he's going to ask me now.

'Has Jade been seeing anyone? Romantically, I mean?'

My pulse accelerates. I knew this question was coming, if only because, in the case of a missing person, there's always a set group of people the police will home in on: parents and other family, colleagues, close friends and... other halves. But it still hits me like a bullet. I know the answer to his question, but I can't tell him the whole truth. Jade made me promise never to tell anyone, made me swear to it. I can't betray her trust. Even though I know that in holding back, I may be dashing my hopes of ever seeing her again. I appease my conscience by telling DI Bailey half the story.

'Yes, but she wouldn't tell me who.'

'Why is that? Do you think he's married?'

'I don't know, maybe.' I shrug my shoulders. Hopefully not so casually it comes across as suspicious. 'I guess it could be someone she works with. I'm not aware of the club's policy, but I know some organisations frown on workplace relationships, so it could be the reason she's kept a lid on his identity.'

'Do you know if they're serious?'

I know she is. She swoons over him like he's God's gift. The strong, feisty, independent Jade I know and love nowhere to be seen whenever his name comes up. I hate that. Hate the way he has this power to reduce her to mush. He is the reason we argued. The reason I've seen an ugly side to Jade I find distasteful. A side that wounded me with her stinging words on Monday. Fuelled the rage in me I've done so well for so many years to contain. Could he be the one who attacked Jade? Could he have taken her somewhere, left her for dead? It would be a big risk for him, but things happen in the heat of the moment. Respectable types do bad things all the time when pushed. I'm so tempted to reveal his name, but I know that if I do, and Jade is then found safe and sound with some innocent explanation, she'll never speak to me again. Plus, her career would be ruined. A career she's worked hard for and makes her happy. So, for now, I hold off, bite my tongue. And hope to God it doesn't come to that.

Just then, DI Bailey's phone rings, and I inwardly sigh with relief. I'm not sure I can stand much more of this. I just want to go home and wrap myself under the duvet.

I watch him answer it. 'I'll be right down,' he says. Then looks up. 'Forensics have arrived. I think we're done here.' I breathe another sigh of relief. This time out loud. 'DS Khan will drive you home.'

I'm thankful. Right now, I can't face walking home in the dark. I'm too on edge, too fearful of who might be watching.

We rise to our feet. I'm a little unsteady on mine. 'You've been most helpful,' DI Bailey says, 'although I'm sure I'll want to speak to you again.'

'Of course,' I nod, my insides churning as I do.

'In the meantime, if anything else occurs to you, anything you think might help our chances of finding Jade, please call me.' He pulls out a card from his inside pocket and I take it gratefully.

'Will you be going to the club tomorrow?' I ask.

'I will, yes. And I'll also be speaking to your fellow class members. Susan, Grace, and so on. DS Khan here will be tracking down as many of Jade's other contacts as possible.'

I give a nervous nod, at the same time wondering what my classmates' reaction to Jade's disappearance will be. Susan's always been one to put on a show, the consummate actress. I imagine her eyes widening in shock, her professing to be devastated at the news.

But thinking about what I know, about Susan's blasé reaction to Jade's no-show, about the underhand comments she's made in the past about her, I wonder if, right now, she's gearing herself up for delivering the performance of a lifetime.

Chapter Fourteen

Susan

One year before
Wednesday, 12 July 2017

The new instructor this evening was good, I'll admit. When she'd first appeared, all smiley and perky, I had felt my skin crawl. She'd reminded me of Bubbles off *Ab Fab*, only with slightly more brain cells. Typical blonde ditzy gym bunny, I'd thought. Perhaps a tad unfairly. But the fact is, I don't trust people like that. People who are too happy, too smiley. Going about life like it's a fucking Disneyland parade. It's not natural. It's creepy. Makes me suspicious.

And so, the thought of seeing her 'happy face' three times a week had made me feel rather nauseous, and I'd practically written off doing another of her classes before we'd started this one. I come to this club to release my stress, not add to it. But then, when the music started – I had dreaded something along the lines of a nauseating montage of S Club 7, Girls Aloud and Steps, just because she looks like she belongs in one of those sugary-sweet bands – it was better than I'd expected. A mix of dance, hip-hop and Ibiza classics – my scene spot on. Reminiscent of better days: girlie holidays to Playa d'en Bossa or Mykonos with Tam and the crowd, clubbing until the early hours, sleeping till one, followed by an afternoon of pool parties, cocktails and sex with hot guys. Those were the fucking days. What I wouldn't give to turn back time and do it all again.

Anyway, thank goodness Jade stopped grinning inanely once she got going and was done with her overlong intro on the stage, which nearly sent me to sleep. Fifteen minutes in and she was practically yelling at us to *work hard, push ourselves, and remember – excuses don't burn calories!* That was a good one, I thought. For such a tiny thing, she certainly has a pair of lungs on her.

Looking around, I could see that everyone else was getting into it and enjoying themselves. Particularly the few straight men there. She's so fit, I can't blame them. Once upon a time they'd have looked at me that way. She'd look damn hot in a bikini, I bet. I'd probably fancy her. I mean, all women have 'female crushes', even though most won't admit it. I've kissed a woman before, back in my late teens. It's natural to experiment, though some people can be so prudish about it. I often find they're the biggest weirdos. I mean, it's always the quiet ones, isn't it? Jade must have some faults. Maybe she picks her nose in front of the TV, or chews with her mouth wide open.

Speaking of weirdos, even that oddball she arrived with seemed to lighten up. I mean, I've seen some sights since joining this club, but she really takes the biscuit, sets a whole new record for contender for the 'least likely to set foot in a gym' award. Talk about a fish out of water. And for someone who's apparently only just met Jade, she seems to idolise her. Like she's known her for years as opposed to a few days. I saw the way she was staring at her, as if she wanted to be her, and I couldn't help but wonder if it was out of genuine admiration or blind envy.

The class finished a few minutes ago, and I'm just taking a slug of water, the sweat still pouring off me as I contemplate who I can corner for a drink in the bar. Lance is out tonight with clients, Michael's on a gap year in Australia and Stella's over at her boyfriend's. She's only seventeen but I can't stop her, even though the boy's a bit common for my liking. The barefaced truth is that it would be hypocritical of me to criticise; I was the same at her age – worse – much to my parents' dismay. I'd also hoped that being 'cool' with her choice of boyfriend would draw us closer together, that me being laid-back about who she chooses to hang out with or shag might make her warm to the idea of going shopping with me, or us chilling out on a spa day together. Having not really taken to my kids as babies, I'd hoped we might become closer as adults. But my lax approach doesn't seem to have made any difference. If anything, we're more distant than ever. I know I've never been the hands-on mum she had perhaps wished I'd be, but she's never wanted for anything, and neither has Michael or Cameron. Stella's more of a daddy's girl, I guess. Lance has always been the more tactile of us both, the one who did the hugs and kisses and bedtime stories. So I suppose it's only natural she'd prefer him to me. Plus – and I know you should love your children equally – secretly I've always preferred Michael. Boys are just so much less trouble; no raging hormones to worry about, no diva-like strops, while there's also something more accommodating about the middle child. That's why I'm not so worried about him going off to Australia with his best mate, Steve. He's a sensible boy, and I'm sure he'll be fine. I can't spend all day worrying about him; that won't do me any good, and it'll only give me wrinkles, rendering my six-monthly Botox top-ups redundant.

'Did you enjoy the class?'

I glance over the rim of my bottle to see a slim, fair-haired woman standing there. I noticed her when we were waiting to go in. I'd never seen her before, so I realised she must be new. Also because of the way she was standing there by herself, leaning against the wall and staring at her phone the way people do when they don't know anyone or find themselves alone in a crowded place. It struck me that there was something of the self-conscious about her, as if she was trying to appear nonchalant, but lacking the confidence and presence of mind to really pull it off.

She flicks her side-swept fringe as she asks the question. Even though she approached me, and did so cheerfully, there's a fretfulness in her expression that tells me she has a lot on her mind.

'Yes, I did. Surprisingly,' I say. 'I'm Susan. Not sure I've seen you before. Have you recently joined?'

'Yes. I'm Grace. This is my first class. Had my gym induction with Martin last night. I'm new to the area.'

'Whereabouts do you live?'

'Cobham.'

Cobham's not exactly local. It's a good twenty-five-minute trek down the A3 or along the river road via Esher. Posh area, though. WAG territory. My interest in making friends with this woman is suddenly piqued.

'You didn't think about joining a club round there?' I ask. 'It's a gorgeous area, so classy. Not like Kingston. It's become so scummy in parts, too many bloody students and cheap pubs. Too many chains. I love the boutique shops in Cobham, the chic restaurants like Sixty-Third and First, and The Ivy, of course.'

'Oh, really?' She cocks her head. 'I quite like Kingston, it's such a lovely spot by the river. I'm from the coast originally, so I do miss the water. But you're right, Cobham's lovely, and nice and quiet, which is what we wanted. Even though it's kind of pushed our budget to the limit, and I really couldn't justify joining a club around there. Not on a freelance journalist's salary.'

Not super-rich then. I can't help feeling a pang of disappointment. I'd set my hopes on meeting a new group of minted housewives. Had already pictured Bellini brunches at The Ivy, wine-fuelled book club meetups at someone's gated estate, five-course dinner parties, charity balls, and so on. My life has been sorely lacking in that department of late. I could so do with livening it up.

'The River Club was more affordable,' Grace continues. 'It was recommended to me.'

'Oh yes, who by?'

'Oh, just a friend, I doubt you know her. And she's since left the area.'

Odd, slightly rushed response. I let it go. Not worth my time.

'Anyway,' she goes on, making it clear she wants to get away from the subject, 'I'm guessing you live outside Kingston if it's not your cup of tea?'

'We're on Coombe Hill Road. More towards Wimbledon than Kingston, thank goodness. I don't mind coming here to shop once in a while, if I have to, that is. The cobbled part of town, you must know where I mean – the area with Reiss, Whistles and Karen Millen? It's more acceptable than the other end where Primark is and all those wretched buses congregate – although of course I prefer the King's Road or Bond Street. Kingston really is a last resort, when I don't have time to get into town, that is.'

Grace smiles at me pleasantly. I can't quite tell what she's thinking. Whether she's impressed, intimidated or amused by me. It's a little disconcerting. There's something in her eyes that's not all there. 'I find Central London a bit much,' she says, blowing that rather irritating fringe of hers away from her freckled face. She still looks rather flushed from the class. Perhaps because of her pale skin. 'A bit too frenetic for me,' she goes on. 'Too many people, too many crowds, it kind of overwhelms me. I'm not good on the Tube either, always seem to get lost, and I have a crap sense of direction. Jim's much better at finding his bearings. Whenever we go on holiday, he's always the navigator, while I'm the one dragging the kids around after us, bribing them with ice cream and their electronic devices once we get back to the hotel.'

Jeez. She does go on. Maybe it's nerves.

'Right,' I say, not wanting to prolong the topic.

'So, if you don't like Kingston, how come you work out here?' she asks. 'Why not somewhere closer to you? There must be lots of clubs in the Wimbledon area. The village is very pretty, and popular with mums, so I hear.'

She was bound to ask the question. People I've only just met always do. And it's a fair one. I lean in as if I'm about to divulge some trade secret, even though only a handful of people remain in the room. Including Natalie. She's talking to Jade on the stage, so thankfully well out of earshot. 'I'll let you into a little secret – we know the owners of this place. Lance, my husband, who's a *City* lawyer, worked on the deal when Lorenzo bought the building. He's a businessman, you see. A very rich, powerful, well-connected businessman.' I pause, mouth the words *possible M-A-F-I-A* then tap my nose. 'Ruthless, but then again you don't get to be in his position by playing nice. As well as this place, he owns several other gyms and an exclusive Italian restaurant in Barnes. Impossible to get a booking less than six months in advance, but I can get you and your husband a table any time, just say the word.' I pat the side of my nose again. 'Anyway, we joined out of loyalty to him.' Closer still. 'Plus, just between us, we get a good deal. Not that we need it, of course, but it would have seemed impolite not to take him up on it.'

Grace is suddenly wide-eyed, clearly in awe of what I just told her. I can't help feeling a glow of satisfaction.

'Wow, I see, well, that makes a lot of sense. And it's so nice of you to support a friend.'

Yes, I'm all heart. I don't tell her that Lorenzo's possible gangster connections scare the shit out of me, and that I therefore see it as the safer option to keep him onside. Then again, once you've earned his loyalty, he'll do anything for you. Anything at all.

'Anyway, I'd better go now. Need to be home in time to tuck the kids into bed.'

My heart sinks. She has kids that still need tucking in. *How dull.*

'OK, then,' I force a smile. 'See you at the next class?'

'Definitely,' Grace says. Then quickly adds, 'As long as I can get away on time. Six thirty is always a bit awkward, with the kids' tea, and so on, but luckily, with Jim on leave from work right now I can usually get away.'

'Thank the Lord for that,' I say, hoping she doesn't register the sarcasm in my voice. I manage to refrain from rolling my eyes.

'And what's he on leave from, if you don't mind me asking?'

I'm thinking not law, as she would have said so when I mentioned Lance being a lawyer. Please say City banker, or better still, film producer.

'Teaching.'

Kill me now.

I wonder why he's on leave, but don't want to pry too much at this stage. Plus, I'm not sure she's of enough interest for me to care. We don't appear to be on the same page.

'He was head of physics at an all-boys' private school in Southampton before we moved here. Hopes to go back to face-to-face teaching someday, but for now is content to do some online tuition and work on the book he's always wanted to write.'

I want to ask why he gave up face-to-face teaching, as I sense there's more to the story than simply fancying a break and trying his hand at writing. But I also sense she's not keen to divulge that bit just yet.

Last chance to save herself where the writing's concerned, though. Please say it's crime fiction or something I might be remotely interested in. 'What's it about?'

'The principles of physics.'

I want to laugh out loud, but I think of falling into a pit of snakes, my greatest fear, and manage to remain grim-faced. 'Well, good luck to him on that one. Even so, it shouldn't matter if he's working or not. I never let the kids get in the way of my workout schedule. That's what childminders are for. I went through at least five while Cameron, Michael and Stella were growing up. No chance I was going to let them interfere with my lifestyle. It's how I've stayed sane all these years.'

Grace smiles weakly. 'Yes, maybe that's where I'm going wrong. I've always been the type to take on too much. But I guess you can't do it all, can you? Neither should there be any shame in that.'

Her gaze settles on me, in such a way that I'm not quite sure whether she expects me to answer her. It feels more like a rhetorical question.

I give up on the idea of asking Grace if she fancies a drink. There's no point; I can tell she's keen to get back to hubby and the kids. Plus, I'm not convinced I'd be entirely comfortable just me and her drinking together. She's nice enough, but her life sounds terribly humdrum. And there's something about her I can't quite put my finger on. A certain look in her eyes that tells me there's more to her than surface appearances would suggest.

'See you next week, then,' I smile. Then contemplate the rest of my evening in front of the Kardashians with Mr Shiraz.

Chapter Fifteen

Grace

Saturday, 21 July 2018, nine a.m.

The doorbell goes, stirring me from my sleep. It's not a natural sleep. I've not slept naturally since sometime before we lost the kids. It's a diazepam-induced slumber. I try not to take it in the day like I used to, because I know how it makes me feel, how I lose my inhibitions, my grip on reality, become a danger to others. That's the last thing I want to be. A while back I made a pledge to myself that I wouldn't take it at all. Promised others that I had kicked the habit. But I can't seem to stop entirely. The nights are the worst. When I have nothing else but my thoughts to occupy my mind. When there's no one around but Jim, and I am a danger to no one but myself. I need it to numb the pain, to stop my mind from turning over and over, thinking about my precious boys, my babies, a searing pain piercing my heart as I remember what it was like to hold them, cuddle them, kiss their hair and smell their childlike scent. How I miss the sound of their voices calling for me, even though there were times when the sound of them shouting 'Mum, Mum' at the tops of their lungs would drive me round the bend; how I even miss the sound of them squabbling over stupid, pointless little things that mean nothing in the grand scheme of life, but which I'd now do anything to hear again. Every night is torture, when I have nothing else to think about besides my loss. And so that little pink pill is a godsend, one that for a blissful seven or eight hours enables me to drift off and feel nothing.

But it does mean I don't wake up feeling refreshed despite having had nine hours according to the clock on my bedside table. I turn over on my side, my eyes still shut, instinctively feel for Jim. But his side is empty. He said he'd follow me up when I announced I was off, but I suspect he never did. I'm guessing he decided to work on his book a bit more, like he often does. Either that, or he stayed asleep on the sofa, or napped in his study. His pillow is untouched, as is his half of the duvet. Maybe it was so late by the time he'd finished work he didn't want to wake me, knowing how I need my sleep. I'd like to imagine that's the case, that he was being thoughtful. It assures me he still cares for me even though the way he acts sometimes, it feels like he doesn't. But it also saddens me. That he can make such a practical judgement. That his desire to feel the warmth of my body, cuddle up to me in bed, no longer overrides his desire to be practical about things. Losing the kids has changed both of us. We are no longer the people we were, him especially, and I resent the fact that he blames me, when I see him as the one at fault. The one who caused us to end up in this perpetual cycle of torture.

There it goes again. God, that doorbell is loud. Who the hell can it be at nine a.m. on a Saturday? It's too early for the postman. And why hasn't Jim gone to answer it? He never bloody well does! It's always me. Once he's asleep, it's like he's in a coma. I wish I could sleep that deeply. A rocket might have taken off outside our house and he still wouldn't stir.

As I force myself upright, my head has that familiar spaced-out sensation to it, and I feel slightly queasy as I swing my legs off the side. It's like the entire room is on a tilt, and I'm seeing the world almost in slow motion. I rub my face hard as if to rouse me from my lethargy, press my palms into the mattress to propel myself up, shuffle to the door and grab my dressing gown off the hook before making for the landing.

'For fuck's sake, I'm coming,' I say under my breath, holding onto the banister in a bid to steady myself as I trundle down the stairs. I feel stiff, more stiff than usual, perhaps because I didn't get my usual Friday-night yoga fix.

'Jim,' I call out in irritation. It's instinctive, I guess. I'm just so used to calling out his name in frustration. 'Jim, are you awake? If you are, why didn't you get the door!'

No response. It infuriates me, and this must show on my face as I open the front door and see two men standing there. They're both in suits, and I notice a black Vauxhall Astra parked up behind them next to my Toyota. We only have the one car. With Jim working from home, and no kids to ferry around, we saw two cars as a need-less luxury. Besides, Jim has his bike to get out and about. There are lovely green open spaces and woods in the Cobham/Oxshott area. He says he prefers biking or walking to driving anyway. Says it keeps him fit. That he needs the exercise, stuck in the house at his desk all day. I can't disagree with that. I'm more on the go than him, while my exercise classes at The River Club keep me in shape.

'Grace Maloney?'

'Yes.'

I get a sick feeling inside. And a sense of being here before. Strangers coming to deliver bad news. I think of Mum, wonder if they're here because of her. But surely the home would have called? It's not like they allow their patients to go wandering the streets. The dizziness returns, and as if on autopilot I lean to the left and prop myself up against the doorway.

'I'm DI Donovan Bailey and this is DS Javid Khan.'

Detectives. Both men flash me their badges, and I feel the colour drain from my face. But I quickly tell myself to calm down, rather than jump to conclusions as to why they are here.

'Don't be alarmed, we just need to ask you some questions.'

I feel a mild sense of relief. Even so, what questions? 'Questions?' I repeat. 'About what?'

'About Jade Pascal.' *Shit*. 'We understand you attend her classes at a social club in the Kingston area. The River Club, I believe it's called?'

My nausea returns. 'Yes. What's the problem? It's not something to do with the fact that Jade didn't turn up to the class last night, is it?'

'Yes, I'm afraid it is. Miss Pascal hasn't been seen or heard from in thirty-six hours, and we're now treating her disappearance as suspicious. Particularly as her phone and car keys were found inside her flat, her car still parked on the road outside. We understand she taught a Zumba class on Thursday night, and we're assuming she drove straight home afterwards.'

My heart flutters again, a burning sensation spiking my gullet. 'I see, how awful.'

'May we come in? I'm sorry to have disturbed you at such an early hour on a weekend.'

'Oh, that's quite all right,' I stammer, feeling a bit ashamed that I'm not dressed yet. It's not that early, and he was clearly being tactful. I usher them through. 'Please excuse my state,' I say. 'I had a bad night, didn't drop off until gone one.' They follow my lead into the living room, and I offer them a seat on one of the sofas. I'd half expected to see Jim still slumped there, which would only have served to heighten my embarrassment. But to my relief, he's nowhere to be seen.

'Oh dear, how frustrating,' DI Bailey sympathises. 'My wife has nights like that, while I tend to sleep like a log, which annoys her somewhat.' He grins, and I grin back, feeling slightly more relaxed. At the back of my mind, I wonder where the hell Jim is. I hate it when he disappears without a word. It unsettles me. Perhaps he's gone for a bike ride, or a run in the woods. He does that sometimes on Saturday mornings. Sometimes he'll stay out for hours. It's his way of coping with our loss, the way pills are mine.

'I totally empathise with your wife. My husband's the same,' I say, attempting to keep the mood light.

'Glad it's not just me. Is your husband at home?'

What do I say? That I have no idea because we only talk when it suits him? Either he's locked in his study, or disappears for hours on end, never telling me where he's going, me never knowing when he might return. That he blames me for the loss of our children, even though he's the one who was at fault. That I tell everyone at the club and the care home that we have two wonderful boys who keep us on our toes. Just because I want to appear normal, *feel* normal, when I'm there. That I don't want to be treated as some pitiful charity case.

Think quick. Be assertive. That's how you've got away with your stories this long. 'Do you know, I have no idea where he is. As I said, I had a bad night, and when I woke up he was nowhere to be found. I think he must have gone out for a run. He tends to do that most weekend mornings.'

'Good for him, puts me to shame,' DI Bailey smiles. 'And do you have children? I take it the answer is no, only because it's awfully quiet. Also, and forgive me for saying so, incredibly tidy. My living room looks like it's been hit by a nuclear bomb.'

I laugh. Briefly consider telling him the truth. But instead perpetuate the lie I've told everyone at the gym, just because I can't bear to rehash all that, least of all with these two police officers, even though I know there's a chance they'll find out if they choose to dig deeper into my life. I can't think why they would, though. It's not like Jade and I were known for being best friends. Not like her and Natalie. Soon he'll realise that and leave me alone. Focus on Natalie, and no doubt all the men Jade's shagged.

'Actually, we have two boys,' I say. 'But they were at a sleepover last night. At their best friend's house. The mother's offered to take them to karate club, so I'm a free agent until lunchtime. As for the tidiness, that's only because I cleaned yesterday morning. Come back Monday and it'll be a tip again.'

Please don't come back Monday! Why did I say that?

'I can relate to that. I offer to help with the cleaning, but my wife prefers to do it herself. Doesn't trust me.'

Can't say I blame her. Trust is a risky business.

'Do you mind if I throw on some more suitable clothes?' I say. 'I feel a bit weird in my dressing gown.

Also, I might just grab myself a coffee, not had my daily fix yet. Can I get you gentlemen one too?'

'Of course, take your time,' DI Bailey says, 'and don't worry about us,' he glances at his partner, 'we had one on the way over.'

I smile, assure them I'll be as quick as I can before plodding back up the stairs, feeling a little steadier on my feet, but still sorely in need of caffeine. Fully alert is exactly what I need to be with two police officers here to ask questions about Jade. I can't afford to place myself on the radar of suspicion. Hopefully, once I've answered their questions, they'll realise I can only be of limited help and go away.

I can't have them prodding deeper into my life. Everything will come out if they do. And then I'll be forced to run again.

Chapter Sixteen

Susan

Saturday, 21 July 2018, nine a.m.

'Where are you going?'

I'm sitting on a stool at our glossy kitchen worktop, having some breakfast, Capital FM on low in the background, when Lance appears in the open doorway. Looking rough. It wasn't him in the spare room as I'd first thought when I pulled up in the car last night. I realised that one of us must have left the light on in there at some point yesterday because the house was empty when I finally plucked up the courage to step inside.

Lance came home at least an hour after I went to bed, and so this is the first time I've seen him in twenty-four hours. He looks hung-over, has that blotchy-faced, bleary-eyed look about him I see in the mirror only too often. There are puffy purple bags under his eyes, and a manic restlessness about him that alarms me. He comes through and heads straight for the filter jug of coffee I've recently brewed. The delicious aroma of Ecuadorian coffee beans permeates the air around us, along with the smell of my toast. I feel like saying, 'Hands off, make your own bloody coffee,' but I know how petty that would be of me. Especially as it's his earnings that pays for the damn machine. Pays for everything in this bloody place. I know that's what he'll say in response and quite frankly, I can't bear to hear it. It makes me feel so worthless, like I'm some kind of parasite, even though, when I think about it, he wouldn't be far wrong. I know what I am, know I haven't been the mother or homemaker I should or could have been. I've milked Lance's pay cheque for as long as we've been together, and he knows that. As do our children. So I keep tight lipped. Despite a part of me wanting to throw the damn coffee all over his perfect face. I watch him lift one of our Fortnum & Mason mugs from the rack on the wall, fill it to the brim, then take a swig. He's always taken it black, unsweetened. He avoids dairy and sugar like the plague. Such a fucking health freak. Unlike me, who pretends to be one once in a while but can never stick it out for more than a couple of weeks at a time when my will finally caves and I find myself reaching for the carbs and the sugar. Although, as I said, today he's not looking so healthy. Today it's obvious that last night he went on a bit of a bender. And I'm pretty sure I know why. He knows I have him by the scrotum and that I won't hesitate to twist until he squeals like a pig should he fail to keep to our agreement. Should he fail to keep his mouth shut.

'To play golf,' he replies without bothering to look me in the eye. Like he can't stand the sight of me. Like what I made him do turns his insides. He removes a cereal bowl from a cupboard, grabs the unsweetened muesli from another, then proceeds to fill the bowl before going over to the fridge and finding his revolting unsweetened almond milk which he pours on top. I wonder, if I doused it with insecticide, would he notice the difference? Or if there are any poisonous liquids that don't show up on autopsies? I daren't google it in case Big Brother is watching and I draw undue attention to myself. This is so not the time to be doing that. It's tempting though.

I'd expected the golf response, just because of the way he's dressed. Nike polo top, Calvin Klein bullet stretch golf trousers, the same loafers he always wears to the club before changing into his spikes. Besides, he often plays on a Saturday morning, so it should have been obvious, and therefore I'm not sure why I bothered asking. Perhaps because, having not spoken to a soul since leaving the club last night, I'd felt the need to engage someone in conversation. Michael's still in bed – I heard him roll in at three a.m. and I doubt he'll make an appearance before midday – and Stella won't be back from Jason's much before then, if at all. Lance is my only form of human contact right now. As excruciating as that is to admit.

I can't help myself. Can't help saying something deliberately provoking. 'Are you sure you're up to it, darling? You're looking a bit pale, like you're about to throw up.'

For the first time since he appeared Lance makes eye contact with me. Glares at me, more like. I watch him force down his cereal. He'd be much better off with a fry-up, but his body is a temple and all that crock. 'Oh, I woke up feeling fine, dear. But then I walked in here and saw you.'

His words cut me to the quick. I feel the urge to react, but don't rise to the bait. I must maintain my dignity, my ice maiden act. He's the one at fault, who's got himself into the miserable situation he's found himself in.

'You want to be careful, Lance. Should think about being a little nicer to your wife, now that I know your dirty little secrets. What would the partners say? Your clients? You'd be dead meat at the firm. I can just picture it now on the front page of *The Lawyer* magazine – top partner Lance Hampson embroiled in…'

Before I can utter another word, Lance is on me like a panther. He comes right up, his nose almost pressing against mine, grabs my neck, squeezing it ever so slightly, causing my throat to seize up, the remnants of my toast stuck fast.

'And you want to watch what you say to your husband. I'm betting you have some dirty little secrets of your own, Susie.' He hisses this last sentence, and I can smell the alcohol of last night on his breath, making me nauseous. 'In fact, I know you do. And I think that's why you played the card you did. Because you're scared. Scared of the despicable things you've done coming out.'

He releases his grip, and I rub the circulation back into my throat, my heart pounding like a drum. For all his faults, I hadn't thought him capable of violence. But maybe I was wrong. Maybe in doing what I've done, in being the wife I've been, I've let the demon out of him.

I want to come back at him with some smart, witty retort, but he's caught me off guard and my usual composure seems to have abandoned me.

'I'd think carefully about what *you* say or do, Susie, from now on. I ceded to your demands, to your pathetic, twisted attempt at blackmail. I did what you told me to because unlike you, I care about people, about my children. I feel a duty to protect them. I don't want our kids to suffer for my mistakes. I did this for them, and only them. The one good thing to come out of our miserable marriage.' Again, his words sting me like salt on a chapped lip, just because deep down I know he is right. I'm always looking out for number one, I've been that way since forever, and it's too late to change. In forcing his hand the other night, I wanted to have control over him, wanted him to beg me for my forgiveness, acknowledge me as the victor in our very own War of the Roses, admit that I have him over a barrel. But now he's gone and turned the tables, made himself out to be some kind of humanitarian, acceding to my demands for the sake of our children. As usual, he's a bloody Saint to my Satan. There's something else that rattles me, too. Something in his eyes that tells me he's keeping something from me. Some ace up his sleeve he's waiting to play. In some ways I wish he'd just come out and play it. But perhaps he's challenging me. Challenging me in the ultimate battle of wits, wanting me to be the first one to buckle under the weight of my own guilt.

He goes back over to his breakfast, takes a last mouthful, chews it, swallows, then places the bowl in the sink. 'You've won this battle, Susie,' he says, looking up at me, 'but you have not won the war. Sooner or later the truth will come to light, and when it does, I plan on having a front row seat. You remember that.'

I feel cold all over as I watch my husband leave the room. I thought I had silenced the only person who could ruin me. But I'm starting to think I was wrong.

Chapter Seventeen

Grace

Saturday, 21 July 2018, 9:30 a.m.

'Are you sure I can't get you both some coffee?'

I look at the officers expectantly, hoping they might change their minds now that we've moved to the kitchen, so as to give me a bit more time to wake up and think about what I'm going to say. But to my dismay they decline again, exacerbating my nerves. I sip my coffee, willing my brain to engage and make sure I say the right thing. I'm also aware that my breath must smell rancid as I've not had time to brush my teeth. Just as well we're not sitting too close; hopefully the coffee will mask my morning breath. Jim always comments on how foul it is. Not that his smells like roses.

'So, how long have you been attending Miss Pascal's classes?' DI Bailey asks.

'Oh, about a year now,' I say. 'I was at her launch event, a Body Attack class back in July of last year. The class and gym coordinator, a guy named Martin Tyler, recommended it to me at my induction. I jumped at the chance, to be honest. I'd much rather work out with other people than on my own. I find it motivates me to work harder. I'm not very good in my own company. You'd think I would be, being an only child, but I guess I'd always wanted a sibling, and spending so much time alone as a child has made me appreciate being with other people. Crave it, really.'

Stop gabbling, I tell myself. He didn't need to know that. And he definitely doesn't need to know your life history.

Then again, I do want to appear as friendly and open as possible. Like I have nothing to hide. That's the plan, anyway. Hopefully, if I do that, he'll leave me alone.

'And after that you became a regular at Jade's classes?'

'Yes,' I nod. 'I go three times a week, pretty much without fail. Unless I can't get away because of the kids. But with my husband working from home it's never normally a problem.'

'And how about you? Do you work?'

'I do a bit of freelance writing, gives me flexibility with the kids.'

I notice DI Bailey's gaze switch to a shelf built into the far wall, a framed photograph of Casper and George taking prime position in the centre. 'Nice-looking boys you have.'

I smile broadly, the love for my children filling my heart. I miss them like crazy. And yet I manage to keep up this charade that they are still with us. In some warped way, it gives me comfort. To pretend the unthinkable never happened. To pretend they still roam the house. It makes me feel normal. God, how I wish I'd appreciated them more at the time, cherished the simple things in life instead of moaning, letting it all get on top of me. I should have asked for help, shouldn't have been afraid to say no to things. But it's too late now. 'Yes, they're my pride and joy. Despite driving me crazy every now and again.'

Both detectives give a hearty chuckle. From DS Khan's expression, it's clear he also has kids, that they drive him nuts like mine once did, but also that he couldn't imagine life without them. Or before them. Children are such a blessing; a blessing not to be taken lightly.

'And would you say that Jade is popular?' DI Bailey asks. 'I assume she has other regulars at her classes, like you?' A pause, then with a solemn face he adds, 'I should tell you now that it was Jade's friend, Natalie Marsden, who I understand is another regular at The River Club, who called us to her flat, having gone over to check on Jade after she failed to turn up to last night's class or answer her phone calls. She was concerned for Jade's well-being, said it wasn't like Jade not to show without telling anyone.'

'I agree,' I say. 'Jade's never done anything like this before, to my recollection. Obviously, she's had holidays, but she's always made sure she has cover. Poor Natalie. She's such a lovely girl, got a heart of gold. Dotes on Jade. From what I've seen, Jade's really brought her out of her shell.' I take a breather, then add, 'And in answer to your initial question, Jade was very popular…' *Too popular for her own good.* 'There was nothing not to like about her. I just can't imagine who'd wish her ill. If that's the case, that is.'

'Can I ask what time you left for the class last night?'

'Five fifty-five. I always allow myself half an hour as the early-evening traffic can be a real nightmare.'

'Can anyone verify that?'

I pretend to think. 'No, Jim went out for a late-afternoon bike ride, and the kids were at a sleepover, as I already mentioned.'

'And what were your movements during the day?'

'I cleaned first thing in the morning, then spent most of the day with my mother. She has dementia and is in a care home. It was a very trying day, if truth be told, so I was especially sorry to miss the class. I could have done with it.'

'I'm so sorry to hear that.' DI Bailey smiles kindly. 'I can't imagine how hard that must be.'

I give a grateful smile in return. 'It's not easy, I can't deny it. Seeing the one you love, who brought you up and knew you better than anyone become someone you don't recognise, is tough beyond belief. But she has her good days, and I cling to that.' I don't add that sometimes I think very wicked thoughts and wish she'd pop off peacefully in her sleep. It's a terrible thing to think, but then again, she has no quality of life, it just all seems so pointless. Would it really be such a bad thing?

Both men offer sympathetic smiles. 'It must be very taxing, but I'm sure in her own way your mother appreciates it,' DI Bailey says. Again, I smile gratefully, thinking he really doesn't have a clue. She doesn't appreciate a thing because she has no idea what I do for her, doesn't remember what she had for breakfast, let alone anything else. He pauses, as if the subject of my mother's mental decline deserves a few seconds of silent reflection. Then, 'You mentioned Natalie coming out of her shell since attending Jade's classes. Can you tell us more about that?'

'Oh, well, I just mean I've noticed a change in her since that first class a year ago. She had quite a nervous air about her when we first met, hardly made conversation, looked like she'd rather be anywhere but there. But over time, and especially in the last six months, she's really blossomed, become more confident, more relaxed. Jade's to be commended for that, taking Natalie under her wing, like a big sister I guess, even though I think they're around the same age. She's also lost a ton of weight, at least a stone and a half I'd say, over the last twelve months. Changed her hair, got contact lenses.' I pause. 'Poor thing, she must be worried out of her mind. I should give her a call.'

DI Bailey nods. 'Yes, I think she'd like that. Mrs Maloney, I must tell you, we found blood on Miss Pascal's bath mat. We're still waiting for forensics to come back on whether it's Jade's. Of course, there could be a harmless explanation, but what with her phone and car keys being found in her flat, her car parked outside and her not being seen or heard from in thirty-six hours, it's worrying.'

I gasp out loud. Am quick to place my hand over my mouth. 'Blood? Really? Oh my God, that's awful.'

'Yes, and the more time that passes, the more concerning it is, and we'll have no choice but to make a press statement and appeal to the public.'

'Right,' I nod. *Fuck*, I think.

'We know Jade covered a Zumba class on Thursday night, and of course her car is parked outside her building, so we're assuming whoever attacked Jade, if that is the case, did so after she'd returned home from teaching. According to Martin, who you mentioned earlier and who I spoke to first thing this morning, that would have been around ten p.m.'

I do my best to appear devastated at the idea Jade may have been attacked. 'This is just so shocking. I can't think who'd want to hurt Jade. I'm assuming it could be a random intruder or burglar?'

'Yes, it could. We can't rule out anything right now. And it might explain why the phone was left where it was. Then again, nothing appears to have been taken. Apart from what we found in the bathroom and a few of Jade's clothing drawers left open in her bedroom, the rest of the flat was intact.'

'Oh, that is rather odd. Then again, if it wasn't random, you'd have thought her attacker would have taken the phone.'

'Yes. Unless he or she knew there was nothing on there that could connect them to Jade's assault. Better still, that it contains information which might incriminate someone else, or show Jade herself up in a bad light. It depends how smart her kidnapper is. How well he or she knew Jade, what their history is. There are so many ifs and buts, but hopefully we'll have a better idea once forensics have got into the phone.'

'You think perhaps this could be a kidnapping then?' I ask. 'Rather than, well, I don't want to say the word.' I lower my eyes, shake my head slowly.

'Murder?' DI Bailey says bluntly.

'Yes,' I look up, my voice barely audible.

'I'm afraid I have no idea. As we already discussed, the blood on the bath mat could have an innocent explanation. And as I told Natalie, before a body's been found, there's always hope the victim may still be alive. But that's why we need to act quickly. The more time that passes, the less chance there is of finding her alive.'

There's a moment of silence as all three of us contemplate this possibility. 'And how did Jade seem to you on Wednesday?' DI Bailey breaks the hush. 'Natalie mentioned you'd been at her Body Attack class.'

'Fine,' I say. 'She seemed her usual warm and upbeat self.'

'Really? Natalie mentioned she'd seemed distracted. Not quite right.'

I swallow hard. 'Well, Natalie knows her better than I do. She may have noticed something that completely passed me by. I was too busy concentrating on the class rather than studying Jade, like Natalie.' I hold DI Bailey's gaze and let that nugget of information sink in.

'Can I ask where you were on Thursday night?'

Why do I suddenly feel like he's treating me as a suspect? I tell myself to stay calm. That it's routine, that I mustn't appear rattled. Even so, I am rattled, because if he probes further, checks out my life before I came here, the real reason I uprooted myself and moved to Cobham, I'm done for.

'I was at home.'

'Alone?'

'Jim was upstairs working in his study. The kids were in bed.'

'I see. One last thing, do you socialise much with Jade outside of classes?'

'No. Like I said, Natalie's the one who's particularly friendly with her. I went to her thirtieth last month. But that was a pretty big do, and most of her regulars and then some went along. It was good fun, and she seemed to have a great time. Got made a real fuss of by Barry, the manager. All the men seem to have a soft spot for her. Which isn't surprising, looking the way she does.'

DI Bailey moves to get up, DS Khan following suit, and I want to sigh out loud with relief that the questioning is finally over. I can almost feel Dad's presence by my side, telling me I did well, that he's proud of me for being so strong. God, how I miss him.

'Thank you for your time, Mrs Maloney, you've been most helpful,' he says. 'Just one more thing.'

What now? 'Of course, anything to help.'

'Why join a club all the way over in Kingston? It's not exactly local to here, is it? Bit of a hike.'

I should have expected this. It's the same question I get all the time from strangers. So I'm well prepared to give the response I concocted long ago. 'I just like it. A friend, who unfortunately has moved up North, recommended it to me, said it was great value for money and had a fun, friendly vibe to it. I gave it a go, and saw that she was right. I'm not so fussed about swanky gyms that cost an arm and a leg, I just want to go somewhere I feel relaxed and can have fun.'

Both men smile. 'Makes sense,' DS Khan says. 'Can't stand pretentious gyms myself. I work out at my local council-run gym, and it does the job, suits me fine.'

I smile back, and a few minutes later close the door on my visitors.

Peace at last.

'What was that about?'

Or so I thought. I nearly jump out of my skin, swivel round to see Jim standing there.

'You were here all along?'

'Yes.'

'Why didn't you answer the door, for Christ's sake?'

'You know why,' he growls. 'And you should be grateful.'

'I should?'

'Yes. Because the last thing you want is me speaking to the police.' His gaze drills through me. 'Christ, it makes me sick how you manage to maintain that travesty of a story. How you can believe no one's going to find out. You're sick, you know that? You need to get off the pills, stop living in that deluded world of yours. Every time you lie, you're devaluing our kids.' A pause, then he adds,

'Remember, I'm the only one around here who knows the truth. What you did.'

How can I forget? He'll never let me forget. He'll torment me until my dying day. I watch him turn round before disappearing up the stairs out of sight.

Chapter Eighteen

Natalie

Saturday, 21 July 2018, 11:30 a.m.

'Thank you for seeing me at such short notice, Dr Jenkins. And on a weekend. I know it's a huge inconvenience. I just felt like I was going stir-crazy at home. The last sixteen hours have been so stressful, I needed to talk things through with someone I can trust.'

I'm sitting opposite my therapist in her office in Richmond. I call her my therapist because I don't like using the term 'psychiatrist'. Despite knowing there's nothing wrong with the word, and that a lot of people see 'psychiatrists' to cope with perfectly normal everyday issues like divorce or bereavement. But for me, perhaps rightly or wrongly, the title always seems to equate with the word 'crazy' and I don't want to think of myself as crazy. I think of myself as someone who's been through a lot in their thirty years, someone who had it tough as a child, did some things she regrets but that were in no way her fault and therefore needs a bit of guidance, a bit of TLC every now and again, to get through life. That's what I tell myself anyway.

'That's quite all right, Natalie, you know I can always make time for you. It's also the advantage of being divorced with no kids. I have no ties.' She smiles warmly, and although I know she's trying to inject a bit of humour into the conversation, I can't help feeling sorry for her. She's such a lovely person, the least deserving of a rotten cheating husband who left her for his secretary. It's so sad she can't have children of her own because I know without a shadow of a doubt that she'd make a great mother. At fifty-one her time has sadly passed, although I guess she could always adopt or foster. God, what I would have given to have had a foster mother like her, rather than being lumped with the foster parents from hell. Even though Estelle and John, who came after, were OK. Christ, it was like living with Mary and Joseph after what came before.

It's been just shy of a fortnight since I was last here. I was supposed to be seeing her this coming Wednesday, but the stress of the last two days, the last week, in fact, has made me feel rather desperate, and I know it can't wait. Of course, she knows all about my friendship with Jade, what goes on in the classes, about my work at the library, my history, but there are two major things I haven't told her, and one of them has been troubling me since speaking to DI Bailey.

It's a much sunnier day today. An arrow of sunlight shooting through the half-open shutter and bouncing off her desk to the left of where I am sitting. I always feel calm when I'm here. It's not just Dr Jenkins' soothing voice that gives me a zen-like peace; the entire decor of the room is designed to deliver an air of serenity, from the immaculate nutmeg walls to the temperature kept at a pleasant sixteen degrees. Just behind her shoulder there is a fish tank containing brightly coloured fish so pretty they should, to my mind, belong in a piece of artwork. She's had fish as long as I've known her. Which is about eight years. Since I moved to Kingston from Lambeth, south London, where I was born and spent my childhood and early adulthood. Watching Dr Jenkins' fish always calms me, and it's the reason I now have Ernie.

'Well, it's still good of you,' I say. 'I wish I could buy you lunch or something.'

She smiles, takes off her glasses and removes a speck of something from the corner of her right eye. 'That's a kind thought, but you know I can't accept gifts from patients.'

'Yes,' I say with a gentle nod, 'I know.'

'So, you said on the phone that Jade's gone missing and the police are investigating. That's troubling news. Can you tell me anything more?'

For a brief moment, just seeing a kind, familiar face, being in a calming environment, I'd managed to blot out the dark cloud that's suddenly descended on my life. But then, with this question put to me, the darkness envelops me once more. Sending a chill through me.

'Yes, it is troubling,' I say quietly, blinking back tears. *Tears are for losers. Are you a fucking crybaby?* I can still hear Cath's words as if she'd only uttered them yesterday.

'Natalie, are you there?'

I shake my head, as if to shake away Cath's voice. 'Yes, sorry.'

Dr Jenkins smiles kindly, then sits back, the tip of her ballpoint pen poised on the open notebook resting on her right knee in front of her, which is crossed over her left. 'Can you go over what happened yesterday in a bit more detail? Context always helps.'

I take a deep breath, then tell her everything I told DI Bailey. Including the fact that Jade didn't seem right during Wednesday's class. But I add one thing I didn't tell him. Or even admit to myself the full extent of the problem until now. The fact that lately I've not been sleeping well. That it's been going on for some time now, and that it seems to have got worse these past few nights since my row with Jade on Monday evening after the class.

'I see, that is worrying. What did you argue about?'

'The man she's been sleeping with.'

Dr Jenkins knows Jade's lover is married, but not his identity. I just can't bring myself to betray Jade's trust. But I also know that before long I may have to. If I want her back safely.

'Because he's married?'

'Yes, that's a big part of it. It's never going anywhere, but she can't seem to accept that. It's like she's infatuated with him. Like he has this hold over her. She seems to think he's going to leave his wife and they'll be able to run off into the sunset together. That's what he's told her, apparently, but I reckon it's hot air. They're from two very different worlds, and she's kidding herself. He has too much to lose. And their being together would hurt too many people. Damage too many reputations.'

'Have you ever caught them together?'

'No, I only know what she's told me. They're very careful, and I only found out because she told me one night, after they'd argued about his wife, and she needed someone to talk to. I mean, I only ever see Jade at the club or at her place. It's not like I track her movements 24/7. I'm not some stalker, for God's sake.' I pause, having real-ised my tone has become somewhat defensive, aggressive even. I feel my face burn. 'Sorry, that came across as a little aggressive. I'm just frustrated and worried for her.'

In my mind, I worry Dr Jenkins thinks I've become a little obsessive about Jade. And so I'm keen to set the record straight. OK, so I do talk about her a lot in my therapy sessions, but surely that's not a bad thing? Surely Dr Jenkins knows I'm just grateful for Jade's friendship. After all, she's the first real friend I've had since losing Jack. She's special, like family. And everyone talks about their family, right? It's only natural.

'Are you worried her lover might have hurt her? That he could be behind her disappearance?'

'Yes, I guess. I mean it's possible, I just don't know. I don't know the guy, never spoken to him. From what she tells me, he's gentle and kind and loving with her. Makes her feel special. She says he's trapped in an unhappy marriage. But it could all just be an act. Maybe he says the same thing to a ton of other women. Or maybe he's a bit screwed up, needy. Who knows?'

'Why would you think it could be an act?'

I shrug my shoulders, like it's so obvious I shouldn't have to explain. 'To get sex, of course. That's what men do, they've got sex on the brain. It's all they can think about. And I should imagine they're even more desperate as they get older, when their wives no longer excite or satisfy them.'

'I think that's a bit of a generalisation, Natalie. You can't put all men into the same category as your father. What he did to you was horrific, the worst crime imaginable, but not all men are like that.'

The mere mention of my father causes my insides to flip, images flashing through my mind. Painful, hideous images I thought I'd blocked out through years of therapy. Memories that caused me to do unspeakable things. And then, just because I'm suddenly reliving that trauma, and it's Dr Jenkins who I see as responsible for this, I say something I instantly regret. 'Really? I'm surprised you'd say that, based on your own experience.'

Dr Jenkins has been nothing but kind to me; for Christ's sake, she's given up her Saturday morning for me, and all I can do is take a cheap shot back. To her credit, she remains unaffected, on the outside at least, although I'm sure my words must smart on the inside. She's only human, after all.

'I'm so sorry,' I say, almost feeling the urge to get up and hug her. Although I know that's strictly off limits.

'It's OK, but I am concerned, Natalie. Concerned the aggression's starting to come back. You've done so well to contain it all these years. Long before I've been treating you. I can't help thinking you made a mistake joining that club after all. I should never have encouraged you. It only seems to have exacerbated your stress levels. Stress you didn't have previously, living a simple existence. Your brother always warned you about that, advised you to live a simple life with him no longer around to protect you. You've told me that on many occasions, and he knew you better than anyone, of course.'

I swallow hard. She's voiced out loud the same concerns I've had these past weeks, even though I've tried to push them to one side.

'Please don't blame yourself, Dr Jenkins. It was my decision to join the club, ultimately, and let's face it, until recently it's done me the power of good. I'm physically more fit than I've ever been, more confident. And to be honest, I was leading a pretty dull life. A bit sad when you think about it. I mean, what's the point of living if you have no fun at all? I know Jack meant well, but perhaps it was time I started to think for myself, go with my intuition.'

'True.'

'It's the lack of sleep,' I say. 'That's why I'm so tetchy. You know I need my sleep. Everything goes haywire if I don't get enough.'

'Yes, but why aren't you sleeping? It's stress, isn't it? Stress owing to the fact that you and Jade haven't been getting along as well recently. It must be. I can't help feeling that before, when you kept yourself to yourself, you were able to maintain more of an even keel. You never had trouble sleeping back then as nothing was worrying you.'

She's right. But as I just pointed out to her, what kind of a life was that? I might as well have been dead. For so long, I'd resigned myself to living the life of a hermit, to staying out of people's way, but having had a taste of something different, of something of a life, I'm not sure I can go back to how it was before.

Dr Jenkins moves on. 'And has your insomnia got worse in recent days, would you say? Since your row with Jade?'

'Yes,' I admit, 'I would say so. I was just so upset, and even though we made it up on Tuesday over the phone, it still continued to niggle me because, despite her saying she was over it, that it was all in the past, done and dusted, there was just something in her voice that irked me. A hardness I'd never heard before. Like she didn't care about me any more, like she was…'

'Like she was what?'

I swallow away the bile creeping up my throat. 'Like she was sick of me. Or sickened by me. It reminded me of Cath.'

'Your foster mum?'

'Yes. You know how she used to talk to me as if I was dirt. How she treated me and Jack and the other kids under her care. She made us feel like we weren't worth the ground she trod on, and it hurt to hear almost the same contempt in Jade's voice, my supposed best friend. The only friend I've had since Jack.' I pause for breath. 'Plus I couldn't stop thinking about what she said to me on Monday when I told her she needed to be careful, that the man she was seeing wasn't Prince Charming who was going to whisk her off into the sunset so they could have babies and live happily ever after. Like he promised her.'

'What did she say?'

I feel the tears gather, try to stave them off, but can't stop one from escaping my left eye and rolling down my increasingly hot cheeks. 'She accused me of being jealous. Said I needed to grow up and back off. That just because I wasn't pretty enough to bag a hot, intelligent man, I shouldn't begrudge her for doing so. That I was becoming too clingy, and that maybe I needed to find another friend to follow round like a puppy.'

Just saying the words out loud, five days later, still hurts. It's excruciating to remember them, in fact. She'd never spoken to me like that. Never glared at me in such a way that made me feel so worthless. The way my father and Cath made me feel. It wasn't the Jade I knew and loved; she was like a different person, vain and full of herself. It upset me more than words can say. And it maddened me. God, I can't remember feeling that mad in a long time.

I confess all this to Dr Jenkins because I know that whatever I say to her won't leave these four walls. But having done so, she then launches the killer question I'd expected would follow.

'Natalie, have you started sleepwalking again?'

Chapter Nineteen

Susan

Saturday, 21 July 2018, 12:05 p.m.

'Nice of you to make an appearance.'

It's a little after midday and, as predicted, my twenty-two-year-old son has just rolled out of bed. Still wearing pyjama bottoms and a Nirvana t-shirt, he ambles zombie-like into the living room where I'm sitting on one of our cream leather sofas casually flicking through *Vogue*. I'm meeting my friend, Siobhan, for a late lunch at Beaufort House on the King's Road at two p.m., and then we're getting a mani and pedi at Sarah Chapman, so until I need to set off in around forty-five minutes, I have some time to kill.

Michael's dark hair is an utter mess, matching the unruly stubble framing his jawline. It's just so unseemly, and I can't understand why he'd want to hide such a handsome face. I've never been one for beards. Always liked my men clean-shaven, as Lance was back when I met him, and remains so to this day. I notice Michael's also put on a bit of weight around his midriff. Too much junk and beer and not enough exercise. Having played all manner of sports at Oxford – rugby, rowing, captain of the hockey team – he's really let things slide since coming back from his gap year in May. In two months' time he starts as a trainee solicitor at a top law firm in the City, following in his father's footsteps, but looking at him now it's hard to imagine him fitting in. He looks like he should be selling *The Big Issue* or something equally demeaning. I badly want to say something, have this desperate urge to tell him to stop being such a slob, do some exercise, get a haircut and put the brain cells he's been born with, along with the extortionate private school fees we forked out on, to better use than all-night gaming. But somehow I manage to restrain myself. My husband detests me already; I can't bear adding my favourite son to my list of haters. Even though I fear it may already be too late.

'Good one, Mum,' he grunts. 'I see you're filling in your time as productively as ever. What, no lunch with Siobhan today, no spa treatments planned?'

I smile sweetly, even though it's obvious my son sees me as utterly predictable. Nothing but a pitiful cliché. I wonder, what happened to the sweet little boy who once looked upon his mother with adoring eyes? It's as if the moment he turned eighteen, he wised up and saw me for what I am. Even so, my middle child will always be my soft spot. No matter how much his love for me appears to have waned.

'And what are *your* big plans for today then?' I retort. 'An afternoon of gaming? Or perhaps trying to decide which pizza parlour to order from? It's a hard life doing nothing, I know.'

Two can play at that game. He glares at me but it's obvious he knows I've only gone and pointed out the truth. Still, he doesn't take it lying down. 'Well, after *working* my way around Australia, I deserve to chill out and indulge a bit, don't you think? Before long, I'll be a slave to the City like Dad for pretty much the next forty years of my life. That's the difference between us, Mum. This summer is a one-off for me. Whereas your life is just one long extended vacation.'

'How dare you,' I say, slamming the magazine on the coffee table in front of me.

'It would be different if you did something useful with your time,' he goes on. 'I don't know, some charity work or something. Write a book, do an art class, learn a language, anything, really. But as far as I can tell your life revolves around coffee mornings, lunches, dinner parties, the gym, shopping and visiting the spa.' I feel my face turn crimson, just because I have no quick-fire response. And because I know he's not far wrong.

He's on a roll, and it makes me wonder if Lance has been putting words into his mouth. 'And you weren't even a hands-on mum, a proper homemaker, when we were little. You palmed us off to the nanny or the childminder at any given opportunity, and we've had a cleaner for as long as I can remember.' His eyes fix on me with disdain. 'Don't you feel empty, Mum, don't you feel like your life is missing something? I just wish you'd do something worthwhile for once, but you can't bear to get your mani-cured nails dirty once in a while, can you?'

We lock eyes for a few seconds, and I'm on the verge of responding when the doorbell rings.

'I'll get it,' Michael says. 'Wouldn't want you to get up.'

As I watch him leave the room, I blink back the tears that have collected in my eyes. I am not the crying sort, but hearing Michael's words, realising just how useless he believes me to be, really hurts. He has no idea what it's been like all these years, being married to a man who never loved me, forever in the shadow of his beloved Ellen.

Even if I only have myself to blame. I fill my life with fun and frivolity to mask that pain, that emptiness, even though he thinks it's purely because I'm without feeling. That it's entirely my fault he and his brother and sister were brought up under the umbrella of a loveless marriage. It *is* my fault, in so many ways, but I did try in the beginning, I did try to love Lance. But he didn't want my love because his heart already belonged to a dead woman.

I hear the door opening, then muffled voices. My heart flutters as I wonder who it could be. Quickly, I wipe away the tears from my eyes, get up and check in the mirror over the mantelpiece that my mascara hasn't run and turn round just in time as Michael walks back into the room, two men in suits following behind.

He almost grins as he announces, 'Mother, these two detectives are here to speak to you. About the disappearance of someone called Jade Pascal.'

Chapter Twenty

Natalie

Saturday, 21 July 2018, 12:30 p.m.

Dr Jenkins' question, although not unexpected, causes my entire body to stiffen. I let it hang in the air, almost too afraid to respond, knowing the pain it will cause me to relive that time all over again. I take some deep breaths, squeeze my fists until the whites of my knuckles can be seen.

'It's OK, Natalie,' Dr Jenkins says, 'keep taking deep breaths, try to stay calm. I know this is hard, mainly because we'd hoped you'd put that aspect of your life behind you for good, but in light of recent events, together with the fact that you haven't been sleeping well and are clearly under a lot of stress, you must see why it's important I ask the question. You argued with your best friend, someone you think the world of, someone you've opened up to after years of shutting yourself off from people just because you felt it safer to do so. But from what you said she hurt you badly, so much so you can't seem to let it go.' She pauses, then says more softly, 'We know what can happen when you're under stress, even though I know that was a long time ago. A different life, in fact. So, I feel I have to ask the question – is there any chance you may have started that up again? Along with the dreams? It's important we address this now, before you might do something you regret.'

I don't respond immediately. Think back to the early hours of Friday morning, waking up in my day clothes having fallen asleep on the sofa. I was upset all day with Jade for not calling me back, still feeling hurt by her curt manner on the phone on Tuesday, for taking off without so much as a goodbye on Wednesday night. I can't bear thinking about it, but is it possible I sleepwalked my way to her house on Thursday night? That I might have started all that up again like Dr Jenkins suggested? Could I have…?

No, stop it, I can't allow myself to go there.

'Natalie, what are you thinking?'

Dr Jenkins knows almost everything that happened in my past, but there's one secret from my childhood I've not told her, nor any of my therapists for that matter. Just because I know if I do tell her, there's every chance she'll feel obliged to break her duty of confidentiality to me. But suddenly it's as if the weight of carrying such a burden all these years is catching up with me, almost proving too much to bear, so much so I am desperate to tell her. But in the end I don't. I can't put my freedom in jeopardy after all this time.

'I really don't know,' I say. 'Without anyone catching me in the act, how would I? When I did it before, I was a child, in foster care, around people, with my brother. He was always the one to find me. Guide me back to my bed. Now that I live alone, there are no obvious witnesses. So again, how would I know?'

'OK, I get that. But have there been any signs? For example, have you woken up in your day clothes? In your shoes? We know that's happened before.'

'No,' I lie. And yet I can't brush off the thought of yesterday morning. I'd like to think I'd been asleep on the sofa all that time, that I didn't move from the spot. But what if I did? What if I rehashed what I did as a child? What if I sleepwalked out of the house and did something bad?

I suddenly feel like I'm going crazy. It's killing me having this blank in time. The not knowing. The speculation. The feeling that I'm losing control.

Dr Jenkins holds my gaze, and it's hard to tell if she believes me or not. 'Sometimes you can smell the outside on yourself. Perhaps there was some dirt on your clothing, your shoes, even your hands, that wasn't there when you went to bed?'

'Nope.' I shake my head, again failing to mention that I never actually went to bed that night. At least, not until around 3:30 a.m., after I'd had some water, a savoury biscuit, checked the doors were locked. Loaded the dishwasher. Noticed I'd failed to tick off my day planner like I usually do before bed. 'Nothing like that.'

'And your rota is intact? Nothing missing?'

'No, nothing amiss there.' Another lie, and the deceit is starting to get to me, an uncomfortable twisty sensation mauling my guts, making my insides burn. What am I here for if I can't be truthful with my own therapist? What good is this time with her going to do me if I don't tell her everything? All my worries, fears, doubts.

Secrets.

But still I go on, spouting more lies, just because I'm too afraid of the police digging into my childhood. I can't have all that dredged up again: the night Jack caught me attacking our father after he'd passed out on his bed blind drunk, having come to my bed earlier and abused me; the night I trashed Cath and Brian's bedroom while they'd been down the pub, leaving us kids to fend for ourselves. And all the other times when I walked out of the house, roaming the streets. Totally oblivious to what I was doing. Jack was always the one to find me, bring me back, calm me down, take care of me. He always made things better. Dr Jenkins knows about these incidents; she just doesn't know the one thing that could turn my life upside down if the truth were to come out.

In any case, no one's come forward accusing me of sleepwalking, of doing anything bad in my sleep. I say this to Dr Jenkins, and as I do I almost convince myself that there's no chance I'm falling back into old habits.

Almost.

Dr Jenkins gives me one of her warm smiles, makes a note of something on her pad.

'Natalie, have you ever told anyone about your life in foster care? Or the four years you spent with your father after your mother died? Before they put you and your brother into care when you were ten? Other than Jade, I mean. Anyone at the gym, any of the regulars, or at work? I'm just wondering whether that might have triggered your anxiety, on top of your fight with Jade. Whether someone said anything to upset you, possibly made light, or made fun, of your troubled background.'

'No,' I shake my head fiercely. 'I haven't told anyone else about my past for precisely those reasons. I don't want their pity. I don't want them looking at me as if I'm damaged goods, even though we both know I am.'

I think about my drug addict mother who died of an overdose when I was six, leaving my brother Jack and I in the 'care' of our deadbeat, abusive dad. Never knowing when he was going to come home drunk, taking out his rages on me and Jack. Doing unspeakable things to us. Me especially. And then later, when Dad died of alcohol poisoning and we got placed into foster care with Cath Porter, a horrible woman, together with her equally repellent biology teacher husband Brian, never knowing when my next beating would come, when Jack or I would get our next hot meal. Jack would secretly get food for me. He was my knight in shining armour. It was only chocolate and crisps, and it's where my junk food addiction started, why I never lost weight. But it was food, nonetheless. And I was grateful, never went hungry, unlike the other kids. To the world, our foster parents professed to be upstanding citizens, taking in traumatised and abandoned kids out of the goodness of their hearts. But behind closed doors they were the foster parents from hell. There were five of us in total: Jake, Daisy and Paul, as well as me and Jack. They seemed to take a particular dislike to me and Jack, though, from day one. I can still remember Brian sitting us down on our first night there, telling us how lucky we were to have a roof over our heads, that we were damaged goods, going nowhere fast in life and that their rules were to be obeyed with no exceptions if we knew what was good for us. How Brian became a teacher I'll never know. I guess anyone is capable of fooling the outside world if they have enough guile in them. But I remember as clear as day Brian preaching the rules of 'natural selection' to all of us, saying that Hitler had been right about white people being the superior race (he'd shot poor little Daisy, whose parents had been from Ghana, a look of disgust when saying this), but also that humankind was inevitably split into the weaker and stronger of the species. He told Jack and I that we were the former, born to degenerate addict parents, that our lives would amount to nothing, and that we were to do his and Cath's bidding if we wanted to have any hope of survival. They would lock us in the basement for no good reason, other than us asking for clean clothes or some decent food. That's why I hate basements so much, why I shudder at the thought of getting stuck inside one. It had felt like the worst possible punishment, being locked underground with the mice and rats and the spiders. Where it was cold and damp and dark. I remember feeling so scared. Of course, to the social workers, when they came round to check on us, Cath and Brian were as nice as pie. Dressing all five of us up in the smart clothes they kept for such occasions, while the rest of the time we'd often wear the same knickers for weeks on end because Cath couldn't be bothered to wash them, making us sit beside them on the sofa while we offered the social worker tea and cakes and politely answered all of their questions, nodding and smiling in all the right places and telling them how happy we were and couldn't ask for better foster parents. Although we kids were desperate to say something, to tell them about the beatings, the starvation tactics, the general neglect, when it came down to it we were too scared. Just in case it did no good, and we ended up staying put and making things worse for ourselves. We wanted to tell our teachers. I remember the other schoolkids teasing me, saying I smelt. It was urine, of course. On account of me wearing the same knickers day after day. But when Cath got called in to school, she claimed I had a bladder control problem, that I still wet the bed, traumatised by what my father had done to me. And they believed her. I remember Cath's fake tears as the teacher empathised with her, saying what a great job she and Brian were doing, and that they were saints for taking in such a damaged child.

Is it any wonder I've suffered from anger issues since our mother died? That the stress caused me to experience vivid dreams, to sleepwalk and do things I'd never do when awake and in my right mind? That I found it difficult to trust people and form new relationships? That new places, new people and especially confined spaces stressed me out? I'm not excusing myself – it's a medical fact. That's what the child therapist I was assigned to had said when we eventually escaped Cath and Brian's clutches after two years of hell. Even though the circumstances under which we'd escaped were equally if not more hellish, not to mention the reason the trembling, the palpitations, the panic attacks got worse. They'd assured me it wasn't my fault, that I was a victim of childhood trauma, carrying the kind of stress a child shouldn't have to bear, but that with therapy and the right coping mechanisms I could overcome my anger, my anxiety, my sleepwalking and learn to live peacefully as an adult. They worked with me throughout my teens and beyond until I found my dream job as a library assistant in Kingston, and advised me to find a therapist nearby to keep me on the straight and narrow.

'I only told Jade because she had a shitty childhood, like me. She understands me in a way no one else can,' I tell Dr Jenkins. 'We're both damaged goods, even though on the outside she looks so perfect.'

'Did you tell her that Jack killed Cath after she beat you?'

I don't answer immediately.

'Yes.'

'What did she say?'

'She was sad for me. And for Jack. She knew it was self-defence. That he did it to save me, save us all. Scared

152

that the next time she might kill me. I told her what a good brother he was, the best. He didn't deserve to be put away. Cath was an evil bitch who deserved to die and rot in hell. He did us all a favour by stabbing her through her fat neck. If it wasn't for him, the authorities would never have known what they did to the children in their care.'

I catch the hint of alarm in Dr Jenkins' expression as I say this. Then she glances at the calendar on her wall. 'It's coming up to the anniversary of Jack's death, isn't it?'

How could I forget? In three days' time it will be fifteen years since Jack was killed in prison. Or rather the 'children's institution', as they liked to call it. Where they were supposed to educate and rehabilitate young offenders. How they could have put him in the same place as genuinely disturbed child killers, I'll never know. Children with a different mindset to him, who showed no remorse for their crimes. Children like Albert Cross, who picked on Jack in the canteen and ended up beating him to death. I remember the moment I learned of his death as clear as day. I was with Estelle and John by then, of course. Two policemen had come to the door, and I had screamed so loudly the whole street must have heard me. Before collapsing to my knees, my head bent over, and sobbing into the floor with Estelle and John looking on helplessly. Jack had never once complained all the time he was inside. He always put on a brave face on the few occasions I was allowed to visit; wrote me chirpy letters telling me he'd always be there for me, warning me to be on my guard, that the only people we could trust and count on in this sick world were each other. Hearing how he died, I realised then how bad things must have been for him. And I had wished more than anything that he had told me, talked to me. Thinking that perhaps if he had, I might have been able to help him. But I knew why he hadn't. And that only proved to me how he remained as selfless as ever until the day he died.

'Yes,' I say. 'I'll go and lay some flowers at his grave on Tuesday, like I always do. It gives me some peace, going to see him, telling him I'm sorry.'

'Sorry? Why should you be sorry?'

I hesitate.

'Natalie?'

'Oh, it's nothing, just a figure of speech. I just meant I'm sorry in general, for all he went through, for his having had such a sad childhood, for the fact that his life was filled with so much suffering and I could do nothing to save him in the end.'

'I see,' Dr Jenkins nods kindly.

Just then, my phone rings. I quickly reach inside my jacket pocket. 'Sorry,' I mutter, 'thought it was on silent.'

Being the understanding person she is, Dr Jenkins doesn't look put out. 'It's OK, do you want to see who it is?'

'OK, just this once, just in case it's Jade. Thank you.' I quickly pull out my phone, study the caller ID, but don't recognise the number. It could well be a scam caller, but instinct tells me to answer it, just in case it's Jade calling from someone else's phone, or from a police station.

'Hello.'

A voice answers. It's not Jade's. It belongs to DI Bailey's assistant. I listen to what he has to say, answer a couple of questions, then hang up.

'Who was that, Natalie? Everything OK?'

I meet Dr Jenkins' gaze. 'That was an officer on DI Bailey's team. The blood on the mat was definitely Jade's. They identified it from a recent blood test she had.'

'Oh, heavens.'

'But he said until a body or a weapon's been found there could still be a harmless explanation. Like she cut herself, something like that.'

'Yes, of course.' Dr Jenkins tries her best to sound reassuring, even though we both know that Jade appearing to have vanished off the face of the planet without taking her phone or car keys makes an innocent explanation less likely.

'Her neighbours knew nothing,' I go on. 'Mrs Denby claims to have been asleep, while the others were away for the weekend. Still no sign of her house keys, either. Hard to know what to make of that. There was a call to her landline around eleven p.m. on Wednesday night, apparently. From a mobile number that wasn't programmed into Jade's phone. The officer read me the number – DI Bailey was keen to know if I recognised it – but I didn't. He said it could have been a cold caller. They tried tracing it but had no luck, so it may well have been unregistered. They found nothing untoward on Jade's mobile either. Not so far, anyway. No threatening messages or emails, apart from my gazillion missed calls and texts.' I worry again that it makes me look more like some kind of stalker than a genuinely concerned friend. And looking at Dr Jenkins' expression, I wonder if she's thinking the same.

'Even so,' she says, 'I wouldn't worry. It just shows you were concerned about her.'

Yes, but where was I between seven p.m. Thursday night and three a.m. Friday morning? I can't stop the question from going round and round in my head.

'They did find something, though,' I say. 'When they were searching her place.'

'Oh, what's that?'

'A diary. A diary I had no idea Jade kept.'

Chapter Twenty-One

Susan

Saturday, 21 July 2018, 12:30 p.m.

'Yes, I knew Natalie planned on going over to Jade's place after she didn't show up for her class. She told us all. Me, Grace and Vivien, while we were having a drink in the bar. And you're right, they do seem rather close, although they make a rather odd pairing in my humble opinion.'

I'm trying my best to appear as helpful and polite as possible, but the police turning up on my doorstep unannounced has knocked me for six. I mean, I'm not even a friend or relative of Jade's, I'm just someone who attends her classes, so why single me out? I hadn't planned for that, and it's totally thrown me. I bet it's Natalie who's led them here. I'll kill her if she makes me miss lunch with Siobhan, along with my mani-pedi. They're what's kept me going through what has to have been one of the most stressful weeks of my life.

'How so?' the more senior detective asks.

'Well, forgive me for sounding superficial, which, believe me, I'm not, but Jade's a very attractive girl. She's fit and confident and popular, while Natalie, you might say, is the total opposite.'

'Well, opposites attract, as the saying goes,' DI Bailey remarks. 'Perhaps Jade enjoys having a down-to-earth friend she can rely on. Someone solid.'

'I'm not sure "solid" is how I'd describe Natalie.'

I seize my chance to help Natalie dig her own grave.

'Oh?'

'She's a nice enough person, don't get me wrong. I mean, I *think* she is.'

'You think?'

'Well, you can never know what people are really like, can you? I can't deny how worried she was about Jade last night – we all were – but…'

'But what?'

'But she's a little odd. Dare I say it, disturbed.'

'Disturbed? In what way?'

'Well, she just has these weird rituals, like she suffers from OCD or something. For example, she always stands in the far left-hand corner nearest the exit doors in the class, she'll wear the same outfit for specific days, she doesn't touch alcohol…'

'I'd hardly hold that against her.'

'Yes, yes, you're right. Nothing wrong in that at all. It's just, well, there's just something about her that's not right. Something unnatural. And what's most worrying…'

'Yes?'

I go for the kill. 'Well, I hate to say this, but I think she might have some sort of fixation with Jade. I've seen the way she looks at her, stares at her more like, almost like she wants to *be* her. It's rather… creepy. Makes me think of that film. What's it called, now? Oh yes, I remember, *Single White Female*.'

It's not like I'm lying, it's the truth. But I also know that placing doubts about dear Natalie in DI Bailey's head will divert any suspicion Natalie might have laid away from me.

'I see. Natalie said you didn't seem too bothered by Jade failing to turn up, even though it was very out of character. She thought *that* was rather odd.'

Scheming little bitch. I keep my cool.

'Did she now? Well, why would I be that fussed? So the instructor didn't turn up, big deal. There could have been any number of reasons. She's my class instructor, we don't socialise outside of the club, she's not a close friend. OK, so I went to her thirtieth, but so did half the members! I barely know Jade other than as being a decent fitness trainer. I've got enough to worry about aside from my yoga teacher failing to turn up for one class. Natalie's close to her, like I said. Maybe she knew something we didn't, which explains why she got so agitated. But I certainly wasn't aware of anything. She's not a friend of mine, like I said. She just happens to teach the gym classes I attend.'

Hope I haven't overegged that one. I tell myself to shut up.

'So, you deny latching onto her at her birthday do last month? Several people I've spoken to remember you and her deep in conversation that night.'

Again, I manage to keep my composure, even though I can feel the steam rising from my head. *What will it take to silence that troublemaker?*

'As I told Natalie, I was as drunk as a skunk, I can't even recall what I said. Probably nothing of consequence! I probably didn't even register it was Jade at the time.'

'OK. And can you tell me your whereabouts on Thursday? What you did that day?'

I'll tell you some of them, but not all.

'I went shopping in the morning, had a massage mid-afternoon, stopped at Waitrose on the way home for a quick shop around five, and then spent the rest of the evening at home.'

'Can anyone verify that?'

No, but that's not my fault. I'm ready with my response.

'No, Lance was out with clients. My children were also out. I think they all rolled through the door around eleven-thirty or possibly midnight.'

I don't tell him about the unexpected text message I received that same night. He doesn't need to know about that.

'OK, just one more question, Mrs Hampson. Did Jade seem out of sorts to you at Wednesday's class or, more generally, over the last few weeks? Like something might have been worrying her? Natalie mentioned her not seeming herself on Wednesday evening. That she dashed off straight after without a word to anyone, which was unusual for her.'

'She seemed fine to me. I'm afraid that's just another example of Natalie's – dare I use the word – *obsession* with Jade. I'm not sure you can take much of what she says seriously. I think she's prone to letting her imagination run wild, and it's hard to tell with her what's real or not. So, no, I didn't notice anything out of the ordinary regarding Jade's behaviour, but you might want to question the others in the class, just to make sure I didn't miss something glaringly obvious.'

'Grace Maloney, who I questioned earlier, did in fact say the same.'

Good old Grace, I smile inside. 'Well, there you go then. We can't both be wrong.'

'Yes, that seems unlikely,' DI Bailey responds. 'OK, thank you for your time, Mrs Hampson.'

'Oh, it's no problem at all. And please call me Susan. Anything to get dear Jade back safe and sound. I would hate to think she's been hurt or is in any kind of danger.'

A few minutes later I close the door on my visitors, then look up to the ceiling and breathe a sigh of relief.

But when I turn round I see my son standing there, his gaze piercing mine like he doesn't trust me as far as he could throw me.

And I can't say I blame him.

Chapter Twenty-Two

Jade

Before

We catch each other's eye the moment I walk into the room. He's talking to someone I don't recognise, but it doesn't stop him looking up and holding my gaze, causing a volt of electricity to charge through me. It's as if he'd sensed my presence before I'd even appeared, knowing, or rather hoping, I was going to show, the anticipation of that possibility keeping his senses sharp, the way it did mine. Our eyes linger on one another. An intense longing in them. Symptomatic of an unstoppable force between us that propels us towards one another and blocks out the rest of the world as if everything and everyone in it is immaterial. I'm wearing the silver heart pendant he gave me. He smiles with his eyes as I casually brush my fingertips over the chain. I know how happy it makes him to see me wear it.

I know our affair is wrong. Because he's married, spoken for. Has a family, responsibilities. The rational side of my brain reminds me of this constantly. But the heart is stronger than the head, and I just can't seem to stop myself. Can't resist smiling coyly and letting my eyes drink him in.

I know I am asking for trouble, that this cannot end well if we continue our affair rather than put a stop to it before anyone gets hurt. But that's partly the problem. In some warped way, it's the naughtiness, the immorality of it all that makes it so addictive, so goddamn electrifying.

But there's another reason I can't bring myself to stop. That I tell myself it's OK to carry on. That I'm even justified in doing so. It's the simple fact that I know I make him happy. He was miserable when I met him. I could see it in his eyes. That neglected, hollow look. Almost like a lost little boy trying to put on a brave face, rather than a grown man highly respected in his field. He was hungry for affection before he met me, and I have since satisfied that hunger. She doesn't understand him the way I do. She'd sucked all the life out of him, obliterated any hope of him being happy, with her self-absorbed, controlling ways. Her needs always take priority, no thought given to what he might want.

And that's why we won't stop seeing each other. I fill a void in him, as he does in me. A void I've felt for a long time now, since my early teens, when I lost someone special to me. He needs me, as I need him. I just have to hope that somehow, we get our happy ever after.

Even though stories like these rarely end well.

Chapter Twenty-Three

Grace

Saturday, 21 July 2018, three p.m.

'Hey, Natalie, how are you?'

I've just turned up on Natalie's doorstep. I called her earlier, after DI Bailey and his partner had left and I'd gone through the shower, to see how she was doing. I promised DI Bailey I would, and I like to keep my promises. Not like some people I know. She seemed surprised to hear from me, I guess because I've never phoned her before, despite our swapping numbers a while back. It also sounded like she was out, perhaps in a rush on her way somewhere. I suggested that I come over for a cup of tea and a chat. She was a bit reluctant, as if she didn't want me invading her personal space, but when I said I just wanted to make sure she was OK, and that I wouldn't stay long, she agreed.

I'm keen to dig a bit deeper as to what the detectives said to her. Also, to hear things from Natalie's perspective. DI Bailey could have been hiding something from me for all I know. So, if he is, I'm hoping I can prise it out of Natalie. I need to have all the facts to hand so that I can be prepared. Even though I've covered my tracks and am certain nothing can be traced back to me. I'm not acting purely out of self-interest, though. I am genuinely concerned for Natalie. She's a nice person, despite being a little strange. Not to mention naive. Easily taken in by the likes of Jade, who she idolises. Like I was taken in by her, to be fair. Before Jade showed her true colours, the person I'd always suspected she was.

'Hi, Grace, I'm OK.' Natalie lets me inside and I follow her into her compact living room. I'm struck by how tidy her place is; everything is just so, as if she runs her home with military precision.

'Can I get you a drink?' Natalie asks. 'Afraid I only have water, or decaf and herbal teas.' She looks at me almost apologetically and I feel an urge to mother her. There's such a frailty about her, and I can't help thinking something profound must have happened to her to make her this way. She told me once that Jade's the only friend she's had since childhood, so I imagine her disappearance is killing her inside. She already seems more timid, less confident than she was two days ago. As if Jade brought out the plucky side in her. But now, with her best friend missing, that side has retreated back into its shell. She also looks dog-tired. The way I used to look before diazepam became my friend and saviour. A pasty, drawn-out look. The look of an incessant worrier and a chronic insomniac.

'Whatever you're having suits me,' I smile.

She smiles nervously back. 'Come through to the kitchen, it's a bit cosier in there and we can sit at the table.'

I follow her lead and five minutes later we're seated around her table, sipping camomile tea. It was a good choice of hers in the end. I needed something calming to settle my nerves; something other than pills or wine. Something natural that doesn't screw with my mind or thought process.

'So, how are you doing?' I ask. 'You must be worried sick about Jade.'

She nods, her eyes fretful. 'I am. It was awful, Grace. Finding her clothes and phone lying there, seeing the blood on the bath mat. Her car keys still there, drawers flung open. But no sign of her house keys. I didn't know what to think. I mean, I knew before I went inside that something was wrong, what with her car being parked outside but her failing to pick up any of my calls or texts. I'm still hoping there's some innocent explanation, but with every hour that passes it seems less likely. It's frustrating there's no CCTV outside, or in her building.'

'Yes,' I nod, 'it is. It's not a main street though, is it, plus it's a converted Edwardian house, not one of those modern gated developments.'

'True. I'm guessing if she was attacked, her attacker knew that.'

'That would be my thinking, yes.'

'What did DI Bailey say to you?' Natalie asks.

I relay the gist of our conversation. Then say, 'And you? What exactly did you tell him?'

'Just that Jade had seemed preoccupied on Wednesday, like something was troubling her, and...'

'And what?'

'Look, don't think I'm a bad person or anything...'

Christ, what's she going to say? 'I could never think that.' I swallow my fear and smile sweetly, affectionately placing my hand over hers.

'I told them I didn't think Martin seemed that bothered.'

I'm shocked, and a little cross with Natalie, despite feeling sorry for her. Martin's a lovely guy, and I know for a fact he's got nothing to do with Jade's disappearance.

How could she cast him in a bad light, lay the finger of suspicion on him?

'Why would you mention that?'

I watch Natalie chew her bottom lip, nervously turn her mug anticlockwise.

'Because he's in love with her, I'm sure of it. But she's never reciprocated his advances and I think his ego's taken a bruising.'

A burning sensation fills my guts. A feeling like I've been here before. What is it with Jade and men? Why do they seem to be drawn to her? Like bees around a honeypot.

I chuckle lightly. 'You sure you're not letting your imagination run away with you, Natalie?'

She looks at me crossly, like I've offended her, her gaze steely. 'No. I've seen the way he looks at her. And it's obvious how uncomfortable it makes her feel.'

'And did you tell the police this?'

'No.' She shakes her head. 'I didn't want to go too far. Wanted to wait until a bit more time's passed before I say any more. Even though, in doing so, I may be endangering Jade.'

'Look, I'm sure you're not. Martin's a decent guy. He wouldn't do anything stupid or reckless. He's got too much at stake, too much to lose.'

Natalie appears to think on this. 'I guess,' she mumbles.

'And let's face it, there're probably a number of guys miffed at Jade.'

'How do you mean?'

'How do I mean?' I repeat. 'I mean, she's gorgeous. I bet she's broken a thousand hearts.'

'Guess that's true,' Natalie nods, sipping her tea.

'I'm almost sure it is.' I pause, wonder if I might be pushing things a bit with my next question, but in the end can't resist asking. 'She must have mentioned someone special to you, though, surely? With you being good friends and all. Must have talked about current boyfriends, and previous flings too? Perhaps from her time in Southampton. That's where she lived before, right?'

Natalie patently clams up at this question. Like I've hit a sore spot. It's telling. Indicates to me that she knows more than she's letting on. Especially as she can't seem to look me in the eye. But more importantly, has she told the police anything significant?

'Natalie?' I press.

'No, no, she hasn't.' She again fails to make direct eye contact. 'Jade's very private in that respect, and I've never liked to pry too much. Either into her current love life or her past. She told me once that she looks upon her time in Southampton as almost another lifetime. One she's completely moved on from.'

Relief washes over me. And a little anger. But I try not to let it show, mask my feelings by sipping my tea.

I move on. Making sure I continue to appear interested in Jade's welfare. 'But who would want to hurt her, do you think? The police don't seem to think it could have been a random attacker because nothing was taken. Which means it has to have been someone who knows her. Has some gripe with her. Wouldn't you say?'

Natalie nods. 'Yes, I agree, it has to be.'

'Which is why I'm thinking a boyfriend, past or present. Or someone she's been seeing on and off. A crime of passion, perhaps?'

'Yes, perhaps.'

Having steered Natalie's mind to this possibility, I ask the one question that's been playing on my mind since I got here.

'Did they find anything else at the flat?'

Natalie frowns. 'Like what?'

I shrug my shoulders. 'I don't know. Anything, I guess. They'll want to check her laptop, phone, all that kind of stuff, won't they?'

Natalie doesn't say anything for a while, and this unnerves me. Then, finally, she looks me in the eye and says, 'Yes, I'm sure they're probably still checking all that as we speak. They did say they've not found anything telling on her mobile.' I inwardly sigh with relief. 'Apparently there was a call made to her landline on Wednesday night from what appears to have been an unregistered mobile that wasn't stored in her contacts. When the police tried it, it was out of service.'

'Odd. Perhaps it was a scam caller?'

'Yes,' Natalie nods, 'I guess that's possible. Anyway, it's not even been twenty-four hours since they started searching her place. They may yet find something relevant.'

'True.'

She pauses, then says: 'There was one thing.'

'Oh, what's that?'

'DI Bailey's assistant mentioned they found a diary.'

My heart skips a beat. 'A diary?'

'Yes. He said they have someone going through it now. Said DI Bailey would let me know if they find anything potentially useful.'

'Great.'

I tell myself not to panic. OK, so it's true that diaries are like a window to the soul, an account of a person's innermost thoughts, feelings, hopes, fears. An account of the truth. But other than a minor altercation at the start, Jade and I have got on since we first crossed paths at the club. I've never given her reason to think I bear her any ill will. And I've always kept up my end of the deal. So really, I don't know why I'm worrying so much.

Perhaps it's just indicative of a guilty conscience.

Chapter Twenty-Four

Natalie

Sunday, 22 July 2018

She opens the door and steps into the pitch-black darkness, fumbling for the switch on the wall to the right, sighing with relief when the light comes on. She heads straight for the bathroom, ignoring her growling belly as she does so, taking her mobile phone with her, laying it on the bathroom stand.

She turns on the shower and strips off her clothes, taking a second to admire her naked body in the mirror as it starts to steam up before untying her long blonde tresses and stepping inside the cubicle.

She closes her eyes and tilts her head up to the ceiling, enjoying the sensation of the water running over her, trying to blank out the last few days. The feeling that she is being hunted.

She hears nothing but the sound of the powerful jets rebounding off the cubicle's tiled floor.

Not the bathroom door opening. Nor the footsteps approaching. Nor a voice saying 'filthy bitch' under its breath.

But she does hear the cubicle door crashing open.

Her attacker repeating the same vile words.

And with that, her fear is so great she cannot find her voice to try and save herself.

No one will hear her.

And very soon, she hears nothing at all.

I wake up with a start. Covered in sweat. Gasping for breath. It was a dream, I tell myself, just a bad dream. My worst fear playing out inside my head. I haven't dreamt this vividly since I was thirteen; when the doctors prescribed a low dose of lorazepam because my sleepwalking had got out of control. After what happened at Cath and Brian's, then being parted from my brother, I started roaming Estelle and John's house two, sometimes three times a night. Although I never hurt anyone, they worried I might do some harm at one point, either to myself or to others. The pills helped initially; helped me sleep, got me into more of a settled, regular pattern, until counselling and other more natural treatments and techniques helped me to completely overcome the disorder. I remember dreaming of my mother while I was on the pills, watching her die in front of me, holding her frail hand which would gradually slip away into a dark abyss. I remember the recurrent nightmare of my father beating me, coming to my bed, touching me. Of Cath locking me in the basement, cajoling me, calling me Fatty, telling me I was a crybaby and that I had better shut up if I didn't want another beating. All of my dreams had felt so real because they had represented my worst nightmares. Just like now, I'd wake up in a cold sweat, crying for my brother who was no longer there to comfort me. Just as I have no one here to comfort me now.

I glance at my bedside clock which, to my dismay, reads five a.m. I had so wanted to sleep through till seven. But I guess it's the stress stopping me from doing so. Even pills appear to be no match for my anxiety. I prop myself up on my left side and reach for my glass of water on the bedside table. I take a greedy gulp, my heartbeat gradually becoming less erratic as the liquid swims down my gullet and cools my overheated body.

Despite luxuriating in a warm bath an hour before taking to my bed last night, I had still felt on edge; felt sure sleep would not come easily to me. That, along with the fact that I still have no idea if I've started sleepwalking again, meant I thought it best not to risk things, especially with an investigation into Jade's disappearance under way. I'd wanted to ensure I got a proper night's sleep so I could face the next day with a clearer head, try to regain the control I've taken years to attain over my turbulent life.

I'm certain my anxiety is why I dreamt of Jade driving home in horrendous weather on Thursday night, of her being attacked in the bathroom where I found her clothes and mobile. Her disappearance is consuming me now, my imagination running wild thinking about the possible course of events based on what I found in her bathroom not forty-eight hours ago. And is it any wonder that my worst fears should haunt my dreams? That I should hallucinate so vividly, especially having taken a medicine which is known to cause such side effects? That's what I tell myself anyway, although there's a part of me that wonders if there's another reason my dream felt so real. Another reason I saw her movements on Thursday night in my dreams so clearly, and that I heard the venomous words spoken by her attacker: *filthy bitch*, as if I'd been in the room myself. Words spoken by someone who considered Jade to be easy, a flirt; someone who resented her messing around with a married man. Someone envious of her beauty. Someone angry with her for treating others with seemingly little regard for their feelings.

They are words that could so easily have been uttered by any number of people.

But do I dare to consider myself one of them?

I shake my head, attempt to brush the thought aside, tell myself to lie back down and shut my eyes, try to drift off again. But it's no use. I'm too frightened to, lest the dream returns to haunt me. I'd sat watching TV last night, not really taking the images in, all my thoughts focused on Jade, wondering who could have taken her, wondering what the police will find in her diary. Whether she mentions our argument, along with intimate secrets about me. Secrets I told her in confidence about my child-hood, my foster parents. About Jack. And which pertain to my history of violence. The police will automatic-ally see me as someone who can't be trusted, someone unstable who could easily have lashed out at her best friend after arguing with her, feeling let down by her. As I'd sat there and considered these possibilities, my mind had gone into overdrive. Imagining them questioning me about my argument with Jade, about my past, leading them to perhaps speculate that I attacked Jade without even knowing I had done so.

My heart tells me I didn't. That I loved her too much to have done such a thing, despite her cutting comments. And so, if my instinct is right and that is the case, I can't just lie here and do nothing. I need to take the bull by the horns and do some digging for myself before suspicion falls squarely on me.

Chapter Twenty-Five

Susan

Sunday, 22 July 2018

'Grace, to what do I owe this pleasant surprise?'

It's 1:30 p.m. on Sunday afternoon, and fortunately for Grace I've just got home from an early brunch at The Bingham in Richmond with some of the women I invited to be part of a little book club I started up a few months ago. I quite like reading, but sadly lack the patience for it, so in truth I do it more for the socialising than the culture value. We're much more into commercial fiction than Booker Prize winners. More the *Fifty Shades* than *Midnight's Children* kind of readers. We want something page-turning and gripping – preferably with a bit of steamy sex thrown in for good measure. Six menopausal women aren't particularly interested in highbrow literary fiction; we want something to distract us from our dull lives, our erratic hormones, something juicy, shocking even, something we can sink our teeth into and devour late into the night when sleep proves elusive. So really my club is a chance to gather a band of well-to-do peri and menopausal women, all experiencing similar issues in their lives, all at that no-man's-land stage as the kids go off and you find yourself in a big, empty house with no idea what you should be doing with your time now that you're past the hireability stakes. Of course, a woman's inability to make any kind of rational choice about her life going forward is not helped by the fact that night sweats, insomnia and a gradual increase in forgetfulness render such a decision nigh on impossible. I'm a bit older than the others in the group, so not as bad as I used to be, but I still take HRT on the sly because I'd feel too low, too knackered without it. When you think about it, from the moment that little red patch appears in our knickers we women have it tough – periods, pregnancy, childbirth then menopause. What a fucking party. Men, as usual, have no idea what we go through, no idea what suffering really means; they've no frigging right whatsoever to complain about a bit of nose or cheek hair. Wimps, the lot of them. OK, so Lance is fit, but I'm stronger in mind, always have been. And that's what's most important. Willpower can move mountains. Having that drive to achieve a means to an end. Whatever the cost.

'Come through,' I say. 'Michael's gone to the cinema, while Stella's locked herself in her room. She's meant to be writing an A-level history essay, but my guess is she's on the phone to her boyfriend, avoiding me like the plague.' I don't mention that I haven't a clue where Lance is.

I grin, just to make light of it, even though inside I'm not smiling.

Grace gives me one of her classic half-smiles. It's a bit weird her turning up unannounced, especially on a Sunday, what with her kids at home, and so I'm thinking whatever she has to say must be rather important.

And something tells me it's linked to Jade's disappearance.

'Jim was OK with you dumping the kids on him?' I ask.

She gives a nervous chuckle. 'Yeah, they're growing up now. Less trouble than they used to be. Both have homework to be getting on with.'

'And they don't need you for that?'

Grace appears to hesitate. Gives a little shrug. 'Maths and science. Not my strong suit, more Jim's bag. I was always hopeless at all that.'

'Me too,' I say truthfully.

Grace surveys her surroundings as I lead her through the house to the smaller of our two reception rooms, joined to the kitchen, which overlooks the garden. 'Wow!' She looks at me wide-eyed. 'Every time I come here I never tire of saying that. Your house is stunning.'

'Thanks,' I say. For a fleeting moment I remember when the children were small and they'd play out there – water guns, pool parties, cricket, et cetera. Fun, carefree days. Always supervised by the nanny, of course. Sometimes I look back and wish I'd appreciated the chatter of their voices more, that I'd actually gone outside and joined in the fun the way Lance used to. Rather than downing Pimm's with my mum friends. But it's too late for second chances. I made my bed long ago, and now I've got no choice but to lie in it. We'd all turn back time, do things differently if we could, I guess.

The smaller living room is carpeted, which I find cosier, while the sofas are blue crushed velvet and incredibly comfortable. The kind of sofas you can sink into and never want to move from. 'I'm sure yours is too, only I wouldn't know because you've never invited me. You know how much I love Cobham. There are some fabulous houses around there. And you must have some nice mum friends to hook up with for coffee and lunch. No doubt it's yummy-mummy central.'

Too much? I can't help it, it had to be said after a year of biting my tongue. I settle my gaze on Grace. Although I've wanted to raise the issue with her several times before, this had felt like the perfect moment. To her credit, she doesn't frown or get cross, but I do see a faint flicker of apprehension in her eyes, along with a jolt of her shoulders. Clearly my comment has rattled her. And I haven't a clue why.

'Oh, I would have you over,' she says, 'but it's a bit of a trek for you, and I'm not sure the mums would be your cup of tea. They're a bit ditzy to be honest, more like WAGS than the intellectual women you socialise with, which I guess isn't a surprise given the number of foot-ballers who live in the area.' A chuckle. 'Plus, Jim's so funny about noise in the house when he's trying to work.'

I secretly love the fact that she refers to my friends as intellectuals. Even though in saying this it's clear she doesn't know me or the women I socialise with at all. Either that or she's using obsequious flattery as a means to fob me off. That's the thing with Grace. She's not easy to read.

'Even as a one-off?' I say almost incredulously. I know Lance wouldn't give two hoots. But then again, he's out most of the day. This Jim sounds like a right royal tyrant. For fuck's sake, I wasn't proposing a rave through to three a.m., just coffee!

I invite Grace to sit down next to me on the sofa, but then, having realised I haven't offered her any refresh-ments, quickly spring up again to go and make us a pot of tea. I'm back within five minutes, along with a tray of shortbread, and waste no time in getting down to business.

'So, I get the feeling this isn't just a social call. Is it to do with Jade's disappearance, by any chance?'

Grace picks up her cup and saucer and languidly stirs her tea with a spoon as if to give herself extra time to think about how best to phrase her response.

'Yes,' she finally replies, 'the police came over to the house yesterday morning, spent quite a bit of time asking me questions about Jade and my relationship with her. Whether I had any idea who might have wished her ill, or noticed anything up with her of late.'

Her eyes fix on me like she's trying to read my mind, making my heart tremor. 'And you said?' I say.

'I said I had no idea at all. That, from what I can tell, she's popular with both the staff and the clientele, and as we don't know much about her background, there's not much else I can be of help with. I did say Natalie's probably the best person to ask, what with them being good friends and all, and the fact that they socialise outside of the club.'

Phew. 'Yes, indeed, that's exactly what I said. The police mentioned you didn't think Jade looked particularly out of sorts during Wednesday's class. I'm glad I'm not the only one, I thought the same. I don't know what Natalie's banging on about but, as you say, she's a good friend of Jade's and perhaps she knows things we don't. I'd love to know what they are, though.'

One thing in particular.

'Me too. I did ask Natalie yesterday what she and DI Bailey talked about. Whether she had any idea what the police have found so far. Tried to prod her a bit on Jade and her past.'

My ears prick to attention. 'You went to see Natalie at her place? What was it like?'

'Very neat and organised.'

Why am I not surprised?

'She has this planner on her kitchen wall I couldn't help but notice. I think she ticks various items off as she goes through the day, keeping track of her movements, for some reason.'

I frown. 'Hmm, that is odd. Why would she feel the need to keep a checklist of what she's done? Either she has a bad memory, or it's tied up with this OCD thing she has going on. You must have picked up on it?'

Grace nods. 'Yes, it's hard to miss.'

'Anyway, you asked her what the police have found so far. Anything on Jade's phone?'

'No, nothing on there, apparently. There was a call made to her landline on Wednesday night from a mobile that didn't appear to be programmed into hers. But when the police tried it, it was out of service.'

Ah, the beauty of the burner phone.

'Must have been some scam caller,' I say.

'Yes, maybe. They did find something, though.'

'Oh?'

Grace puts down her cup, looks at me with her deep-set eyes. 'A diary.'

I almost choke on my tea. I don't know why it hadn't occurred to me, but I guess I never imagined someone like Jade to be the type to keep a diary. Me prejudging people, as usual. I try not to let my worry show.

'Gosh, I wonder what she writes in there. Some people just keep a note of what they need to do in diaries, don't they? You know, like pay a bill on a certain day, or visit the dentist.'

Grace nods, laughs. It feels a bit forced. 'Yes, that's true, hadn't thought of that.'

I study her face. 'You're not worried, are you?' I can't think what Grace would have to feel worried about, but then again, she is the secretive type.

Another nervous laugh. 'No, course not.' She picks up a shortbread but doesn't bite into it just yet. Using it as a distraction rather than for pleasure. 'If she mentions us, the classes, it's probably in a tongue-in-cheek way. I don't know, something like, Grace still looks like a gormless giraffe doing tree poses, or no matter how many star jumps Jill does she still hasn't lost a pound.'

'Ha ha. Good one.'

We both laugh heartily, while inside I pray to God that Grace is right.

Chapter Twenty-Six

Natalie

Sunday, 22 July 2018

It's two p.m. and I'm sitting on a train to Southampton. Facing forward in a two-seater row, my bag my only companion, my gaze scarcely leaves the window as the changing scenery flies by, ranging from lofty high-rises and dense clusters of houses to sparser, greener landscape, while more passengers get on and off at various stops: families out on day trips, noisy teenagers moving in packs, solitary travellers like me – some chatting with strangers, some with their noses buried in books, some listening to music, some just staring into space. The latter is also me, as I contemplate my purpose in trekking seventy-odd miles to visit Jade's former flatmate, Megan Stanley. I know they lived together for nine years, first as students, then having landed their first teaching jobs following a gap year spent travelling. Jade soon after realising that teaching wasn't for her and retraining as a fitness instructor. But that's all I know, and so I'm hoping Megan can tell me more, fill in some gaps.

I think back to, maybe, six weeks ago, when Jade came round to mine after a Friday-night class and we'd ordered a Chinese. She'd told me then about Megan, with whom she'd shared a flat in a development near the waterfront overlooking the River Itchen. She'd even given me her address. I'd thought it a bit strange at the time, seeing as that part of her life was behind her, but she'd said that Megan was a friend she could trust and that if I was ever in trouble and something happened to her, I should call Megan. It makes me wonder whether, even back then, there was something bothering Jade. I wonder, did I fail to spot the signs? Did I mistake Jade's curtness with me for something else that was weighing her down but which she couldn't risk telling me about? Did I fail her as a friend?

'But why would anything bad happen to you?' I'd asked, feeling a bit scared.

Jade had given me a reassuring smile. 'Course it won't, there's no reason why it should. I just wanted to tell you about Meg, in case. Say I have to go away, or something. Don't take this the wrong way, but I sense I'm the only one you can rely on. Your brother is dead, you have no other living blood ties as far as I know, so it occurred to me, if ever you were in need of a helping hand, you should know about Meg. I lived with her for nine years and she's a good person. A very private, discreet person you can trust.' She'd grinned. 'I've told her about you, you know.'

'You have?' I'd said, at the same time feeling ashamed about the pang of jealousy that had struck me on hearing Jade speak so fondly of Megan. Someone who'd known her far longer than I had; someone with whom she'd no doubt shared many secrets and wonderful moments.

'Of course,' Jade had smiled. 'How could you think I wouldn't? You're my bestie now.'

A tear rolls down my face as I think back to that moment. I'd never felt more loved and special hearing

Jade's words, and it brings home to me how I can't imagine life without her.

So that's why I'm sitting on this train. Thinking maybe Jade spoke to Megan recently, voiced any fears or worries she may have had to her; stuff she hadn't felt able to tell me just because things had been a bit frosty between us lately. Jade said she's the one person, aside from me, she's felt able to trust with her secrets. This brings me comfort, some level of assurance that I'll feel able to speak with Megan candidly and in confidence.

And if she did tell Megan something, I'm hoping it might shed some light on her disappearance, offer some clue as to who might have taken her or wished her ill. Alternatively, some trouble she may have got herself into. Perhaps an argument she'd had with *him*. The police still haven't made Jade's disappearance official. But they will soon, and I can't help wondering what *he's* thinking. Whether he's worried about her, assuming he's tried to get in touch and realised she's missing. Or whether he's deliberately keeping his head down, more worried for himself and what the police might find. For all his faults, I still can't believe he's behind all this. He'd be risking too much.

After a time, the train pulls into Southampton Central Station. As it's the tail end of summer and a brighter day than of late, there's quite a crowd pouring onto the platform, no doubt seeking some last-minute coastal sunshine, and it takes me a while to navigate my way out of the station and find a taxi.

Having hailed one, I give the friendly cabbie the address and before long we pull up outside the gated development where Jade once lived with Megan.

I'm cursing myself for not ringing ahead. There's a porter's lodge adjacent to the gate, and there's no way the guy manning it is going to let me in without first speaking to Megan. What if Megan's away, and I've made all this effort for nothing?

I pay the driver, then get out of the cab. It's the middle of the day so she may well be out. But it's also a Sunday, and Jade mentioned Megan works long hours at the university so enjoys relaxing at home on the weekends.

I saunter up to the porter's lodge, put on my best smile. 'I'm here to see Megan Stanley.' I'm expecting a surly look followed by a grilling, but to my surprise the porter is both friendly and apologetic.

'Ah, I'm sorry, love, but Meg popped out an hour ago. Not sure where she was off to, as it's unusual for her, being a Sunday and all, but you may have a wait on your hands. Was she expecting you?'

My heart sinks. I *have* come all this way for nothing. I'm just contemplating how to respond when the porter's face lights up. 'Well, what do you know, there she is coming through now, laden down with shopping. Meg, love, did you not think to take the car? There's someone here to see you.'

I swivel round to see a petite brunette standing there. She's carrying two bags of groceries, one in each hand, and looks a bit flustered with the load, but still manages a smile.

'Thanks, Gerry, but I fancied the exercise.' She looks at me directly. 'Can I help you?'

'I'm Natalie Marsden. A friend of Jade's. Jade Pascal. Jade said she'd mentioned me to you.'

The smile becomes broader. She sets down the shopping and offers me her hand. 'Yes, yes she has. Oh, it's so lovely to meet you. Jade's told me so much about you.' A warm feeling floods my insides as she says this, but at the same time it makes me tearful.

Megan looks aghast. She comes closer. Puts her hand on my shoulder. 'What's wrong? Has something happened to Jade?' Her brow creases with concern as she says this and I feel bad for ruining her Sunday, but I need answers and I'm hoping Megan might have some.

I can barely look her in the eye as I say, 'She's missing. Didn't turn up to her class on Friday and hasn't been seen or heard from since Thursday night.'

'Oh, God.' Megan covers her mouth in shock.

'You've not heard from her then?'

She shakes her head slowly. 'No, no, I've not spoken to her since last weekend.' A pause, then, 'You'd better come up.'

I offer to help Megan with her shopping, then follow her through the gates and across a grassy courtyard to the block in which her two-bedroom flat is situated.

We take the lift to the third floor, and once inside, she guides me through to the kitchen. 'I'd better put this away first, got some frozen items, hope you don't mind.'

'No, of course not, go ahead,' I say.

I look around, and her flat in many ways reminds me of Jade's. It's small but neat, tastefully decorated, and yet has a homely feel to it. I can just picture Jade living here.

I watch Megan put the last of the food items away. 'I've not seen anything on the telly,' she says while bending down over the fridge before standing again and turning to face me.

'Well, it's not been forty-eight hours since I reported her missing. I think if we've not heard anything by this evening, or by morning at the very latest, she'll be officially declared missing and the police will launch a public appeal.'

That's what DS Khan told me when he drove me home on Friday night.

'Oh, I see. Did you mention me to the police?'

'No. Jade said you're a very private person and I didn't want to disrespect that.'

'Thank you,' Megan smiles. 'Still, I expect they'll track me down soon enough. And that's fine. I want to do anything to help find Jade. Look, let's go through to the living room, we'll be more comfortable in there. Have you eaten? Can I make you some lunch? Nothing fancy, just a sandwich or something.'

I haven't eaten, and I'm starving, but I'll feel really ungrateful if I tell her it has to be wholemeal bread. Thankfully, she saves me from my embarrassment. 'Brown bread OK? With some plain cheddar and pickle?'

I tell her that's perfect, and before long we're seated at a small table in the living room set against a window overlooking the water. I can hear the call of gulls as we sit there eating our sandwiches, making me wonder why Jade would have wanted to swap this peaceful existence for the more fast-paced, smoggy hub of London.

'So, tell me everything that's happened since Friday,' Megan says.

Megan has a soft, ultra-feminine look and manner about her. She has long chestnut-brown hair and is wearing a baby pink V-neck jumper matched with blue skinny jeans. Her voice is clear and articulate, which I guess shouldn't come as a surprise given her profession.

I proceed to relate all the facts so far, omitting the bit about me not sleeping well and my history of sleepwalking. I don't know if Jade's told her about the latter – I'd be upset if she has as I told her in confidence – and see no point in bringing it up. I also don't want word getting back to the police, although I'm still none the wiser as to whether Jade mentioned it in her diary. I mean, there's no reason she should have done, but I can't be certain.

I do tell Megan about our argument on Monday, though, and that Jade's lover has been causing tension between us for a while now, because I don't approve of him and warned her it would all end in tears. I also mention it's crossed my mind that he might have something to do with her disappearance, even though it would be a big gamble for him.

'Unless something happened in the heat of the moment,' Megan says. 'When emotions are running high, when it's a matter of love and sex and passion, the most rational of people can become animals. Lose control. Especially if they're deeply unhappy for other reasons. Crimes of passion happen all the time, I hate to say.' She bows her head and I see that her eyes have welled up. Jade clearly means a lot to her.

I reach out and squeeze her hand. She gives me a grateful smile in return. 'Does she talk about him much to you?' I ask after a time. 'I mean, has she seemed happy of late, when you've spoken to her?'

Megan sits back, looks wistfully out of the window. 'She does seem happy. And he's all she thinks about.' My spirits plummet as she turns her gaze back in my direction. 'I know that's not what you wanted to hear, but she genuinely cares for him, and something tells me the same is true in reverse.'

'Yes, but how can it ever end well? With him being married. I worry about the wife finding out, causing trouble for them both. Who's to say she hasn't already, that she's not the one behind Jade's disappearance?'

'People get divorced all the time. And from what Jade's told me, his wife isn't a saint. She's done some bad things in her past, apparently. Things he's finding increasingly hard to live with.'

'Really? Do you know what they are?'

'No, no I don't,' Megan says quickly, looking away again. 'But it can't be easy, living with someone you despise.'

'Yes, I guess that's true.'

'But you have a point about the wife perhaps causing trouble,' Megan goes on. 'She sounds unstable to me, and I often wonder what she might do if she were to find out.'

'Do you think I should tell the police who he is?' I ask. 'Jade made me swear to keep it a secret but now that she's been missing for some time, I don't think I can. It may harm our chances of getting her back.'

Megan's eyes become hard. 'Let's put it this way: if the police come knocking on my door, I won't hesitate to tell them.'

I'm struck by the conviction in her voice. But I'm also glad of it. She's made me realise I can't hold back any longer. Even if it comes to nothing, it's best out in the open. I don't think about the fact that I'm a hypocrite for saying this. A hypocrite for not mentioning to DI Bailey that I've not been sleeping well, that Jade and I had an argument, that I have a history of being violent in my sleep.

'OK, I won't hold back any longer. For Jade's sake,' I assure Megan. 'Hopefully the police will be discreet until they know for sure whether or not he's got anything to do with her disappearance. I wouldn't want there to be any unnecessary collateral damage. That's always been my worry about revealing his identity. Aside from my promise to Jade to keep it a secret.'

Megan smiles, seems relieved. Then adds, 'That aside, Jade has generally seemed fine to me. Still enjoying her classes, putting the bad memories behind her.'

I immediately tense. Caught off guard by the rather blasé way Megan referred to Jade's bad memories, as if I should know what she's alluding to. 'Bad memories? How do you mean? Here, in Southampton? She's not told me much about her student days. Just that she enjoyed uni but realised teaching wasn't for her and wanted to get back to London, where the action is.'

I hold Megan's gaze and can see from the look in her eyes that I've only been told part of the story. Even so, she seems reluctant to elaborate further.

'Megan?' I press.

She hesitates. 'I-I shouldn't have said anything. There's a reason Jade buried that part of her life, and I'd hate to think I'd betrayed her wish to keep it buried.'

'I understand that,' I say, 'but Jade is missing and anything you can tell me might help. Could even be the key to her disappearance.'

Megan gnaws on her bottom lip as I look at her with pleading eyes, willing her to go on. Finally, she relents with a heavy sigh. 'OK.' I inwardly exhale with relief, then listen anxiously.

'Jade loved uni, we all did. We had a blast in halls. But after that Jade's life became a bit more complicated.'

'How do you mean?'

Another laboured sigh. 'I'm guessing Jade told you the reason she became a fitness instructor was because she realised teaching wasn't for her after she got a placement at a local school?'

I nod. 'Yes, she did. Why? Isn't that the case?'

'No, I'm afraid not. Jade loved teaching. She loved helping kids, making a difference. She wanted a job in a state school, wanted to help less fortunate kids, but you can't be too picky these days, can you? Not a lot of jobs came up by the time she'd qualified, and her tutor at uni encouraged her to apply for a post at Dashwood Boys, a private school on the outskirts of Southampton. Jade took his advice, got the job and loved it.'

I'm puzzled. Why on earth would Jade tell me that she realised teaching wasn't for her? 'She did?' I say.

'Yes. I think it meant a lot to her to be the teacher she never had at school. Maybe she told you she was picked on at school by her head of PE, bullied for want of a better word.' I nod. 'She was a nasty piece of work by all accounts, but ironically it was she who spurred Jade into teaching.'

'So what went wrong?' I ask. 'Why did she give up teaching and retrain as a fitness instructor? Did something bad happen? Is that the real reason she left Southampton?'

Not for the first time, Megan hesitates. I don't blame her. I'd be the same. Afraid of breaking my best friend's trust. But I impress upon her that this could be a matter of life or death, and it does the trick. 'Yes, something bad happened. Jade had an affair with a teacher at the school. He was married.'

Not another one. It's all I can think as Megan drops this bombshell. *What is it with Jade and married men?*

'This guy was, how can I put it, he wasn't only after sex, in the throes of a midlife crisis, like a lot of men are. His marriage had been on the rocks for some time, and he was lonely and desperate for affection. After a lot of mutual flirtation, countless looks across the corridor, in staff meetings, you know how it is, he texted her, asked if she wanted to have a drink sometime. She knew it was a strict no-no. But what can I say, it's hard to reason with attraction, and she couldn't say no.'

I can hardly believe what I'm hearing. And it makes me wonder what other secrets Jade might have kept from me. I'm cross she didn't feel able to tell me, and yet at the same time, maybe she was ashamed of her past, perhaps fearful of how I'd react. 'So, what happened? How long ago was this?'

'It started when she was in her second year at the school. She was twenty-five as I recall, and it went on for two years. Not sure how they hid it for so long. They would meet in secret, at low-key bars, hotels, and she fell in love with him. And he with her. She was happy, the happiest I'd seen her in a long time. I think he genuinely loved Jade, she's that kind of person, isn't she? Easy to like, to fall in love with. He said he wanted to leave his wife for her.'

'And did he?'

'It wasn't that simple. His wife had a history of depression. She was on antidepressants – hardcore ones, as I recall – and he was finding it increasingly hard to cope with her behaviour. She'd drink quite a bit too. But they had children, so he felt stuck. Plus, he worried what she might do to herself if he left her. Both her parents were ill, which didn't help matters.'

'What happened?'

'Although they were always careful, one night a friend of the wife's spotted them in a bar in the New Forest. He'd told her he was going on some kind of work bonding getaway, when really, he and Jade had gone away for the weekend together. The friend took photos and showed the wife. She went mental at him when he got home – they were college sweethearts, apparently, and I think he was everything to her even though he no longer felt the same way. He made the mistake of telling her this, that he didn't want to be with her any more, and that night, when he was asleep in the spare room, she took the kids from their beds, dosed up on booze and benzodiazepines, strapped them into the car intent on going God only knows where and crashed into the side of the road. The weather had been horrendous, plus she'd been going way too fast.'

'Oh Jesus,' I say. 'Were they OK?' I can hardly bear to hear Megan's response.

'Yes, thankfully. All three of them lived. The wife and one of the kids got away with cuts and bruises, suffered some concussion and fractured ribs, but it was touch-and-go with the other child for a while. He was put into an induced coma and was in the ICU for some time. But that's not the whole story.'

'Tell me.'

'The hospital called the husband in the middle of the night, told him what had happened. He jumped in the car, clearly distraught, wasn't focusing and by then the weather had turned even worse, causing him to veer off his side of the road and have a head-on collision with a fuel tanker coming the other way.'

'Fuck. What happened? Did he make it?'

Megan's eyes are suddenly steeped in sorrow. 'No. The car exploded. He died instantly. The wife was already on antidepressants, like I said, but this was kind of the last straw, and she had a full-on breakdown, spent some time in rehab. Anyway, as you can imagine, the press was all over it in a shot, and Jade's name came out. The other woman who broke up a happy marriage and caused the poor wife to go completely loopy. Jade was beside herself; the guilt almost ate her alive, and she nearly went mad herself. It all got too much for her and she decided to leave town, make a fresh start. She spent a couple of years back in London retraining as an instructor before moving to Surbiton.'

'Did Jade ever meet the wife?'

'No,' Megan shakes her head. 'She never even knew what she looked like until the crash happened and it made the papers. The husband never wanted her knowing about that part of his life. Didn't want Jade feeling guilty. It's easier, isn't it, to feel less guilty, when you aren't able to put a face to a name. But of course, as I said, once the accident happened, it was all over the press.'

She pauses. Then says, 'There's one other thing. Jade's real name is Annabel Richards. After all this happened and Jade decided she needed a fresh start, she changed her name.'

I feel utterly blindsided. And not a little betrayed. I mean, how could Jade have kept something so huge from me when I've told her so much about my past? That said, it's such a ghastly business, perhaps she blames herself for what happened and couldn't bear to rehash it all. Perhaps she was worried I wouldn't want to know her any more. No wonder she didn't want to hear me berating her for being involved with a married man.

'So,' Megan says, 'now you know the real reason Jade left Southampton.'

'You don't think the wife could have something to do with her disappearance, do you?' I ask. 'I assume she's out and about now?'

Megan shakes her head. 'I doubt it. Jade's never mentioned coming across her again. But that doesn't mean she hasn't, I guess. I do know she left Southampton, just because the press intrusion was so bad, and everywhere she turned she was hounded. She lost her job, of course, and I imagine there were memories everywhere she turned. I can't see why she would bother doing anything to Jade now. Plus, Jade changed her name – she'd be harder to find.'

'Because she blames her for everything she lost?' I say. 'Her children, her husband. I mean, she wasn't right in the head before all this happened from what you've just told me. What if she still isn't, despite getting help? There's no telling what she might do.'

Megan is silent, and it's as if what I just said has hit home with some force. I see fear in her eyes.

'What were their names, by the way?' I say. 'The wife and husband. I know you're probably trying to protect Jade, the way I have been in not telling the police everything, but if this woman is a possible danger to her, you need to tell me.'

Megan doesn't answer straight away, her face pensive, as if debating whether to tell me. Then, finally, she looks me in the eye and says, 'The wife's name was Grace. Grace Maloney. And the husband's name was Jim.'

Chapter Twenty-Seven

Jade

Before

I'm still in denial. Still can't quite grasp the fact that he's gone. Despite his death being splashed across the local news, despite me being pursued by local reporters who'd prostitute themselves for a quote from 'the other woman'. I can't leave the house for fear of being set upon, branded a home-wrecking whore by those who only see what they want to see. Those who know nothing of his pain, the miserable life he'd led with her, the purity of our love.

Only last week he was telling me how much he loved me. Now, besides the pendant he gave me, all I have left of him is a voicemail I couldn't bear to delete.

I wonder, why does someone up there seem to have it in for me?

Why does it feel like I'm destined never to be happy? For some reason, whoever's calling the shots seems determined to take anyone I choose to care about away from me. Is it me? Am I cursed?

Megan told me that I need a good cry. Need to let it all out. But for some reason I can't. Perhaps because I feel I don't deserve to cry. He wasn't my husband, after all. He was hers. And perhaps, if he'd never met me, he'd still be alive.

I can't stay here, I'll go crazy. And besides, there's no way the school will have me back. They'll want to distance themselves from the scandal as much as possible. I couldn't show my face there again anyway. Not just because of the looks I'd get — I've no doubt both the students and staff would make my life impossible — but because it would be a constant reminder of him. Even though I'm doing myself no favours on that score by continuing to wear his pendant. I just can't bring myself to take it off.

I need to get away from here, make a fresh start. In a place where my past cannot haunt me.

A place where Annabel doesn't exist.

Chapter Twenty-Eight

Natalie

Sunday, 22 July 2018, 6:30 p.m.

I'm back home, but I might as well be locked in one of my nightmares. Shock doesn't feel like a big enough word to describe what I'm feeling. I can't believe Grace has been lying to everyone at the club all this time. Making out to be married with kids, pretending she has her hands full with a family and job on top of her ailing mother. I wonder if that part is even true, whether her mother having dementia is another fabrication rather than reality. Whether she works at all. I intend to find out what's real and what isn't. But right now, that's the least of my worries. What's more puzzling, and what I can't get my head around, is why Jade never said anything. How she and Grace have managed to be civil around each other all this time. How is it that Jade didn't freak out the minute she saw Grace turn up to her first class a year ago? Surely she must have been scared, wondered what the hell Grace was up to? It's clear from what Megan told me that Grace hasn't been right in her mind for some time, and the fact that she's been lying to us all, making up this fantasy world, tells me her time in rehabilitation hasn't helped. Hardly surprising, I guess, given the trauma she's been through. But why did Jade go along with her lies?

All this makes me fearful. Fearful of what Grace might be capable of, of what she might have had on Jade to guarantee her compliance. She'd certainly looked more harried than usual on Friday night when Jade failed to show. Was it guilt rather than worry I saw carved across her face? And now I realise why she was so keen to come round to mine on Saturday afternoon. She was scared of the police finding out about her past, and her previous connection to Jade.

As for Jade, what happened in Southampton isn't something she could have just forgotten about with a change of name and residence. Granted, it might have helped, but it couldn't possibly have eradicated the horrific scars of the past, including the loss of the man she loved. Especially when the person who played a large part in that turns up in the very place where she'd hoped to start afresh.

How could either of them stood not to say anything? More's the point, *why* did they choose not to say anything? Why keep up this pretence? How could Grace not have wanted to scream blue murder at the woman her husband cheated on her with? Likewise, how could Jade have held her tongue and not lashed out at the woman responsible for driving her lover to his death? Could it really be a coincidence that Grace happened to join the same club where Jade worked as a fitness instructor? It's hard to believe that's the case, and again it makes me wonder what her intentions were on joining. It's weird and it's twisted, and I need answers, but there're only two people who can give them to me.

And one of them is missing.

There's only one option left open to me. I have to pin Grace down tomorrow and confront her. Demand the truth. It's not a conversation I'm looking forward to, but I can't avoid it. I need to give Grace a chance to explain before I take this to DI Bailey.

Chapter Twenty-Nine

Grace

Sunday, 22nd July 2018, seven p.m.

I'm so uptight I can't keep still. I keep thinking about what Jade, or rather Annabel, might have written in that diary of hers. Up until last month, I wouldn't have worried. Would have told myself I had nothing to be concerned about, because we had resolved our differences a while back, and Jade had made a solemn vow to me that she'd never tell anyone my secret. I'd made my peace with her, was healthier in mind and body for it. But then something happened to make me realise she never had any intention of changing.

A leopard never changes its spots, after all. And neither does a Jezebel like her.

I remember the look on her face when she spotted me in the gym the day before her launch class a year ago. It had literally turned white, as if she'd seen a ghost. Or rather, her worst enemy. After all, I was the woman she abhorred with a passion. And no doubt she knew the feeling was mutual. I guess she'd thought I wouldn't find her after she'd changed her name, dyed her hair from brunette to blonde. That was her plan, of course. To start afresh, pretend to be someone else, leave her complicated past behind her. But I'm a reporter, after all. Despite losing my job, I have my ways. I'm cannier than her, and eventually, after six months of looking, I tracked her down.

It gave me such a fabulous sense of satisfaction seeing her face drop. Seeing the fear in her eyes. My insides had positively burned with delight. I'd never met Jade in the flesh before. But I knew what she looked like, of course, from the photos my friend had sent to me. Photos of her and Jim canoodling in a bar; photos that had fired a level of pain through my chest I hadn't thought possible.

I'd confronted Jim that same night; the night I took the kids, the night Jim died. A night that changed all our lives forever. I'd taken a heavy dose of diazepam along with a large glass of wine and I wasn't thinking straight. Was completely out of it, in fact, and should never have been behind the wheel of a car. After the accident, they charged me with two counts of dangerous driving, but rather than send me to jail they'd imposed a hefty fine, taken my licence away for two years and sentenced me to fifteen months rehabilitation because I'd demonstrated remorse and it was felt I hadn't been in my right mind. Which I hadn't, of course. And after Jim died, things only got worse. I had a full-scale nervous breakdown and was admitted to a psychiatric ward. There, I experienced all kinds of delusions, which was terrifying. My in-laws were granted custody of the kids because the courts felt I wasn't stable enough to be a proper mother and look after them. It was at this point that Mum went into a care home because the day carers were no longer enough and I wasn't around to fill the gaps; she needed full-time supervision. Somehow, over time, I convinced the doctors I was better. And in many ways, I was. I was certainly more in control. They kept me on a low dose of diazepam, just for night-time because I still had trouble sleeping, but it was strictly controlled in such a way that I couldn't take more than I needed. When I came out, I knew I couldn't be in Southampton any more. The kids had been taken from me, and everywhere I turned there were memories of them and Jim and the life we'd had. Plus, I'd lost friends, my job; there was nothing left for me there.

And in my mind I knew it was all because of *her*. It's why I knew I had to find her, seek her out, make her admit what she'd done, make her pay. If I didn't do that, I knew I'd never have peace, never stop seeing Jim. Something I've not told the doctors about. There's no way they'd have let me out if I had; I was smart enough to know that. I started seeing Jim during my first week at the hospital. He still stalks me like a ghost because he blames me, wants me to feel pain and remorse for what I did, every minute of every day. I know the doctors will tell me that my husband is a hallucination, and that's why I never mentioned it in the hospital. And maybe they're right. Maybe I am delusional. But it's what I deserve. I deserve to hear the bitterness in his voice, see the revulsion in his eyes. In death he has made it his mission to keep me in a state of purgatory, and I know this will be my lot in life until the day I die. I guess there's also a part of me that needs to see him, talk to him, even though I know he hated me at the end, cheated on me, died because of me, because I can't bear the thought of him being gone. I've never been very good on my own, like I told the police.

In joining The River Club, I knew that somehow I had to get Jade onside if I didn't want her telling everyone about what happened in Southampton. Once my gym induction was over, I'd left the club, fully expecting her to follow me out to the car park and confront me. And she had. Cornered me right up against my Toyota and asked me what the hell I was playing at. Why I wasn't locked up in some psychiatric ward. Naturally, I'd acted all contrite, burst into tears, told her over and over how sorry I was, that my parents' illnesses had overwhelmed me, that for a long time I hadn't been myself, that that's what depression did to a person, that I had a history of it – which was true, it's quite common in only children who have a habit of seeking perfection – and that I was overcome with remorse for what I had done; for taking the children, endangering their lives and causing Jim to lose his. All that was true, of course. But I'd also made it clear to her that she wasn't innocent in all of this. That Jim had been my husband, and despite this she had willingly entered into an illicit affair with him, knowing he had a wife and two young children who needed their father. I saw the shame on her face, and realised that her shame, her guilt for what she had done was largely why she'd left Southampton. She was deeply ashamed of what she'd done, of the heartache she had caused. And unlike me, her mind had been perfectly sane throughout the time she was doing it. She'd asked me if I'd come here to make her life miserable, to seek revenge, and I'd said no, of course not, she was the last person I'd ever wanted to set eyes on again. Plus, she'd changed her name, so how could I have known she was teaching here? It was chance, coincidence, I'd said, but now that we'd found ourselves in this situation, perhaps it was a sign. Perhaps someone had brought us together to confront our demons, finally make peace with the past, neither of us being innocent.

All that was bullshit, of course. I had tracked her down and moved this way to check her out. Fish out some dirt on her. Make her pay for destroying my marriage, my life.

And I had chosen Cobham because it was quiet, out of the way, where people were less likely to ask questions. But still near enough to Surbiton, where I knew she lived. But naturally I didn't tell her that; I'd said the club had been recommended to me by a friend, the same story I've told everyone since, and that I had moved to a peaceful area so I wouldn't be hounded, so I could make a fresh start. Just like her. I had promised to keep quiet if she did the same. She'd asked me why I was so desperate to keep up this pretence of being a wife and mother, of working as a freelance journalist, and I had told her the truth. That it was comforting to believe I was still a mum, still a wife, still employable, that people would be less likely to ask questions if I led the kind of life so many women in the area lived, that if I made out I was a busy part-time working mum to two young kids it would make sense that I didn't have time for anything else in my life. I wanted to be seen as normal; that was and remains so important to me. All I've ever wanted was a loving husband and kids; a secure family unit. And even now, after all this time, I can't bear to accept that I've lost that. For good.

Thankfully, Jade agreed to keep quiet – I guess she was scared of her employer discovering her past – and we managed to stomach the sight of each other. And then, after a time, and to my surprise, instead of growing to hate her more, I saw that she wasn't all bad, learned to live with what she had done just because, I guess, I knew in my heart of hearts that I had done something worse. I realised that letting go of my hatred was the only way I was going to heal. And one day Jade had come over to the house, and she'd explained about her childhood, about what a horrid woman her mother had been, about her bulimia and insecurity issues. How she'd missed out on a father figure. And I had even started to feel sorry for her. Forgot about my desire to make her suffer. I realised she was broken in so many ways, that she wasn't some scheming gold digger who made a habit of stealing husbands. I realised how unhappy Jim had been, and that she'd genuinely loved him. And as much as it had killed me to admit it, I realised my own behaviour had driven him away.

But then something happened. Something which made me see her for what she is. Made me realise she'd been fooling me, along with everyone else, all this time.

Something which made me mad, reignited my desire for revenge. Forced my hand to do something which I now realise may have grave consequences for us all.

Chapter Thirty

Natalie

Monday, 23 July 2018, three p.m.

The library is usually my haven of tranquillity. Where I feel most peaceful. As a child, after Jack and I were parted, books became my escape. I'd get lost in magical worlds and adventure stories, while the characters became my friends; friends I could trust and who would never betray or talk back to me. It's why becoming a librarian was so appealing. A job that required a love of reading and storytelling, and where I could be surrounded by books, soothed by their smell and comforting texture.

But today, thinking about Grace, about confronting her this evening after the class, I'm as jittery as a squirrel. I know Martin's got a temp in; I got a message from the club to say so. I'm not sure how I'll get through the class, not knowing what's happened to Jade, telling myself that it's she who should be putting us through our paces, and that this nightmare shouldn't be happening.

I need answers, and fast, just because I feel like I'm going slightly mad with it all. Plus I'm still worried about what Jade might have said about me in her diary. I try to put my fears to the back of my mind for now, focus on one thing at a time, Grace being my priority. I phoned her earlier, on the off-chance she was going to be at yoga this evening. I'd have preferred to have avoided the club, but I couldn't meet her in the day, with work – I didn't want to let Jane down again even though she's been kind and said she understood if I needed some time off. Grace had sounded so normal over the phone, said although it felt slightly weird going to a class knowing something awful might have happened to Jade, she needed the exercise to take her mind off things, especially as the kids had been particularly hard work of late. Fuck, what a head screw. How I managed to bite my tongue and stop myself from saying *you don't have any kids because you nearly killed them, drove your husband to his death, and yet you go around pretending you're this normal wife and mother*, I'll never know. But somehow, I did. I guess a part of me feels sorry for her, understands her reasons for keeping quiet, for wanting to blend in and appear normal, keep her past a secret. Just because it's exactly what I've been doing for the best part of eighteen years. Anyway, the phone wasn't the best medium for this type of conversation. I need to look her in the eye, perhaps suggest a drink after the class, and hope to God Susan won't poke her nose in and invite herself along. Not that I don't still have my suspicions about her, too.

'Everything all right, Nats? You're staring into space there.'

Great, it's Sam. Just what I need. She's right, I was lost in my thoughts, but it's also typical of her to comment on it. I wouldn't mind if she did so because she cares. But the tone of her voice is drenched in condescension, and I'm spot on in foreseeing her next remark.

'Aww, is it about your friend, Jade? Awful business, her disappearing like that.' The police went public with Jade's disappearance last night, and it made the front page of the *Kingston Guardian*. 'Although she did seem the impulsive type. A bit too big for her boots, if you ask me.'

I'm suddenly a fuse about to blow. I've never told Sam how close Jade and I have become. No doubt she's been eavesdropping on my conversations with Jane, who I feel comfortable opening up to.

'How do you mean? Because she stood up for me when you were being rude about my figure and lack of fitness?'

Sam looks astonished. It's the first time I've answered her back, and it felt so bloody good. Before, I was happy enough in my personal life to be able to tolerate her condescension. But now Jade's missing and my life is in disarray, I can no longer hold my tongue.

'What the hell's got into you?' she snaps.

'You, that's what! I'm not the mealy-mouthed loser you think I am. I'm sick to death of your snide comments, of you putting me down. You're just a librarian, like me. No one cares about you, you're nothing special, you're ordinary.'

Sam's face has gone red; she looks to be on the brink of tears.

'Jade's turned my life around for the better, she's the best person I know, and I'm worried sick about her. So don't you dare come out with opinions on stuff you know nothing about! You are nothing compared to her, NOTHING, so why don't you just piss off and die! And stop calling me Nats! Only my brother called me that. And he's fucking dead!'

I realise I'm shouting now, and that the whole library floor is staring at me. Including Jane, who doesn't look best pleased. For that, I can hardly blame her. But to my dismay, as I look beyond her shoulder, I realise someone else is watching.

It's DI Bailey, and he's also looking less than impressed.

Chapter Thirty-One

Natalie

Monday, 23 July 2018, 3:30 p.m.

I'm sitting across from DI Bailey in Jane's office, which she's kindly allowed him to use. He's in her seat, and I'm in the chair opposite, a chair I've sat in many times before, but right now it feels very different. In fact, I might as well be in an interrogation room at Kingston Police Station; the atmosphere is so stifling I can barely breathe, and while I've not yet been accused of anything, it's like a veil of suspicion is hanging over me.

'So, tell me, Natalie, what was all that about?' he asks. 'You seemed very different to the quiet girl I met the other evening. There seemed to be a lot of anger stored up inside you.'

I wonder where this is going, but I tell myself to stay calm, count to three in my head, say the mantra.

'I'm just upset about Jade. And Sam, who's always picking on me, said some mean stuff about her, and I'd had enough. I'm just a bit stressed. It feels like it's all getting on top of me, and I'm not feeling as calm as I normally do. Usually I just ignore Sam's spiteful comments, but I'm tired, and I guess my fuse was a little on the short side today.'

'Is that what happens when you're tired, Natalie? You get stressed, angry? Explode, even?'

His eyes bore into me, Mr Nice Guy no more, and I instinctively flinch. Who's he been speaking to, I wonder?

'What do you mean?'

'I take it you saw the press conference last night?'

'I did.'

He pauses, as if to rack up my discomfort, make me wonder what's coming next. 'Well, we had a call from a member of the public who claims they saw someone matching your description walking along Jade's road on Thursday night. Around ten thirty p.m. Presumably after she'd got home from teaching her class.'

'What?' I can barely get the word out. Then give an uneasy laugh. 'But that's impossible. Whoever this person is, they must have been mistaken. Don't you think I'd remember something like that?'

'We brought the person in, showed them your photo, and they confirmed it was you who they saw.'

'But I took a sick day on Thursday. I was at home all day.'

I don't mention the fact that I woke up on the sofa in the middle of the night wearing the same clothes. That I don't recall going to bed.

'And were you wearing blue joggers and a matching sweatshirt, along with black Adidas trainers?'

I can't lie. I was. And I can tell he knows it too. 'Yes.'

'Our witness described the person they saw wearing the exact same clothing, which seems like a bit too much of a coincidence, don't you think?'

I say nothing. What can I say? My mind is spinning as I desperately try to think of a way out of this, but at the same time it's too muddled to be capable of rational thought. All at once a sense of dread overwhelms me. Because I now have confirmation of what I'd been fearing most. That I've been sleepwalking again.

'Why were you off sick?' DI Bailey asks.

'What do you mean? What kind of a question is that?'

'It's not a hard question. Why were you sick? What was wrong with you? We spoke to your supervisor, Jane, and she said you're rarely off sick, but that you have seemed rather "off" of late, not yourself. Tired.'

Why does it suddenly feel like the world is conspiring against me? All I want is for Jade to be safely returned to us, but instead I'm being made to feel like a key player in her disappearance.

'I-I...' As much as I want to, I realise I can't take a chance and lie. There can be no more lies. Enough lies were told in my childhood. 'Because I haven't been sleeping well. I was tired, and I couldn't face work.'

Even if I have been sleepwalking, I still can't believe I'd have harmed Jade. It was different with Dad. With Cath and Brian. I hated them. Hated them with every fibre of my being. But not Jade. I loved her like a sister. OK, so it hurt badly when she accused me of being someone who didn't know what it felt like to be loved. And her thought-less words made me angry. As did her failure to call me back. But I can't believe I could have unconsciously hurt her. I mustn't let the doubt creep up on me just because of what happened in my childhood. I'm a different person to who I was then; I have to believe that, even though, since Jade went missing, it's felt like I'm trapped in some twisted mind game, being tested. The trouble is, I'm not sure I'm strong enough to come out on top.

'Natalie, my officers have been through Jade's diary for this year, retracing her steps, as it were, trying to ascertain whether it gives any indication as to what might have happened to her. Along with her mindset of late.'

'OK,' I say calmly. 'And have you found anything useful?'

It's like I do and yet don't want to hear the answer.

'Much of it is general day-to-day stuff. But there are three entries of particular interest. One of them refers to an argument you two had last Monday.' *Shit.* 'Three days before Jade went missing. Over a man she's been seeing. A man you don't approve of. Why didn't you mention you argued when we spoke on Friday night? That's a pretty big oversight, wouldn't you say?'

I swallow hard. There's no other way to respond to his question other than to admit I was scared. Scared of painting myself in a bad light, making it seem I was jealous, that I had a motive for harming Jade having only argued with her three days before her disappearance.

'I was scared, OK? My friend was missing and I didn't want you to think I had something to do with it, that I'd deliberately called you there to take the suspicion off me. Surely you can understand that?'

'And yet now you've only gone and made things worse for yourself because, as it turns out, Jade kept a diary divulging all kinds of secrets. A diary I'm assuming you knew nothing about?'

All kinds of secrets. I wonder what he means by that? Wonder if Jade mentions Grace and their history in her diary, the fact that Grace has been lying to us all since joining The River Club, and that she has a motive for hurting Jade? I hope so, and yet I am clearly not off the hook. How can I be when I've been spotted on Jade's road the same night she went missing?

214

'We know from Jade's diary that you'd been getting on her nerves for some time, and for various reasons. She refers to you as being needy, clingy and resentful of her having a boyfriend.'

'I wasn't needy or resentful! I just told her she was making a mistake with him, that I couldn't believe he was going to leave his wife for her like he claimed he would. That he was just using her for sex.'

'Why would you think that? Because of your child-hood?'

My shoulders tense. 'My childhood? What do you know about my childhood?'

'In her diary Jade alludes to you having had a hard time growing up, first with your father who abused you, and after he died, your foster parents. We've since looked into your background, and we know your brother killed your foster mum after a particularly bad beating you'd suffered one night.'

I'm mortified Jade broached the ugly details of my childhood in her diary. The sleepwalking is one thing, but the abuse I endured is another. Mortified the police have seen fit to delve into my past, like they've already branded me a suspect. Then again, how can I begrudge Jade for writing her thoughts down? Perhaps she found it cathartic to put her thoughts on paper, the way I keep a rota of my day to stay on top of things, maintain some semblance of control. All the same, I can't help feeling a sense of betrayal.

'It's true I had a tough upbringing, and it affected me. It would affect any child, the stuff I went through.'

'Affected you how? Your temper? Mood swings? Is that what caused the sleepwalking? Caused you to attack your father and trash your foster parents' bedroom while they were out? Caused you to undergo countless hours of therapy to overcome years of trauma and the fact that your sleepwalking had got out of control?'

'How do you know all that? From Jade's diary? I can't believe she'd have gone into such detail. What's all this got to do with her going missing? Shouldn't you be focusing on Jade's lover? Or more's the point, his wife? Jade wasn't all squeaky clean, you know, there's stuff in her past she was ashamed of. Stuff that got her into trouble, caused her to run away.'

In my mind I know exactly what my childhood has got to do with Jade's disappearance. And that's why I need to shift the focus to Jade's past, steer DI Bailey in the direction of others.

But even before DI Bailey answers my question, I realise how he knows so much about my past. He's spoken to Dr Jenkins. Although I now see her privately, when I first moved to the Kingston area my GP referred me to her when she was working as a consultant for the NHS. That must be how he found out about her. By delving into my medical records. But how could she have betrayed my confidence? There's only one explanation I can think of, and it frightens me. She must see me as a potential danger to myself and to others, thereby overriding her duty of confidentiality to me as her patient.

Am I dangerous? The very idea scares me, even more so now that I know I sleepwalked out of the house on Thursday night. I can only assume I was heading for Jade's. But why? To harm her? Or to warn her? I just wish I could remember.

'You can tell me about Jade's past in due course,' DI Bailey says. 'There are definitely hints of something bad having happened, of some trauma she'd tried to put behind her in relocating to Surbiton. But for now, let's focus on you.'

Fuck.

'I spoke with Dr Jenkins over the phone earlier. I can assure you she was not in the least bit happy divulging confidential information about a patient, but when I made it clear to her that a girl's life was quite possibly at stake, and that you'd been spotted on Jade's road the same night she went missing, together with the fact that you'd argued earlier that same week, she accepted it was a matter of public interest for her to assist us with our investigation.'

I shrug my shoulders. 'OK, we argued. So what? Friends argue all the time. It doesn't mean they kill each other.'

'I said nothing about killing.'

Jesus, he's twisting my words. I feel like he's placed a noose around my neck and is gradually pulling it tighter. 'I didn't mean it literally, it was just a figure of speech. I just mean there are other people you should be looking at rather than pursuing me, her only real friend around here, who genuinely wants her back.'

'Other people? Like Susan Hampson?'

I recoil in my seat. Realise Jade must have mentioned Susan in her diary. That DI Bailey knows something. But what and how much does he know? I need to tread carefully. 'Well, yes, but also Grace Maloney.'

'Why her?'

'If you stop attacking me, I can explain.'

'Take it easy, calm down, I'm not attacking you. We'll get to that in a minute. I appreciate you had a traumatic childhood, and I am truly sorry for that. I also know you've worked hard at overcoming your anger issues and haven't, to anyone's knowledge, experienced as an adult the kind of episodes you had as a child.'

'Yes, that's true. I have worked hard. And living an ordered, peaceful life has allowed me to do that.'

'Until you met Jade and your ordered, peaceful life was thrown off course?'

'Is that what Dr Jenkins said?'

'She mentioned you've changed since meeting Jade. That in many ways it's been a good thing, but that she thinks you became a little obsessed with her.'

I feel my face go red. 'I'm not in love with her, if that's what you mean. Neither am I a stalker.'

'You lost a brother. That must have hit you hard.'

I nod. 'What's that got to do with anything?'

'I'm just wondering whether Jade perhaps filled the gap he left behind. Only, in her case as a sister. Whether she started controlling your every move, not intentionally, but just because you relied on her so much? The way you relied on your brother.'

I can't believe what I'm hearing. He's making our friendship sound twisted. 'Jack always protected me. When he killed our foster mother, he did so in self-defence, because she'd beaten me that same night. He couldn't stand to see her hurt me any more. Feared she might kill me. But they made him out to be a murderer, a monster, when all he was doing was protecting his little sister. They locked him away in a children's prison with kids who actually were seriously messed up, who were a danger to society, and one day he paid the price. I miss him terribly, and yes, maybe to a certain extent you're right. Jade was the first person since Jack who was truly kind to me, who accepted me for me and tried to help me, defend me against bullies who see me as some kind of freak. Just because I'm not beautiful and smart and from a good background.'

'I'm sorry about your brother, Natalie,' DI Bailey says kindly. His tone more like the first time we met. It's hard to believe that was only three days ago; somehow it feels like three weeks. 'But isn't it possible, Natalie, that unknowingly, you might have harmed Jade, lashed out at her while sleepwalking, not realising what you were doing? The way you did as a child? This type of thing has been known to happen. People having blackouts, harming the people they love without having any recollection of doing so. Killing them, even.'

I feel tears, and before long I can't stop them coming fast and furiously. 'No! No, it's not! I only ever lashed out at people who harmed me. At my father who raped me, at my foster parents who were cruel to me. Despite our argument, I know I would never hurt Jade. She was my best friend.'

'Was she?'

'Yes, why would you think otherwise?'

'It's clear from what Jade wrote in her diary that you saw her as that, but I'm not certain she felt the same way. And I'm thinking you perhaps picked up on that when you argued last week.'

I'm desperate to read Jade's diary. Desperate to see what exactly she said. Not just about me, but about Grace, about Susan. I need to see it with my own eyes. 'Will you show me the diary?' I ask boldly.

'Perhaps. But for now, please answer the question.'

'Yes, I suppose I did. I guess the way she spoke to me made me feel like I was more of a pity case to her, rather than her equal. But it's only lately that she's made me feel like that. We've had so many laughs together, so many fun nights. I'm not stupid. She genuinely liked having me as a friend because I liked her for her. She knew that. It's him, he's twisted her mind, he's been a bad influence. I'm sure of it.'

'Who is he, Natalie? Jade only refers to him and to others by their initials. Not unusual in diaries. Still, I'm almost certain I've figured it out, based on the information I have from you and others to date. But I want to hear it from your lips, Natalie. As the person she confided in. Tell me, for Jade's sake.'

Before, I'd felt such loyalty to Jade. She'd trusted me with her secrets, as I had trusted her with mine. But now everything is out in the open, it's like that trust has been broken, and is meaningless. By her own hand, she has forced me to divulge what she had begged me to keep a secret.

And so, because of this, I don't hesitate to reply: 'Lance Hampson. Susan Hampson's husband.'

Chapter Thirty-Two

Jade's diary

July 2018

Monday, 16th July So today was both the best and the worst. The best because L said he's finally going to leave her for me. I was so happy! It was like music to my ears. He said he can't stand the sight of her any more. That he does everything possible to avoid spending time with her, that all they do is argue when they're in the same room, and that he can't forget the bad things she's done and which she appears not to give a shit about. He said it's made him realise life's too short and that he needs to get on with his life, make the most of it. I can't begin to express the joy his words brought me. We'd met in the usual place, and I threw my arms around him, and we'd hugged long and hard and he had made me feel so loved and wanted. The way I'd always yearned to feel, growing up. The way only two other men in my life have made me feel. Both equally special to me. Good, kind men who genuinely loved me, and whose memory will never fade in my heart. I can't help hoping this is third time lucky for me. It has to be. This is my time for happiness, finally.

If only N hadn't gone and spoilt it. That's where the crap part of today comes in. Earlier tonight we argued after my yoga class. You'd think she'd be in a good mood after a class. I mean, it's meant to make people calm, but it seems to have the opposite effect on her. It freaks me out, to be honest, just because of what I know about her childhood. The usual crowd was there. It felt like L's wife was giving me the evil eye every so often, like she knows something. Hates my guts. G was looking at me a bit funny too. Of course, we both share a terrible secret, a secret I've promised to keep quiet about because I see how much she wants to put the past behind her, but the way she looks at me sometimes, I'm starting to think she's not over it. Her and S make a good pair when I think about it.

Anyway, after the class was over, N hung about, as she often does, only because she has nothing better to do, I guess, and sees me as her only friend. I don't mind it as such – after all, I'm the one who convinced her to join the club, and I want to be as helpful and supportive as possible. Especially as I know she's had it tough. But she's been a bit off recently, a bit short with me, and it's starting to get on my nerves. I was debating whether to tell her my good news, and in the end I did, only because I was so happy and I wanted someone to share in my happiness. It's not like Mum cares. So I told her he wants to be with me but she didn't believe it. Said he was just saying it, that he'll say anything to get sex. She's said the same thing before. Kept on and on about how I'm making a mistake and he's never going to leave her for me. That I was delusional. Ha! What does she know? She's never had a relationship. Never known love. She has no idea what it's like to love a man, so how can she comment? Everything she says is a product of her own hang-ups; the fact that her father abused her, and that she doesn't trust men because of that.

The fact that her foster mum used to beat her. For her to accuse me of being delusional is rich, too, based on the stuff she did growing up. I mean, I know it's not her fault she sleepwalked, she did go through a lot, but even so, she has no right to lecture me.

Sometimes I wish I'd never told her about him. I only told her because I was pissed off with him at the time, because he'd said something that got my back up that day. He'd gone on about S not being right in the head, that she hadn't been a good mother to his children, and that he was finding it hard to live under the same roof as her, and yet, when I'd told him to leave her, that he was wasting his life on her and that if he'd only just take a chance on us he could be happy again, he'd snapped at me, said it was OK for me, that I was from a different world, didn't have the kind of responsibilities he had. He'd hurt me when he said all this, made me feel like a child, and that's why I'd told N one night when she came over for takeaway and I'd had a bit too much wine. Just because she was there at the time and I needed someone to rant at. Of course, she'd been lovely and supportive, but when he and I made up I got the feeling she was disappointed. Said I was a sucker for punishment. That I was treading on thin ice carrying on with him and that his wife was bound to find out sooner or later, and then my reputation would be in the gutter. And I realised then the reason she had been so lovely and supportive was because she was glad we'd argued, perhaps hopeful we'd split up and then she could have me to herself. It's not like I think she wants anything sexual. I just think she's a bit odd and insecure and needy, and that I'm the only one who's bothered to be a friend to her so she's worried about losing me.

I wish we hadn't fought tonight, as it's really put me in a bad mood. In the end, I told her to butt out of my life, that it was none of her business and that she was jealous. Her face went red and she stomped off. It wasn't kind of me, I realise that now and I feel bad. I'm going to try and call her tomorrow, make it up with her. But I also intend to be firm. She needs to realise she can't control me or my life. And if she can't do that, then I'll tell her we can't be friends any more.

July 2018

Wednesday, 18th July I've decided to resign at the end of the week. I'll come in Friday, for my usual class, only a bit earlier, and hand in my resignation to Martin. I can't be around these women any more. They're stifling me. And L's wife is psycho. She knows about us. I'm not sure who she found out from, as we've been so careful, but she confronted me today before the class started. Came up to me on the stage, when there was no one else about, and said through clenched teeth that she knew I was screwing her husband, that someone had sent her photos anonymously in the post to prove it, and that if I didn't put a stop to it now, she would show the photos to Martin and Barry, destroying my credibility as an instructor and any chance of me getting a similar post elsewhere. She said she was going to confront L about it this evening after the class, threaten to tell his stuffy law firm that he'd been sleeping with a gym bunny twenty years his junior, making a laughing stock out of him amongst his colleagues and clients. She said she could pretty much guarantee he'd choose salvaging his reputation at the firm he's devoted his life to, over a slut like me. That his kids' well-being would always take precedence over mine. I was shocked, felt so sick, and could barely focus on the class. She said she'd also make it her mission to dig up dirt on me, which scared me senseless.

It made me wonder if she and G have been talking. I can't believe G would say anything, just because she wants to keep that part of her life a secret too. I kept an eye on her throughout the class, and there was nothing in her body language to suggest she was behind all this. Then again, I know what a good actress she is, so who can tell?

I could sense N knew something was up. She was staring at me as usual, could see the fear in my eyes. I'm sure she was pissed off when I took off so quickly after Monday's class, had probably expected a heart-to-heart chat after we made it up yesterday on the phone. But I was in no mood to play sister to her this evening. She doesn't know the burden I've been carrying since my party. And how the hell do I know she's not the one who sent the photos? How do I know she's not been stalking me and L?

I suppose it's possible that changing my name wasn't enough to stop nosy types digging up dirt. S said she only found out about L and me this week. But maybe she was lying. Maybe she's known for some time and has been looking into my past, waiting for something to come up which she can use against me, waiting for the right moment to strike. She had a coldness in her eyes that freaked me out. And I saw exactly what L meant when he said she was a reptile in human form. Still, even though she scared the shit out of me, I tried not to let it show. Played a card of my own. A trump card, in fact. She was so drunk the night of my birthday, I guess she didn't remember. Didn't remember confessing the vile thing she did, something that shocked me but which I've kept close to my chest all this time. Although it's been hard keeping it from him, I've not told L because I didn't want to cause him unnecessary pain if I could help it. Also, I couldn't be sure she hadn't made it up, she was so wasted. But we're too far gone for that now. If I want to be with L, I have to do what's necessary to hold onto him. So, I have done. I told the bitch I wouldn't hesitate to tell the world what she told me. That I would expose her for the deceitful, heartless cow she is. And when I said that, I could tell from the fear in her eyes that what she'd confessed to me that night was true.

June 2018

Sunday, 24th June Woke up this morning with the hangover from hell. Can't remember feeling this hung-over in a long time. Vomited three times before nine a.m., and for once it wasn't me sticking two fingers down my throat, but totally unforced. Guess I shouldn't be surprised – it was my thirtieth, after all. That's how you're supposed to wake up after a milestone birthday do, isn't it? Everyone told me that. Even so, I hadn't thought I'd drunk that much. I'd stuck to single spirits mixed with diet lemonade after the first glass of complimentary bubbles Barry laid on, and usually, if I do that and avoid wine, I'm fine.

I was so thankful today's a Sunday, and I didn't have any classes. There's no way I'd have been able to teach. I mostly lounged around on the sofa, watched old episodes of *How I Met Your Mother* and gradually by five p.m. felt more human. I know I'll be fine for tomorrow night's yoga, although I'm slightly dreading it after having the most disturbing conversation with S last night.

I hadn't especially wanted a big fuss made over me, but everyone at work had egged me on, as had N. S also said I'd regret it if I didn't do something to mark the occasion. She told me my thirtieth is the last time I'll wake up not thinking I'm old and past it, wishing I'd done things differently. Wishing I'd made fewer mistakes. That come forty, things will change inside and out, and I'll realise I'm halfway through my life, not young any more and that time is running out. Talk about being the voice of doom and gloom. I've always had the feeling she's jealous of me, and it was almost like she wanted me to feel bad despite pretending to look out for my well-being. Anyway, after her depressing advice, I kind of felt obliged to have a party, even though it makes me think of J and how we could have been celebrating together if we'd been more careful and things hadn't gone pear-shaped in Southampton.

To be honest, it was nice people making a fuss over me yesterday, just because I wasn't used to all that, growing up, didn't have a proper eighteenth because Mum had kicked me out by then. Before that, the only fuss she made was over my weight, like if it had gone up by one pound or my handstands weren't precise enough. I thought about Dad last night, too. Wishing he could have been here to celebrate with me. Thinking about how he'll never get the chance to walk me down the aisle, play with his grandchildren. Even though there are times when I'm not even sure that's going to happen, just because the guy I'm in love with won't commit. Hasn't given me reason to hope. Fuck, it's true turning thirty has brought back all kinds of painful memories. Made me think about this boy I used to know, back when I was in primary school. Guess he was sort of my first love, we had such a special connection. He'd take my mind off the fact that I was so unhappy with Mum and the nasty things she said to me. He understood me better than anyone, and then one day he was gone. It's been the story of my life. Losing people. I try not to dwell on it most of the time, but it's occasions like last night that make me remember the people I've loved but who aren't around to share in my happiness.

N was on good form last night, thank God. She's a good friend, but she can be a bit of a mood kill sometimes. I know we have this connection, at least she thinks we have, because we've both had crappy childhoods, but I've not done some of the weird shit she's done. My mother was a cow, but looking back, it was better than foster care. I guess I'm more a glass half-full person, while N's definitely a glass half-empty sort. Understandably, losing her brother, etc. But she can be a bit suffocating, and I'm never quite sure what she's thinking, whether she's being totally honest with me. I can't babysit her forever. I hope she realises that. I have to get on with my life, and I hope she doesn't get worked up about it. Sometimes I feel like I'm walking a tightrope with her, she's so temperamental.

Anyway, she was sweet and said I deserved a big party, to be made a fuss of, especially as I work so hard. I'm not sure that's true. I'm a fitness instructor, for God's sake. It's fun, not exactly long, taxing hours or rocket science. I miss teaching at the school, but I can't go back to that. Besides, not sure anyone would hire me. Still, I appreciated her saying I deserved it, and it made up for the fact that lately she's been getting on my tits. It almost feels like she's jealous rather than looking out for my best interests. I'm not so sure she'd be OK with me seeing anyone, quite frankly. Married or not. I bit my lip, though – didn't want to get into an argument and upset her. Just because I know how fragile she is mentally and I didn't want her flipping out.

I keep thinking about that day at the library. She was such a timid, frumpy thing, so lacking in self-confidence, so out of shape. I felt sorry for her, wanted to help her. Because I recognised the 'victim' in her. I saw the way her cow of a colleague had put her down, tried to make her feel small, as my mother had done to me. I enjoy rooting for the underdog, taking a stand against pushy, unfeeling women, just because my mother's one such woman. S reminds me of Mum, so it's hard to feel pity for her when she moans about L ignoring her. Even more so after what she told me last night. I may have been pissed, but it's not something I'm likely to forget in a hurry. I promised I'd say nothing, and I'm tempted to write it down here. I've always written journals, I find it cathartic and no one's going to read this, so why should I care? But I can't bring myself to. Because what if she made it up? What if she exaggerated? I wouldn't put it past her – she was pissed. I guess I'm worried in case L finds my diary one day even though I keep it hidden away. I don't want to cause him needless stress if it's a load of bullshit. Or get S into trouble for something she didn't do despite the fact I hate her guts.

Anyway, thank God N was fine last night, didn't say a word about L, although it did at times feel like she was following me around like my own shadow, making sure I didn't make a twat out of myself.

I know she's only looking out for me. But sometimes it really does feel like she's trying to be my mother, and that fucks me off as I don't need another mother who strangles the life out of me. At one point I felt like I couldn't breathe, so I escaped outside to get some fresh air. But then I got cornered again. Only this time, I didn't mind the intrusion. It was L. Somehow he'd managed to escape, and hopefully no one saw. We'd been snatching sneaky glances across the room all night, and he'd noticed S latching onto me, saw how uncomfortable I looked, followed me outside to ask what she'd been saying. I wanted to tell him, but also couldn't bear to hurt him. Just said she was drunk and talking a load of nonsense. Telling me to make the most of life while I was still young and not let chances slip by. He was so sweet. Told me he was sad that I didn't seem to be having a good time. I assured him I was, and that even though we couldn't be together as such, I was glad he was there. Feeling his presence was enough. We've always had that connection. From the moment we set eyes on each other in the gym, when we knew we had to be with one another. I'll never forget our first embrace in the corridor. So risky, but also thrilling. We've been more careful since, but whenever I see her in the class, I can't help wondering if she suspects anything. It's my guilty conscience talking, I suppose.

Anyway, I'm glad I had the party, and need to keep the faith that everything will work itself out. Even though, after Southampton, keeping the faith's not always been easy. Life can be so shit, just because people make it so. We're all so fucked up in the head. I still love working at the club, but I'm not sure I want to hang around there much longer. Thinking about looking elsewhere, maybe moving back to Central London where I can get lost in the crowds. Surbiton's a bit too much like Southampton, where everyone knows everyone's business. Plus, although I thought I was OK with seeing G every day, deep down I'm not. There's always this feeling lurking inside me that she's planning something. I mean, how can she be OK with what I did? I made my peace with her because I didn't want her bad-mouthing me, but I've never felt right about it. There's too much history between us. I just hope L will follow me wherever I end up. I can't bear to be parted from him. Can't lose another man I love.

I know it's not an easy decision for L. And I know that when S finds out about us, she'll probably want to kill me.

Chapter Thirty-Three

Susan

Monday, 23 July 2018, 7:30 p.m.

I'm feeling unnerved after last night's press conference, knowing Jade's disappearance is now public knowledge. So unnerved I've just poured myself a large measure of gin with a splash of tonic. It was hard to conceal my delight at her no-show last Friday, but now things suddenly seem to be spiralling out of control, including my own composure, and that's not something I had planned for. I know I should probably act like everything's normal, which includes going to my class, but I'm finding it tough keeping up my typically nonchalant facade, and I don't want to give Natalie any excuse for running to DI Bailey. Plus now that Jade's been officially labelled a missing person, it might look a bit cold of me to attend a class like nothing's happened. Even though I could do with the endorphin release. I also can't stop thinking about last night. Another altercation with Lance, and in front of Stella to make matters worse.

I was having my usual Sunday-night glass of wine, no different to any other night, to be honest, except on Sundays I stick to the one rather than several, and had decided to order in. After my slightly worrying discussion with Grace that afternoon, I was just contemplating something exotic like Thai or sushi to take my mind off things, when Stella had sauntered into the living room. 'What's up, Mum?' she'd asked, slumping down on the sofa next to me just as I was logging on to Deliveroo.

She'd had her earbuds in when she first appeared, but she'd peeled one out just as she'd asked the question, even offered me a half smile. Clearly, she'd been at a loose end and had nothing better to do than sidle up to her fuddy-duddy mother. That's what I'd thought at the time. Only because usually at that time on a Sunday night she'd be out with friends, or the boyfriend, or on her phone to one or the other in her room. Rarely do we share a sofa together and actually talk. Lance was locked away in his man cave in the garden, which is strictly out of bounds to the female species – God only knows what he does in there, he either claims to be doing DIY or watching sport, but I reckon he jerks off to porn – while Michael was down the pub, as usual. So I thought maybe this was my chance for a girlie night with my daughter. Maybe we could order in together, watch a movie with some hot men in it, pretend like we were close, like mothers and daughters should be.

'I'm about to order in. You hungry? Fancy some sushi?' I'd asked.

She didn't respond at first, appeared to give it some thought. Then said, 'Sure, why not?' with a shrug.

I'd felt an unfamiliar glimmer of joy at her response, having expected her to pass. I'd wondered if I could coax her into a movie as we waited for the order. Thinking how I needed something to take my mind off Jade and that diary of hers, still wondering whether she might have mentioned me, and not in a good way. We'd settled on a sushi bar we liked the look of and placed our order.

'Fancy watching a movie?' I'd taken my chances, making sure to strike while the iron was hot.

'Sure, but I'll choose. Nothing from the dark ages, OK?'

I had smiled. I was just so thrilled that my daughter was paying me some attention. I'd have watched *The Exorcist* to keep her there. It had me wondering, though, if she had an ulterior motive, as sad as that is.

Stella had clicked on the Netflix app and settled on a romcom featuring Zac Efron. Suited me fine. But just as she'd pressed play and I was getting an unfamiliar fuzzy feeling in my belly, a nice, pure feeling that took my mind off all the other unpleasant stuff stored in the back of my brain, Lance had come storming in, the door crashing open and rebounding against the wall with such force I thought he might have caused serious damage. Stella was up like lightning. 'What the fuck, Dad?'

The look in Lance's eyes had told me he wanted to kill me. And not for the first time I had felt frightened by what he might be capable of. Not to mention what he might have found out. I'd told myself not to panic, to play it cool as usual.

'What's wrong with you?' I'd yelled. 'Frightening Stella like that.'

'Like you care. Turn on *BBC News*,' Lance had bawled.

Stella was still holding the remote, and seeing the look on her father's face, she hadn't dared disobey him.

Even before the channel had flipped, I'd sensed what I was about to see, and with that, my appetite had waned.

The news channel was showing a press conference led by DI Bailey, with DS Khan at his side, a sea of reporters listening intently to what they had to say. An image of

Jade was on the screen behind him. And it appeared that we were catching the tail end of the show.

'Jade was last seen on Thursday night at The River Club in Kingston upon Thames, where she works. We understand from her manager that she left the club at around nine fifty p.m. that night, having taught a class from eight thirty to nine thirty p.m. Based on the fact that her car remains parked on St James Road in Surbiton where Jade lives, and her car keys along with her phone were found inside her flat, we believe Jade made it back to her flat, but after that, her whereabouts are unknown. It also appears she may have had her house keys with her. As Jade has now been missing for seventy-two hours, there are growing concerns for her safety, and it is therefore imperative for members of the public to come forward with any information they may have. Thank you.'

Just like that, Lance had darted over to Stella and snatched the remote control from her, before switching the TV off. 'Stella, please leave the room. I need to talk to your mother.'

'But...' she'd begun.

'Now!' Lance had barked back.

Stella had given him a sulky look, then slinked out the door. Damn you, Lance, I'd thought to myself. Finally, I was having a moment with our daughter and you had to go and ruin it.

'Do you know anything about this?' he'd demanded, once he was sure Stella was out of earshot.

'What?'

'Don't you "what" me! HAVE YOU GOT ANYTHING TO DO WITH JADE GOING MISSING?'

I'd folded my arms. 'No, of course I haven't.'

'You're lying,' he'd growled.

'I'm not fucking lying. How could you think such a thing?'

Bit of a weak argument coming from me, I knew that as soon as the words had left my mouth. And based on his response, he knew it too.

'Oh, I don't know, because you're a spiteful, cold-hearted bitch, jealous of Jade and what we had? Frightened of losing the lazy lifestyle to which you've become accustomed?'

I had held my tongue. I couldn't afford to let my guard down.

'I know you were out at the time,' he'd gone on.

'What?'

'Stop saying "what", pretending like you're innocent. I know you were out on Thursday night, around the time they're saying Jade would have got home, because I called the landline,' he'd said.

'I wasn't out. I can't have heard the phone.'

'Hmm, likely story.'

'Why on earth were you calling? You never call, you're not that considerate.'

'I was calling to tell you I had an email from Cam. He's coming home this weekend.'

'What? Why? And how am I only hearing this now?' I had studied his face, and then the realisation had dawned on me. 'Oh, I see. You were pissed off I didn't answer your call that night, so you wanted to punish me by keeping quiet.'

'Don't be so juvenile, Susie. Since then, Cam texted to tell me not to say anything, that he wanted it to be a surprise. But judging by your reaction it's not a welcome one. Nice to know how keen you are to see your eldest son.'

'Oh, fuck off, you know I didn't mean it like that. It's just a bit short notice. I've got nothing prepared.'

'Don't worry, he's staying in London, it's a business trip, but when he emailed I thought you should know. That's not the point. What were you doing when I called?'

'I don't know, maybe I was having a poo, is that what you want to hear? And where were you at that time, may I ask? How do I know you're not involved in Jade's mysterious disappearance?'

He'd given me an incredulous look, appeared almost fit to burst. 'Me! I broke things off with Jade over the phone on Wednesday night. Like you told me to. No, make that *blackmailed* me to. You fucking watched me while I made the call, if you remember. After you came home pissed as usual. You told me that if I was to go within a hundred yards of her again, you'd take me to the cleaners and ruin her life. Tell me, Susie, is that why you insisted I use that pay-as-you-go phone you'd especially acquired for the occasion? Because you didn't want anything being traced back to you?'

'Don't be absurd,' I'd retorted. In my mind I'd said to myself he was spot on. I'd been told it was crucial that nothing could be traced back to us, should it come to that. 'And anyway, coming back to you, so what if you broke things off? How do I know you kept to your promise? That you didn't secretly meet up with her again? Maybe she convinced you to, begged you to have it out with her face to face, or perhaps one last shag for the road, and you had some sort of lover's tiff. Maybe she threatened to kiss and tell if you didn't take her back, and you lost your cool.'

Lance had glared at me with a hatred that might have turned me to stone. But there was also something else in his eyes that had scared me. Something had changed, I could feel it. He knew something, I was sure of it. But I didn't dare ask the question in case I was wrong.

'You know I wouldn't hurt her,' he'd said. 'But you, you're a different story. I know you did something. So, tell me, what was it, Susan?' He'd come closer, his eyes still shooting daggers. 'What did you do?'

'What I had to!' I had snapped back.

'And what the hell does that mean?'

'It means I made sure the little slut won't be showing her face around here again. But judging by that press conference, I needn't have bothered. I'd call that karma, wouldn't you? Clearly someone wanted the tramp gone as much as I did!'

Lance's face had turned scarlet as he'd lurched forward towards me. So close I could feel his breath hot on my face, making me want to retch.

'I don't believe you for a second. I know what you're capable of. Of the lengths you'll go to get what you want.' He'd paused, then, 'You'd better hope they find her alive, or else I won't hesitate to go to the police.'

I'd shuddered at his threat, just as I shudder now thinking about it. I was so sure he'd do anything to save his reputation at the firm, the family name. His children's reputations especially. But maybe I was wrong.

'You wouldn't dare,' I'd said. 'You know I won't take it lying down. I will contact every newspaper up and down the country and let them know you were shagging my fitness instructor, a girl twenty-two years your junior. How nice for your children to wake up to that story, to read the sordid headline in their morning newspaper over breakfast, or better still, out with friends, on the Tube, or at work, or even once Michael starts at the firm next month. He'll be blacklisted, jeered at. His career over before it's even begun. His dad a smarmy cheating sugar daddy. Is that what you want?'

'Why *you*!' Lance had reached out with his hands, as if wanting to take hold of my neck and strangle the life out of me. I knew I deserved it, but I'd come this far and I couldn't allow myself to falter. If I did, I knew I'd crumble to nothing and he'd see through my lies. So, I hadn't moved from the spot, stared him out, and he had edged backward.

'You have nothing,' he'd said. 'Just a couple of photos of us embracing and one of me kissing her forehead. We're not even kissing on the mouth, let alone shagging. You can't prove anything. Jade was smart, she would have known that too. She probably told you so to your face. And that got you worried.'

'Ah, but that's what journalists are for, darling. Don't you know they are excellent at twisting the truth?' I'd bitten back. 'A bit like you lawyers. Only in this case it's not twisting the truth because it *is* the fucking truth!' I couldn't contain my anger any longer, picking up my empty wine glass and hurling it at Lance. He'd ducked just in time for it to narrowly miss his head.

'You're a fucking psycho,' he'd growled. 'And I don't care about your stupid photos. I did what you asked of me and broke things off with Jade for her good, for the children's sake, and certainly not to please you. That should have been enough for you. You don't love me, you never have. You were just scared of me cutting you out of my will.'

'And why shouldn't I be? I've devoted over thirty years to this marriage, I'm owed that.'

'Really? The entire time we've been married, you've contributed nothing of value to it. Your sole contribution as far as I can tell is to have drained all the money I earn every month. Tell me, what good are you to anyone?'

His words had stung me, but still I'd replied: 'I gave you three kids. Doesn't that count for something?'

'Yes, and I've said it before, they're the only good thing that came out of our shambolic marriage. But mark my words, if I should learn you haven't been entirely truthful with me, I won't hesitate to contact the police and tell them who I think might be behind Jade's disappearance.'

I had watched him leave the room. Such a fool. He is a man, after all; they're all fucking gullible fools, the lot of them. Of course, I hadn't been entirely truthful with him, I never have been, so why would I break the habit of a lifetime?

And now, as I sit on my sofa, alone again, I give myself a rallying cry. I refuse to let him or any man, including DI Bailey, ruffle me. And I refuse to allow that weirdo Natalie to vilify my character, as I've no doubt she's continuing to do. I've not heard from DI Bailey since Saturday, so I'm hoping they know nothing about my husband's extramarital activities. Jade wouldn't have wanted to chance anyone at the club finding out about her affair with a client, I'm certain of it, so there's nothing for me to worry about. Before long, they'll give up and it will all blow over. That's what happens in the majority of missing persons cases. I've read up on it. I've done my research. And that's what this is. Just another missing person. Hundreds of women go missing, and the fact that Jade's gone missing the same week I happened to accuse her of sleeping with my husband is pure coincidence.

I reach for my gin and down it in one. But resist the temptation to pour another. I need to keep sharp, and I need to watch my step with Lance. One false move or slip of the tongue under the influence, and I'm toast. And that would be such a shame.

Having come this far. Having got more than I bargained for.

Chapter Thirty-Four

Monday, 23 July 2018, nine p.m.

She's not sure how long she's been here now. Time has no meaning in this place. It might be the break of dawn, it might be the dead of night. She has no idea because there are no windows, and therefore no way of making any kind of informed judgement. She has no watch, no phone, nothing that might allow her to keep track of the time. It's disorientating, and it's sending her a little mad. She mustn't panic, she must stay strong, stay hopeful. Hopeful that someone will put two and two together, realise she is here and rescue her.

She hears noises every so often: human footfall, the TV, although she cannot tell if the voices she hears are male or female, one person or several. Everything seems to merge into one. She tells herself she must survive, keep well for when, by God's good grace, she will emerge. Free again.

Her captor must pay for what they have done. They cannot be allowed to get away with their crime.

As she sits there in the near darkness, rather than contemplating her death, she contemplates this person's demise. Because that's what fighters do. They don't submit to domination. They become the dominator.

They go for blood.

Chapter Thirty-Five

Natalie

Tuesday, 24 July 2018

I bend down and lay the flowers against my brother's headstone. Read the words inscribed across it.

> *The best brother a sister could ask for. My friend and saviour, my heart. May you rest in peace.*

They are words no fifteen-year-old girl should have to write about their brother, and because of this I cannot stop a tear from falling and landing on the grass. I took today off, like I do every year. So I could visit Jack's grave in Lambeth Cemetery, spend some time with him, talk to him, say I'm sorry and make peace with his death even though I know it will always haunt me.

The last few days have drained me, and so quiet reflection is what I need, even though it's moments like this, when I have time to think, that I can't help wondering what happened on Thursday night. The not knowing is torture, and it looms over me wherever I go.

After DI Bailey witnessed my flare-up at the library, and our conversation that followed, I never made it to the club. I was too exhausted to face Grace, or Susan for that matter, and in any case, now that DI Bailey knows about Jade and Lance, about Jade's history with Grace – I couldn't allow him to leave without telling him about my conversation with Megan – it's no longer for me to confront Grace. I'll leave that job to the police. Something DI Bailey said he intends to do today.

I slowly stand up, pause a moment or two, my eyes still fixed upon my beloved brother's grave.

'I'm sorry, Jack,' I say. 'I'm sorry our parents were losers. I'm sorry our mother was a druggie, our father an alcoholic abusive arsehole. Sorry we ended up with the foster parents from hell. I don't know what we did to deserve all that, but that's life, I guess. It's not fair, it's shit. Sorry I was the weak one, that you had to be strong for the both of us. Sorry you ended up in that prison, that the system failed you. Sorry you didn't feel able to tell me how hellish it must have been in there, keeping a brave face for me, as you always did. I will always be grateful to you, you will always have a place in my heart, and I hope one day we will meet again even though, with the life we were dealt, it's hard to believe there's a God. Hard to believe there's a benevolent being when the world is full of so many shitty people, when life can deal the best of people the cruellest of hands. Rest in peace, dear brother. I'll see you next year, same time, same place.'

'That was beautiful.'

I turn with a start at the unexpected voice, having thought I was alone. There was certainly no one about when I last looked, and it's as if the elderly woman I see before me has appeared from nowhere. She must be in her late seventies, early eighties. She's wearing a light mac, tights and sensible flat shoes, along with a headscarf – overdressed for the time of year, the way older people often are. She supports herself with a stick in her right hand and has watery blue eyes that seem to cut through me and see into my soul.

'Thank you,' I stumble.

'Whose grave is that?' she asks. 'If you don't mind me asking.'

'My brother's,' I reply.

'I'm so sorry,' she says. 'I only ask because I often see flowers laid by his grave and suppose he must have been very loved. I come here to visit my daughter's grave, just over there.'

She gives a slight tilt of her chin to the right, to indicate where her daughter is buried.

'I'm sorry for your loss,' I say, somewhat absent-mindedly, just because I'm too busy wondering who could be leaving flowers at my brother's grave.

'Thank you.'

'Hope you don't mind me saying, but I'm a little confused,' I admit. 'We lost our parents very young and only had each other. Jack died when he was sixteen. I can't think who would be leaving flowers at his grave.'

'That's heartbreaking,' she sighs. 'The death of a loved one is always sad. But the death of one so young is a tragedy. I speak from experience.'

'Your daughter was young when she died?'

'Twenty-two. Not much older than your brother.'

'I'm sorry, that's very sad.'

'Thank you.'

'I don't suppose you've ever seen who's been leaving flowers by my brother's grave?' I ask hopefully. 'Whether it was a man or a woman?'

She shakes her head. 'No, I'm sorry, I haven't. I only noticed the flowers because they're always so striking. The most exquisite spray of red and white roses.'

'I see,' I say, still puzzled.

'Whoever it is, whoever they are,' she carries on, 'they must have cared for your brother deeply.' She gives me a kind smile, as if to reassure me that my brother was loved. But there's also something of a mischievous glint in her eyes that sets me on edge. Makes me wonder if she knows more than she's letting on.

'I must be going,' she continues. 'But can I leave you with one last thought? A bit of free advice from an old woman and the voice of experience, as it were.'

I wonder what on earth she's going to say. 'Sure, please do.'

'Don't go to your own grave with a cloud hanging over you, with any regrets or burdens weighing you down. Free your mind and clear your conscience. Always speak the truth. Perhaps if your brother had done that, he'd still be with you today.'

She lets that digest, the same twinkle in her eye, then turns around and leaves. I watch her walk off. It's hot today, the midday sun beating down across the back of my head and neck. But it's the unmistakeable air of menace in the old woman's voice that has me perspiring. It's as if she's read my mind, knows the burden I've been carrying all these years and is daring me to confess it.

It's like she's saying that if I don't, I'll never be free.

Chapter Thirty-Six

Grace

Tuesday, 24 July 2018

'Hello, Mum, how are you?'

I study my mother for a moment. She still looks like my mother. The mother I've always known. The same hair, same mouth, same oval-shaped face. Albeit a little frailer, a little more shrunken, a little more wrinkled and bent over. But when I look into her eyes, that's when I know she isn't the same person. She is there in body, but not in mind. It's like her spirit has been wrenched out of her, and in its place all that's left is an empty shell of a woman. Who neither laughs nor cries, expresses neither joy nor sadness, but always gives the same blank reaction.

When she speaks, when I try to engage her in a conversation, it's like talking to a robot. There is no inflection in her voice. Just a drab monotone. She has no opinions, shows no emotion. It's like she's forgotten *how* to feel. As if the disease that's ravaging her brain has robbed her of her humanity. And after all, it's emotion, feelings, that make us human. The ability to feel: to love, to desire, to hate, to crave. Whether good or bad, the better or worse side of human nature, without emotion, without the ability to feel something, we humans aren't really human at all.

Even when she eats, I can see she's not really savouring her food; she shovels it in and that's that, job done. Sometimes I feel like prodding her, taking her by the shoulders and shaking her violently, as if doing so will shake the life back into her, bring back the mother I once knew. The mother I would shop with, who'd plait my hair and help me with my homework, who'd soothe me when I was down, who'd congratulate me when I was high, who'd engage in conversation and offer a rational opinion. In all honesty, I hate coming here; I'd rather not, because the mother I knew is dead to me and I know I'll never see her again. But the humanity in me knows I must. Because I'm the only one who will come to see her, and because I suppose it appeases my conscience for what I did. Plus I know it's what Dad would have wanted.

There's another reason I come here, though. Visiting Mum is like visiting a confessional of sorts. I can sit with her and tell her my secrets, confess my sins freely and without fear of them being exposed. She won't tell anyone because nine times out of ten she doesn't really hear me. And even if she does, she won't remember what she heard the next day.

'Fine, thank you,' she replies, staring into space in the direction of the TV, which is showing old episodes of *The Chase*. She's not really listening to the questions, so there's no chance of her having a clue about the answers, but the TV, the radio, have become routine, white noise, a kind of comfort blanket to her.

'Have you eaten?'

'I have.'

'What did you eat?'

'I don't know.'

Marvellous. I try not to get frustrated.

'Where's Jim?'

She asks this every time I visit.

'Working,' I reply.

'As usual.'

'Yes, as usual,' I nod.

'Why didn't you bring the boys? Not seen them since last week.'

I try not to cry. 'Maybe next time.'

'OK then.'

'Mum, can I tell you something?'

'Yes, dear.'

I think of the press conference given by DI Bailey on Sunday night. Reporters, cameras, the gravity of the situation made all too real. Jade's disappearance now in the public domain. A national story. And one the press will latch onto like a kettle of vultures. A sexy gym instructor gone missing, a potential scandal waiting to be unearthed. They'll tail the police until Jade is found, dead or alive; they'll continue to dig and pick away until they've found something. And before long, they'll discover her real name and the whole scandal with Jim will be reopened. I'm a reporter, I know what they're like.

Fuck, my head is spinning. I just want to break free of this incessant mental torture. And which only seems to be escalating. It was never meant to go this far. All I wanted was for her to be taught a lesson.

'I did something bad, Mum,' I say. 'Something I'm starting to regret. Something that's got out of control.'

'You did?' She's still staring at the TV. 'What did you do, dear?'

'I think I may have sent a young woman to her grave.'

Chapter Thirty-Seven

Grace

One month before
Saturday, 23 June 2018

It's nice to be out, at a social event, I mean. Even if it is a bit risky potentially widening my circle of friends. I'm thankful it's something other than working out or the supermarket. Or sitting alone in my study writing fictitious freelance articles, imagining some publication will take them on even though the last thing I need is to draw attention to myself. Something other than talking to my dead husband all day, or worse, the four walls.

Because I'm at pains to keep my past a secret, I deliberately limit my socialising. I never mingle in the immediate area where I live. I've chosen not to frequent any places that might attract 'friends' or 'gossip' or any kind of interest in my life. I never even get a food delivery because I don't want the delivery driver snooping into my life. I know how some of them like to chat, ask you questions about your personal life, and I can't take that risk. I shop at the massive Sainsbury's off the A3 where there's no chance of getting to know anyone. The only place I've let myself go a bit is here, at the club. But even here I'm careful. When Karen on reception asked me why I don't get a family membership so the kids can use the pool and my husband and I might play tennis at weekends, I tell her Jim isn't into working out, and that the gym is my 'zen' time. That with a hectic home life, I need something that's just for me, away from the kids and my husband. She didn't see anything odd in that. And neither did anyone else. Least of all Susan, who positively applauded me for reaching such a decision. Of course, Jade knows my secret. Knows that I am all alone. That I have no one left in my life aside from my senile mother. It's funny, having come here to study Jade, to see what it was about her that made Jim cheat on me, to make her feel uncomfortable, to plot my revenge, I have found myself liking her more and more. She's not the hard-hearted slut I thought she was. I've watched her come and go, leave her flat, go jogging, shop in town, and not once have I seen her with another man. I mean, yes, she flirts a little bit with men at the club, but we all toss our hair and flutter our eyelashes every now and again, and I've never noticed anything overtly sexual in her mannerisms. She's not the shallow, reckless man-eater I had taken her for. One day, maybe a month after I joined the club, during which time I'd been tracking her movements, thinking about how I might punish her, she asked me to have coffee with her. I was somewhat shocked, as this hadn't been part of my plan. So I invited her over to mine. The first and last of my guests. And we'd talked. She said she was sorry for the pain she had caused me. That she hadn't set out to take Jim away from me. That he'd told her he was unhappily married and lonely. And hearing all that, although it broke my heart, I realised I had neglected him over the years, fretting over the kids, over parties and World Book Day, over Dad and Mum; that I had failed to see how he was hurting too. How he'd also needed my care and attention. I was so consumed with me, with life getting on top of me, I had stopped being the girl he fell in love with. The girl who'd always suffered from depression, who'd always been a bit of a perfectionist, but who had allowed him to help her, loosen her up and enjoy life. I so wanted to be angry with Jade, but I realised she wasn't to blame. She was caught between Jim and I, an innocent really, and if it hadn't been her, it would no doubt have been another girl's arms he'd have fallen into.

I tried to make it up with Jim the other day; tried to tell him I was sorry and that he needed to forgive me so we could both have peace. But he refuses to forgive me, says that I'm selfish, that in continuing to take the drugs I've not learned anything, that I must pay for what I did to our children, and that I will eventually burn in hell.

I haven't told Jade I see him. If I do that, she'll think I'm crazy. I want to stop taking the pills, but I'm just not strong enough. Can't seem to move on, break the cycle. And that's why I can't bring myself to broach a reconciliation with my kids. How can I look them in the eye and tell them I want to be a part of their lives when I still pop the same pills that caused one of them to end up in the ICU, and me to hallucinate about their dead father?

I've no idea if Jim's parents will entertain the idea, but in my heart I'm not even sure I'm worthy of my boys' love, knowing it was my actions that drove their father to his death. What would I say? Would they even want to see me? The thought of them wanting nothing to do with me is nigh on unbearable, and so I'd rather not risk that possibility just yet.

The function room is decorated with gold and silver balloons, the number thirty emblazoned across them in honour of Jade's birthday. There are banners hanging from corner to corner of the ceiling, a fully stocked bar and a table of delicious canapés lined up alongside it to the left. There must be around eighty people here; maybe thirty odd attend Jade's classes, while the others are staff and some Jade said she doesn't know. It's sad she has no family, and it's another reason I've come to forgive her. I realise she's lonely, like me, despite being young and beautiful. That her harsh upbringing did her no favours, and that despite what happened to my marriage, my childhood is something to be thankful for; I was blessed with loving parents who always put me first and never put me down the way Jade's mother did.

'Hello, Grace.'

It's Natalie. She looks quite nice this evening. Has actually made an effort to wear something more befitting her age. A simple black dress, not strapless, of course, but it shows a bit of knee, and the top half doesn't rise all the way to her collarbone. She's definitely grown in confidence since we first met. And I can tell Jade is the reason. Natalie told me the story of how she came into the library nearly a year ago and gave her snotty colleague an earful. Again, when she told me this, I realised that the girl I had come to torment didn't deserve that. That Jade has a good heart. Which is why Jim fell for her, as much as it still pains me to admit.

'Hi, Natalie, you look lovely.'

Natalie blushes, touches her hair self-consciously as I pay her the compliment. Evidently she's not used to being complimented on her appearance, and doesn't know how to react. 'Thank you,' she says awkwardly. 'So do you.' She looks around the room, Bruno Mars' 'Uptown Funk' ringing in the air, causing us to have to raise our voices to be heard. I see she has her usual soft drink, while I'm clutching my second glass of wine. I tell myself to slow down. Loose lips will never do.

'Jade looks stunning, doesn't she,' Natalie says, her eyes motioning to the other side of the room where Jade is talking to Martin and Barry. I've noticed the way Martin looks at Jade, but it's clear from Jade's body language that she doesn't feel the same way. It's strange; if I were her age I'd be in there like a shot, he's so handsome, but he might as well be the plainest man on earth for all the attention she gives him. Maybe she hasn't got over Jim. That makes two of us.

'Yes, she does,' I agree. Jade is wearing a blue halterneck chiffon dress which shows off her toned arms and tiny waist to perfection. I notice Susan and Lance standing nearby talking to Vivien and her husband, Frank. It's been obvious to me for some time that Susan and Lance's marriage isn't a happy one. The frostiness between them is palpable, and when she's talking, him a silent bystander, I can see the look of irritation in his eyes, as if he can't stand the sound of her voice, as if he wished she'd shut the hell up. I sense it in Jim's voice when he deigns to appear and talk to me. To be fair, he has good reason to hate the sound of my voice, but what about Lance? What is it that Susan might have done to make him loathe her company so much? Is it the fact that she's so fake and full of herself? So shallow and money-orientated? Or is there something else? Some other secret between them that's festered over the years like a scab that won't heal. A putrid pus of animosity that's become more and more infected as time has worn on.

She already seems quite pissed, waving her wine glass around as she gesticulates with her hands. Both men look really bored, while Vivien's trying her best to appear interested, none of them getting a word in edgeways by the looks of things.

'Susan's had a few too, I see.' Natalie stirs me from my thoughts.

I chuckle. 'There's a surprise. Her husband's not looking amused.'

'No, no, he's not.' Her response is noticeably clipped.

'Have you ever spoken to him?' I ask. 'I have a couple of times, and he wasn't very forthcoming.'

'I haven't,' Natalie shakes her head. 'Probably thinks himself too good for the likes of me. Being a hotshot City lawyer.'

'Don't put yourself down,' I say.

'Oh, I'm not. I'm not bothered at all.'

It doesn't sound like it. The tone of her voice suggests she hates his guts, a little too much for someone she barely knows, hasn't even spoken to. I wonder what that's all about, or maybe I'm reading too much into things. Natalie is a bit odd, to be fair, even though she's a little less strange than when we first met.

I find myself talking to a few new people this evening who naturally ask about my line of work and my family circumstances. I spin the usual lies – it's become so easy now, like second nature – but as I know none of these people matter in my life, that I may never see any of them again, it doesn't cause me any concern.

It gets to about ten p.m. and a few people are starting to leave. But generally the night is still going strong, with quite a crowd on the dance floor, the usual classics like 'YMCA' and 'Dancing Queen' attracting a number of pissed women. Jade seems to be having fun. She's been up to dance a few times, but I can't see her now. I squint through the throng and to my amusement spot her sitting at a table in a far corner with Susan. She looks like she wants to be anywhere but there, and Susan is clearly very drunk, her arm around Jade's neck, talking into her ear about God knows what. Probably a load of meaningless nonsense, knowing Susan, although at one point I see a look of alarm shrouding Jade's face, as if Susan's just told her something rather shocking. I happen to look around and see Lance standing with Frank. I watch him nodding a lot but it's clear where his line of vision is focused. It's directed at Susan and Jade, and he doesn't look happy. No doubt it's the usual thing. He's embarrassed about his wife, and wishes she'd leave the poor birthday girl alone. I can't help but empathise. After all, Jade's here to have a good time and not be bored to tears by Susan waffling on about herself. She always has to be the centre of attention. Even in the classes. I don't think I've been to a single class where she hasn't tried to dominate, show off, talk about herself, or make some 'witty' comment. It's the same when we go for coffee, or on the couple of occasions she's invited me over to hers. She's a crowd-pleaser, pure and simple, feels the need to be loud and overbearing to mask that emptiness in her life.

Eventually, Jade manages to prise herself away, still looking uncomfortable. I think she's had quite a bit to drink too, so maybe she's not feeling too well. I watch her disappear out of the room, presumably to the Ladies. I think about going after her to check she's all right when I see Lance slip out of the room too. OK, so he also needs the loo, no big deal. I leave the room myself and head for the Ladies, check inside but Jade's not in there. It's a warmish evening and the doors leading out to the pool and tennis courts, a little way down from the Ladies, are open. I wonder if Jade's gone outside to get some air, just because I would have passed her en route back to the function room.

Curious, I go to explore. Amble down by the side of the pool until I reach the tennis courts which are lined by netting and foliage to the right. And that's when I hear whispered voices. I creep along, careful not to make a sound, crouch down and spot a man and a woman locked in an embrace. It's Jade and Lance. They're not kissing but he has his arms wrapped around her, and I can hear him saying, 'I'm sorry you had to listen to her rabbit on.'

Jade breaks free and takes his hand in hers, smiles and looks up at him adoringly.

'It's OK, I've dealt with loony middle-aged women like her before. Worse, in fact. The certified psychotic kind. The trick is to keep them sweet. Pander to them, stroke their egos, make them think you care.'

A sick sensation envelops me as I hear her words. *Loony? Psychotic?* She's talking about me, I know she is. Has to be. I mean, call me paranoid, but it would be the coincidence of the century if she knows any other middle-aged women who'd spent time on a psychiatric ward. How could I have been so stupid? Believing she felt sorry for me, that she forgave me, was now my friend. It was all an act. She's been playing me for a fool, laughing at me behind my back. How do I know she didn't target Jim from the start, seduce him with sex, twist his mind against me? The way she's clearly seducing Lance behind Susan's back.

An anger I've not felt since my friend showed me photos of Jim and Jade together consumes me. I act on instinct. Retrieve my phone from my bag, take several photos of Jade and Lance holding hands, then embracing once more, him kissing the top of her forehead.

I see her for what she really is. A heartless, conniving harlot who preys on married men, steals them from their wives. Like she gets some sort of kick out of it. Some kind of sick pleasure in breaking up families. I don't care that her mother was a bitch, that she had an unhappy childhood. If that's even true. And if it is, it seems being a bitch is in the genes.

I'll keep these photos safe. And I will continue to be Jade's friend. Be pleasant, attend her classes. And, when I feel the time is right, I will use them to expose Jade for what she is.

Chapter Thirty-Eight

Susan

Tuesday, 24 July 2018

'DI Bailey, how lovely to see you, please come through.'

It's not lovely to see him, he's the last person I wanted to see, so I'm not entirely sure why I said this. It's just who I am, I suppose. The flawless actress. I've faked my way through life this long, I'm hardly going to stop now.

'Thank you.'

Unlike the first time we met, there's no smile or pleasantries. His manner is curt. And he declines refreshments with an abrupt, 'No, thanks.' All this sits ill with me, and it's clear he's keen to get to the point once we are sat facing each other in the living room. Luckily Lance is at work, and both Michael and Stella are out too.

'Mrs Hampson, we know that your husband was having an affair with Jade Pascal.'

Fuck. I try not to appear flustered, hope the colour hasn't drained from my face.

'What?' I say.

It's a stupid reaction, but I can't think of anything more eloquent on the spot. 'How do you know this?' I say, trying to keep my voice measured.

'It's been confirmed from several sources. The first, a diary Jade kept.' *Fuck.* 'The second, by Natalie Marsden, her close friend.' *That meddling cow, Jade must have confided in her after all.* 'The third, by your husband.'

I can't believe my ears. Lance has dropped me in it. He's determined to get me into trouble. But why would he risk his reputation like that? Maybe he thinks I was bluffing about going to the papers. And the bastard son of a bitch would be right. I've been a shit mother, always put myself first, but I could never do that to my children. Having said that, there is another, more selfish reason why I don't want the press delving into our dirty laundry. And now I can't help wondering if Lance knows what it is.

'My husband?' I say.

'Yes. I spoke to him at his firm this morning. And just so you know, he has an alibi for Thursday night.'

'Does he now?'

'Yes, several colleagues have confirmed that he was with them at a bar in Fenchurch Street. And this has been further verified by CCTV.'

'I see.'

'He also claims that you asked him to break things off with Jade on Wednesday night. That he made a phone call to her right in front of you, around eleven p.m., using an unregistered mobile phone. Is that true?'

I hadn't believed it possible, but I hate the fucker even more.

'Yes, it's true.'

'Why unregistered? Your husband said you insisted he use the burner phone you'd purchased if he knew what was good for him. Do you still have the phone?'

I hesitate.

'Mrs Hampson?'

'No, I don't have the phone. I got rid of it.'

'Why? Why the secrecy?'

I can't tell him the truth. I'll get myself into even deeper water if I do, and the police will be the least of my worries.

'I can't say.'

'Why?'

'Let's just say I have my reasons, and it's safer if I keep them to myself.'

DI Bailey looks positively pissed off by my response. But he can't force me to come clean, even though my holding back has made him more suspicious of me than ever. He moves on. 'I'll ask you the same question I asked when we first met last Saturday, Mrs Hampson – where were you on Thursday night? Between the hours of nine thirty and midnight, when your husband says he got home. He told us he called the house twice, but no one picked up.'

I'm tempted to insist I was home, but something tells me that's exactly what he's goading me to do.

'I went for a drive.'

'A drive. Why? And don't lie, Mrs Hampson.'

'I couldn't think straight. I was reeling about the photos, about the fact that my husband had been cheating on me with my fitness instructor. No one was home and I was jittery.'

'Did you pay Jade a late-night visit, by any chance?'

'No!'

'Think about it, perhaps?'

'OK, yes, maybe I did, but I didn't act on it, I drove around then came straight home.'

'What do you think you would have said to Jade had you gone to see her?'

I don't respond. So he does the talking for me. 'Might it have had, by any chance, something to do with the fact that Jade refused to accede to your attempts at black-mail? Something, I'm guessing, you failed to tell your husband about. You confronted her on Wednesday night before the class, threatened to release photos of her and your husband you had somehow obtained, and when she made a counter-threat of her own, you were taken aback. Panicked, for want of a better word.'

I'm stunned. Stunned that Jade would have recorded all this in her diary. 'No, it most certainly did not,' I say defiantly, 'Lance broke up with her. Anything she's claimed in that diary of hers is pure fantasy.'

'How do you know about the diary?'

'Grace Maloney told me. She heard from Natalie.' I smile. 'Women talk, DI Bailey, don't you know that?'

His expression remains stern. 'Mrs Hampson, what is it you told Jade on the night of her birthday party last month? We know you told her a secret, and that Jade threatened to spill it last Wednesday night after you warned her to stay away from your husband.'

My head is about to explode. How can this be happening? I feel like my world is closing in on top of me.

'I told her nothing. I was drunk, goodness knows what I said. I can't remember much of that evening, to be honest. I told you, she's making it up.'

DI Bailey gives me another deadpan look. 'I don't believe you. I think you told her something pretty devast-ating, I don't know why but you did, and because she threw it back in your face you went to her flat on Thursday night, you had an argument and...'

'No, I told you, I only went for a drive. I never went to her flat.'

'But you went near it.'

I swallow hard.

'We have your car captured on CCTV driving along Victoria Road, the main high street running through Surbiton, around ten thirty on Thursday night. St James Road, where Jade's flat is situated, runs directly off Victoria Road and although it doesn't have CCTV, we do know your car made a left turn onto it. So, Mrs Hampson, are you still telling me you didn't pay Jade a visit that night?'

This is really starting to get to me now and I almost can't breathe. 'Look, I know it sounds like a crazy coincidence, but while I was driving I got a text from Michael, my son, telling me he'd got into a fight and that he needed me to pick him up on Maple Road, where he'd been drinking in a pub with his mates. You may know that Maple Road meets the bottom end of St James Road, so it was natural for me to turn down the latter. Funny thing was, I didn't recognise it as his number, but I knew it was him because he signed off with M and a peace emoji, like he always does. I was worried, it was so unlike him to want anything from me, so I drove there straight away in a panic. I thought maybe he'd lost his phone in the fight and was using a friend's. But when I got to the pub where he claimed he'd been drinking, there was no sign of him. I rang the number back but there was no response. It really freaked me out, and I drove straight home, feeling even more panicked, but hoping he'd perhaps made it home after all. But he wasn't there. I rang his usual number, and he answered, sounded perfectly fine. I was cross, asked him what he was playing at, but he swore he'd never sent me a text. I figured he'd been spammed, or his friends were playing a joke on him.'

Now I'm wondering if the joke is on me. This is all getting rather sinister. I never meant for things to get this far, but it's as if I'm being put through a roller coaster of emotional torture. And with DI Bailey's next question, the torture continues. 'Let me see the text.'

Fuck. 'The text?'

'Yes, the text, show me.'

'I deleted it.'

'You deleted it?'

I give an awkward nod.

'So, first you got rid of the burner phone. Then you did the same with this alleged text. How convenient.'

I'm suddenly hot all over and I'm certain my face must have gone bright crimson. 'I–I was alarmed when Michael said he never sent it. Although I hoped it might be one of his friends, I couldn't be sure, so I deleted it and blocked the number.'

'I see.' It's clear he's finding my explanation hard to believe. Like I'm scraping the barrel for excuses. And who can blame him? The interrogation goes on. 'How did you obtain photos of your husband with Jade? Did you have him followed?'

'No, they were sent to me. By email. I didn't recognise the address, and I've no idea who took them.'

'Did you ask your husband who he thought might have sent them?'

'Yes. He hadn't a clue either. I'm assuming you've already asked him.'

'Yes, he said the same. I need you to forward the email to me. It's possible it's encrypted, but my team will hopefully be able to work through that. Of course, if it was

264

sent from some random internet cafe, that makes tracing it back to an individual user harder, but we can try, see where it takes us.'

'Fine.'

DI Bailey leaves soon after and I sigh with relief. But my ordeal is by no means over. Not for one second did he believe me when I denied telling Jade my secret. He knows I'm lying, and I can't help wondering if there's anyone else who knows it too.

Someone who knows that I've been lying through my teeth all this time. And wants me to pay for it.

Chapter Thirty-Nine

Natalie

Tuesday, 24 July 2018

Since leaving Jack's grave I've not been able to stop thinking about the old woman who approached me. The fact that it was almost as if she could see into my soul, feel the hurt, regret and guilt I've been carrying all these years. I've heard of psychics reading people's thoughts before, but I'm not sure that applies here. She was kind enough, but there was also something unsettling about her, something I can't quite make sense of.

It's just gone two p.m. as I sit on a train at London Waterloo, waiting for it to set off. I'm not on my usual line back to Surbiton, though. I'm headed for Richmond. To see Dr Jenkins. I know if I go home I won't be able to relax. I've got too much on my mind, and it's making me feel on edge. Not just the old woman and what she said, but being caught on camera in Jade's street. It's disconcerting not being able to remember, and I'm frightened about what I might have done. Desperate for some clue, some confirmation I've got nothing to do with Jade's disappearance. Hopefully, Dr Jenkins can help me work through that.

Forty minutes later, I'm seated across from her. I want to admonish her for letting the police into my past, but I know how unfair that would be. She isn't to blame, and I need to stop being angry with people. Especially those who have been good to me. Like her, like Jade.

'Why did you lie to me, Natalie?' she asks.

'I didn't lie,' I say.

'You told me you hadn't been sleepwalking again.'

'No, I told you I didn't *think* I'd been sleepwalking.'

'But you knew you hadn't gone to bed that night. You woke up in your clothes, didn't you?'

'Yes,' I admit. 'I was scared. I couldn't bear to think I might have had something to do with Jade's disappearance. I still don't think that I could.'

'Why?'

'Because with my father, with Cath and Brian, they'd been cruel to me. They deserved it.'

'So had Jade, you said so yourself. You said you'd seen a side to her you'd never seen before, when she'd claimed you could never understand what it was to love a man, that you needed to butt out of her life. And you said she'd still been hostile on the phone, even though you'd made peace.'

She's right. She had been cruel. It was like a switch had been flicked. Almost as if she was intentionally being unkind. Like she was encouraging me to flip. After all, she knew about my past. Knew it could trigger all sorts of hang-ups from my childhood.

'That's true,' I nod. At the same time, I can't seem to get the old woman's voice out of my head.

'What is it, Natalie? Has something happened? How did this morning go? At Jack's grave.'

In my heart I know this is the reason I am here. I can't hold back any more. Can't run away from the truth.

Lately, since my argument with Jade, since her disappearance, since learning I was there on her street last Thursday, it's like my past is chasing me, catching up with me, bringing me to the point of confession.

So I tell Dr Jenkins about the old woman, about someone laying flowers at Jack's grave, about her parting words.

'Who do you think may have left the flowers?' she asks.

'I don't know,' I say.

'Could it have been you, without realising?'

The thought has occurred to me. 'I don't know.'

'I can see this woman has thrown you. Why is that?'

'Because it was almost as if she could sense my inner turmoil, see the burden I've been carrying all these years.'

The tears are forming now, my chest burning, my pulse accelerating. Dr Jenkins can tell I'm in pain, that I'm struggling. She's not meant to touch me, but just then she does something she's never done before. She gets up from her seat, comes over and kneels down in front of me. Takes my trembling hand in hers and squeezes it tight. 'Tell me, Natalie, tell me what you've been hiding all these years.'

This is the point of no return, and I know that once I tell Dr Jenkins, I'll have no choice but to tell DI Bailey too. I cannot bury my sins forever. That's what the old woman was saying to me.

Even so, I'm not brave enough to look her in the eye as I say, 'It wasn't Jack who killed Cath. It was me. He was branded a murderer because of me. He died because of me.'

Chapter Forty

Grace

Tuesday, 24 July 2018

I enter my house and drop the keys on the hall table. I feel exhausted. I always do after visiting my mother, but especially so today. Because of what I told her. She didn't take it in, of course. After I confessed to seeing Lance with Jade that night, to the renewed hatred I'd felt for Jade, she'd asked me if Dad was coming over for tea later. Part of me had wanted to cry, but the other part had found it almost comical. In fact, I'd almost envied her. Living in her own world, oblivious to everything. Human emotion is such a double-edged sword. To love and feel real joy being one of life's great pleasures; to feel pain and regret the way I do, a never-ending cycle of torture.

'I'm guessing you went to see your mother.'

I look up to see Jim standing there.

'Why are you here?' I say. 'I know you're not real. I know you are dead, so why are you here? Why do you continue to torment me?'

'Because that's exactly what you deserve.'

I put out my hand. 'Go, get out of my sight, get out of my head.'

I shut my eyes, shield them with my hands, tell myself he's just in my head, that I see him because I feel that I deserve to be in pain, to hurt, to suffer, to be reminded of what I did. It had been getting better for a while, I had been seeing him less, but since Jade's birthday last month, the visions have worsened.

'Don't walk away from me. I know what you did. Have you learned nothing? And now it seems you may have driven someone else to their death.'

'She deserved it. She told me she felt sorry for me, that she had forgiven me, had genuinely loved you. But she was a liar and a slut. A scheming slut who made a habit out of stealing husbands like it was sport to her.'

He's glaring at me now. 'She did love me. And I allowed her to love me because you stopped loving me. Stopped noticing me. You tried to take everything on, like some kind of hero, when you didn't have to!'

I put my hands over my ears, squeeze my eyes shut. 'Shut up, shut up!' I yell. 'Go away, leave me alone.' He's right, I know he is. I stopped being the person I was when it was just him and me, when we were young and had so much energy, fewer responsibilities. I did take on too much, and I shouldn't have done, but I also know I can't be the only woman in their mid-forties to have done so. We could have got through it, weathered the storm, we could have got counselling, but he was weak, the way men of a certain age can be. He betrayed me as much as I betrayed him. 'You aren't blameless in all this!' I scream. 'You stopped seeing me for me, the woman you fell in love with. How I wanted you to say come on, Grace, let's go away for the weekend, let's go out for a meal in London, get a babysitter, you get dressed up and we'll paint the town red. But you never did, it was too much effort for you and easier to look elsewhere rather than remember what we once had. I wanted to be made to feel special again, but you didn't see that. All you cared about was your own bruised ego, the fact that you weren't getting enough attention from your wife who only ever wanted the best for her family. Whose only crime was to love them!'

Silence. I daren't move or speak. Then, after perhaps ten seconds, I slowly remove my hands from my ears, open my eyes. He's gone. Thank God. But then the silence is shattered by the doorbell.

I retrace my steps back towards the front door, take a deep breath, then open it.

'Hello, Grace, may I have a word?'

It's DI Bailey, and from the look on his face I think I know why he's here.

Chapter Forty-One

Natalie

Tuesday, 24 July 2018

Looking at Dr Jenkins' expression, it's hard to tell what she's thinking right now. She's very good at hiding her feelings, it's part of her skill set, but there's perhaps something in her eyes that tells me she's in shock.

I can't blame her. In fact, she has every right to hate me, strike me off her patient list, pick up the phone to DI Bailey without a moment's hesitation and tell him she's been treating a liar and a murderer. Dr Jenkins is the one person I'm meant to confide in, reveal my darkest secrets to, things I'm ashamed of and need to let go of in order to fully heal. But I have committed a cardinal sin. I have kept the biggest secret imaginable from her, just as I have from the police and all my other therapists over the years. Partly because I was scared of what would become of me if I told the world what really happened that night, partly because it's what Jack had wanted; it was his plan after all, his plan to save his little sister, so if I told the truth, wouldn't that be dishonouring his wishes? Wouldn't that be rendering his death even more senseless than it already was?

Or is that just an excuse? An excuse because I am afraid of what might happen to me after I confess, and because it appeases my conscience to think he went down that path with his eyes wide open, that I never pushed him down it. In truth, although I've always told my therapists that living a reclusive, ordered lifestyle was my way of dealing with my anger issues, of containing my sleepwalking, I know there's more to it than that. Living a sheltered life before meeting Jade allowed me to hide from the truth. And the fewer people I mixed with, the less chance there was of my secret ever coming out. But meeting Jade, and now her disappearance, has upset the balance of things, and here I am, brought to the point of confession, scared in case it was me who attacked her last Thursday night, the way I attacked Cath in my sleep.

'This is quite an admission, Natalie,' Dr Jenkins says. She's moved away now, is back in her seat. Keeping her distance from a self-confessed murderer.

'Are you scared of me?' I ask, feeling the tears gather. Her body language is suddenly hostile and I already feel like a criminal. A monster even.

'Should I be?'

'No,' I say. 'I'd never harm anyone when I'm awake. It only happens when I'm stressed, when I sleepwalk. I wouldn't attack some random person, only someone who's hurt me. I feel certain of it.'

'Like Jade? She hurt you.'

As much as I want to refute that, I know I can't. Just because I don't have any concrete proof. 'I don't know. Yes, maybe, I guess I can't rule it out. Although my gut still tells me I didn't. Yes, we argued, yes, she said some cruel things, but not on the scale of what my father or Cath did to me. They physically abused me, for God's sake. I was a child. And besides, since then I've had lots of therapy, I'm a grown woman. I'm more in control.'

'And yet you were spotted on Jade's road the night she went missing.'

She has me there, and I can hear the doubt in her voice. I can't blame her after I've been keeping something so huge from her.

'Tell me what happened that night, Natalie. Tell me how Jack came to take the blame. Lie down on the couch and close your eyes if it helps.'

The last thing I want is to relive the memory of that hideous night, but I have no choice. I do as Dr Jenkins says and go over to her couch in the corner of the room, lie down and close my eyes.

'Take a few deep breaths before you start, Natalie.'

Her voice is more soothing now, and it gives me the courage to continue.

'The night I stabbed her she'd beaten me badly. Brian had been away, and she had taken one of his belts, stripped off my nightdress, forced me to stand facing her bedroom wall, my palms flat out in front of me and then proceeded to whip me across my bare back until it was red-raw and bleeding. I can still remember the sound it made as each stroke attacked my skin. That heart-stopping second as I waited for another one to be inflicted, the pain growing worse each time. She made everyone watch, including Jack.

"*That'll teach you not to steal, you filthy girl*," she'd said, a self-righteous grin spread across her face, her eyes glistening with delight at my suffering. All I had done was take an extra bit of bread for one of the other kids. Daisy. She was only six, a tiny, frail thing. I didn't tell Cath that, of course. Daisy was the sweetest little girl with the most sorrowful black eyes. I couldn't bear for her to punished, so I said the bread was for me. "*Like you need any more*

274

bread," Cath had scowled before striking me once more, at which point I had screamed out in agony. The other kids had watched in fear, including Jack. I'd glanced left between strikes to see him standing there and I could tell from the mad look in his eyes that he'd wanted to kill Cath himself. But he and I, we had an understanding, we knew each other's expressions, what the other was thinking without having to speak. And it was like he knew I was saying to him, "No, don't do anything stupid, Jack, it won't help, you'll only make things worse."

'I could see how it had killed him not to be able to defend his little sister, could see how powerless he felt, that he wanted to take control, and it had touched my heart. Knowing Jack was always there, that he cared for me – it's what got me through my early childhood.

'Later that night, when Cath was in bed, he'd fetched a cloth and some warm water with salt, along with some Savlon from the kitchen drawer where he knew Cath kept it, and he had bathed my wounds as I lay hunched in pain over the bed we were forced to share, despite the fact that by this point I was twelve and Jack had just turned thirteen. It took every effort not to scream because we didn't want to wake Cath, and I remember Jack giving me a pencil to bite down on, while he'd sung, "You Are My Sunshine" softly under his breath, the way he had done after my father abused me. The same song my mother would sing in one of her rare lucid moments. It's the only nice thing I can remember about her, her singing that song.'

'I'm so sorry, Natalie.' I don't need to open my eyes to see Dr Jenkins' expression. I can feel it from the tone of her voice. Gone is the hostility my confession had roused in her. And in its place, I hear sympathy and a profound

275

sadness. But I don't want to open my own eyes just yet. Lying down while I keep them closed is the only way I'll make it to the end of my story.

'So what happened after that?' Dr Jenkins asks. 'How did you come to kill Cath?'

'I remember eventually falling asleep that night on my side, because lying on my back was impossible. Jack had opened the jewellery box he'd given to me as a present for my tenth birthday to soothe me to sleep. I remember the little ballerina inside would stand and pirouette to music when you opened the lid. I'm not sure how he'd acquired it, I never asked and he never told me because I'm guessing he didn't want me to think any less of him. Not that I ever could, but that's how considerate he was, how important it was to him to give me some joy in my life. I loved that box, I still have it. Still play it when I'm feeling down. Even so, despite Jack's attempts to settle me with the lullaby it played, I know my sleep was always fretful. That I regularly got up around ten thirty and that Jack was always the one to find me and bring me back to bed. Anyway, going back to that night, the next thing I remember is being woken by Daisy's piercing scream early the next morning. The shrillest of sounds that I knew had come from tiny lungs. We'd all rushed to Cath and Brian's room – saw Daisy standing over Cath, shaking uncontrollably. I'd nearly vomited, there was just so much blood, it was everywhere. I'd stabbed her in the neck and the heart. At the time, I didn't know it was me who'd killed her, even though, perhaps intuitively, I worried I might have done. And although I felt sick, I remember also rejoicing inside that Cath was dead. Knowing that this might just be our ticket to freedom. Jack had said nothing at that point, but I realised later at the police station, after he'd taken the rap for me, that he'd found me, brought me back to our room, washed the blood off my hands and my nightie, before cleaning the knife and burying it under the floorboards.'

'And what happened then?'

'Being the oldest, Jack took charge. He was so kind, calming poor little Daisy down, as well as the others. He told me to take her hand, reassure her everything was going to be OK. The four of us had followed him downstairs, noticed that the back door was open, various cupboards too. But at that point we hadn't spotted that a knife had been taken from the block on the kitchen sideboard. We found the living room in a similar state of disarray: books overturned, drawers flung open. Although a part of me had felt relieved, just because it had all the classic signs of a break-in, the other part had still worried that I might be to blame. After all, I'd left the house before, attacked Dad, trashed Cath and Brian's bedroom. But I kept quiet because Jack said nothing to the effect that it could have been me, and I trusted him to do what was best, trusted him to take control. Which he did. He rang the police and they were round in a shot, surveying the scene as Jack guided them round, spotting the missing knife. Being kids, they were gentle with us. They wrapped us in blankets, took us to the station, had social workers come in to comfort us, make sure our mental health was OK, that we weren't suffering from PTSD or anything.

'And then, after a couple of hours had passed, they interviewed us in separate rooms. I was so scared, I'd never been left with a stranger before without Jack. I asked for him, but they said they needed to speak to us all separately first, but that a social worker would be allowed to stay with me. She was nice – Helen. She helped me a lot in the aftermath of Jack's arrest.

'I wasn't brave like Jack, and I was terrified of what lay ahead for me if it turned out I'd stabbed Cath and he wasn't around to comfort me. Helen had sat beside me while a police officer questioned me. I told him everything I knew, which was very little. Said I'd been in bed the whole time, fast asleep, and that hearing Daisy's ear-splitting scream had roused me from my peaceful slumber. I didn't dare tell them how Cath had beaten me the night before. Although I was only twelve, I understood enough to realise they'd think I'd have a motive for harming her. I didn't know that by this point, Brian was back, hysterical. That he'd named me as the troublemaker, told them about my history of violence and that, by definition, it had to have been me who'd killed his wife. The police officer went away after a time and then, after what felt like forever, he came back, having heard what Brian had to say. The other kids told the police how Cath had beaten me badly, so thankfully it wasn't long before he got his comeuppance. The trouble was that this, along with Brian's statement, meant the evidence pointed heavily towards me being the one who'd killed Cath. And as much as it had terrified me to admit it, my gut had told me I was guilty.' I pause, just because it's so painful reliving that time.

'What then, Natalie?' Dr Jenkins probes gently.

I think back to that moment. The moment that changed my life and ended Jack's before he'd had the chance to reach adulthood.

'I was in a state, shaking. Helen had tried to calm me down, told the police officer to bring Jack in. She could see that I was scared and needed my brother. Which I did. Badly. They told Jack what they thought had happened, and that's when he made the ultimate sacrifice. Like I already mentioned, he and I were so close we knew what the other was thinking just by looking into each other's eyes. And as he'd looked into mine, I knew what he was trying to say. He was telling me it was OK, that it wasn't my fault, that he knew I'd never intentionally murder another human being, which is why he'd tried to cover it up. And that's when he told them he'd done it. He knew I wouldn't be strong enough to survive what was to come if they arrested me. He told the police that seeing Cath beat me the previous night had been too much. That he was worried she might kill me, kill one of the others one day. He said he had stabbed Cath to death so she wouldn't hurt any more kids, and we'd all be free of her and her husband's evil clutches. He even gave them the location of the knife, which he had buried under the floorboards. Wiped clean of my fingerprints, of course, so that nothing could be traced back to me. I'll never know how he managed to get the blood off my nightie, but somehow he did. He also told them he'd opened the back door to make it seem like there'd been a random intruder.'

I stop for a while, feel emotionally drained, and yet it's a relief to get it all off my chest, this burden I've been carrying for eighteen years.

'Are you OK, Natalie?'

'Yes, Dr Jenkins, I'm OK.'

'I'm so sorry you went through all that.'

'Thank you, but I'm the one who should be saying sorry.' I open my eyes, slowly raise myself to an upright position, slide off the couch and go back to my chair facing Dr Jenkins.

'I wrote to him in the children's prison where they locked him up. I still can't believe they treated him like a murderer. I mean, yes, he killed someone in their eyes,

279

but surely they should have seen that he was driven to it? I had expected them to treat him differently, realise the trauma we'd all been through at Cath and Brian's evil hands. Allow some leniency for that. But for some reason they didn't. Jack always wrote back to me. He never let me down until the day he died. Never gave any hint of how miserable he might have been. He remained true to his word, as strong as ever, telling me he was OK, that one day he'd be out of there and he'd be able to look after me again. That it would always be him and me, until the end.' I pause, then add, 'He had such a way with words, he convinced me it would be OK. Just because I knew how smart, how strong he was. But he wasn't as strong as he'd thought he was. He was a boy in his teens, after all, stuck in a place with kids far more dangerous than him.' I pause again, tears streaming down my face. 'If I'd spoken up, Jack would still have been alive. He'd have a wife and kids, a brilliant job, another fifty years of his life to look forward to. I was weak, and I let him suffer, when I should have been the one to suffer.'

'But you have been suffering, Natalie, you've been suffering ever since he took the fall. But that was his choice, and you cannot blame yourself entirely. Jack was smart, as you said. He knew what he was doing.'

'Jack was a boy!' I yell. 'Yes, he was mature for his age, the life he'd been born into had forced him to be. But he was still only thirteen when they took him away. A gentle soul who wouldn't hurt a fly. But that's not how he'll be remembered. He'll be remembered as a murderer because of me.'

I'm suddenly sobbing hysterically, nearly two decades of guilt pouring out of me.

'You can change that, Natalie,' Dr Jenkins says.

I slowly look up at her, and seeing the expression on her face, I know exactly what she means.

'Yes, I know,' I say, the old woman's words at the cemetery echoing through my mind. 'Don't worry, I know what I have to do. I'm going to tell DI Bailey everything.'

Chapter Forty-Two

Grace

Tuesday, 24 July 2018

'Why did you lie to me, Grace?'

There's no point playing dumb or innocent. It's clear to me that DI Bailey knows the whole story, and I've been such a fool for thinking I could keep my past from him all this time.

'You've been delusional,' I hear Jim whisper into my ear. 'Delusional for thinking you could keep a secret like that all this time.'

'Grace, did you hear what I said?'

I don't mention to DI Bailey that right now he's competing for my attention. Just as Natalie was at the club last Friday when she asked me if I'd said something. I had heard Jim's voice in my ear telling me what a spiteful thing I did, sending photos of Lance with Jade to Susan. That I'd get found out. Deep inside my heart, and in that bit of my brain that's still capable of rational thought, I know I'm not well; I've not been well for a long, long time. Even before Jim and I were married, to be honest, although it was Dad's death and everything that happened after which accelerated things, not helped by the pills, of course. But the thing is, I have these wonderful moments of lucidity;

moments when I see everything so clearly, like I did earlier with Mum, moments when I almost feel like the Grace Jim fell in love with. And it's confusing. It makes me think I'm OK, when really, I'm not. Far from it.

'Why do you tell everyone that you live with your husband and children? Have a job. I know what happened in Southampton, so there's no point in denying it.'

I don't answer immediately. Then I say, 'You have a family, DI Bailey, you told me so.' He nods. 'And isn't it the greatest feeling, doesn't it make your heart swell with pride to talk about your wonderful wife, your beautiful children? Above everything else in your life – your job, your achievements, your time at college with your friends – isn't it your wife and children who you are most proud of? For whom you'd give up all that other stuff in a heart-beat?'

Another nod. 'I would.'

'I enjoy talking about my husband and my kids to people who don't know me from before, don't know what I did, what I lost, because it brings me solace. Just for that time, when I am at the club, having a drink with the women there, exchanging stories about our days, I can pretend all is well, pretend to live that life again, because there is no one there who knows otherwise. Until I come back to this empty house and the reality hits me like my heart's been ripped out.'

'But there is one person who knows otherwise, isn't there, Grace?'

I swallow hard. I suppose this means Jade wrote about me in her diary. I guess I shouldn't be surprised, now that I know what a compulsive liar she is. How could I ever have trusted her to keep her mouth shut? And yet, the guilt I can't help feeling, and which I confessed to my

283

mother, is still there. Fermenting inside me. All because I never intended for Jade to get hurt. I just wanted her humiliated, run out of town.

'Yes,' I say calmly. 'Jade.'

'Jade? Or do you know her better as Annabel?'

I flinch. 'I guess you learned that from her diary, too?'

'In answer to your question, we learned very little about your history with Jade from her diary.'

'Oh.' I feel a twinge of guilt. It's like the universe is conspiring against me to make me feel bad about myself. I'm guessing DI Bailey must have taken it upon himself to look into my past. With Jade missing all this time, he was bound to check out the background of everyone she associated with.

'Natalie Marsden gave us the initial heads-up, and my team has since dug deeper into your past.'

'Natalie? Jade told her? How long has she known?'

I'm puzzled, just because I've never sensed any bad vibes from Natalie. Always had the feeling she quite liked me. This is all getting stranger by the minute. Or is it my mind telling me that? Just because I haven't been able to think straight in a long time.

'You know how close Jade and Natalie are, how worried Natalie's been about her. She took it upon herself to visit Jade's old flatmate in Southampton to see if she might be able to shed any light on Jade's disappearance. A woman named Megan Stanley. Jade never told Natalie about what happened in Southampton.' He gives me a stern look, as if to say he knows it's crossed my mind that she might have done. 'Or spoke ill of you in her diary. She did say you both shared a painful secret, hinted at you acting slightly off with her, as if she'd done something to upset you, but she couldn't think what it was.'

I bite my tongue, try not to react. I thought I'd disguised my feelings well. But clearly not.

'According to Natalie, Jade was never very forthcoming about her time in Southampton. Simply said there wasn't much to tell and that it felt like another lifetime ago. Jade lived with Megan for nine years. So they were very close. Knew everything there was to know about each other.'

I sense where this is going and my palms are suddenly clammy. I want to rub them together, just for something to do, but I know it will only draw attention to my awkwardness. 'With nothing else to go on, Natalie went to see Megan on Sunday afternoon. Before my press conference. So Megan knew nothing about Jade's disappearance. She'd been alarmed, of course, eager to help in any way she could.'

'And?' I'm desperate, and yet almost too scared for him to get to the point.

'And Megan told Natalie that, contrary to what Jade had told everyone, she didn't quit being a PE teacher because she realised it wasn't for her. In fact, she loved her job at Dashwood Boys, it was everything she'd imagined it to be. The reason she quit was because of the tragedy she found herself a part of, following the exposure of her affair with the head of physics. Jim Maloney. Your husband.'

I feel my face burn, can't speak.

'I won't go into any more details because I realise how painful this is for you and we don't need to rehash all that. But I was hoping you might fill in some gaps. Like how you happened to end up joining the same health club where Jade worked, seventy miles from Southampton. We know Jade went back to London, changed her name and retrained as a fitness instructor, before getting a job at The

River Club two years after leaving Southampton. But how about you? How is it that, having been discharged from a psychiatric ward where you received fifteen months of treatment, you came to be living in Cobham, and yet attending your dead husband's ex-lover's classes at a club not in the least bit convenient to your new location? And before you answer that, Grace, I don't believe in coincidences. Not in cases like the one I'm dealing with right now. The truth, that's what I want. No more stories or fantasy worlds. Just the honest truth.'

I keep my head down, too full of shame and remorse to meet his gaze. Not just a detective facing me, but a father who no doubt thinks I must be Satan's spawn to have nearly led my children to their deaths. Even though I was out of my mind at the time.

I try to justify my actions to him. Tell him that Jim had been perfect to me in every way, just as I had thought I was perfect to him. But that I let things get on top of me. 'I neglected him,' I say. 'Took sleeping pills, drank too much, because despite being ready to drop and at the behest of everyone, I was too wired to sleep. Sex was the last thing I was interested in, and it pissed me off that he didn't seem to get what I was going through with my parents. I guess he picked up on that. And eventually looked elsewhere.'

'So you grabbed your kids from their beds in the middle of the night high on drink and prescription medication and drove them off the road to get revenge?'

At this, I feel the anger and pain consume me. 'Of course not, that was never my intention! I was angry, distraught on learning that the love of my life was having an affair with a young and beautiful woman. I'd taken diazepam, as you said, and I wasn't thinking straight. Everything I believed in came crashing down on me and it was like I was no longer capable of rational thought. All I thought about was taking the kids from him, teaching him a lesson, making him suffer. Not a day goes by when I don't regret what I did, when I don't suffer for it, but it was an accident. And the courts knew that. They knew I never meant to harm my kids. That's why they didn't put me in prison. That's why I spent fifteen months on a psychiatric ward.'

'You still haven't answered my question, though. Why did you join The River Club?'

'To study her, to see what it was about her, besides the obvious, that made him want her. But also, to make her life hell,' I answer honestly.

'And did you make her life hell? Why didn't she freak out? How did you convince her to go along with this pretence?'

I tell him about my encounter with Jade in the car park. How apologetic she'd been, how we'd reached an understanding to tolerate one another even though I'd been lying at that point and was merely looking to bide my time, study her life, her movements, so as to formulate a proper plan of revenge. 'One day, we had coffee, at her suggestion,' I explain. 'She opened up to me. Told me about her childhood, her mother, losing her father, and for the first time I felt sorry for her, and I realised that in many ways I'd been so much luckier than her. That she wasn't to blame for what happened with Jim. That she'd been filling an emptiness in both their lives.'

'But something happened to change your mind about Jade, didn't it, Grace?'

He knows about the photos. But how?

'You saw Lance Hampson with Jade, didn't you? On the night of her birthday party. You took photos with your phone and you sent them to Susan Hampson. You thought Jade had changed, but when you saw her with another woman's husband, a woman of a similar age to you, you got angry. You figured she'd been fooling you all along. Pretending to like you, but really laughing about you behind your back, just as she was laughing behind Susan's back. And all the memories of Southampton came flooding back, and this time, you couldn't allow her to get away with it. You couldn't say anything to Susan, or to anyone for that matter. You were too afraid of your past being exposed. So, you had to find another way. You had to make sure Susan received the photos, but anonymously, so it couldn't be traced back to you and someone like me wouldn't find out about your past. You knew how Susan would react. Unlike you, unlike Natalie, she's no shrinking violet. And she has money and means and powerful contacts. She is someone you knew would do anything to make sure Jade paid for her actions, who would metaphorically, and perhaps even physically, bury Jade for sleeping with her husband and threatening her lavish lifestyle.'

'I never meant for her to get hurt,' I protest. Right now, all I want is for the ground to swallow me up because that's where I belong. 'I just wanted to see her humiliated, exposed for the husband stealer she is. I wanted Martin, who worshipped the ground she walked on, and everyone at the club, to know what kind of woman she is, in the hope she'd be forced to leave with her tail between her legs. But now it's looking like something much worse might have happened to her, and it's all because of me, and the guilt is killing me.'

'You sent the photos from an internet cafe in New Malden, didn't you?'

'What?' I hear my voice, as fragile as glass.

'We traced the IP address to the Spring Cafe, showed your photo to the staff there, and one of them made a positive ID that you were sitting at a PC in the far corner last Tuesday from ten to ten twenty a.m. We have a copy of the email sent to Mrs Hampson attaching the photos sent at ten fifteen. Don't even try to deny it.'

'I don't deny it,' I say. 'But it was never my intention for Jade to go missing, to be physically harmed,' I repeat. 'I just wanted her to be humiliated, the way she humiliated me. I wanted to teach her a lesson. Wanted her to stop thinking it was OK to steal innocent women's husbands.'

'You think Susan Hampson is innocent?'

'She didn't deserve to be cheated on.'

'Didn't she?'

He knows something I don't. And to be fair, Susan isn't innocent. I've seen the way she leers at the young men at the gym, and not for one second do I believe she'd pass up on the chance to screw one. She was patently hiding something last Friday when Jade failed to show up and Natalie was asking questions. And it made me think that perhaps she had blackmailed Jade into quitting her job. I'd never thought her capable of taking things to another level, but now I'm starting to wonder if I've been naive in that regard. Perhaps she's committed a crime far worse than blackmail. I shudder at the thought, again can't help feeling guilty for what I've done now that I know Jade never told Natalie about our history. She kept up her side of the bargain, whereas I betrayed her trust in sending those photos to Susan. In truth, I didn't send them because I felt sorry for Susan. I sent them because I was still feeling sorry for me, because I needed to quench my own thirst for revenge.

Chapter Forty-Three

Susan

Wednesday, 25 July 2018

It's 6:15 p.m. and I've just arrived at the club. I couldn't sit at home a second longer. I need to let off some steam, release my stress in some other way than through alcohol. It's also important I show I've got nothing to hide, having stayed away on Monday because it had felt a bit too soon following Sunday's press conference announcing Jade's disappearance. I'm thinking of Vivien and Jill in particular, each of whom texted me earlier to see if I was coming tonight. They've both been questioned and have alibis, as does pretty much everyone else at the club, including Barry and Martin, making it even more important I act normal. OK, so the police know I confronted Jade about her and Lance, that I got Lance to break things off with her on Wednesday night. But that's all they know, and it doesn't make me a criminal. Doesn't mean I went to her flat on Thursday night and attacked her. Or that I got anyone else to. They have nothing that enables them to make that connection, from what I can tell. Jade might still have been the victim of a random prowler for all they know. Sure, she wrote something in her diary about me letting her in on a secret, and maybe they assume she threw that back in my face when I told her to stay away from Lance. But that's all they have – assumptions. It's my word against a missing girl's. They have no evidence, and they have no way of knowing or proving what I told her that night at her party. Plus, we were surrounded by witnesses. Witnesses who will testify to the fact that I was blind drunk. I can't let the situation get to me, can't let it ruin my life, screw with my mind. I need to carry on as normal, face everyone and act as if it's just another day at the gym. It'll seem more suspicious if I steer clear of the place.

As I walk through the turnstile, I spot Martin up ahead. He's perfectly pleasant, which reassures me he has no idea the police have been questioning me again about my possible role in Jade's disappearance. He looks worried, though. Poor thing. It's clear he's smitten with the girl. If only he knew what a conniving little bitch she was behind that Shirley Temple veneer. Acting like butter wouldn't melt to all and sundry, making everyone believe she had their best interests at heart, including Natalie. Ugh, speak of the devil, there she is up ahead, walking down the corridor.

I hadn't expected to see Natalie here again, though; certainly not tonight at least, not even a week since Jade's disappearance. I didn't think she'd set foot in the place again without her beloved Jade teaching the class. I'd expected her to be holed up in a dark corner crying her eyes out. I wonder why she is here. To spy on me? It's clear from what she's told DI Bailey she's out to poison his mind against me.

I won't avoid her, much as I want to, much as I can't bear the sight of her. If I do that, she'll think I definitely am hiding something.

I up my pace until I'm right alongside her. 'Hello, Natalie.' I project my voice deliberately and she jumps out of her skin. I try not to laugh.

'Sorry to startle you.' She stops short, looks me in the eye. Something of a fire in hers. I hadn't expected that, and I have to say it throws me.

'Are you?' she growls.

I give a forced laugh. 'What's that supposed to mean?'

'Well, you always say that, but I'm not stupid. It's obvious from the tone of your voice that you're not sorry, so why maintain this ridiculous charade?'

Again, her sharp retort is unexpected. And it makes me angry. Angry that this little freak has managed to make me feel stupid. ME! I don't like being made to feel stupid. Lance made me feel stupid years ago, and I showed him. More recently, his little slut made me feel stupid. And now her minion is doing the same. I need to get some level of control back, but somehow it feels like I'm losing my grip.

'Listen here,' I put my face up close to hers, 'what gives you the right to speak to me in that way?'

She doesn't budge. 'I could say the same. Just because I don't have your money, your rich husband, your big house, doesn't make my life worth any less than yours.'

I swallow hard, once again taken by surprise. It's almost as if rather than make her cower back into the hole she came from, Jade's disappearance has made her bolshier.

'What's come over you?' I ask.

'Let's just say I've realised that suppressing things, allowing myself to be trodden on, is doing me no good.'

I see my chance to get my own back. 'You're not referring to Jade, are you?'

She frowns. 'How do you mean?'

'That's exactly what she did to you, isn't it? Trod all over you, I mean. You allowed her to dictate your life, you followed her around like a doting puppy, rather than seeing yourself as her equal. Because you knew she didn't see you as her equal. Tell me it isn't true.'

She knows I'm right, and I can also tell from the look on her face, which is gradually becoming redder, that she knows something else. Something about Jade she's not letting me in on. I always knew she was hiding something, and now I'm desperate to find out what it is.

'What is it you know about Jade? You found something out, didn't you?'

'She did.'

I swivel round in surprise to see Grace standing there.

'Grace,' Natalie says, looking equally alarmed. 'I didn't expect to see you here.'

'I'm sure you didn't. And I could say the same. But perhaps you were secretly hoping I would be. As I'd hoped you would be too. I think we need to clear the air.'

'What the hell's going on?' I ask. Clearly these two are in on some secret information I'm not a party to.

I look at my watch. 'The class is about to start.'

'Forget the class,' Grace says. 'The three of us need to talk.'

'What about?' I ask. Like Natalie, Grace seems different. There's a conviction in her voice I've never heard. Suddenly, I feel the most vulnerable one here. How is this happening?

From her tone, I can tell she's not taking no for an answer. 'Let's go to the bar, it's quiet in there at the moment,' she says.

Five minutes later, we're seated around the table in the bar that's furthest away from the counter. Only a couple and another group of four sitting far enough away for us not to be heard.

I'm the only one who's ordered booze. Grace and Natalie both opting for diet lemonades.

'I sent you the photos of Jade with Lance,' Grace says.

I'm flabbergasted. And it makes me wonder what else she knows. 'You? Why?'

Grace proceeds to explain, and after she's finished, I can't speak.

Finally, I say, 'You *knew*?' It's obvious to me from her impassive expression that this hasn't come as a surprise to Natalie.

'I knew about Grace and Jade's history, yes. But not about the photos Grace sent to you. Now it's starting to make sense.'

'What do you mean, it's starting to make sense? How do you know about their history?'

After she's done explaining, the sliver of regret I was starting to feel with regard to Jade has been pulverised to oblivion. I feel no remorse whatsoever. She got exactly what she deserved.

'What have you done with her, Susan?' Natalie asks.

'Is that why you came here tonight?' I say. 'To interrogate me?'

'Ever since Jade didn't turn up last Friday, you've displayed no concern whatsoever,' Natalie says. 'You seemed positively pleased about it.'

'Why should I have been concerned? She's not my best friend. And judging by what you've just told me, it's good riddance.'

'No, she's not your best friend, she's your enemy. She was sleeping with your husband, so of course you'd want to be rid of her.'

'The police know you told her to back off and that you used the photos as leverage. That was my intention, I'll admit,' Grace says. 'But it was never my intention for her to get hurt. I just wanted her run out of town.'

'You told Jade something at the party that night, didn't you?' Natalie says, her eyes icy. 'And when you threatened to show the photos to Barry and Martin and God knows who else, she made a threat of her own, didn't she?'

I pick up my wine glass, take a big gulp. Right now, it's like swallowing acid.

'Who are you, fucking Miss Marple?' I say.

'Answer the bloody question!' Natalie demands, getting up from her seat. It almost feels like she's going to attack me.

'Sit down, Natalie.' All three of us turn to see DI Bailey and DS Khan standing there, before making their way towards us.

'Thank God,' I say. 'This girl is nuts. You might want to think about arresting her.'

'Susan Hampson, I'm arresting you on suspicion of the abduction of Jade Pascal. You do not have to say anything...'

'What the fuck?!' I scream, edging back as the room seems to shrink, everyone looking my way.

'...but it may harm your defence if you do not mention when questioned something which you later rely on in court. Anything you do say may be given in evidence.'

He grabs my arm, places the cuffs around my wrists, proceeds to lead me out like a common criminal. Natalie is shooting daggers at me, while Grace is giving me an equally stern look. The same look my son gives me. A look to say I don't trust you.

Chapter Forty-Four

Natalie

Wednesday, 25 July 2018

I'm dumbstruck, and yet, for the second time in less than two days, I feel some level of relief. It's as if two great weights have been lifted from my shoulders. The first, confessing to Dr Jenkins that I was the one who killed Cath. The second realising that I can't have had anything to do with Jade's disappearance. Although I don't know the grounds on which Susan has been arrested, the police must have strong evidence to have made such a move. I just hope and pray Jade's alive and that they find her soon.

It's just on eight p.m. as I switch on the kettle. After the police took Susan away, I didn't hang around long. I would have left sooner had Grace not asked me to stay a short while so she could explain.

At first I'd found it hard to look her in the eye, knowing she'd lied through her teeth; lied about her husband, her children, her job. What she'd done, her history with Jade. But then I realised how hypocritical that would have been of me, having killed someone with my own hands, having been indirectly responsible for my brother's death, even though I was persuaded by him that it was the only way. I've yet to tell the police. I promised Dr Jenkins that I would, and I will. I'm just not quite strong enough to do that yet. I will, though, once I know for sure what's happened to Jade. Once the whole business is sorted and I am fully in the clear. Hopefully I won't have to wait too much longer now.

As I listened to Grace tell her story, hearing the regret in her voice, I couldn't help feeling some level of sympathy for her. She loved her husband, really loved him, and she didn't deserve to be cheated on. He was at fault too; he was weak, he should have talked to her, told her what he was feeling, just as my brother should have talked to me. Not that my brother was weak. He was the strongest person I knew, and I've no doubt the reason he never told me how bad things were inside the prison was because he wanted to shield me from all that. That was his mission in life. To protect me. Even so, I wish he'd let me in that one time. Allowed me to help him.

All this time, I've tried to keep my life, my temper, in check, with rules and rituals. But now I realise this was my way of burying my secret. By focusing on routine, my mind had no time to focus on anything else, including my guilt. It's not the doctors' fault; I hid the truth from them, made them believe it was my father and foster parents' abuse that made me angry, and then later, my brother's untimely death. They didn't know I was carrying another form of anger, an anger that was consuming me inside – anger with myself for allowing Jack to take the blame. For allowing him to die. It's funny how it's taken Jade's disappearance to bring that out of me. I only wish I could see her again, tell her I'm sorry for not being truthful with her, sorry that she didn't feel able to confide in me about her past.

I take my herbal tea into the living room and switch on the TV, already tuned to the news channel, my attention immediately caught by the reporter who's standing in front of The River Club.

'A fifty-two-year-old woman has been arrested in connection with the disappearance of fitness instructor Jade Pascal. I'm standing in front of The River Club where Jade worked and was last seen on Thursday evening, having taught a Zumba class. According to the police, important evidence came to light earlier today connecting the accused to Jade's disappearance. If anyone thinks they may have seen or heard anything, or have any information whatsoever relating to Jade's disappearance, they should contact the number appearing at the bottom of the screen now.'

The image reverts back to the newsreader in the studio and as it does, I get a stabbing sensation in my head. Blurry images flashing through my brain. I press the palm of my hand against my temple and realise it's just stress. The stress of not knowing what's happened to Jade. It's why I've been dreaming of her in the shower. It's my mind imagining what might have played out that evening, rather than what actually did.

Hopefully, the wait will be over soon, and one way or another we'll know the truth.

Chapter Forty-Five

Susan

Wednesday, 25 July 2018, 8:30 p.m.

I wait for the interrogation to start. DI Bailey and DS Khan have just sat down in front of me, having made me wait on my own in the confines of this dreary interview room for thirty long minutes. No doubt they've been conspiring with one another as to how to play things with me. I'm betting DS Khan will start the ball rolling, playing good cop, and then DI Bailey will step in, try to break me. I know, I've watched enough police dramas on TV to imagine the set-up. I'm prepared.

I wonder if Lance knows yet. Wonder if he's told the children. They're probably doing cartwheels in the living room, throwing a party. Then again, me being arrested isn't going to do Lance's reputation at the office any favours, or Michael's at the firm he's not even started at yet. I don't care about Lance, but I do care about my children, no matter what they might think. That's why I still can't believe Lance confessed to his affair with Jade.

'Mrs Hampson, we asked you before why you were out driving late on Thursday night, and you claimed you just went for a drive to clear your head before receiving a message from your son to say he needed picking up outside a pub on Maple Road having got into a fight, but that when you went to fetch him he wasn't there, causing you to drive home.'

'Yes, that's right.'

'And you said you returned home around eleven p.m.?'

'Yes,' I nod.

'And when you got home, no one in your family was in the house.'

'Correct.'

'OK, leaving that aside, I want to show you something.' There's a folder in front of DS Khan. He opens it up and pulls out an A4-size sheet of paper. From upside down, it appears to be a printout of an email.

'What's this?'

He swivels it round.

'My officers have been trawling through Jade's emails and found this in a subfolder of her inbox marked "Miscellaneous".'

I feel like I'm going to be sick, having scanned the contents of the email. It's from me to Jade threatening to have her killed – not in those exact words, but the meaning is pretty clear – if she didn't back off and 'keep to her word'.

But the thing is, I didn't write it. So who the fuck did?

'I didn't write this!' I protest.

'This is your email address, correct?'

'Yes, but…'

'Sent at two p.m. on Thursday afternoon.'

'Yes, I can see that…'

'"Keep your mouth shut or I'll get someone to shut it for you."'

DS Khan holds my gaze, having recited what's written, and my chest is beating so fast I feel like I'm on the verge of a heart attack.

'I did not send this.' I try to keep my voice calm but it's a struggle. 'I must have been hacked.'

DS Khan leans forward ever so slightly, and now I can't even breathe.

'This is a clear threat on Jade's life. Tell me, did you follow through with your threat, Mrs Hampson?'

'No!'

Now DI Bailey cuts in. It's all been perfectly staged, perfectly timed, to this moment.

'Are you arguing with what's written here? With your own email address?'

'No, I mean, yes! Why would I be so stupid as to send a threatening email to Jade from my own email account? Someone is trying to frame me. Have you talked to Grace, to Natalie? There's something not right with them, and you know it. You know Grace is certified insane. She nearly killed her kids, for Christ's sake. Drove her husband, who you also know had an affair with Jade, to kill himself. Surely it's her you should be talking to. How do you know she isn't trying to frame me to get away with killing Jade? She's the one who sent the damn photos to me, for God's sake.'

I let that sink in as they sit back, appear to mull over my very valid point. I feel a mild sense of triumph. I can tell my idea doesn't seem so far-fetched to them, but I also realise they need something more if I am to solidify my case against Grace.

'Look, I already confessed to blackmailing Jade with the photos, to warning her to back off, to telling my husband to break things off with her. But that is all I did.

I had no idea the very next day she would go missing. But maybe that was Grace's plan. She sends the photos anonymously to me, knowing it would rile me, knowing I'd have it out with Jade and my husband, giving her free rein to do whatever she did with her, while casting aspersions on my character, knowing you'd somehow figure out Jade was having an affair with my husband.'

Again I let that settle, the air thick with tension.

'It's a good theory,' DI Bailey says. 'But it's still not enough to be able to release you. The fact is your car was caught on CCTV driving around that night, and we have an email sent from you to Jade that very afternoon threatening her life.' He pauses, then says, 'Is there anything else?'

I can't hold back any more. I have to tell them everything in the hope they'll believe I had nothing to do with Jade's disappearance, even if I was glad about it. 'OK, I wanted to make sure Jade was gone, wanted to force her to resign, stay away from my husband. I wasn't sure Lance telling her it was over would be enough. I don't want to name names, DI Bailey, but let's just say I have friends with influence.' I think of Lorenzo, Lance's client, his richest, most loyal client, but, more importantly, a man who can get things done. A man I know has used less than salubrious means to get what he wants, to become the powerful businessman he is today. 'Rich, powerful friends,' I continue, 'who have people who take care of things for them. I asked one such friend for a favour. Asked him to send Jade a message.'

'Message, what kind of message?'

'A message to the effect that if she didn't cut all ties with Lance and keep her mouth shut, someone would shut it for her.'

'The exact same wording you used in your email. What a coincidence.'

'I agree, it is a coincidence! But why the hell would I send her an email if I'd already got someone to do the job for me? It doesn't make sense.'

'So you're admitting you had some thug threaten her life? How did they do it?'

I take a deep breath, then say, 'I'm not an expert in these things, and I don't know the details, but I'm guessing they cornered her on the street or near her home. It's always more effective in person, so my contact tells me. But they didn't follow through with their threat to harm her. It was too soon. I wanted to give Jade a chance. They wouldn't have acted that same night, and my contact swore to me they hadn't laid a finger on her.'

DI Bailey looks at me like he doesn't believe me. As if to say my supposed email trumps my other convoluted explanation. 'Why go to such lengths if Lance broke things off with Jade over the phone right in front of you, and knowing you had photos you could show Jade's employers? There's only one explanation I can think of, which is that Jade had something on you. What is it, Mrs Hampson? I think it's about time you told us the secret you disclosed to Jade on the night of her party. A secret I think she planned on revealing to the world after you blackmailed her.'

Chapter Forty-Six

Susan

June 1988

I watch her from across the street, coming out of Wimpy, a takeaway bag in one hand, a paper cup in the other. She's a pretty little thing. Prettier than I'd cared to imagine. Raven-haired, petite and waiflike, so fragile it's almost as if, should a gust of wind come along, she'd be blown away like *Dorothy*. Even with that unsightly bump of hers on full display. I'm guessing she's popped out on her lunch break, and now she'll be heading back to her father's jewellery store, one street away, where I know she works part-time to pay her way through nursing school. Such a good girl, such a hard worker, such a *do-gooder*. So unlike me. I wouldn't be here, bothering her, if I hadn't heard from Tam that Lance has secretly been trying to win her back. Tam said her spies saw them meeting up for a drink in a cosy corner of a wine bar in Putney – she was on the OJ, of course – and that he'd looked completely love-struck, his hand every now and again taking hers, folding it like a precious jewel he couldn't bear to let go of. He never told me any of this, of course. After seven months of seeing each other, our dates have become more and more infrequent, and lately, after sex, he gets up and leaves, rather than staying over. He's short, distant, and I can tell he's working up the courage to end things, the initial passion having fizzled out, and has only let it go on this long because Tam scares the shit out of him. Alan, his good mate, is good mates with Tam, and perhaps he's afraid of them making trouble for poor, sweet Ellen. Hearing about their rendezvous was bad enough, but learning she's also carrying his child had made me green with envy, and I realised then that there was no time to lose, that I had to act now or lose him forever. And so, Tam and I had made a plan. A plan I am now going to put into action.

Like a powerful and unstoppable gust of wind, I'm going to blow dear little Dorothy away, and out of our lives for good.

I very much doubt he's mentioned me to her; he wouldn't want to do anything to risk losing her again. Even so, I am slightly nervous as I wait, maybe half an hour, just to give the poor thing some time to eat her lunch. What if she does know all about me, what I look like, and the plan backfires? I tell myself I can't think like that. That I must act confident, make out I have no idea who or what she is to Lance.

Thinking she must be done with her lunch by now, I make my way towards her father's shop. A sly glance through the door and I see to my delight that she's behind the counter serving a customer who's checking out various silver bracelets. I stick to my plan, go inside and head over to a display cabinet offering a selection of men's wedding bands. After a time, the customer leaves and she and I are alone. I look up, catch her eye across the shop floor. She smiles at me pleasantly, comes over, says, 'Can I help you, madam?'

'Yes,' I smile brightly, the smile of a woman in love. Then gush, 'My boyfriend asked me to marry him at the weekend.' I hold out my left hand, the four-carat diamond and platinum engagement ring I borrowed from Tam glimmering under the lights of the shop. I do my best to look elated, and her face lights up like the brightest of stars. A slight guilt tugs at my insides, but I force it down.

'Oh wow, congratulations!' she says. 'You must be on cloud nine, it's SO exciting.'

'Yes, it is.' My gaze travels to her bump. 'This time next year I hope to be in your position. When are you due?'

'Ah, not for another eight weeks. Still cooking.' She pats her stomach and I want to vomit.

'Aww,' I say. 'Anyway, I couldn't wait to check out some men's wedding bands. Obviously I'd like to bring my fiancé with me at some point, but I wanted to get a head start. Just so excited.'

'I can understand that,' she says with the same grin. 'I'd be the same.'

'You're not married?' I say, my eyeline resting on her bare ring finger, before returning to her bump. 'Sorry, couldn't help but notice you're not wearing a ring.'

She blushes. Poor thing must feel so embarrassed. Shame. 'Afraid not. Bit complicated. I split up with the father just before I found out I was pregnant. I didn't want him feeling sorry for me, didn't want him to think he owed me anything, so I never told him.'

'Oh, I'm so sorry.' I pull a sad face.

'Oh, it's OK, we're back together now.' She smiles.

'You are? How wonderful. I'm sorry to pry, but it's such a lovely story, do tell all. I so love a happy ending.'

'Oh, don't be silly,' she giggles. 'I quite like telling it.'

I bet you do.

'Go on then, I'm dying to hear.'

She proceeds to tell me how Lance had rung her up out of the blue around a month ago. Said he was desperate to see her, that he hadn't stopped thinking about her, wanted to talk things through. She'd been reluctant, couldn't bear the thought of getting hurt again. Apparently, they'd split up ten months ago over his choice of friends, her feeling that he'd changed since falling in with the law crowd, who she viewed as shallow, money-orientated and full of themselves. But he'd realised his mistake, realised he'd been an arse, that his glossy new life was superficial nonsense (no doubt he included me in the same category), and all he wanted was for her to give him another chance. So, she'd agreed to meet him. At the wine bar Tam's friend had spotted them in together. He'd been shocked to discover she was pregnant with his child, of course, but when he'd got over the shock, Ellen had seen the tears in his eyes as he'd told her that he'd never wanted anything more than to be a part of his baby's life. Not just his baby's life, but her life. He wanted them to be together, as a family.

So touching. So moving. So finger-down-the throat nauseating.

'Oh my gosh, that really is the stuff of fairy tales,' I say. 'Have you set a date?'

'No, I want to have the baby first, lose all the weight.'

'Oh yes, of course, for that *dream* dress. I'd be the same.'

I let that settle a moment or two and then we spend the next twenty minutes looking at men's wedding bands. I tell her I think I know which one he'll go for, but reiterate that I'd like to bring him into the shop one day to have a look for himself. 'He's not that great on surprises,' I say. 'So I think it's better to be safe than sorry.'

'Absolutely, you want to be sure he'll like it.'

'Indeed. We're quite different. Unlike him, I enjoy being surprised. Are you the same? I think all women are.'

I receive an enthusiastic nod. 'So, I take it you'd like him to choose your wedding band?'

'I would,' I grin. 'I mean, I *adore* his choice of engagement ring,' I thrust out my ring finger again, 'he just knows me so well, so I'm sure I'll be equally as thrilled with the wedding band. I was a bit cheeky, actually, told him to surprise me again.'

'Oh yes, he definitely has good taste. And it fits your finger like a glove.'

'It does,' I gush once more. 'And I think it's so romantic when men go to so much trouble. It proves how much they love you, don't you think?'

'Definitely, you've got a keeper there.'

'I think so,' I nod. 'But it has to be said, I've seen a few here I adore. Your shop has some real gems. If you'll excuse the pun.'

'Thank you, the business has been in the family several generations.'

'And it shows. That's why I'm going to recommend he come here to look. Rather than some soulless chain or overhyped store on Bond Street. I'd much prefer you having our custom.'

Another sweet smile. 'Thank you, that's very kind.'

'Not at all.'

'Do you have a photograph?' she asks.

Bingo.

'So I can recognise him when he comes in. Also, I don't work Wednesdays, and in case he comes in that day I can make sure whoever's covering looks out for your fiancé. You've been so lovely, I want to make sure we provide the best possible service.'

'Ah, how amazing. So kind. Yes, of course I do.'

My heart thumping with anticipation, I delve into my handbag and pull out a photo of Lance and me taken at one of Tam's parties around two months ago. As usual we'd drunk too much, our cheeks pressed up against each other. Seemingly joined at the hip. No one would be able to tell that he was already tiring of me. He hadn't said anything, I just knew, could feel it, the way only the female of the species can.

'Here he is,' I sigh. 'The love of my life.'

I watch her face fall. Her eyes awash with shock, all the colour fading from her blooming cheeks.

And then, before I can say another word, she faints before my very eyes.

My work here is done.

Chapter Forty-Seven

Susan

Wednesday, 25 July 2018

I never expected to feel relief, but I do. I've carried this secret, this burden for so long, it had become a millstone around my neck. It's ironic, really. I wanted Lance to be free of Ellen so that I could have him to myself. But ever since that day, rather than feel free, I've felt trapped. Trapped within my guilt, within a never-ending cycle of self-loathing over the consequences of my actions. And yet never finding it in myself to confess, to seek forgiveness.

'I didn't mean for her to die,' I say. 'Didn't mean for her to go into early labour and suffer a massive haemorrhage on the operating table, for the child to die from complications too.'

Both detectives eye me like I'm scum. Not unlike the hatred I'm used to feeling from my husband and, to a lesser extent, my own children.

'What did you intend?' DI Bailey asks.

'Just to get her out of the picture, for her to think Lance was a liar and had been playing her for a fool and that she was better off without him.'

'Lance must have been heartbroken by her death, along with the death of his child. How did you convince him to stay with you?'

I'm sickened by myself as I say the words I've known to be true all this time, but had never confessed to anyone. Besides Tam. 'I told him I was pregnant. Which I was.'

'With his child?'

'No, I had a one-night stand after I found out he was trying to get back with Ellen.'

'Cameron, your elder son?'

'Yes.'

'And I'm guessing he doesn't know Cameron isn't his?'

I shake my head vehemently. 'No, and he must never know, it'll kill him.'

'Are you sure that's what you're worried about?' DI Bailey asks. 'Or are you more concerned about him killing *you*?' I open my mouth to speak but he doesn't let me finish. 'Rather than express remorse for your actions which, without doubt, led to the death of a young girl and her child, rather than confessing your sins to Lance, you took it upon yourself to capitalise further on his loss and your unexpected pregnancy by lying to him once more. Tell me, how were you able to live with yourself, Mrs Hampson?'

My hands are shaking now, and I can't help but flex my jaw to stop my entire body from shaking. The answer to his question is that I'm not sure. Maybe it's just how I'm built. Some defect in me that allows me to carry on despite the guilt metastasising in me day by day. But it's caught up with me now. And soon Lance will know, and I'll have lost everything I was so desperate to hold onto.

'Why did you tell Jade?' DI Bailey stirs me from my thoughts. 'Why tell a relative stranger, someone you've said yourself was "just your class instructor" something so big, when you knew it would be disastrous for you were she to reveal your secret?'

'I'm not entirely sure how it happened,' I answer truth-fully. 'I mean, I didn't know she was sleeping with my husband at the time, for a start. I was very, very drunk, I know that, and I tend to say things I shouldn't when I've had too much. I'd also had a bad fight with Lance before the party. It had almost felt like he'd deliberately set out to pick a fight with me. I remember him calling me petty, and useless, that I only married him because I wasn't smart enough to stand on my own two feet. That I was too selfish and incapable of bringing up a child on my own. He'd made me feel so small, so stupid, like I had no brain. And I guess I was angry, and Jade could tell I was upset about something, and she'd asked me what was up, that she was good at keeping secrets – something we now know is true, based on her history with Grace – and so I guess I just couldn't help spilling the beans. I don't remember telling her about Cameron, though. Just Ellen, what I said to her in the jewellery shop that day. What happened after.'

'And what did she say?'

'She was shocked, of course, but promised to keep it a secret.'

Just then, there's a knock on the door. DI Bailey looks up and over my shoulder, gives a slight nod of his head. I turn around and see a police officer I don't recognise standing there. 'Sir, you're needed.'

DI Bailey gets up, tells DS Khan to accompany him, and once again I am alone. Left to stew. Left to wonder what fate awaits me.

Chapter Forty-Eight

Natalie

Wednesday, 25 July 2018

Having gone to bed early feeling shattered, I'm having the best sleep in a long time – no nightmares, no tossing and turning – when a banging on my door wakes me with a start. For a moment, I think I must be dreaming, but when the banging doesn't stop and I look around and pinch myself, realise I am awake, then I know this is real. For a fleeting moment, I wonder if it's Jade. Back in my life, alive and well. But when I go to the window and peer down at the street, a sense of alarm rushes through me. It's not Jade.

It's the police.

Perhaps they're here to deliver bad news or, on the flip side, tell me they've found Jade safe and sound and that she's asking for me? I wonder what Susan told them, whether she buckled under pressure, confessed to being the one who attacked Jade, perhaps in a fit of rage. Who knows? It's hard to believe even Susan would intentionally go to Jade's place to kill her. And how would she have got the body out? I suppose she is rich, possibly has friends in all the right places. There's no point me speculating, I need to go and find out.

I rush downstairs as the doorbell goes. I'm still half asleep, can only get down there so fast and find myself nearly tripping over in the process.

Finally, I'm at the door. I open it, see DI Bailey and DS Khan standing there.

'What is it?' I ask, almost breathless. 'Have you found Jade? Did Susan confess?'

'No. We no longer believe Mrs Hampson is behind Jade's disappearance.'

Both detectives are wearing grim expressions.

'You don't?' I say.

'No, we do not. Miss Marsden, do you have a basement?'

My heart jerks. Why are they asking me this? 'Yes,' I reply.

'May we take a look?' Before I know it, both detectives are inside my house. They push past me, eyes everywhere.

I don't want to believe it, but at the same time I realise where this is going. They think I've got Jade trapped downstairs in my basement. But I never go down there. I hate basements, have done ever since Cath and Brian would regularly banish me to theirs as punishment. Where it was dark, damp and cold, full of spiders and rats. I'd never go down there in the cold light of day, let alone at night. I'd be too afraid. But just as I contemplate this, the most hideous scenario occurs to me. I'd never go down there intentionally, but what about when I'm sleepwalking? Would I do so then?

'I need you to take me to your basement now.' DI Bailey's voice is harsher still, an iciness to his glare that tells me I need to do as he says without complaint.

Panic takes hold of me, and it feels like something's trapped in my windpipe as I steer them to the door adjacent to the living room which leads down to the basement. There's a bolt across the top as well as a Chubb key which I always keep in the lock. I turn it, unbolt the top lock, push the door to, switch on the light at the top of the stairs, but before I can say another word, the detectives have pushed past me and are racing down the stairs, calling out Jade's name.

I daren't go down there, I'm too afraid of what I might find, and as I wait for them to reappear, hearing their voices continue to call out Jade's name, I want to be sick.

'Here, sir.'

Shock and utter despair rip through me as I hear those words telling me they've found something, and I can't stop myself from falling to my knees as the ghastly truth is laid bare.

Chapter Forty-Nine

Natalie

Wednesday, 25 July 2018

Jade's alive, and I should be rejoicing. But all I can think about is her shell-shocked appearance at the top of my basement stairs. Knowing that I am responsible for her incarceration. I look at the photograph DI Bailey has thrust in front of me. An image of me with Jade last Thursday night. We're standing outside my house. Jade is in front of me and appears to be unlocking my front door while I lag just behind. I can't believe it. There's no arguing with what I'm seeing, I just wish I knew what happened. Unlike the night I attacked Dad and Cath, I want to remember because I still can't believe I'd have hurt Jade.

'This photo was sent to us anonymously.'

'That's odd, isn't it?' I say. 'Why would the sender want to stay anonymous?'

'It's a police investigation. We get hundreds of anonymous calls and messages. That's not the point, Natalie, because you can't argue with what we're looking at here. You say you don't remember Jade bringing you back to your house that night after you turned up on her street?' I shake my head. 'But I'm guessing that's what happened here.'

Tears are streaming down my face as I reply, 'I don't remember. You know I sleepwalk, you know my history from Dr Jenkins, I don't remember the things I do when I'm asleep.'

'Like killing Cath Porter?'

My heart stops. 'You know?'

'We spoke to Dr Jenkins. Why didn't you tell us?'

'Because I was scared. I only told Dr Jenkins yesterday. I was going to tell you, please believe me.'

'When? After Susan Hampson was charged? Taking the suspicion off you?'

'No!'

'Did you hold back in the hope Susan was charged because you hated her for belittling you, because you hated her husband for having an affair with your best friend, and you wanted to bring down their entire family? Cause them untold misery?'

'What? No!'

'Susan made you feel small, didn't she? And so did Jade when you argued last Monday. She betrayed your friendship, talked down to you the way Susan did. So you made a plan to punish them both in one fell swoop, didn't you? You hacked into Susan's account on Thursday afternoon and sent a threatening email from her to Jade to frame her.'

I shake my head, run my fingers through my hair, unable to believe what I'm hearing. 'What? No, I did not! I don't know the first thing about hacking. I told you, I don't remember anything of that night. That's what happens when I sleepwalk. I don't remember!'

DI Bailey sits back in silence, as if pondering my response. I wonder, was he testing me just now, wanting to gauge my reaction? Looking at his expression, I get

317

the feeling he believes me when I say I genuinely don't remember the events of Thursday night. That nothing about what I may have done was premeditated. 'OK, let's assume I give you the benefit of the doubt about not being able to remember. In that case, let me tell you what I think happened. I think you sleepwalked to Jade's house, and that she realised you weren't yourself. She took you home, but then, when you got inside, you turned on her, threw her in your basement to punish her for the way she'd treated you. The way Cath would punish you. Isn't it possible that's what happened?'

I want to say no, it's not possible, because I would never hurt Jade. But how can I say that, based on the terrible things I've done while having no recollection of doing them?

'And what does Jade say? Is that what she said happened?'

'We've not been able to speak to her properly yet, she's too weak, having survived on the tinned food and bottled water you keep down there. Well, the ring-pull ones she was able to open and weren't out of date or inedible. We noticed an excess of toilet rolls and soap, too. What's all that about, Natalie?'

'I like to be prepared in case of an emergency, some kind of national crisis. I've got no one else to look out for me. It's just been me since Jack died and I left foster care.'

'How long have the provisions been down there?'

'Since I moved in. I didn't even put them there, I got the delivery driver to do it for me. I avoid the basement at all costs.'

Silence, as both detectives continue to stare at me like I'm guilty as charged. Which I might well be, despite having no recollection of that night. I just wish I could have spoken to Jade, but she could barely open her eyes, and they'd whisked her off in an ambulance before I'd even had the chance to try.

After that, they'd arrested me, and now here I am in a holding cell at Kingston Police Station. Being interrogated and made to feel like I'm not fit to be a part of society.

Perhaps they are right.

Chapter Fifty

Susan

Thursday, 26 July 2018

I should feel relieved to be home. To be free and off the hook for Jade's disappearance. But prison might well have been a better option. Last night, when I got home from the station around midnight, after the police released me based on further evidence that had come to light, and which I have since learned led to Natalie's arrest, Lance was waiting for me.

Sitting on the sofa, a glass of Scotch in one hand, he'd demanded the truth. Why I had been arrested in connection with Jade's disappearance, what I had told the police. There was no running away from it. He would have found out eventually, and I didn't have the energy to keep it from him a second longer. I realised it was karma for my sins. My penance for lying to him not once but twice all those years ago. For ruining a girl's life, for ruining Lance's, all because of my own selfish thirst to be part of a society I wasn't born into, but which I had craved like water in the desert. As Lance had sat there, his gaze burning through me, the detectives' faces after I'd told them my secret had flashed through my mind. Looks of pure and utter scorn for who I was and what I'd done, and for the first time in my life I had felt genuine remorse.

I'd carried this burden around with me for so long, and yet I'd never admitted to myself that I was truly sorry for my actions. That I was to blame for Ellen dying and losing her child. For causing Lance a lifetime of unhappiness with a woman he never loved. And in the end I'd also admitted that Cameron wasn't his child, but that I had pretended he was to secure the trap I'd planned to perfection.

As I'd expected, he'd erupted, and at one point I thought he might actually kill me, but somehow, he'd restrained himself, telling me I deserved to rot in hell. It's strange, he'd almost seemed more shocked about Cameron than about Ellen, perhaps because unlike Ellen, unlike his dead child, Cameron isn't someone who only exists in his mind. He is someone he must face every day, a constant reminder of my deception and the last thirty years being based on a lie. I suppose it was as if I had caused him to lose two children in the space of the fifteen minutes in which I had revealed my sins to him, and for that, I can never forgive myself.

He'd risen from his seat, walked my way, stopped a few inches from me, and I can still hear the words he'd whispered into my ear with a venom that took my breath away.

'I'm filing for divorce tomorrow, and you will agree to a quiet settlement and the bare minimum. You will leave this house, you will relinquish your five-star holidays, your Mercedes and your spa sessions. You will get a job and live a frugal life. And if you do all that, I won't tell our children what you did, and I will continue to love Cameron and be the father he's always known. Do we have an agreement?'

I was shaking as he'd said this, but I didn't dare disagree. I'd simply nodded, waited for him to leave the room, and then I had collapsed to the floor and wept.

It's eleven a.m. now, and the children, who know nothing of our divorce just yet, are out. As usual, Lance is at work. Before he left this morning he told me he wants me out by the weekend, but the fact is I have nowhere to go. The disgrace is too much, and I know that for all my bravado, without money, without the material things in life that have kept me going all these years, I am nothing. I can't bear to live that kind of life; it's too late to mend my ways and be a good person. I was never built for that, I cannot change.

So I take the only option that's left for me. Stella always comments how I pop paracetamol like smarties. Well, now I'm going to prove her right. I unscrew the bottle of gin and pour myself a large glass, neat, then gather up the two dozen capsules I emptied from the stash I keep in my bedside drawer for hangovers, stuff them in my mouth and wash them down with the mother's ruin.

My final thought being how true that saying is.

Chapter Fifty-One

Grace

Thursday, 26 July 2018

It's three p.m., and I've just arrived at Kingston Hospital where Jade is being held under observation. There's nothing much physically wrong with her; it's the psychological scars that will take time to heal.

'I'm here to see Jade Pascal,' I say. The nurse on reception asks for my name and I give it to her. I called ahead to check if Jade was OK with me coming to see her. I'd half expected her to tell me to go to hell, having learned that I was the one who sent the photos of her and Lance to Susan. But to my surprise she'd told the nurse on duty it was fine for me to pay her a visit this afternoon. I try not to glean too much comfort from this; perhaps she plans on telling me to get lost to my face.

Anyway, here I am, not quite knowing what it is I'm going to say, terrified of what she might say to me, and yet curious to learn more about the circumstances that have led her here.

Since coming clean about my past, my fake life, I've stopped seeing Jim. It's as if no longer pretending to live a life that I lost a long time ago has freed my mind.

I cancelled my membership at The River Club. I can't face going back there again after all that's happened, and anyhow, I need to move on, make a fresh start. I intend to make contact with Jim's parents, try and make them see that I've changed, ask if they'd be willing for me to come and see the boys, for even just an hour a week, on the condition I get regular therapy. If they agree, I'll move their way, move Mum to a home nearby, of course, but as yet I've not decided where exactly.

I still can't believe Jade's been a prisoner in Natalie's basement all this time. I always thought Natalie was strange, but I had no idea what a troubled past she'd had. Jade was a good friend, good at keeping other people's secrets, it seems; she had never once mentioned Natalie's terrible childhood to me, or her history of sleepwalking. But perhaps if she had told someone, we might have found her quicker.

The nurse tells me Jade is in room six, then lets me through the controlled doors. I reach Jade's door, give it a gentle knock, hear a faint voice telling me to come in.

Hospital doors are never locked, I know that from experience. I turn the handle and push the door open, immediately spy Jade lying on the bed, a drip in her arm. She looks pale, a haunted air about her.

She turns her head to look at me. 'Hello, Grace.' Tentatively, I approach the bed. 'Come, sit,' she beckons.

I sit in the chair next to her. Seeing her lying in the hospital bed, I feel a twinge of guilt, but I tell myself it's not my actions that have led her to this state. In the end, my sending Susan the photos had nothing to do with her disappearance. Natalie is the one who took her, because she was angry and jealous and didn't know what she was doing at the time. Acting out her subconscious thoughts in her sleep.

'I'm sorry I sent the photos to Susan,' I say. 'But I was so mad. You told me you loved Jim, that you didn't make a habit of stealing husbands, but when I saw you with Lance, when I heard the things you said, about being able to fool women like her, psychotic women, in fact, it felt like you were talking about me, and that the friendship we'd created had been a lie.'

'I know, and I am sorry for that,' she says. 'I guess it's a defect in me. That old sugar daddy cliché. I have a habit of falling for older men. And I saw a pain in Lance the way I saw a pain in Jim. Only the circumstances were different. Unlike Susan, I know you're a good person deep down. I know you feel remorse. And I know you never meant for your children to get hurt, or for Jim to die.'

'So why did you say those things?'

She hesitates. 'I-I guess I wanted to reassure Lance I could handle things.'

As she looks into my eyes, I get the feeling she's hiding something.

'Can I ask what happened? With Natalie, I mean?'

She props herself up slightly on the bed, asks me to hand her the glass of water on her bedside table, which I do.

'I came home from the class around ten p.m. Natalie and I had had a falling-out over Lance on the Monday, and I was pretty awful to her, it has to be said. She was livid, and I could tell our argument had affected her badly. Things had already been a bit tense between us because she didn't approve of Lance, and she'd admitted she hadn't been sleeping well for some time. I knew about her history of sleepwalking, that she'd done some violent things in her sleep like attacking her Dad without realising it, and it had worried me. Scared me, to be honest. She just

325

seemed so wound up. I didn't want to rock the boat too much, though, so I set my mind on calling her on Tuesday, to smooth things over. But she beat me to it. I answered her call and we made up. OK, so I didn't feel completely comfortable with it, and there was still some tension between us, but we made it up all the same.'

'Natalie had mentioned you not seeming yourself on the Wednesday night. At the class. Was she right?'

'Yes, she was right. Susan confronted me about Lance before it started, threatened to show the photos you sent her to Barry and Martin if I didn't give up Lance. I was so upset, especially as he'd only told me two nights before that he wanted to be with me. I made some threats of my own and she backed off, but it still upset me and I left without chatting to Natalie like I usually do. I suspect that got her back up. I was going to call to explain what happened as I felt bad, but then Lance phoned around eleven the same night. From a number I didn't recognise, although now I know why – Susan didn't want to chance anything being traced back to her. Lance said he couldn't see me any more. I was mad and upset and I didn't feel like speaking to anyone afterwards. Especially Natalie, who'd warned me off him. I couldn't bear to hear her telling me she'd been right all along. I ended up ignoring her calls all day Thursday, also because something else happened to completely terrify me. Well, two things, actually. I was at home most of the day, feeling down and taking it easy before my class that night – covering for Shona – but had popped out for some groceries around two. I was walking home, maybe forty-five minutes' later, had reached my door when some thug approached me and backed me up against the wall. He said if I didn't keep my mouth shut about Susan, if I didn't leave Lance alone and quit the club,

326

he'd shut it for me. I realised Susan was behind it, that she was frightened of me divulging her secret to Lance, and it scared the crap out of me. It was obvious he wasn't kidding.'

'Oh my God, that's awful,' I say.

'Yep, which the police told me is why Susan got Lance to split up with me using an unregistered phone. She'd already planned on sending the heavies round the next day after I threatened to spill the beans on her secret earlier that night at the class and, like I said, couldn't risk anything being traced back to her should they ever have seen it through with their threat to harm me. Lance didn't know this, of course – if he had, he'd have gone ballistic. Believe me, after that, as much as I wanted to expose Susan, I was too frightened to say anything, and it was my intention to resign on the Friday before the class. To make matters worse, I got an email from Susan that same afternoon while I'd been out, reinforcing what the thug had said. I'd thought it a bit risky of her to do such a thing, especially having got that piece of meat to do the threatening for her. She denied it, of course, as did Natalie. Who knows what the story is there. Perhaps we'll never get to the bottom of that one.

'Anyway, I put on a brave face for Shona's class that night, but I was still so upset I didn't want to speak to anyone, couldn't face calling Natalie back. Despite a dozen or so missed calls I'd had from her. I remember coming home, going to the bathroom for a shower, putting my phone down on the side, then having a nosebleed. I managed to stop the bleeding, then got undressed, was about to get into the shower when my door buzzer rang. I thought it might have been Lance, hoped it was, at least. Hoped he might have told Susan to go to hell, that he had come round to make up, tell me he wanted to be with me after all and we could get out of town. Pretty naive, I know. I remember dashing to the hall, naked, pressing the intercom, then hearing Natalie's voice. "Let me up," she'd said, "let me up now, or I'll tell everyone at the gym about him." She had sounded really weird, like she was in some kind of trance, and I freaked, ran to the bedroom, flung on the first clean clothes I could find, grabbed my house keys, which had my set of Natalie's keys on there too, and raced out the door. I was so stupid, totally forgot about my phone. I guess I panicked she might start shouting outside in the street or something. I found Natalie standing on the doorstep, but just as her voice had sounded weird on the intercom, I knew from the look on her face that something wasn't right. I tried to put my arm around her but didn't attempt to wake her. I knew it wasn't safe to wake someone who's sleepwalking. I told her, "Let's get you home." And I remember walking her back to hers, unlocking the door, then going inside. I said, "Let's get you back to bed," and in that split second I had turned my head towards the stairs, she went for me. Tried to strangle me from behind. I somehow broke loose and ran for the basement door, where I knew she wouldn't follow me. It was stupid, but it was the nearest door to hand, and I managed to get inside before she could attack me again. I shut the door, frightened she'd follow me down there, then heard the bolt being drawn. I knew I was trapped. I'd never been down there, I knew she hated basements because her foster parents used to lock her up in theirs. She'd told me all about her keeping food down there in case of an emergency. Since her childhood, everything she does is about having control. Being prepared.'

328

Jade pauses, tears streaming down her face. 'She's so full of anger, and I know she can't help it, despite all the therapy she's had. But she shouldn't be out in the world. She needs full-time professional help, I realise that now. Care I wasn't able to give her.'

'Why didn't you scream for help? The waking Natalie would have released you, surely?'

'I was too afraid. How did I know that for sure? How did I know which Natalie would appear if I did? Even if she'd been in her right mind, I was scared she'd be too afraid to admit what she'd done, worried I'd go straight to the police, which I would have done. All I could do was hope someone would find me eventually.'

Listening to Jade, I can't imagine how scared she must have been. What she went through is horrifying, and yet she appears so strong, so together. So smart. I guess growing up with a mum like hers has hardened her, made her into a fighter, a survivor.

'Are you going to see Natalie?' I ask. 'I mean, if it wasn't "her" as such who attacked you, you can't really blame her, can you? It's an illness, it's not her fault, you must know that. That's what mental illness does to a person. I know that only too well. It wasn't the real me who took the kids and drove that car into the side of the road. I wasn't myself; it was the pills and the breakdown I had suffered. People like Natalie need kindness rather than punishment.'

'I know that,' Jade nods. 'And yes, when I feel stronger, I will go to see her, and I hope that in prison she'll also get the treatment she needs. I've no doubt her lawyer will argue for a reduced sentence based on lack of capacity. But like I said, right now she's not fit to be out in society. She needs to be treated in a controlled environment. Needs to atone for what she did. Not just to me, but to others in the past. We can't just let her off because we feel sorry for her.'

I can't blame Jade for feeling this way; I'm sure I'd feel the same if I were in her shoes. Nevertheless, I leave with an uneasy sensation in the pit of my stomach. Something just doesn't feel right.

Chapter Fifty-Two

Natalie

Monday, 30 July 2018

I'm sitting in a visitors' room at Tolworth Hospital in Surbiton, waiting for Dr Jenkins to arrive. Having been charged with actual bodily harm and kidnapping, the court decided to send me to a psychiatric unit for a report to be made on my mental health, rather than allow me out on bail or keep me in prison on remand. Based on my lawyer's submission, they've agreed that evidence from a doctor is required as to whether I am fit to plead and what my sentence should be. I expected this, and to be honest I'm glad of it. I don't want to go home. For one, because I've got no one to go home to and I'm scared I might sleepwalk again if I'm stuck at home alone and stressed. And two, because I can't bear to be in the place where I kept my best friend a prisoner. Where I attacked her. As for the other option, prison terrifies me, even though I realise that's where I might end up after my trial, depending on what the court rules.

The decor is pristine white, like heaven's waiting room, even though right now I feel like I am in hell. There is nothing in here except for a table and two chairs. And right now, I am being watched by a guard in case I try to harm myself.

Eventually, the door opens, and I'm immediately comforted by Dr Jenkins' familiar face.

She gives me a faint smile, then tells the guard to leave, that she'll be OK and sound the alarm if she needs him. I know it's routine, but it makes me feel like a psychopath. There's no way I'd ever harm her, not awake, at least. She knows that, I can see it in her expression. Even so, it's not nice being made to feel like I'm some kind of wild animal that she may need protection from.

Once we are alone and she's sitting across from me, she asks me how I am.

'OK,' I say. 'As well as can be expected. The last week or so has felt like a blur. I was so convinced it was Susan, that I'd done nothing wrong, so when they turned up at the house and found Jade, it felt like I was stuck in some nightmare. When I was a child, Jack was always there – he was the one to find me, catch me in the act. I remember him reassuring me it wasn't "me" as such who did the things I did, that it was my subconscious thoughts playing out in my sleep. Acting out stuff I'd never do if I were awake because I'd know it was wrong. I mean, we all think things about other people when we're awake, don't we? We may dislike a person and wish them ill in our minds, but we don't act on our feelings, just as I'd never act on my feelings when I'm awake. But clearly something happens to me when I sleepwalk. It's like another side to my personality takes over. And yet…'

'And yet what, Natalie?'

'And yet I still can't believe I would have attacked Jade. I never hated her, never wished her any harm in my mind. Not like I did my father or Cath. I loved her like a sister, and I just can't think I'd have gone round to her place intending to hurt or trick her.'

332

'But you were angry with her. You'd argued, and it unsettled you. You knew things still weren't right.'

'It's true, I did sense things weren't right between us. But I'd also sensed there was something else bothering her. And that's why I called her repeatedly. Not to stalk her, but because I was worried about her. And now we know I had good reason to be worried. Because Susan had threatened her.'

I pause for a moment or two, deep in thought. 'What is it?' Dr Jenkins asks.

'You mentioned to me in the past about using hypnosis to try and help me overcome the sleepwalking. To remember what happened when I attacked Dad and Cath. What I was thinking at the time. I declined before, because I hadn't been honest with you, hadn't told you I was the one who killed Cath, and I was afraid of my secret coming out. But now I have nothing to hide or fear. All I want is the truth.'

'What are you saying, Natalie?'

'I'm saying I want you to hypnotise me, Dr Jenkins. I want to remember what happened. Not just on Thursday night, but with Dad and Cath. I need to know what was going through my mind when I attacked them. But especially when I attacked my best friend.'

Chapter Fifty-Three

Jade

The present
Tuesday, 31 July 2018

I pull back the thick powder-blue curtain a fraction and peer out of my bedroom window, see the familiar black Vauxhall Astra pull up and come to a standstill. I wait with bated breath. No sign of its passengers just yet, causing my tension to rise, my mind to wonder what they might be talking about, why they are here.

What they may have discovered since I last spoke to them only three days ago.

Finally, the driver and passenger doors open, and I see the detectives exit the car, serious expressions etched across their faces, not unusual in their line of work, but there's something about their demeanour that worries me; a kind of singularly determined look that tells me something's changed, that they've made some kind of breakthrough.

I watch them cross the road, eyes darting left and right as they do so, then approach the front door. I watch the more senior officer raise his right hand and press the bell.

It's so quiet in my bedroom, the sound seems to reverberate around me in one thunderous echo. It's grey outside today, chilly too; more like mid-autumn than late summer, and I've even had to turn on the central heating. But it's the sound of my bell being pressed by my visitors that sends a shiver up my spine rather than the cool temperature.

I cannot dither a moment longer. Even though the last thing I want is to go downstairs and open the door to my visitors. I leave the bedroom, being sure to close the door behind me, then slowly make my way down to the hallway, the sound of my breathing and the natural creaks of the building all that can be heard. Then I inhale deeply before opening the door to my callers.

They're standing there with grave expressions and when I ask them what's happened, how I can be of assistance, they say there's been a development in the case and enquire if they might come inside.

I cannot refuse them. I must stay calm, act surprised, exude an air of innocence. Be the best actress I possibly can. It shouldn't be hard; I've been doing that for so long now it's become second nature, donning another face for the world. Hiding the truth, my past. The things I've done and kept secret from others. In any case, I'm not the only guilty one here. Far from it.

I latch onto that thought, flash my most congenial smile, say, 'Yes, of course, officers, anything to help,' then lead them inside and say a silent prayer that my secret is still safe.

Up in my flat, I offer DI Bailey and DS Khan refreshments but they both decline.

'How are you feeling, Jade?' DI Bailey asks.

'Better,' I say, 'much calmer.'

He says nothing. Just stares, like he's trying to read my mind. It spooks me.

'So, do you have any news on Natalie's trial? Is that why you're here? Has she been assessed yet?'

'In a manner of speaking.'

His cryptic response alarms me. I try not to show it. Simply say, 'I'm not sure I follow.'

DI Bailey leans in across the kitchen table, but again I try not to appear flustered even though I know something is wrong.

He pauses, then says, 'Why did you set Natalie up, Jade?'

My heart stops.

'Why did you make out she attacked you, forcing you to hide in her basement when you know as well as I do that you went in there willingly?'

'What?' I say out loud. *Fuck, fuck, fuck*, I scream inside.

'We're not disputing her sleepwalking her way to yours on the night in question. We have eyewitness confirmation of that. Neither are we disputing you walking her home, before opening her front door for her and taking her inside. We have photographic evidence of that too, albeit sent to us anonymously by a mysterious witness. But that's where the truth ends, and the lies begin.

'When you got inside you made Natalie a cup of camomile tea, knowing this always calms her down. She was still asleep, but you sat her on the sofa and got her to drink it while you watched.' He pauses, as if to heighten my anxiety, then, 'We know this because yesterday Natalie underwent hypnosis.'

'What?' I exclaim. 'Hypnosis? What a load of tosh. How do you know she was really under? She could have made up any old story to try and get away with what she did. Surely that's not even admissible?'

'Do you know what I think?' he says, ignoring me. 'I think you waited for her to drift off, and when you were sure she was asleep, you got your accomplice to lock you in the basement where you knew she kept food because she'd confided in you about it.'

'What?' I repeat. 'That's utter crap! My accomplice? What the hell?'

'We know you had help. We know you cut your accomplice a key to Natalie's house. That she was waiting inside for you to arrive with Natalie that night. That she's the one who took the photo of you and Natalie outside her front door and sent it to us anonymously. Once you got into the basement, she locked it, then went home. But we also know there was another player in the game, someone who deliberately cast suspicion on his wife. That person is Lance Hampson. Using a different burner phone to the one Susan got him to call you with on the night he broke up with you, he sent a text from Michael to Susan that Thursday night knowing her car would be captured on CCTV in this area, although not having anticipated she'd already be out and about, thereby putting her under suspicion and giving us reason to question her. He also sent a threatening email from Susan to you, making it look like she may have been the one who attacked you and therefore amplifying that same suspicion. You both knew these two things taken together would give us cause to bring her in, scare her, wheedle her secret out of her. It was all part of the game. The psychological warfare you waged on the three women you hated with a passion.'

I laugh out loud, even though my insides are turning. 'How can you possibly have come up with such an outrageous notion? And who is this mysterious accomplice you're claiming I have?'

337

'I think you deliberately argued that Monday with Natalie to upset her, to get her worked up, to get her to start sleepwalking again. You knew she didn't approve of your so-called affair with a married man and you played on this, knowing her history of anger issues, of stress, of violence. And it worked. She'd been doing it for a few days now, you'd been watching her walk to your street, hover outside, then turn back again. So you decided Thursday would be the perfect night to put your plan in motion.'

The room has started to spin.

'And why would I do that? Why would I want to set Natalie up?'

'To punish her for letting her brother, Jack, take the fall for killing their foster mum. You knew each other as kids. Jack was your friend, your only friend, and one day he was gone. He wrote to you, didn't he? After he got charged with Cath's murder. He said he was miserable, that the kids there were making his life hell but that Natalie could never know because she wasn't strong enough to hear it. He told you he knew you were stronger than her, and that he could trust you with the truth, which was killing him inside. He didn't want you to think he was a killer, didn't want you to stop caring for him. And so he told you what had really happened that night, and made you swear not to tell a soul. You did as he asked, hopeful that one day you might be reunited. But he got into a fight with another kid and he died. Something you have never got over, something you wanted to punish his sister for. Walking into that library last July wasn't a coincidence. You sweet-talked your way into Natalie's life, made her feel special, only to break her again, make her confess to a crime she'd lied about all these years.'

'And how could you possibly know all this?' I ask.

338

'Natalie told us about the woman she met by Jack's grave.'

I flinch.

'The same woman who told her about someone leaving flowers at Jack's grave. You. She warned Natalie that she shouldn't go to her own grave with secrets. Put the idea into the mind of a woman she knew was fragile at your command. We know that old woman is your grandmother, whose maiden name was Pascal. The mother of Ellen Walters, your mother. Lance Hampson's former sweetheart.' He pauses, then lets the final bombshell drop. 'Lance Hampson is your father, isn't he? Isn't that the truth, Jade?'

It's over, I can't lie any more, as much as I want to. Not now that DI Bailey's clearly put two and two together. Natalie's recollection under hypnosis may not have stood up in court, but I'm guessing it was enough to make him suspicious of me and question her further.

He goes on. 'We found your mother, or should I say adoptive mother, Rachel, still living in north London. Her husband, Gary, was a good man, and he worked for your grandfather at his jewellery store. Ellen died in childbirth, but the child, you, survived. Your grandmother was so heartbroken having discovered from Ellen on her deathbed that Lance had lied to her and was marrying Susan, that she didn't want you to have anything to do with Lance. She made out you'd died too, when in fact you were secretly given up for adoption. And it was Gary and Rachel who took you in. Named you Annabel. Annabel Richards. Gary was kind, but he died when you were small, leaving you with Rachel, who treated you badly and no doubt helped turn you into the troubled, vengeful woman you are today. You were lost without

Jack. Rachel put you in a private school for girls, and there you were bullied by the head of PE who resented you for being better at gymnastics than her daughter. Another spiteful woman intent on making your life hell. You quit gymnastics at seventeen, went to Southampton University, far away from your mother, and all thoughts of Natalie were put out of your mind. You thought maybe you could turn a corner, be happy, especially when you met Jim Maloney at the boys' school you found a teaching position at. You fell in love with him, but once again it ended in tragedy, and your part in a scandalous love triangle came out. It was all over the press and your grandmother saw the story, knew it was you as she'd been watching you from afar all this time, keen to know how you were doing, that you were OK. She sought you out and told you about your real mother, about her being in love with a man named Lance Hampson who broke her heart. She told you about Susan, what she'd told Ellen that day, and you made it your mission to seek her out. You stayed in Kilburn for a time, visited Jack's grave in Lambeth, retrained as a gym instructor, feeling you couldn't go back to teaching after all that had happened. But at the same time, desperate for a father figure, you revealed yourself to Lance. He told you how much he'd loved your mother, had never wanted to marry Susan. He'd had no idea Susan had visited Ellen that day but believed it couldn't be a coincidence, felt sure she had done something to upset her. Together you made a plan to destroy Susan and make her confess to what she'd done all those years ago. You engineered that at your party, having changed your name to Jade Pascal and become an instructor at the same club she belonged to, and you made sure to leave a trail of breadcrumbs in the fabricated diary you left for us to find. Filled with other more mundane entries, but three particularly telling ones you knew would attract our attention.'

'How do you know all this?' I say.

'Because we found your grandmother, from the description Natalie gave us. We got her to tell us the truth. Armed with all the facts, we then paid Lance a visit, who confirmed you to be his daughter. Interesting, in the photos Grace took all you're doing is holding hands, him kissing the top of your forehead, and now we know why. It was enough to make Grace, another woman you had a problem with, think you were having an affair, enough to make Susan think the same, but really it was a moment of affection between father and daughter. You wanted Grace to see you together, to hear you, knowing she'd most probably tell Susan, to get you into trouble. I'm guessing you never knew Grace would turn up at the club, that was never part of the plan, and you were perhaps a little alarmed at first. But then you thought, bingo, let's punish three women at the same time, implicate them in your disappearance. They deserved to be miserable, to be driven stir-crazy, because that's what they had done to the men in their lives, the men who'd been innocent, the men you had loved but lost.'

I can't fail to be impressed by DI Bailey's powers of deduction. I'd planned it all so perfectly from the moment I found out from my father where Susan worked out, realising Jack's little sister lived less than a mile away. Two for the price of one. And DI Bailey is right: I was rattled by Grace. Rattled by a woman I'd hoped never to set eyes on again, having sent a man I loved passionately to his grave. And when she told me how she was living a lie, asked me to keep her secret, I was sickened. Sickened by yet another woman running from the truth, pretending like it never happened. And I decided I had to force her hand, too, make her come clean. That's why I told Natalie about Megan. Dropped her name into the conversation a few weeks before the plan was put into play. Meg was the only woman I trusted besides my grandmother, and she knew everything I was planning and agreed to help me. I knew Natalie would seek her out, that Meg would tell her the truth, and that in doing so Grace's secret would be exposed.

'Tell me, Jade, why Natalie? Why choose her rather than Susan to take the hit for your fake incarceration? Surely it's Susan you despise the most? Surely it's her you wanted to end up in prison?'

'Because it would have destroyed my father, his reputation and his career, along with my siblings' lives too. Even if they are half of *her*, it wouldn't have been fair on them to be forever tied by blood to a criminal. Cameron was a different story, of course, but it's not his fault his mother was a conniving bitch. I mean, she called on her mobster friend to use one of his thugs to threaten my life. That was totally unexpected and scared the crap out of me, I have to say, but in the end it turned out to be an added bonus. My father was just as shocked as I was to find out Cameron isn't his. Heartbroken, in fact. But he won't tell him, knowing it would break Cameron's heart. Her coming clean was enough – that's why I got Dad to send a threatening email to me from her account, I needed something more to force her hand, even though that was probably the weakest part of my plan because I know Susan wouldn't have been so stupid as to draw attention to herself – and I knew that Dad casting her off without a penny would be worse than prison for her.

And what do you know, I was right, because the bitch went and killed herself. As for Natalie, she allowed Jack to take the fall for murder all these years. She had so many chances to confess, to her therapists, to me, but she was too much of a coward, too weak. Dad was worried about me locking myself in her basement in case she found me and went all psycho, but I convinced him that I knew what I was doing and that he could trust me. That there was never any danger of her harming me because she hated basements and never went down there, and even if, by the slimmest of chances she did, I assured him I could handle her. The way I've handled all the women who've been a curse on my life. He'd looked so relieved when I said this. Smiled at me with pride, then removed his snug red woollen scarf and wrapped it around me as we'd sat on a bench in Hampstead Heath, one of my favourite childhood haunts.

'Not for a second do I regret my actions. Natalie deserves to go to prison for what she did, to be punished. If it wasn't for her, Jack might still be alive, and we might have had a future. Jack was an innocent, just like Jim, just like my dad.'

Chapter Fifty-Four

Natalie

Friday, 10 August 2018

'Is it good to be home?'

I've been back home a week now, and Grace has popped round to say goodbye. She's moving up to Manchester where her in-laws live with her kids, Casper and George. They've had some conversations, realised Grace is off the pills, has turned over a new leaf and means to get better. They've agreed to give her a chance to get to know her boys again, and I'm happy for her. For all her faults, I can tell she's a good person deep down, that she loves her children and wants to be a good mum. That's more than can be said for a lot of mums. Mine, for example. Susan. Jade's adoptive mum. The mother–child bond is said to be the most important relationship in the world, and I think that's probably true. When there is one there's nothing more special. But when there isn't, when mother and child fail to bond, it's the child who suffers, pays the price for the rest of their lives.

'Yes,' I say, 'sort of. Although, like you, I'm not sure I can stay round here much longer. Too many bad memories.'

'But you love your job,' Grace says.

It's true, I do. But after all that's happened, I feel like I need a fresh start. Somewhere people don't know me, won't remind me of what's transpired these last few weeks. Right now, I'm on sick leave, but Jane told me to take all the time I needed. 'People know too much about me now,' I say.

'But you've been exonerated. Everyone knows Jade set you up.'

I sip my tea, smile at Grace. 'I appreciate your kindness, but you know what people are like. They can't forget. They make judgements, assumptions, like to gossip. Sam already saw me as a freak, I can't imagine what she thinks of me now. Now that my fucked-up childhood is out in the open. It's stuff like that people will focus on. People like Sam who enjoy ridiculing misfits like me. Because, let's be honest, people can be shits.'

Grace stays another half hour or so then leaves. I realise I'll never see her again. Just like I'll never see Jade again. Although I can never forgive Jade for trying to frame me, for wanting me to suffer the way she believed Jack had suffered in prison, I'm thankful to her in some ways. She brought me out of my shell, encouraged me to socialise, get fitter, live life, even if she did so for her own purposes. There are so many reasons I chose not to live that way for so many years. Childhood trauma, my history of sleep-walking, not wanting to get close to people for fear of getting stressed, triggering the syndrome all over again. It felt safer to live a controlled, ordered, solitary existence, where there was no danger of me getting stressed and hurting anyone.

But now I know different, as does Dr Jenkins after she put me under hypnosis, made me remember. Now I know there was never any danger of me hurting anyone. That

I never, in fact, hurt anyone. That was just something I was made to believe by the one person I had trusted most in this world. The one person I had worshipped, and would have gone to the ends of the earth for. The child psychologists had seen this, and that's why the person who spent his life deceiving me was banished to the best place for him. I just wish I had found out sooner.

Chapter Fifty-Five

Jack

February 2000

It's no use, I can't sleep. I can't possibly sleep after what that bitch did to my sister. Although I also know that my sister's welfare is not my primary concern here; it's really just an excuse for the urges I'm having. The urges that have been with me long before we came to live with Cath and Brian.

I've always had this rage burning through me. A rage I know I can't contain. Don't want to contain. It's simmered at the surface for a long time now. Since our mother left us to fend for ourselves. Or perhaps I'm using my mother's neglect, my childhood trauma as an excuse. An excuse for a genetic fault in my make-up that's as unchangeable as the stars in the sky. As opposed to Natalie, whose sleepwalking syndrome is no doubt the result of the stress and neglect she's suffered. She is a blameless innocent. While I always know exactly what I am doing.

I remember stamping on insects as a five-year-old and enjoying the feeling of crushing the life out of something. The glorious high that came with wielding power over them, knowing I controlled whether they lived or died.

It gave me such a buzz, just as it gives me a buzz to manipulate and control my little sister. I know she worships me, that's always been my goal. Her brilliant older brother, who she'd do anything to protect. Who she sees as special and unique, someone who can do no wrong. How mistaken she is. That's how Annabel sees me, too. I remember chancing upon her in the park one afternoon when I was ten. Her bitch of an adoptive mother was busy chatting to another mum and I was kicking a ball around with some mates who lived her way. She was looking a little lost with no one to play with, doing the odd cartwheel to pass the time. I befriended her and she told me how much she hated her mother, how she craved a father to take her away from it all. So I decided to fulfil that role for her. Meeting her in secret once a week. Pretending to care for her, sympathise with her, even though I didn't much care one way or another what or how she was feeling. I did it to gain her trust, just because one day I knew it might come in handy. And the more puppets you can control, the greater the puppet master, right?

I love that feeling of being able to manoeuvre weaker souls than myself to do what I want, of being hero-worshipped; it's such a rush, gives me a kick like no other. That, and hurting people, seeing the suffering in their eyes. The way I watched my father suffer as I slowly poisoned him to death. Small doses of turpentine in his booze, which gradually saw him off to hell where he belonged. Everyone just thought he drank himself to death. But I know better.

Unlike Nats, who was too young, I can still remember our mother's face – thin and gaunt, the result of too many drugs and not enough food, but still with a kind of elfin grace to it. She was slight all over, reminded me of the ballerina that went round inside the jewellery box I gave

Nats for her tenth birthday, and which she keeps hidden from Cath because the fat, ugly munter would only take it away from her. Nats told me it was the best present she'd ever had. She doesn't know I stole it from a shop. I've never told her this, not because it's the kinder thing to do, but because I worry it might tarnish her saintly image of me. I daren't do anything that might jeopardise her love and admiration for me. I feed off that, and I cannot under any circumstances lose her respect. That's why I've never told her about Annabel. I can't have her being jealous, thinking any less of me. She needs to think I am devoted to her and her alone.

I hate Cath and Brian, like I hated our father. Like I hate a lot of people. It's a struggle sometimes not to act out more. But like I said, it's all about control. And if there's one thing I'm certain of, it's that I'm one hundred per cent in control of my actions. Unlike Natalie. Nats started sleepwalking when she was seven. She's never done anyone any harm in the process, but I made her feel that she had. It's cruel of me, I know. But I don't really care. I feed off her dependency on me, and I can't risk losing that. I knew exactly what I was doing when I attacked our father with the back of his shoe – the same shoe he used to beat Nats and me with – in his bed the night of my ninth birthday. Not two hours after he'd come to our bedroom and abused Natalie, unaware that I was awake and listening. I knew Nats would be up around 10:30 p.m., like clockwork, and so I timed my attack expertly; made sure she was there in the room while I did it, locked in her sleep, unaware of what was going on, but a scapegoat for when Dad woke up and saw the both of us. I made out she'd done it and that I'd intervened just in time to stop something fatal from happening. Hoping they'd both be grateful to me. That my father might actually show some respect for me. I wanted them both under my control; puppets whose strings I pulled to perfection. But our fucking shit of a father was never grateful to me, and so later I killed him. Natalie was grateful, though. Grateful I'd stopped her from causing fatal damage in the nick of time.

After our father died, they sent us into foster care, and we got lumped with Cath and Brian. It wasn't long before I wanted to do them harm, and trashing their bedroom was a form of me acting out on my urges, even though it never gave me the same buzz as taking a life. That was one of many nights they'd stayed out late at the pub, leaving us kids to fend for ourselves. Again, I made out Nats had trashed the room in her sleep, and that I'd been the one to stop her. And they believed me. It's such an exhilarating feeling: not just the act itself, but the deceit – it's the getting away with it that gives me the real buzz. They weren't grateful, though. Just like my father. But Natalie was. And she realised she needed me even more after that.

I look at Nats lying on her side in bed, the side that's taken less of a beating, her sleep restless, as it always is. Even though after Cath banished us to our room I tended to her wounds and soothed her to sleep with her precious ballerina's lullaby. I know she'll get up soon, start walking, just because she follows the same pattern every night. The beating was especially bad today, and I can't stand for it any more. One day I think Cath might go too far and kill her, and I can't have that. I can't lose the person who worships the ground I walk on. And that's why I'm going to make sure that never happens. Although this time will be different. This time I won't place the blame on Natalie because murder is a different story, and I can't risk losing her to some children's prison's control. She'll never survive, and so I need to be smarter about things.

I look at my watch. It's nearly 10:30 p.m., nearly time for Nats to get up and wander. I have to be quick.

I strip down to my boxers to avoid having to endure the tedious rigmarole of disposing of any blood that might spray onto my pyjama bottoms or t-shirt. I can easily wash blood off my skin with a hot shower. Then, I quietly crawl out of bed and make for the door. As I do, a familiar rush of excitement pulses through me; at the thought of hurting another human soul, especially someone I despise through and through. I can't help it, it's like a drug I can't resist. Tentatively I open it, pop my head out, listen for any noise. I can't risk the other kids being awake. Satisfied they're fast asleep, I go downstairs to the back door and open it. The lock has always been dodgy, and I want to draw the police's attention to this when they arrive at the crime scene. I open a few cupboards to make it look like an intruder was here, do the same in the living room, overturn some books and other stuff on the floor, then return to the kitchen and grab the bread knife from the block Cath keeps on the sideboard. It's a bit risky keeping the back door open, but it's a rainy night and hopefully no one will notice or be tempted to come inside. As for my fingerprints, they'll just be amongst the dozens of fingerprints around the house; there's no reason for me to be singled out. Then, I creep upstairs, make for Cath's room, put my ear to the door and hear her repugnant snoring. I close my eyes and think back to about five hours ago – watching her strip Nats' nightie off, making her bend over, whipping her with Brian's belt, making all of us watch. I will do worse to her, and she won't even know it's coming.

I open the door, see her sleeping like a baby. Not an ounce of remorse for what she's done affecting her slumber. Even though, I guess, I am not one to talk. I enter the room. Move closer. Closer still until I reach her side of the bed, can see her fat face, the face she stuffs every day with food she fails to share with the rest of us. I waste no time and raise the knife high above my head, bring it down hard into her neck, hitting the artery. Caught unawares, she has no time to think, to react, but I bring it down once again into her stony heart just to be sure, blood spraying across my bare chest. She is dead, and I am tingling all over with a feeling akin to ecstasy.

I turn around, think I can make it back before Natalie starts roaming, but I see her standing there, watching me, and yet seeing right through me. I know she won't remember what she saw, and I must get her back to bed before they come and find us. I can't have them thinking it was her who killed Cath, that would never do; she'll be sent away if they think she did this. But neither can I get caught. I am the hero in her life, and I don't want her knowing the same rage that consumed our father consumes me. Not that he was a patch on me. Not even close.

I don't try to wake her, but I do guide her back to our room with my unbloodied hand, the knife still gripped in my right. We reach our bedroom and I gently coax her into bed, and before long her eyes are closed. I go to the bathroom and have a quick shower, hoping it won't wake the others, which thankfully it doesn't. At the same time, I rinse the blood off the knife, dry it with a towel, then return to our room before placing it inside a polythene bag which I double-knot, just to make sure it's secure. Then, I crouch down and feel under the bed for the loose floorboard, pull it up and place the bag inside, before replacing the board with pinpoint precision. Part of me was tempted to put the knife back in the block having cleaned it. But I couldn't be sure my DNA was wiped clean, and I wanted it to seem like some random intruder had picked it up on the spur of the moment. I just hope the police fall for it and that I haven't, being only thirteen, although smarter and more mature than most boys my age, miscalculated the situation.

Having done all that, I creep into bed beside my sister and fall straight to sleep.

I'm woken by a piercing scream, as is Nats. It's Daisy.

I act as surprised as everyone, rush to where the other kids have assembled. Daisy is shivering uncontrollably, clearly in shock at the sight before her. Cath's blood is all over the sheets, her face as pale as snow, her body steadily hardening. A quick glance at Nats tells me she's in shock too, but there's also something in her expression that tells me she feels relieved to be free of the bitch lying dead before her. I can't help but smile inside, can't help congratulating myself for being her saviour once more. I tell her to stay calm, to take care of Daisy, then I lead them all downstairs and act shocked, seeing the place in disarray, although no one spots the missing kitchen knife, so I don't mention it.

I take charge, call the police and in no time at all they are here, surveying the scene. Unlike the children, they spot the misplaced knife. It's no surprise, it's what they are trained to do, and I hear one of them say, 'Looks like a possible burglary gone wrong, sir.' Natalie is frightened and I comfort her, tell her it will all be OK, like I always do. We are wrapped in blankets and taken to the police station. Social workers are called, but I am parted from

Natalie. I see the look of horror in her eyes, that it's torture for her not being with me in this strange place. I try to hide the satisfaction that I feel from this. Knowing she can't do without me. But I also worry what she might say without me there to guide her.

I am questioned by a police officer, a social worker at my side. I explain that my sister and I were asleep all night but were woken by Daisy's scream. I point out finding the back door open, the downstairs living room and kitchen in chaos, reinforcing the idea in their heads that it must have been a random intruder as the evidence suggests.

It's some four hours before I see Nats again. They lead me into a different room where she is being held. They tell me Cath's husband has been notified, that they have spoken to him. That they know about Nats' sleepwalking, know she trashed his and Cath's bedroom and attacked our father, which I stopped in time. Know she has been seen wandering out of the house. They also know from the other children that Cath beat her last night. Nats is trembling now, and I realise they think she did this. It's the easy assumption to make, based on the history they've been given. I am angry with myself for not foreseeing this. I know I am incredibly smart, that I read a lot, but I am only thirteen after all. I also know, looking into Nats' eyes, that she's convinced she did this too. I have two choices: I let her take the fall and she is led away and I lose control over her forever, or I say it was me and she sees me as the hero brother who saved her from prison. Prison can't be that bad. Prison will be full of other children I can control. I can make myself master of them all.

I look into Nats' eyes, a look as if to say it's true, you did this, and I'm so sorry, it's not your fault, I tried my best to protect you. But it's OK, I'll take the hit for this, the way big brothers do. I'll continue to be your hero, your knight in shining armour, the one you can always count on. I know that's what she sees in my gaze. But she doesn't see what else I am thinking: that when I go to prison for this you will still love me, still worship me; you will write to me and do everything I ask of you because you will believe I took the rap for you. Deceiving you in the same way I deceived Annabel, telling her I could never leave you because I am the only one who can keep a check on the bad things my little sister does in her sleep. I will somehow get word to her, too, tell her I took the fall for you, because I can't have her image of me shattered either. She will believe me, but she will keep my secret because I will tell her to, and I know she'll never betray my wishes.

I turn to the officer and say, 'It wasn't Natalie, it was me. I killed Cath because of what she did to my sister. I had to make the beatings stop, stop her from killing the only family I have left. You'll find the knife under our bed back at the house. Under the floorboards.'

I know they will take pity on me, take into account my terrible childhood, me being made to watch my little sister suffer. The lawyer men will argue that for me, and they will allow some leniency, point out that this is my first offence. And I will act all sorry, and no one will ever know that behind my repentant facade lies a very different agenda. I will fool the child psychologists who will undoubtedly be called upon to assess me, just as I have fooled everyone all this time.

I look at Natalie and see the adoration in her eyes. She still believes in me, still loves me, thinks I have made the ultimate sacrifice for her.

I am a god to her, while she is the loser sister who doesn't deserve a brother like me.

Being a psychopath, I can't ask for more than that. Other than the exquisite euphoria of extinguishing another human life, of course.

It's what I crave.

It's what I live for.

A letter from A.A. Chaudhuri

Dear Reader, I hope you are keeping well. Firstly, I just wanted to say a huge thanks for reading my novel. This is my second psychological thriller with Hera Books, and I'm delighted to be publishing with them again, following a fantastic experience with *She's Mine*. *The Loyal Friend* explores various themes – friendships, jealousy, revenge, deceit and family dynamics to name a few – but also other issues close to my heart, like mental health. It therefore means the world to me that you have chosen to read it.

I began writing this book in July 2021. I wanted to base it in a setting I didn't feel had been done before in the psychological thriller genre, and with the health and fitness industry having become a key part of so many people's lifestyles – largely owing to the stress we encounter on a day-to-day basis, along with the push given by lockdown to keep ourselves healthy – I also felt the setting would be widely relatable. Having said that, although the backdrop for the novel is a health club, it's about so much more than that, largely centring on the relationship/dynamic between three very different women and the things that are motivating them to act and live their lives in the way they do. Natalie, Grace, and Susan are ostensibly three normal women tackling everyday issues so many women around the world face these days, including being able to keep a grip on their own stress levels and sanity in a world that can push human tolerance to the limit. I have struggled with my own mental health owing to the stress of caring for my elderly parents, while managing a career and young family. The pressures on women to perform and 'have it all' can be intense, and it was therefore something of a cathartic experience to write this book, at a time when I was dealing with a lot of personal stress. It also gave me great pleasure getting lost in the story and characters; this is, of course, why I write, because writing is my passion, and nothing brings me greater joy and peace of mind besides my children. It took me six months to write this book, and then another four months of editing to make it the best version of itself with the help of my wonderful editor, Keshini Naidoo. Aside from the issues it explores, I hope you found it a pacey, twisty, and compelling read that kept you guessing until the end.

The story and characters are completely fictional, although I did live in the Surbiton area for ten years, and pre-COVID used to work out with a lovely group of girls at a local gym. I can assure you, nothing so scandalous occurred there and none of the women featured bear any resemblance to them!

If you enjoyed *The Loyal Friend*, I would be absolutely thrilled to hear your thoughts via a review, which I hope might also encourage other readers to read it. It's such a joy seeing reader reviews; they are hugely inspiring and greatly appreciated in that they give me the encouragement to keep writing and perfecting my craft going forward to the next book and beyond. Incidentally, if you enjoyed this book and haven't yet read my debut with Hera, *She's Mine*, published in August 2021, I'd love for you to look it up. It's available at Amazon, Waterstones, The Works and all good online retailers.

Again, thank you for your support on my writing journey and I hope you'll continue to follow me as I work on new releases.

You can get in touch on my social media pages: Twitter, Facebook. Instagram, Linked In. Also, please visit my website for further information on my books, and latest news/blog posts. I'd love to hear from you if you'd like to talk about *The Loyal Friend*, *She's Mine*, or anything else for that matter. Without readers' support, we authors would be lost; it is the stimulant that keeps us going and helps us to gain new readers, and so I hope you know how much I appreciate your time and trouble.

Best wishes and happy reading.

Alex x

https://www.facebook.com/AAChaudhuri/
https://twitter.com/AAChaudhuri/
https://www.instagram.com/A.A.Chaudhuri/
https://www.linkedin.com/in/
a-a-chaudhuri-55a83524/
https://aachaudhuri.com/

Acknowledgments

I started writing this book in July 2021, just before my debut with Hera Books, *She's Mine*, was published, and finished it in November of the same year. During this time, I was dealing with a lot of personal stress and upheaval but as is always the case when I write, despite the various conflicting pressures, once I got going, I found that getting lost in my book and the characters helped to relieve that stress and proved to be a hugely cathartic, rewarding experience, resulting in a book I am extremely proud of, and in which I have invested many hours of hard work. That being said, there are a number of people I would like to thank, without whom this book would not be possible.

My publisher and co-founder of Hera – editor extraordinaire and all-round lovely person – Keshini Naidoo, for her incredible worth ethic and boundless enthusiasm, and for having faith in me and this book. I was not in a great place before I started this novel, but Keshini was so warm and patient with me, and that really is testament to the kind of person she is. She really is the most fantastic editor to work with, without doubt one of the best in the business, and since being signed up by Hera, I have learnt so much from her, for which I am truly grateful. Keshini and the whole Hera team have been a dream to work with, and a special thanks must also go to Dan O'Brien, Publishing Executive at Hera, for her work on the promotional side of things with *She's Mine* over the last year or so, and Canelo/Hera Managing Director Iain Millar, for his fabulous support and encouragement. I must also thank the copy editor, Jenny Page, whose comments were incredibly helpful, along with the proof-reader, Andrew Bridgmont, for helping to make it as error-free as possible. Thank you also to Ghost Design for all their hard work on creating such a stunning cover – so commercial yet classy at the same time, and none that captures the underlying menace throughout.

Thank you to my wonderful agent, Annette Crossland of A for Authors agency, for always believing in me and lifting my spirits, and for being such a huge support in reading my first draft so quickly. And, of course, for loving the book! I am so grateful for her encouragement and patience with me, for being such a genuine friend as well as my agent, and her legendary eagle eye! It's always a bit nerve-racking sending off a new book, and so I was skipping for joy when her joyous seal of approval popped into my inbox!

Kirstie Long of A for Authors for reading *The Loyal Friend* in its infancy, and for her constant source of support, encouragement, and friendship. Her keen eye for detail and insightful comments these past few years have been invaluable, and I can't thank her enough for always being there to guide and help me.

My best and massively talented author friend, Awais Khan, who is always there to listen and bolster me in good times and bad. And make me laugh! His generous, selfless support is second to none and I feel so lucky to have made such a wonderful life-long friend since we launched our debuts back in summer 2019.

To Sabine Edwards for her support and encouragement and for being so super organised and generous with her time.

To Ayo Onatade, one of the most warm-hearted, respected people in the industry I am privileged to know and who has been incredibly supportive to me and my books since my debut, The Scribe, was launched back in July 2019.

Thank you to Simon Bewick of Bay Tales for his fantastic support with the launch of *She's Mine* last summer; his review of the book at a Bay Tales virtual event helped it to gain traction for which I am extremely grateful.

Thanks to Dr Jacky Collins (Dr Noir) for her amazing support with *She's Mine*. It was such a privilege to be interviewed by someone so respected in the industry, but also one of the nicest people.

Thanks to the CWA and Capital Crime for their fantastic support over the last three years, in giving me opportunities to promote my books and reach wider audiences.

Thank you to all the amazing bloggers, book clubs and reviewers who gave such fabulous feedback on *She's Mine*, who have interviewed me about the book and my writing, helping it to reach wider audiences – and whose support means the world. There are so many of them I can't possibly name everyone even though I'd love to (!), but a very special thanks must go to blogger supremo Danielle Price, everyone on the *She's Mine* blog tour, Jude Wright, Surjit Parekh, Melissa Allen of Female First and The Squad Pod girls whose boundless love of reading and selfless support for my work blows me away. The Squad Pod's choosing *She's Mine* as their January 2022 Book of the Month couldn't have made for a better start to the year and it was incredible fun and richly rewarding to interact with them over that. I love reading every single one of the blogger reviews and really appreciate the care, thought and time that goes into them.

Thank you to all the authors out there who have supported me, particularly those that read and endorsed both *She's Mine* and *The Loyal Friend*. I know how busy they are, so I am indebted to them for finding the time to read my books.

This book, as you know, centres on three women, and so I'd be remiss not to mention some very special women in my life, who make it brighter and always know how to make me smile when times are tough: Chika Ripley, Priya Pillai and Danielle Price. Three very different women, but who are all equally wonderful, talented, and brilliant in their own right, and who I feel very lucky to have in my life. Also, I hasten to add, very unlike the women in *The Loyal Friend*! Thank you for championing my books and always being there.

To my fellow A for Authors writers for being such a kind, quirky and wonderfully supportive bunch. There's a real 'family' atmosphere to the team, which counts for a lot and is really rather special.

The reading and writing community on Twitter and Instagram. Again, there are so many of you who have been incredibly supportive – bloggers, general readers and authors alike, and I am so grateful for all the personal messages you have sent me this past year telling me how much you enjoyed *She's Mine* and are looking forward to the next book. I hope you enjoyed *The Loyal Friend* as much.

Friends and family, who have been a constant source of support and encouragement since the start of my writing career. Thank you for buying my books and spreading the word – it means a lot.

Finally, my beautiful boys, Adam and Henry, my Mum and Dad and my husband, Chris, who are always so patient with me and my writing, who give me the space to 'do my thing' and always believe in me. This book is for you – forever in my heart.